DEADLOCK

A JOHN HUTCHINSON NOVEL

ROBERT LIPARULO

THOMAS NELSON
Since 1798

NASHVILLE DALLAS MEXICO CITY RIO DE JANEIRO

Published in Nashville, Tennessee, by Thomas Nelson. Thomas Nelson is a registered trademark of Thomas Nelson, Inc.

Thomas Nelson, Inc., titles may be purchased in bulk for educational, business, fund-raising, or sales promotional use. For information, please e-mail SpecialMarkets@ThomasNelson.com.

ISBN 978-1-59554-167-3 (tp)

Library of Congress Cataloging-in-Publication Data

Liparulo, Robert.
    Deadlock / Robert Liparulo.
      p. cm.
    Sequel to: Deadfall, 2007.
    ISBN 978-1-59554-166-6
    1. Kidnapping—Fiction. 2. Canadian—Fiction. I. Title.
PS3612.I63D45 2009
813'.6—dc22   2008044443

Printed in the United States of America

09 10 11 12 13 RRD 5 4 3 2 1

To Mark Nelson

Thank you for being a great friend all these years

"A scar nobly got . . . is a good livery of honour."
—WILLIAM SHAKESPEARE, *ALL'S WELL THAT ENDS WELL*

"Battle not with monsters
lest ye become a monster;
and if you gaze into the abyss
the abyss gazes into you."
—FRIEDRICH NIETZSCHE

ONE

The mission was simple: kill everyone.

The complications came in the details, such as the directive to keep it *quiet*. So when a guard stepped around the corner of the house, Michael had to stop him from firing the pistol he was reaching for. Michael brought up his sound-suppressed shotgun and put a sabot slug—which became shrapnel only upon hitting flesh—into the man's chest.

There was no way he could have missed. His helmet contained a face mask that enhanced the quality of everything he viewed. A blue set of crosshairs showed him where his weapon was pointed. The system recognized humans, and the face mask crosshairs turned red when his aim was dead-on.

The man flew backward and struck the corner of the house. But instead of rebounding off it, he continued falling, passing through the bricks as if he were a ghost. The break from reality startled Michael, but only for the five heartbeats it took him to remember another of the helmet's technical capabilities: it could insert avatars—digitally constructed characters—into his field of vision.

Unless the system glitched, as it had just done, it was impossible to tell avatars from the live actors cast to make these training missions as authentic as possible. The face mask's screen rendered people, real or drawn, as photo-realistic cartoons. Sketchy black lines outlined them. Their skin was too perfect, too creamy.

"Crap," Michael said, disappointed in himself for letting the glitch startle him. His teammates—not to mention the officers watching in the Command Center via a live satellite feed—would have caught his hesitation. That was all he needed, being the newest and youngest member of the team.

Here on out, he thought, *make it perfect.*

He felt a nudge on his arm, and the team leader's voice came through his headphones: "That was the warm-up."

Of course. The designers of these tactical games always pulled the same trick: they sent an enemy to confront the team right away. It got the players' adrenaline pumping, their hand-eye coordination aligned, their minds into a kill-or-be-killed mentality.

Michael glanced back. He nodded at his own helmeted reflection in Ben's black face mask. Beyond, at the curb, Anton occupied the team's transportation, a van "commandeered" for the mission. Emile, the last member of their four-man team, would be coming through the back.

Don't shoot him, Michael reminded himself. That would completely blow their chances of outscoring the other teams. He'd never live that one down.

"Get moving," Ben said.

Michael moved quickly up the front porch steps, knelt in front of the door, and pulled a lock-pick gun and tension wrench from a pouch. He felt the deadbolt disengage. He unlocked the door handle and replaced the tools. He rose, readied his weapon, and waited. A red light on his display indicated that Emile had not yet bypassed the home's security system.

Michael considered the scenario they were playing: A rebel leader, whose planned coup would harm U.S. interests, had holed up with guards in a suburban community. Michael's team was to eliminate everyone and make it look like a murder-suicide. That meant no evidence of forced entry, and when they terminated the leader—the High Value Target—the shooter had to be close, the shot placed just right so the wound would appear self-inflicted. They'd been told the HVT had access to the type of shotguns the team was using. The weapons' smooth-bore barrels would make it impossible to prove different weapons had been used.

Ben gripped his shoulder, reassuring him. It only made Michael more nervous. This was Fireteam Bravo's last chance to edge ahead of Team Charlie in frag points, or successful kills. He didn't want to mess up.

On his screen, the red light changed to green. Three deep breaths, and he opened the door.

He stepped into a foyer and buttonhooked around the door. Clear. A living room opened to the right. Farther along the left foyer wall was a French door, partially open. Light shone through the glass panes.

The layout of the house—two stories, central hall on the ground level with rooms on either side—would force him and Ben to separate.

As Ben rushed toward the lighted room, Michael moved into the living room. He panned the gun across the area. Clear.

Behind him came a scream. It was cut off by the distinctive sound of his teammate's weapon: *Thoomp! Thoomp!* Something crashed. Michael fought the urge to rush back.

The scream had been high-pitched, like a woman's, then changed to a deep, guttural growl. Either his headphones had glitched or the guard had shrieked in surprise, then slipped into you're-not-going-to-get-me mode as he'd gone for his gun.

Had to be an actor. What computer-generated avatar would do that?

He ran through the room, toward an archway. Beyond, the surfaces of a kitchen gleamed. A door in the kitchen's back wall swung open. As a figure came through, the sensors in Michael's helmet identified the intruder as another team member—Emile.

Michael turned, absently noticed a table cluttered with the remnants of a meal: dirty plates, silverware, glasses. He started past it and spotted a man. He was standing in a den, on the far side of a couch. Facing Michael, he reached into his jacket.

Michael fired. The man left the ground. He crashed into a television, which rocked but stayed on. The system added spatters of black game-blood to the front of the TV. Cartoon animals danced and sang on the screen, their voices high and merry.

Thousand points right there, Michael thought. *I'm going to be top dog on this one.*

Emile rushed to a sliding glass door off the den, opened it, and stepped out.

Michael went to an opening on the opposite side of the den. The foyer: he'd circled back around. Ben was making his way up a staircase. Michael fell in behind him. At the landing, Ben turned left and swung into a bedroom.

Thoomp!

Michael turned right. At the end of a hall, a man stood in a doorway. Michael snapped his shotgun up. The computer's facial recognition software identified him as the HVT. Michael ran for him. The man slammed the door.

Michael rushed up to it, then remembered why the guy was the High Value Target: rebel leader, preparing a coup. No doubt he was armed, leveling a machine gun at the door. Michael slammed his back against the wall beside the door.

Kick it in. Duck out of the line of fire. Dive back in. Blast away.

Glass shattered within the room.

The window!

Michael kicked open the door. He saw a flash of movement at the shattered window.

No, no!

He jumped onto the bed, over it, stopped beside the opening. He glanced through, pulled his head back. The patio roof extended out from the house below the window, glass and pieces of wood all over it. He stuck his head through to check either side. Nobody.

Emile was just there. He'd gone out the door to the backyard patio.

"Emile! He's in the backyard! Do you see him?"

Michael stepped through the window and scrambled down the incline to the roof's edge. The yard was dark, except right below him, where the light from the house splashed out. A rain gutter had broken away, swinging from one end. He leaped for the grass. His ankle twisted and he rolled. Pain flared up his leg. He brought his gun up, swung it in a complete circle, rotating his body on the grass.

The sliding door into the den was open. Could the HVT have gone back in? Through the house to the front door? Hiding? Again, he spun around. He saw no other clues to where the man had gone. He got his feet under him. His ankle gave out, and he fell to one knee. Felt like glass grinding around inside him.

Forget it. Push it away.

He rose and limped through the door. Swinging his weapon back and forth, he crossed to the foyer. Ben was stomping down the stairs. The front door was open. Emile came through it from outside. He shook his head.

"What happened?" Ben said.

The garage.

Michael started for the door in the kitchen. As he passed another door—narrow: a pantry or coat closet—it opened. A man—not the HVT—bolted out, screaming. He was on Michael, hammering at him with something, cracking it against the helmet.

Static flickered over Michael's screen. The man's image flickered with it, his face seeming to change. He went out of focus, then became sharp again, all eyes and nose and teeth. Michael couldn't get his gun around. He pushed, but the man was clinging to him with one hand while the other continued beating the object into his helmet and shoulder.

Thoomp!

The man gasped and crumpled.

Liquid spattered over Michael's face mask, obscuring his view. Bursts of static on the screen pierced Michael's eyes. He reached for his chinstrap. His fingers slipped over it, wet. He tugged off his glove, got the chinstrap unsnapped, and ripped off his helmet.

At his feet, bleeding out on the floor, gasping for breath, was a young boy.

TWO

The child could not have been more than twelve or thirteen years old.

Unfiltered by the computer, the cartoon aspects were gone. The blood was not black, but bright red. And everywhere. It spurted out of a hole in the boy's side. The kid looked up at Michael, fear and disbelief making his eyes wide. He tried to talk, hitched in a breath. His head pitched back. His chest stopped rising and falling. The air he'd taken in eased out.

Michael dropped his helmet and fell to his knees. He touched the boy's face. The flesh under his fingers was soft. Michael slid his hand down to the wound. Wet, sticky, warm. His finger slipped into the hole. He felt bone.

"What?" he said. He looked up at the helmeted soldier whose shotgun still oozed smoke. "This is *real*! *He's* real! Just a . . . just a boy."

"Michael." The voice was muffled by the helmet, but he recognized it as Ben's. "Put your helmet back on."

"But . . . can't you see? This is real. He's dead. We killed him."

"Put it on, now." Ben shifted his aim from the boy to Michael.

Michael's chest tightened. "Wait!" he said. "This is real! It's not an exercise, it's not a game!" He felt sick. Had he really believed it was all just a game?

Realistic, yes . . . that's what made the Outis Corporation the best at training soldiers. That's why he'd chosen to go with it right out of high school.

But *real*? No, no . . . not now, not here. They had not been deployed. They were still on U.S. soil, he was sure of it. They often traveled, or pretended to travel, to training facilities Outis maintained all over the country. And they had traveled this time, but not far.

"What's going on?" he said. His eyes stung, clouded up. He wiped at them.

Ben was a statue, unmoving except for the finger tightening against the trigger.

Emile darted forward, putting himself between Michael and the team leader. He held his hand up to Ben. "No!" He swiveled his helmet around to Michael. "Put your helmet on. Michael! You *have* to."

For the first time, Michael saw not his helmet but his own pale face staring back at him from the surface of his teammate's face mask. He was accustomed to the helmets, their uniformity and anonymity. But now, with his own off, and a dead boy in front of him, they seemed alien and wrong.

"Out of the way, Emile." Ben sidestepped, reclaiming his target. "You have till three," he said to Michael. "One . . ."

"Michael!" Emile said. "Put it on!"

"Two . . ."

Once again, Emile stepped in the way. He spoke to Ben, words Michael could not hear.

Michael looked down at the boy. About his brother's age. Kind of looked like him too. He spotted what had rolled away from his hand when he fell, the weapon the boy had attacked him with: a family-sized can of chili. Michael felt dizzy. He closed his eyes.

This is what's not real: this dead boy. The game, the exercise, those are real. I got hit on the head, that's all. Jumping off the roof. Some crazy actor's overexcitement when he attacked me. Got me thinking weird. I'll open my eyes, and the boy will be gone.

But he wasn't. The metallic odor of blood and tangy cordite from the gunshot that had shed it stung Michael's nostrils. He started to hyperventilate. He stood. "How could this happen?" he whispered. "This isn't right."

Ben handed something to Emile.

Michael's eyes focused beyond them, to the den. The cartoon characters on the television were doing a cancan through a field of flowers. Red blood ran like claw marks over the screen. He squinted, tilted his head, but he could not quite see the body on the floor in there—only a blue-jeaned leg and sneaker. They were small. He had shot another child, maybe a few years younger than the one at his feet.

He groaned. "What have we done?"

Emile stepped toward him, his hand out, calming him. "It's all right," he said. "It's not what it looks like."

"Not with the helmets on," Michael agreed. "Take them off, you'll see. You'll see what's real."

"We've all had them off at one time or another, Michael," Emile said. He edged closer. "It's all in the timing, man. You took yours off a little too soon, that's all."

Michael looked around Emile. "Ben, who did you shoot in that room over there? Who screamed? Who'd you shoot in the bedroom upstairs?" He started to weep. *"Who did you kill?"*

Emile sprang and seized Michael's wrist. His other hand came around from behind, holding a pistol.

No, no—not a gun, Michael realized. It was the CO_2 injection pistol the team leader carried for hostage-taking.

Michael punched at Emile. He struck his helmet, his arm. He stopped him from swinging the syringe closer.

"No!" he said. "Look, look what's happening. This is real."

He stepped back, and his ankle gave out. He went down hard. His cheek landed in a puddle of blood. The boy's lifeless eyes glared at him accusingly.

Emile's knee dropped into Michael's ribs. He felt the wind forced out of his lungs, but before he could respond—before he could push Emile off or take a breath—the cold barrel of the injection pistol pushed into his neck.

Pppsssshhh.

The nightmares began.

THREE

Denver, Colorado
Three days later

The place was called Casa Bonita. It was the closest thing the Mile High City had to a true theme restaurant, the kind that pocked the landscape around Disney World like acne. Mexico was done here *en una manera grande*: lava-rock walls, thatched-roof gazebos, fake palm trees festooned with holiday lights, what appeared to be an entire street lifted out of Puerto Vallarta. The centerpiece was a lagoon into which "cliff divers" plunged, alongside a three-story waterfall, every half hour. Diners sat at tables in aristocratic dining halls and waterside cabanas, in the caves of the Sierra Madres, even in the darkness behind the waterfall. Kids played games in one of several arcade rooms and crept through Black Bart's Hideaway, a cavern of passageways where lights flashed on to reveal monsters hidden in the walls and where air, accompanied by shrill alarms, shot out at unsuspecting passersby. Parents got caricature portraits made near a wishing well and passed time in the cantina. Somehow, this tour of *la Tierra Azteca* fit in a single building that, from outside, mimicked an oversized Spanish mission.

Laura Fuller gazed up at the black-painted ceilings, where tiny lights twinkled like stars. "I thought our flight was taking us to Denver, not Mazatlán," she said, sipping a margarita.

"Great, isn't it?" John Hutchinson pushed his plate away and leaned back in his chair. He plopped a hand on his belly, groaning. "These all-you-can-eat meals should be illegal."

"I had three plates of enchiladas," said Laura's son, Dillon. He didn't bother to look up from the sopaipilla he was dousing with honey.

"It was a long flight, and we didn't get up in time for breakfast," Laura explained.

Hutch was familiar with the journey.

The day before, Laura and Dillon had taken an eight-passenger commuter out of Fiddler Falls, a speck of a town in northern Saskatchewan. The stomach-tossing, six-hour flight alone was enough to lay seasoned travelers low, but then they had spent the night in Saskatoon and caught a 6:30 AM commercial flight to Denver—another five hours in the air.

Hutch caught the eye of a wandering trinket salesman and waved him over. The man stepped up to the table, bearing lighted spinning butterflies, glowing rabbit ears, and swords that *shling*ed when waved— apparently pirates and conquistadors used the same bladesmith.

"What's your fancy?" Hutch asked Dillon.

"I'm too old for that stuff," the boy said around a mouthful of food. His eyes sparkled at the goodies all the same.

"Ten is not too old for a light saber," Hutch informed him. "Green or blue?"

"Hutch, really," Laura said, "you don't have to."

"If you're going to explore the caves, you gotta have a sword." He pointed at one and handed the man a twenty. He turned the saber over to Dillon.

The boy, all eyes and teeth, accepted it. He swung it around, then held it vertically in front of himself. Its blue glow radiated over his face.

Hutch remembered those eyes, at once vibrant and sad; the mouth that when it smiled made dimpled cheeks and revealed Chiclet teeth and a little tongue that seemed not to know quite what to do with itself. It'd been over a year since he'd seen Dillon. Hutch had bought Laura a satellite phone, the only kind that worked in the wilderness she and her son called home. He'd burned through a few paychecks' worth of airtime minutes, but it wasn't the same as being with them.

They'd met a year ago when hell had staked a claim on Fiddler Falls. A young man named Declan Page and a homicidal gang of youthful followers had attempted to take over the town—for not much more reason than because they thought they could. Laura's husband, Tom, Dillon's father, had died fighting them.

Hutch and three friends had been camping in the hills above town. They had inadvertently crashed Declan's party, and through dumb luck, according to Hutch, or through "survival skills and heroism," according to some news media, they had managed to stop the siege. Hutch had saved the boy's life. In turn, Dillon had *returned* Hutch's life to him, reminding him that despite the nasty divorce he was going through, life was worth living and the children his ex was trying to keep from him were worth fighting for.

Hutch leaned across the table to run his fingers over Dillon's hair and cheek. "I'm glad you're here."

Dillon rolled his eyes. "Finally!" He looked anxiously at his mom. "How long, a week?"

"We head home next weekend," she said.

Dillon frowned. He gazed at Hutch, and his eyes got a little watery.

Hutch felt the same. A week was too short, but he said, "Hey, we can do a lot in a week. You'll see. In a week, you'll be so beat you'll want to go home just to rest."

"I do chores at home," Dillon said.

"He does," Laura said. "It's amazing, how much he helps."

Dillon hung his head. He found the switch on the sword and turned it off.

Laura smiled at Hutch. "We're tired, that's all."

"I'm sorry," Hutch said, bringing his watch up. "I should have thought about that. You need a nap more than you do a crazy place like this." He moved a napkin from his lap to the sauce-smeared plate in front of him.

"No," Dillon said, perking up. "That's all right. I want to see more." As if to prove it, he turned the sword's light on again. "Can I . . . uh . . . ?" His finger pointed this way and that; his eyes roamed elsewhere.

"You sure?" Hutch said. Getting an enthusiastic affirmation, Hutch looked to Laura. She shrugged, as if to say *Kids*. He tossed Dillon a plastic baggie of tokens. "Don't spend it all in one place."

Dillon hefted it in his hand. His smile grew bigger. He stood and looked around, unsure which direction to head first.

"Dillon," Hutch said, gesturing for the boy to draw closer. He whispered, "Check out the area under the bridge in Black Bart's. It's really cool." He pointed, and Dillon ran off. Hutch called to him: "But don't get lost. It's easy to do in this place." To Laura he said, "This is Logan's favorite restaurant."

Logan was Hutch's twelve-year-old son.

"Once, when he was about seven, he ran off like that and disappeared.

We couldn't find him anywhere. Cops came, started interviewing people, checking the security tapes. Janet was freaking out."

"You weren't?" Laura's eyes had grown big.

Hutch smiled. "In my way. Thing is, I should have known. I've been coming here since *I* was a kid. Finally, I had a revelation." He laughed and took a swig from a bottle of Dos Equis. "Black Bart's Hideaway. There's a plank bridge in there. If you're mischievous enough, you can slip between the rocks and get under it. Almost no way to see under there, it's so dark, even with the lights on."

"He got stuck?" Laura said. She looked over her shoulder the direction Dillon had gone. "Why didn't he call out?"

"Uh-uh," Hutch said. "Not Logan. He was hiding."

"That whole time?"

"That's Logan."

"Well, it is called Hideaway."

"Exactly." Hutch drained the bottle into his mouth. He reached for the flag attached to a tiny pole on the table. Raising it beckoned a server. Then he stopped and withdrew his hand. He'd promised himself no more than two beers at a single sitting. After returning from Canada, he'd had trouble with that. It was just too blasted easy to keep going.

He said, "Of course, they'd turned the lights on and even flashed a light under the bridge. Whenever they did, Logan would squeeze himself into a corner."

"Oooh," Laura said.

"His rump was red for a while, I'll tell you," Hutch said. "But worse, as far as he was concerned, we didn't come back for six months."

"No more hiding?"

"You gotta hide when you're here. Only not for three hours."

"So," she said, shifting in her chair, sizing him up, "where are they, Logan and Macie? Not your week?"

"It is, actually. Janet will bring them to the house this evening. You know I've always wanted the two of you to meet them. I think Dillon and Logan will have a blast together. When you see him, ask to see his grill."

"His what?"

"His braces. Not really what the rap kids consider grillz, but close enough for a twelve-year-old suburbanite."

She shook her head. "I'm still trying to get my head around the idea that you're not the Grizzly Adams guy I met in Canada. Of course, I knew you lived in Denver, but I can't shake the thought that you belong in the woods, in some cabin you built yourself. Instead of stalking lynx through the wilderness, you write newspaper columns. Now you tell me your son talks like a . . . whaddaya call 'em . . . gangsta?"

They laughed.

"Something like that," Hutch said. He tried to remember if he'd ever seen her smile in those few weeks he'd spent in Canada while the authorities up there conducted their investigation. Probably she had, if only forcing it for Dillon's sake, but he couldn't recall.

Laura said, "How is it, having them back?"

Hutch nodded. He wished he could say, *We went camping last week and saw a bear!* Or, *You should have seen Macie in the school play. Eight-year-olds everywhere gave up their dreams of stardom, what with her talent sucking up all the accolades.* But truth was he'd won joint custody, and it hadn't gone much further than his kids bouncing from Janet's home to his every week.

He hadn't done all the things with them he'd thought he would. No bike rides or circuses. No taking Logan to the skate park or fishing with Macie. Going out to the movies or the ice-cream parlor—events he'd imaged as everyday occurrences—had become rare. He sometimes wondered, when his mind paused long enough to consider it, whether *getting* time with them had been more important to him than spending time with them.

But instead of addressing it aloud, he said, "Both Janet and I come from broken homes. When we got married, we promised ourselves we'd break that cycle. Guess that didn't work so well."

A spotlight illuminated a stage beside the waterfall, about halfway up. A cowboy spun a six-shooter and spoke into a microphone: "Well, howdy, folks. I'm sheriff of these parts, and I'm looking for Black Bart. Anybody seen that varmint?"

A chorus of kid voices yelled that the evildoer was *right there*, sneaking up on the sheriff from behind the waterfall. He was a cowboy bad guy: black hat, bandolier, and Snidely Whiplash mustache.

Laura said, "I thought Black Bart was a pirate."

Hutch shrugged. "Depends on the context, or what costumes are handy, I guess." He sat up in his chair and saw Dillon run up to a rope barrier on the other side of the lagoon. Hutch waved, but the boy's eyes were too full of the show. He said, "I bet he's never seen anything like this before."

"I never have," Laura said. She touched his arm. "Don't feel that you have to, you know, show us the sights. That's not why we came."

"Oh, come on. Skiing. The Rockies. Mile High Stadium, I mean, Invesco Field. My dad still calls it *Bears* Stadium, and that goes back to '68. Let's see, what else . . . ?"

"John Hutchinson," she said. "You, that's what we came for. I'm just happy you could make time for us."

He nodded. "Got a couple columns banked, so readers won't miss their thrice-weekly dose of the Spirit of Colorado."

His column, which ran in the *Denver Post*, profiled Coloradoans who had triumphed over adversity. Everyone had made a big deal over his entering the ranks of these victors by surviving in Canada. In fact, the story had been picked up by the national media.

Before he had realized what was happening, they'd dubbed him a hero. The story of Declan, the scion of the Page fortune, gone bad and the man who'd stopped him had made it to the pages of *People* magazine and *Reader's Digest*. Heck, even *60 Minutes* had given the drama a twelve-minute segment. Three publishing houses had contacted him about writing a book, but they wanted a "hero's tale," and that didn't interest him.

He simply couldn't take credit, when all he had done was live through it, and when so much tragedy had resulted despite his best efforts. Besides, he was flat broke and couldn't find time for his kids. What kind of hero let his life crumble like that?

"Dillon was hoping the two of you could do a little archery," Laura said. "He's become a regular Robin Hood."

"I hope not the part about—"

The James Bond-like opening of Led Zeppelin's "Kashmir" emanated from his breast pocket. He pulled out the mobile phone.

"—robbing from the rich to give to the poor," he finished. The call was coming from a pay phone. "Hello?"

"John Hutchinson?"

He didn't recognize the voice, strained, rushed.

"Speaking."

"Don't say my name."

"That would be a little difficult, since I don't know—"

The voice said, "It adds up to a dime or more."

Nichols. Dr. Dorian Nichols.

Hutch stood so quickly, his chair toppled backward. "I thought you were . . ." He started to turn away, remembered where he was, and held an index finger up to Laura. She had stopped his bottle from toppling over when his legs had hit the table. He turned away from her concern.

Hutch said, "The cops . . . *everyone* is looking for you. Your family . . ."

"They slaughtered them, all of them." Nichols's voice broke on *slaughtered*, rose in pitch.

"They? Who?"

"Don't use any names!"

"You think what? My line's bugged? Yours? You're calling from a pay phone."

"Yours, absolutely, but they probably have entire area codes covered for me by now. They use a keyword program. It can monitor millions of conversations without anyone having to listen. That's how they do it now."

A señorita brushed past, leading a family to a nearby table. Hutch picked up his chair and stepped around it. He faced a lava-rock wall, lowered his voice.

"You keep saying *they*."

"You have to ask?"

"The news said—"

"I know, that I killed them. That's what they made it look like. Would you expect anything different?"

"Where are you? Why are you calling me? You need to go to . . ."

The man jumped into Hutch's hesitation. "To who? I can't go to anyone. As soon as I do, they'll lock me up. Then Page . . ." The man pulled in air, as if trying to take back the word. "Put me in a cell and I won't come out—they'll get me for sure. The only chance I have to . . . to expose who did this is to blow it wide open."

"I don't understand." But Hutch was beginning to. "Why don't you go to the media? I mean, the big guys? They'd—"

"They'd think I went crazy, like they're already saying. First they'd turn me in, then they'd write a story about how they helped apprehend me."

Hutch closed his eyes. Nichols was right. Hutch had beaten his own head against enough brick walls this past year to know. The man Nichols was talking about—Brendan Page—had insulated himself so thoroughly, was so adept at using his money and influence, that he was nearly untouchable. And *nearly* was Hutch's hope only adding words. If Page had gone after Nichols as ruthlessly as he apparently had done, the doctor must possess exactly what Hutch's investigation needed.

God help me, Hutch thought. *Thinking like this. The man's family. Still . . .*

"What do you have?" Hutch said.

Silence. Finally, Nichols said, *"Xĭ năo . . . Genjuros."*

"What? Wait . . . spell that." Hutch patted his pockets for a pen.

Nichols said, "Do your research. I'll be in touch."

"Hold on. Where are you? I can—"

A clicking sound came through, as though he could hear the quarters Nichols had used dropping through the phone.

"Hello? Doc—" He stopped himself. Bugged? *His* phone? He looked at it, as if some evidence of it would show. The screen told him the call had been lost. He slapped it shut and dropped it into his pocket. He turned to the table, picked up his sunglasses.

"We have to go," he told Laura.

"What is it? Is everything all right?"

Hutch flagged down their server and handed her a credit card. He turned back to Laura. "I'm sorry, it's just . . . Everything's okay. That was a guy I'd been trying to reach. He'd always avoided me, like everyone else. Now he's in trouble and wants to talk. I think he knows something, what I've been looking for."

"About Declan's father?" she asked.

Hutch had always believed the billionaire military industrialist had something to do with the atrocities his son had committed in Canada. The Canadian and U.S. justice departments had ultimately disagreed. Hutch had been digging for dirt—futilely—since returning to Denver a year ago.

He said, "I think so, yeah." He waved at Dillon, still watching the show from the far side of the lagoon. "Dillon!"

Black Bart pushed the sheriff off the stage. The lawman plunged twenty feet into the water. Everyone booed. Black Bart laughed maniacally.

"Dillon!"

The boy glanced over. He grinned and waved.

Hutch beckoned him. The server returned with his card and the bill to sign. Hutch scrawled the odd words Nichols had told him on a napkin and shoved it into his pocket. He said, "He wants me to research something. Said he'd get back to me."

Laura said, "Hey, at least he had the courtesy to call after we ate, huh?"

Dillon ran over. "Can we get more of those roll things?"

"Not this time, honey." Laura pulled his coat off the back of a chair.

"We're *leaving*?"

"I'm sorry, Dillon," Hutch said. He tried to corral his stampeding thoughts. "We'll come back, I promise."

The boy slipped into his coat. He looked around, frowning at all the places he didn't get to explore.

Hutch patted him on the back. "I promise." He slipped around him and headed for the exit. He'd already started the list of things he had to do when he got home, the computer searches, the phone calls.

FOUR

Brendan Page moved through the building like a big cat through a jungle. At fifty-eight he was as fit and agile as most of the twenty-somethings his company sent into the world's hottest war zones.

Staying that way wasn't easy. He worked with a nutritionist to calibrate his diet, a physical trainer to mastermind the perfect combination of aerobic and strength exercises, a dancer to help him stay in tune with his body and movements, and experts in the fields of intelligence and memory, because what good was a powerful body without the mind to guide it? To Page, by the time that good night came, it was too late. Dylan Thomas had it right: it was not death but old age at which you should "burn and rave."

Now, maneuvering through the corridors, he felt everything, sensed everything: the rubber soles pressing lightly on linoleum before receiving his entire weight; the way the lights cast his shadow behind him . . . under him . . . ahead of him as he passed them; the hint of aftershave lingering from his prey's having been there. A few minutes ago, at most. Without looking, he gently, almost absently, tried each door handle he passed: always locked. He checked his Steyr Tactical Machine Pistol—or TMP—an Outis favorite for its firepower, dependability, and compact size. It was chambered and ready, set to full auto.

He detected a high-pitched whine coming through his headphones, so quiet he could have imagined it. He raised his weapon and tapped it against the helmet. The noise stopped. Remembering the flickering image one of his soldiers had recently experienced, he gave his faceplate a hard crack with the weapon. There—a flash of static across his heads-up display.

One of Page's companies had developed the helmet. Earlier versions, less laden with technological goodies, had worked perfectly. In fact, thousands of units continued to function well for his soldiers all over the world. But it seemed that each new feature he requested rendered the helmets less reliable.

He didn't know all that much about how the technology worked; he only knew what he wanted and demanded that his engineers figure out how to pull it off. To Page, war was a business: it had clear objectives; it required certain tools and skills and people to use them effectively. His strengths lay in innovating new tools and skill sets, in conveying his vision and making it contagious, so the smartest minds in the world would rally to make it a reality.

When the tools and skill sets failed, it often resulted in disastrous consequences like those he'd witnessed the other night. But he knew the score: push a technology, a strategy, a human to just beyond the breaking point, then build the infrastructure that supported the improved version. It was the only way he knew to keep advancing.

He continued to move along the hallway, stopping short of a four-way junction. On the map in his heads-up display, the left corridor flashed. He turned left. The direction might prove to be wrong, but the computer was making calculations based on data Page either did not know or could not keep in his head while maintaining a stealthy pursuit. The system had analyzed video and debriefing reports from many of his opponent's previous battles. It also took into account what Outis knew of the man's training and experience. In this case, his opponent was a lifelong military commander. He would have been taught, and seen the advantage of, left-hand turns when pursued on foot.

Roughly 80 percent of the population was right-handed, meaning chances were high that a pursuer's body was also angled that direction. Turning left required the pursuer to swing his weapon and body farther. Even that extra second or two could mean the difference between the quarry getting around the next corner unseen or not. In the absence of contradictory evidence—say, a blood trail or scuff marks heading another way—Page would trust his computer's advice.

Where are you? he thought. He realized he had whispered the words only when a faint snickering came through his headphones. The voice belonged to his opponent, Col. Ian Bryson, a guy as hard and sharp as an obsidian arrowhead. That famous quote about something either killing you or making you stronger? Ian was the kind of guy Nietzsche had in mind.

Page said, "You've got a voice channel open."

"The better to hear you scream," Ian said.

Page paused, hoping to hear the sound echoing in the corridor, through a door. He said, "Not this time, my friend. Let's get on with it."

"Had enough?"

"Of *stalking*, yes."

"All right," Ian continued. "Next door on the left."

At the door, the computer told him there was a 19 percent chance his opponent would attempt an ambush immediately upon his entering. If time were an issue, if he had to stop his opponent from killing a hostage, for example, he would have bet on his four-to-one odds and stormed through the door. This time, however, he could be cautious.

He hunkered beside the wall and pushed open the door. No gunfire, no sounds. He pivoted through, kicking the door so it would slam against the far wall. If it did not, he would shoot through it. A quick 180-degree pan of his head allowed the helmet's optics to find, if it was there to find, the heat signature of even a single finger.

The room was a cavernous warehouse. Crates were stacked to varying heights, forming long canyons between them. Twenty, thirty rows, at least. Mesh-covered lights, hanging from high rafters, failed to dispel the gloom or chase away the deep shadows.

Page ran to a crate and pressed his back against it. He peered around the corner into one of the long canyons. With utter blackness on the other end, it could have extended forever.

The computer flashed a green *E* in the upper left corner of his display. Two lines appeared explaining why the Enemy possessed the advantage: Steyr = short-range weapon. E = long-range marksmanship. Page imagined getting in a firefight between the wooden walls of crates. His aim would not be as sharp as his opponent's; his ammo would fall short. He slipped his weapon over his shoulder and put it behind his back. From the same location he withdrew a Parker Hale Model 85 sniper rifle. The deficiency of his previous weapon disappeared from the screen, but the enemy's marksmanship continued to give him advantage. That wasn't going to change anytime soon. He had to find another way to turn the tables.

Page darted across the opening and to the next canyon. *Straight as a shooting range*, he thought. Precisely the venue of Ian's best advantage. Here Page could never triumph over the former Army Ranger. No, Page preferred close-quarter combat, where his greater agility and confidence gave him the upper fist. He needed to get closer to Ian. As he was trying to figure out a way to do that, the heads-up display suggested a different strategy. Anticipating Page's discomfort with distances and knowing he'd move closer, Ian—according to the computer—would try to circle around.

Page moved back to the open door and slid behind it. He waited . . . three minutes . . . four.

Patience, he thought. *It's not always balls to the wall . . . unfortunately.*

Finally a noise reached the sensitive microphones on his helmet. He watched through the gap in the door as Ian poked his head around the farthest row of crates.

The colonel had taken advantage of retirement, letting his hair— still full and dark at sixty—grow long and shabby, sprouting a mustache and even a soul patch. Ian's work at Outis was another way for him to let his hair down, as it were. The things he helped do there beat in time with his military heart, propelling the contemporary fighting machine into the future; but the Pentagon would never consider dancing on the razor's edge the way Outis did. It was much easier to let a private company get its hands dirty.

Ian ran to the next opening, peered down the canyon, ran to the next. He disappeared between the crates.

Page moved out from behind the door. He angled toward the opening where Ian had disappeared. His helmet beeped. It displayed an arrow moving from the top of the screen toward the bottom.

Page ducked into the canyon next to the one for which he had been heading. The system indicated Ian would anticipate Page's move: he was probably returning to wait for him at the head of the canyon. Page moved deeper into the row. He found a place where the wall was a single crate high. He slung his weapon over his shoulder and hoisted himself up. Testing the top for noisiness, he crawled across to the next row.

Ian had his back pressed against a crate, inches from the end of the row. He held a pistol in one hand, a knife in the other.

Page backed away from the edge. He carefully set down his rifle and pulled a pistol from a holster. He shifted it into his left hand and inched forward. Ian was gone.

He heard a sharp inhalation above him. He rolled to see Ian lunging, both hands on the handle of his BFK knife. Page raised his leg, and Ian landed on his boot. Page fired. The first shot tore a chunk out of Ian's shoulder. The second pierced his neck. The next three caught him in the chest and sent him reeling over the edge of the crate.

Page rose. He holstered his pistol and picked up the rifle. He jumped down from the crate. He straddled Ian's legs, staring down at the bloody mess. He said, "That was too easy, my friend."

Ian's head lifted. He said, "You don't think it's over, do you?"

Footsteps pounded against the concrete floor behind Page. He spun in time to see a soldier charging with a bayonet. Page fired, a .308-caliber direct hit that sent the soldier sailing into the shadows.

Page frowned at the smoke drifting from the rifle's barrel. It formed a perfect circle and drifted away.

Something soft landed behind him. He twirled to see a black-cloaked ninja holding two *kamas*—short sickles with foot-long blades. The assassin skipped toward Page, blurring the *kamas* in front of him.

"Okay," Page said. "That's more like it." He flipped his rifle over his shoulder and withdrew a *naginata*, a long staff with a crescent blade on one end. As Page braced himself, the computer analyzed his opponent's foot movement, body roll, the angle of each arm, the movement of the eyes.

The ninja attacked.

Perfectly reading his helmet's tones and the icons flashing on the display inside his face mask, Page moved: he ducked as a *kama* swung past. He pivoted his leg away as another *kama* struck the floor where his knee had been. He was about to rise when the computer told him not to. He crouched lower as the two blades crossed overhead. Responding to a tone, he thrust his own weapon, skewering the ninja through the rib cage. Blood geysered out of the man, who dropped his *kamas* and continued to spasm on Page's weapon. A choking, gurgling sound issued from his gaping mouth.

Page watched for a few moments, then said, "All right, Ian."

Ian's voice came through the headphones: "Thought you wanted to experience the victory of the kill."

Blood poured from the ninja's mouth.

Page said, "I got it."

"Ain't pretty, is it, Brendan?" Ian said. "Unless you didn't like the guy." Ian laughed wickedly.

The ninja's eyes rolled toward Page's. More blood, more wet noises.

Ian was challenging him, putting it in his face. Page knew the man's position: War was hell. Not that it wasn't sometimes—often—necessary, but it burned hotter when death was easy, impersonal.

Page yanked the *naginata* out of the ninja. Before the man could fall, he swung the blade into his neck. The ninja disappeared.

Page unsnapped his chinstrap. The video flicked off. He pulled the helmet over his head, squinting into the darkness of the circular room around him. He wore a skintight bodysuit on which seventy markers allowed 250 cameras to monitor his every movement. They, in turn, placed him in a virtual reality environment, one of many that were preprogrammed and called up at a controller's whim. The point-of-view of his VR self in that VR environment was then fed back to the heads-up display in his face mask. The controller could introduce millions of details into the viewer's perspective, from people to objects.

Page's companies had been experimenting with putting specific people into the VR worlds, as it had done this time, with Ian. Coupled with Behavior Pattern Analysis software that made the computer-drawn people—or *avatars*—behave the way actual people did, it allowed soldiers to learn to fight opponents before they ever actually faced them in person. The virtual Ian that Page had fought behaved the way the real Ian would have in a similar situation.

Page bent and unsnapped his heavy, ski-type boots. He slipped out of them and stepped off the low pedestal. It was a pad that registered every step, jump, and tiptoe he made. Its resistance-adjusting surface, in tandem with a harness-and-wire system, gave the VR player total freedom of movement, and the *feeling* of actual movement, without his venturing from the center of the VR room—or "Void," as it had become known at Outis.

He walked to a wall of additional helmets and other motion-capture gadgets and seated his helmet into a recharging base. He snapped his weapons prop—which, in his VR display, had been a Steyr TMP, Parker Hale rifle, and *naginata*—into tongs on the wall.

He gazed up at the control room's window, two stories above the Void's floor. Ian sat at a control panel, punching buttons and turning knobs. He saw Page looking and flipped a switch that opened an intercom.

"How was it?" Ian said.

"Your avatar flickered a few times. It hesitated when it was over me with the knife."

"That was a glitch," Ian said. "I wouldn't have hesitated."

"And the eyes still aren't quite right." Page rolled his head around, feeling the muscles in his neck flex and pop. He pushed his fists into his lower back and bent over them.

Snatching a cigar holder off a shelf, he withdrew a vintage Davidoff Dom Perignon, a dark brown stick of aromatic Cuban leaf, made before the manufacturer fled Havana for the Dominican. He rolled the cigar under his nose, appreciating the coffee-chocolaty fragrance coming off the wrapper.

"Oh," he said, catching Ian's eye again. "Was the rifle smoke your idea? How many programming man-hours did you spend on that one?"

"If you want, we can program smoke rings for you too," Ian said.

"I'm not laughing, smart guy." He clipped the foot of the Davidoff and toasted the head over a lighter's mini-torch. His inability to blow smoke rings, despite burning through a dozen cigars a day, was a company joke—though only Ian dared laugh about it to his face.

The great Brendan Page, he'd say, *conqueror of cities, builder of empires, leader of thirty thousand men . . . can't blow a smoke ring.*

Page pulled on the cigar, tasting cedar in the smoke. He glanced up at the empty control room window. He formed his lips into an *O* and pushed out some smoke. An unformed plume billowed into the room.

Ian strolled past the window.

"Ian!" Page called. He waved the smoke away from his face.

Ian nodded at him.

"Let's go again," Page said.

"Anyone in mind?"

Page thought about it. "I think it's time to kick bin Laden's butt again. Put him on, but give him a couple extra bodyguards this time."

FIVE

Hutch held the phone away from his ear as the man on the other end laid into him.

"Where do you come off calling me at home?" the man said.

Hutch said, "Okay, forget about Dr. Nichols." He tapped a notepad on his desk with a pencil. "What about *Genjuros*? Does that word mean anything to you? I think it's G-E-N—"

He heard a *click* and the familiar nothingness that was somehow deeper than silence. "Hello? Dr. Kregel?"

He sighed and dropped the handset onto the cradle, then rocked back in his chair. He gazed at the dry-marker board, the size of a garage door, that hung on one wall of his home office. It was covered with scribbled notes in a dozen colors. Lines snaked around and through words, suggesting tentative connections. Photographs and articles clipped from newspapers and magazines or photocopied from books were taped here and there along its edges, spreading onto the walls.

One of the papers, partially covered by later additions to the wall, was headlined "The Psychological Effect of War on the Adolescent Mind." It was written by Dorian Nichols, PhD. A small picture showed a man in glasses and a bow tie.

Hutch tossed the pencil at it. He said, "What is it, doctor? What did you want me to find out?"

A knock came at the door. Laura peered in, smiling. "You're not talking to yourself, are you?"

"Don't worry, I don't listen." Hutch looked at his watch and realized he'd been holed up for three hours. "Uh . . . I lost track of the time."

"I kind of got that," Laura said. She came into the room, carrying two steaming mugs. "I brought you something from my neck of the woods. *Nahapi* tea."

"Ah, the good stuff. Supposed to be relaxing, right?"

"It means 'sit down' in Cree," Laura said, picking her way though the clutter on the floor. "It's supposed to *remind* you to relax. You look like you can use it." Her foot struck a pile of magazines. She lurched forward, swayed, kept the tea from sloshing out. She handed him a mug.

Hutch opened his arms, indicating the piles of everything everywhere, the wall of notes and papers. "Welcome to my world," he said. "My work for almost a year."

"Your obsession, more like it." Laura read his face and said, "Sorry, I didn't mean—"

"No, you're probably right." He took a sip. Vapors carrying hints of flowers and fruit filled his nostrils. "Almost every waking hour."

Laura walked to the wall. Her eyes roamed over the mass of information.

He fought the compulsion to distract her, to lead her out into the other room where the extent of his preoccupation—he liked that word better—wasn't so obvious. But he'd told her about it over the phone; it was only fair that she witness the hard-copy version.

"This is all about Brendan Page?"

Hutch had never accepted the findings that Declan Page had acted independently when he'd used a satellite laser cannon, developed by one of his father's companies, to terrorize Fiddler Falls and kill more than a dozen people. Hutch believed the elder Page had instigated the assault or, at minimum, had known about it and done nothing to stop it.

Hutch had begun his own investigation. Nothing he'd found implicated Page or his companies—just as the Canadian and U.S. authorities had determined. But to Hutch, that only meant Page was a master at covering his tracks. The deeper Hutch dug, the more he became convinced the man was guilty of all sorts of crimes. Hutch stopped caring whether Page went to jail for playing a role in the tragedy in Canada, as long as he was busted for something.

Hutch stepped beside her and scanned the wall. "Him, Page Industries, Outis Enterprises."

"Outis? The . . . what, military organization?"

"Paramilitary. Some people call it a privatized army. A division of Page Industries. Its tentacles reach into every aspect of defense and security. It trains forty thousand personnel a year."

"Trains who to do what?"

"You name it: U.S. military Special Ops soldiers. Law enforcement officers in tactical operations—handling bank robberies, high school shootings, high-speed car chases. Outis has trained special teams from dozens of countries in aviation security and taking down hijackers. Whatever situation cops, soldiers, the CIA may encounter anywhere in the world, Outis has a program, experts, and the facilities to train them for it."

Hutch lifted his tea, but his racing mind wouldn't let him drink. He absently held the cup near his chin as he went on. "Over the last ten years the company has expanded from simply training other agencies' personnel to contracting out its own teams to do whatever job requires skilled soldiers and massive firepower. It provides everything from three-man bodyguards and a bulletproof car for a corporate executive to thousand-man armies, complete with air support and tank-like vehicles, for diplomat protection in war zones. It has teams breaking up drug cartels in South America, guarding embassies, hunting fugitives. Ten thousand gun-toting, helicopter-flying, combat vehicle–driving soldiers in U.S. military hot spots are actually Outis employees or contractors."

He shook his head. "It's an amazing operation. Other Page Industry companies have always designed and manufactured weapons—from small arms to missiles to the satellite laser weapon we encountered. Now it seems their most cutting-edge developments go right to Outis."

"Exclusively?" Laura said.

"The most skilled personnel, proprietary technology, and superior equipment. You want to make sure a diplomat doesn't get splattered or a fugitive gets captured, you call Outis."

"So," Laura said, "how does any of this make Page a criminal?"

Hutch moved his finger over the wall's collage. "Every now and then, Outis is accused of something . . . let's say *unsavory*." He tapped an article. "Double billing and including profits in expense reports to make profits on profits." He shrugged. "That's a civil issue. No big deal. But . . ." He tapped another article. "Here, Outis soldiers staffing a detainee camp are implicated in mistreating prisoners and torture. There are reports of a dozen similar incidents involving Outis personnel." He waved at a stack of clippings. "Drug smuggling . . . kidnapping a foreign dignitary . . . a bank robbery in Zaire . . . assassination."

"Hutch," Laura said, "if those things are sanctioned by the company, then it's an international crime syndicate."

"Hidden within an impossibly complex organization," he agreed. "And operating under the authority of federal governments, with details classified top secret, which means they can't be looked into without congressional approval."

Laura added, "Not to mention they tend to be engaged in activities where the line between what's authorized and what's not can be blurry." She scrunched her brow. "Right?"

"Blurry or nonexistent." He sighed heavily. "There's always something that exonerates either the accused soldiers themselves or the company. Often there's no proof of who did what. Witnesses have an uncanny way of disappearing or changing their stories. Suddenly it's self-defense—or the soldiers involved acted independently, outside company directives. This, despite witnesses or documents, even money trails, to the contrary.

"One problem is the way Outis gets involved on a legal level. It's not a military entity, so it's outside military law. At the same time, it doesn't move in until its people get immunity from prosecution from the host country. Those protections can be set aside if it's proven the accused were involved in activities outside their stated purpose for being there. But that takes time, often enough time to implement a cover-up."

He started tapping again. "One or two times, okay. Maybe even a dozen, given the size of the organization. But . . ." He stepped back and spread his arms out to indicate the entire collection.

Laura bit her lip, taking it all in. She said, "But, Hutch, hasn't each of these been investigated, and Page Industries exonerated?"

"Most of them," he said. "Some of them are active. Hence, my sixteen-hour days."

"I hate to say it, but it seems impossible trying to prove culpability when Page's companies have already covered themselves to the point that investigators have closed the book. And they have more access than you do. Why not let it go?"

Hutch sipped from the mug, found the tea too sweet, and put it on the desk. "Because when the Roman Empire was strong, it was untouchable, undefeatable. But Caesar wasn't."

"You lost me."

He moved to the left side of the wall. "Read the highlighted part."

Laura leaned in and read: "'Let the record show the witness identi-fied photograph A11, Brendan Page.'"

Hutch said, "That's the deposition of a torture victim. Now this . . ."

She read from a newspaper clipping: "'Industrialist Brendan Page admitted being in the country at the time of the assassination, how-ever . . .'"

"And farther down in the same article." He pointed.

"'A man matching Page's description was seen leaving the building, escorted by two unidentified men. When questioned . . .'"

"He was at the scene when Colombia's foreign minister of finance was assassinated in Switzerland," Hutch said. He started tapping docu-ments again. "Here he is implicated in taking part in the killing of civilians in Beirut. . . . Same thing in Baghdad. . . . Another torture. It goes on and on. Most times, if there's any mention of Page at all, it's lost among footnotes, with words like *uncorroborated* and *unreliable*. Or, again, the witness disappeared or said he'd been mistaken."

"But why? The man's a billionaire. He has people . . . an *army* . . . to do his dirty work."

"Because he loves it!" Hutch said. "He's ex–Special Forces. He made his first fortune inventing a particularly effective antipersonnel mine. He's been known to join his soldiers on the front line in the heat of battle. He gets off on war and fighting and death. I don't even think the money matters to him, except that it allows him to continue doing what he loves. There are rumors that every development that comes out of Page Industries he either thought up himself or personally chaperoned from inception to implementation. He's the Steve Jobs of war."

"Hutch," she said, frowning. "This is huge. Why hasn't anybody put this together before?"

"What I have now is enough to convince *you* Page is up to his eyeballs . . . but it's not enough to convince anyone else, not anyone who could do something about it. There are so many vanished witnesses and documents, so much information shielded by the top-secret designation. I can't tell you how many calls I've made, people I've visited and bribed, hours I've spent tracking down and poring over obscure, redacted, misfiled documents. And I've only got started." Hutch smiled. "Besides, somebody has to be first."

"Somebody whose world was torn apart by Page's weapons and offspring."

"It helps."

Footsteps padded down the hall toward them. Dillon peered around the door frame.

"Hey, you," Hutch said. The uncertainty in the boy's eyes broke Hutch's heart.

Dillon stepped in, and Hutch approached him and knelt, bringing his eyes level with the boy's. "I'm sorry. I've been a terrible host. Even worse, I've been a terrible friend. Will you forgive me?"

Dillon gave him a tight-lipped smile that within seconds became a toothy grin. He nodded.

Hutch leaned in to give him a hug. He said, "You want to hang with me awhile, maybe get some hot chocolate?"

"And popcorn?"

"Popcorn goes without saying."

Dillon slipped out, running toward the kitchen.

Laura crossed the room, avoiding the clutter. She stopped at a plaque on the wall. She read it out loud: "'The world is a dangerous place, not because of those who do evil, but because of those who look on and do nothing.'"

Hutch stepped beside her. He touched the engraved lettering. "David Ryder and I were always challenging each other with quotations. He stumped me with that one."

"Edmund Burke?" Laura said.

"That's what I thought. Turned out to be Einstein. I didn't put an attribution on it, because I like to think it's David prodding me on with it."

She touched his arm. "You miss him a lot."

He nodded. "He was a good man. Best I've ever known. He shouldn't have died the way he did. It was so meaningless, so random." He tilted his head. "Terry too, and your husband. That whole mess in Canada . . . I don't know, I guess this quote carries more weight now than when I first heard it."

She tapped a *Wired* magazine cover tacked to the wall beside the plaque. Brendan Page looked out from it. She said, "What, no bull's-eye drawn over him?"

"Reminds me how smug the guy is," Hutch said. "Look at those eyes, those pursed lips."

In the photo, Page stood casual and confident, holding a cigar near his face. Around him a battle raged: soldiers fired machine guns at unseen targets, a fiery explosion was frozen in mid-destruction, and over his shoulder a sleek tank crested a ridge. Where plumes of smoke obscured his feet and legs was the line HOW THIS MAN IS RESHAPING THE WAY WE FIGHT.

SIX

Brendan Page pulled off the helmet and stepped out of the boots. He unzipped the VR suit, pulling it down to his waist. Perspiration beaded over him like sequins. Close-quarters combat was a strenuous activity, mentally and physically—even in virtual reality. He glanced up at the control room.

Ian sat before a monitor, his hand gliding over a trackball. Brendan's teenage son, Julian, stood behind him. The boy returned Page's nod and returned his attention to Ian's shutdown procedure.

Julian was not a happy child; he hated being housed and schooled on the Outis compound. The only part of it he did seem to enjoy were the VR facilities: learning its programming and control protocols and experiencing the VR environments himself.

Ian caught his eye and clicked on the intercom. "Got some news, Brendan. Come on up."

Page gave the man a thumbs-up. He went into the locker room. Five minutes later, he'd showered, dressed, and was bounding up the stairs to the control room. Julian had left. Page dropped onto a leather couch.

Ian studied a computer screen displaying a map.

"Found a glitch," Page said. "I hit my helmet with the weapons prop and got static, like what's-his-name described the other day. It's systemic to the design."

"You wanted it bulletproof," Bryson said. "You never mentioned anything about soup cans."

"Chili," Page corrected.

"Anyway, that's not the problem," Ian said. "He wasn't ready."

"Nothing gets you ready like doing," Page said. "How many tactical training missions has he completed? How many VR simulations?" He felt his pockets for a cigar case and realized he'd left it in the locker room. "He's our *seed* for Fireteam Bravo. The whole point of getting newbies into fully functioning teams is to eventually have entire teams made up of soldiers who've known nothing else but Quarterback."

Quarterback was Outis's latest project—the human equivalent of pushing the technological envelope. The name derived from QRBO—Quick-Response Black-Ops. They consisted of four-man teams whose sole purpose was to move in quickly, accomplish a task, and pull out just as fast. The plan had been to lease these teams to governments who needed their services, at phenomenal premiums over the everyday soldiers Outis provided.

During their development, Page had encountered his own need for their expertise. Like a drug dealer cooking the purest meth, he couldn't resist sampling his own product. And like that dealer, waking one day under a bridge, covered in vomit, Page had felt the sting in an operation that had gone south.

Ian waved a hand at Page. He had other business on his mind. "Our guy at Purdue intercepted a call from Nichols. You were right: he tried to avoid the keyword system."

"What got him?" Page said.

"He used your name. That, coupled with *slaughtered* within three words of *family*."

"We got a location?"

"Pay phone in a town called Pinedale, California, between Redding and Eureka. Fireteam Alpha's on its way there now. Shouldn't be too hard to find him."

"Who'd he call?"

Ian grinned. "Your favorite journalist."

"Hutchinson?" Page shook his head. "Dog with a bone."

"Eventually the bone splinters." Ian rocked back in his chair.

Page said, "Guy's only been a nuisance until now. But if he's talking to Nichols . . ."

"He won't be . . . not anymore."

"I mean, if he's making this kind of contact, he's wormed his way in. It's only a matter of time before he's calling his big-media friends and the feds to show them what he's found."

Ian pressed his lips together, thinking. "Journalists don't mean anything, Brendan. You know that. Witnesses are one thing. Employees with loose lips an even bigger thing. But the media sniffing around . . ." He pulled on his mustache. "Part of the territory."

"Hutchinson is a witness," Page reminded his friend.

"Of Declan's lunacy, not *yours*." Ian smiled. "None of his suspicions was corroborated. That case is closed. He's nothing."

Page smoothed his hair back, thinking.

"If anything," Ian added, "slip him some cash."

"Not this guy. He thinks he's on a crusade for justice."

"So what are you thinking, take him out?"

Page nodded slowly.

"Might not be such a good idea," Ian said. "Not on the heels of this whole Nichols thing. Besides, who *doesn't* know he's got you in his sights? You're the first person they'll suspect."

Page sighed. Ian was right. The way they'd handled Nichols was a bit of overkill. Reckless. He had simply been too eager to put his men through the paces, to give them the experience they needed and take care of a potentially devastating problem at the same time. He thought again of the methamphetamine cook sampling his own brew. It was never *if* he was going to OD, but *when*.

"Look," Ian said, "we counsel clients about this sort of thing every day. What's the objective?"

Page opened his hands. "Get him off my back. Shut him up."

"He wants to put you away, and you don't want to be put away." Ian pushed himself up in his chair and crossed his legs. "You have a conflict. What are the tenets of conflict resolution?"

Page smiled at his friend's analytical approach. "Diplomacy. Threat. Use of force."

"Well," Ian said, "it's clear your asking him to go away won't work. And you don't think he can be bought off."

Page shook his head.

Ian raised his bushy eyebrows. "Why jump right to use of force, especially when it could cause the equivalent of an international uproar, maybe retaliation?"

"In this case, from the media, the authorities," Page agreed. "But, Ian—guy like Hutch, he doesn't scare easily."

"Neither does Iran or North Korea," Ian said. "You have to find out what he cares about more than he cares about putting you away. You've done your homework; I can't imagine you don't already know the answer. The next step is figuring out how to deliver the message. How loud do you have to yell? Sometimes all the U.S. has to do is send a secretary of state. . . ."

"And sometimes they have to position a fleet of destroyers and aircraft carriers off the coast," Page said.

"Let 'im know you're serious. And have the means and willingness to back up your threats."

"Ian, I knew there was a reason I keep you around." Page hefted himself off the couch. "Get a couple teams ready. Put . . . ah, what's his name, Mitch? Daniel?"

"Michael," Ian said. "I don't think . . ."

"Right back on the horse, Ian," Page said. "Don't start talking like Nichols, now."

"You know me better than that."

"Okay then." Page walked to the door. He said, "Look, we'll ease him back in. This'll be a reconnaissance mission, no contact. Happy?"

"A little better," Ian said. "No firepower?"

"Since when does an Outis squad not pack?" He shrugged. "What good's an aircraft carrier without any aircraft?" He went to the door and turned back. "Remember what Sun-Tzu said. Keep your friends close . . ."

"And your enemies closer."

"I have to get ready," Page said, opening the door. "Company's coming."

SEVEN

Hutch carried a big bowl of popcorn into the living room. Laura had taken a position on the couch, looking comfortable with her leg tucked under her. She watched hearty flames consume a log in the fireplace. Dillon came up behind him, his own bowl in his hands. The boy was warming up to Hutch again, going on about life in Fiddler Falls: how fourth grade didn't seem much different from third, since all of the town's twenty-eight elementary students shared a single room; how last summer he'd helped old man Nelson stock and clean his mercantile—"For real money!"—and how the town was still rebuilding the structures Declan had demolished with his satellite weapon.

Hoping to change the subject, Hutch said, "What did you think of my office building?"

They'd driven by the Denver newspaper agency's downtown digs on their way to the restaurant.

Dillon made a face. "Kinda ugly."

Hutch couldn't disagree. It was an eleven-story structure that looked as if it might have been made out of white Legos. On one side of the facade rose a scaffoldlike structure with green-tinted panels. It could have been stacked balconies off low-rent apartments. "It's nice inside, though," Hutch said.

Dillon scrambled into a big La-Z-Boy next to the couch. He crossed his legs Indian-style and parked the bowl of popcorn in his lap. He said, "In Fiddler Falls, everything is five minutes away—walking! It took us ten minutes just to get from your work to the restaurant, then a *half hour* to go from there to your house. I timed it." He tapped the big watch on his wrist.

Hutch saw that it was his hunting watch, which he had given Dillon before heading home last year. "Hey, you still have it."

Dillon smiled.

Laura said, "Tell him it's okay to change the alarm time, or at least turn it off."

"It's good luck!" Dillon said. He looked at Hutch. "Remember how it woke us up when we were hiding in the cabinet—early enough for us to get away before the bad guys woke up?"

"Early enough? That was—what?—four in the morning?"

"Four in the morning," Laura confirmed, sounding exasperated. "Four o'clock, every morning, *beep-beep-beep-beep-beep*."

Hutch moved around the coffee table and sat on the couch beside Laura. He raised his eyebrows at Dillon, who simply shrugged. He asked, "So do you get up that early?"

Dillon shook his head, an emphatic *no*.

Laura touched his knee. "We went back to the mine. He found one of the arrows you lost there. He has sort of a collection of . . . mementos, I guess you'd call them."

The puzzlement on Hutch's face must have showed. She gave him a half shrug and put her index finger to her mouth in a way Dillon couldn't see.

Hutch said, "You're into a new school year now. How's that going?"

"Like nothing changes," she said. "I'm still teaching third, fourth, and fifth grades, so only a third of the faces are new. I love it. They're great kids."

Hutch said to Dillon, "Does she cut you any slack, being your teacher and all?"

The boy made a face. "Are you kidding? The teacher's kid can't do *anything* wrong. It's not so cool."

A slight lisp still clung to his *S*s, and Hutch smiled at that. To Laura he said, "And you're getting by all right, it seems."

She frowned, but nodded. Her eyes flicked past him to her son. She said, "We're doing okay, aren't we? Some days are better than others."

Dillon said, "We have a new constable. I don't like him."

Hutch nodded. Dillon's father had been the Royal Canadian Mounted Police's only representative in Fiddler Falls. The natural response to Dillon's statement—"Why don't you like him?"—was a place Hutch didn't want to go. Most likely, the boy didn't like him simply because he wasn't his father. Who knew what kind of emotions would come pouring out of Dillon if he tried to explain?

The silence stretched out until Hutch thought his uneasiness would have been obvious to a toddler.

Dillon hopped up. "I gotta pee," he said, running for the bathroom.

Hutch laughed. "I remember when Logan was that age. He always waited to use the bathroom until it was an emergency."

"So he'll outgrow it soon?"

"I think they reach an age when not quite making it in time is embarrassing enough to get them moving sooner." He shifted on the sofa to face her. He whispered, "So what's this about Dillon collecting things? It must be a painful memory for him."

Laura shook her head. "Of course losing his father is painful beyond measure. But right after it happened, I started steering our conversations toward finding the silver lining, you know? Not that there ever could be anything good about Tom's death, not in a practical sense, to a child." She thought a moment. "Not to me either. We talked about how bad things happen to good people, but God has a way of, I don't know, redeeming even the worst things life throws at us."

"'You meant it for evil, but God meant it for good,'" Hutch quoted.

She nodded. "That got us looking for the good things that came out of that horrible situation."

"Like *what?*"

She slapped his knee. "Like meeting you. It may have been during the worst time of our lives, but we met you all the same. You kept Dillon safe, and in the end saved all of us."

Hutch shook his head. "No, it wasn't like that."

"Well, think what you want. You became a good friend to Dillon. You have a lot of the same qualities Tom did. You have a strong sense of right and wrong and a burning need for justice. You're kind and . . . are you blushing?"

"Me? Nah, a little warm's all. The fire's heating up the room too much."

She smiled sweetly, which he was sure only made his face flush more. *Oh man*, he thought. *I have been alone too long.*

Laura said, "Dillon lost his father but found a man who treated him like a son. That you came into his life at the same time his father left us made Dillon bond to you. It took some of the pain away. I don't know, it's just . . . as bad as the bad is, it doesn't mean the good isn't good."

Hutch shook his head. "And then I go and stop calling. What an idiot."

"Don't be so hard on yourself," Laura said. "You invited us here. You're staying in contact with Dillon. And whether you take credit or not, we're alive. That's the biggest thing we're thankful for and what we've focused on since then. We survived. That's why Dillon started his collection. Not because we lost our husband and father, but because we're still here. It makes Tom's sacrifice mean something. Every time Dillon and I do something that makes us feel alive—kayaking down the Fond du Lac or kissing each other good night—we honor his sacrifice, we honor him."

A tear broke free from one eye and streaked down her cheek. A sad smile found her lips, and she wiped her face.

"Why are you crying?" Dillon asked, putting the brakes on his bounding entrance.

"Just talking about Daddy, sweetheart. You know how I get."

He came around the coffee table and wrapped his arms around her neck. They squeezed each other for a long time.

Hutch looked away, but couldn't keep from turning back. He felt both awkward and privileged to witness their love for each other. He had written countless columns about people whose jobs sent them wading into the muck of human misery. Emergency room nurses and doctors, homicide detectives, social workers. Many of them developed bleak outlooks on life and lost touch with the beautiful things that made the horrific ugly in the first place: they spent so much time in the dark, they forgot about the light.

Hutch had become one of them. His children, and Laura and Dillon's love now, were bright flashes in the darkness he'd pulled around him by delving so deeply into Page's world.

Mother and son parted. Laura sniffed and brushed away more tears. She ruffled Dillon's hair. Obviously trying for lightheartedness, she tossed some popcorn into her mouth. She grabbed another handful and stood. "I think I'll go freshen up a bit," she said.

She started around the couch, but was stopped by a pile of unopened boxes. "You moved in *how* long ago?"

"Six months." Hutch eyed the boxes as if they were tattling on him. "Stuff I don't need, I guess."

Laura backed up and crossed between the coffee table and the TV. She said, "But you do need a *lot* of video games, I noticed. How many different systems you got here?"

"Only an Xbox 360 and a PlayStation." He paused, then added with exaggerated meekness: "And a Nintendo Wii."

She tossed a few pieces of popcorn at him.

He threw up his hands. "The *kids*," he said.

"And they get everything they want?" Her mock scowl turned into a knowing smile.

"Well, actually . . ." Hutch said, "yes."

"Whoa," Dillon said. "Cool."

Laura walked on toward the hallway that led to the bathroom. Over her shoulder she said, "You're spoiling them because of the divorce."

"Well . . . *duh*!" Hutch called and smiled at Dillon.

EIGHT

Dillon plopped down in his mother's place on the couch. He scooted closer to Hutch, seeming perfectly content.

"Man, look at you," Hutch said. "You've grown—what?—a couple of feet since I saw you last?"

Dillon lifted his feet, parked them on the table, and waggled them. "Nope, these are the ones I've always had."

Hutch gave him a push. "Sharp as ever," he said. "What do you think of Denver so far?"

"It's *big*."

"Next to Fiddler Falls, what isn't?"

Dillon shrugged.

Hutch said, "Your mom tells me you're using the bow and arrow set I sent you."

Dillon nodded. "I shoot it almost every day, when the weather's good enough."

"So you're getting pretty good?"

"I shot a squirrel," he said, excited. "While it was running up a tree!"

"Really? Wow. Did I tell you I've been working on my moving-target shooting?"

"How? What do you shoot at?"

"There's a bow hunters group over in Golden. They have a contraption that flings plastic Coke bottles in the air."

"And you shoot at them? With a bow and arrow?"

"Well, I do shoot at them," Hutch said. "Hitting them is another story. But I'm getting better."

Dillon shook his head in amazement.

"That's nothing," Hutch said. "Have you ever heard of Howard Hill, the greatest archer who ever lived?"

Dillon's brow scrunched up in thought. "I don't think so . . . You told me about Zhou Tong."

"Oh, yeah. Zhou Tong was something. Taught the Song Dynasty to be the best military archers in history. But Howard Hill, let me tell you." Hutch hopped up, getting into character. "Okay, picture this. People coming from all over to see this guy. He comes out, big, handsome, fit. Kind of like me."

Dillon laughed.

"He looks into the crowd and selects someone." Hutch pointed majestically at Dillon. He grabbed his hand and pulled him up. "He tells the young lad, 'Stand right here, and whatever you do, don't move.'" Hutch positioned Dillon by the living room's back window and squared his shoulders. "He takes an apple . . ." Hutch pretended to polish the fruit on his shirt and place it on Dillon's head.

"That's William Tell," Dillon said.

"Mr. Tell used a crossbow. Doesn't count." Hutch waved his hand, shooing away such nonsense, and strode into the foyer thirty feet away. With exaggerated gestures he nocked an arrow onto a bowstring, raised the bow, and aimed at Dillon. He plucked back on the string and released. His face contorted in horror. He pressed his cheeks between his palms and ran toward Dillon, staring at an imaginary tragedy at the boy's feet. "Oh my goodness, what have I done?"

"Uh-*uh*!" Dillon said. "He didn't do that!"

Hutch straightened. "No, Howard Hill would split the apple. Then he'd do it with a plum. And when the crowd thought they'd seen everything, he'd have someone flip a coin in the air, and he'd shoot *that*."

"For real?"

"I saw him do it in a documentary," Hutch said.

"Cool!"

"I heard of another guy," Hutch said, "who'd shoot *aspirin* out of the air. You can do just about anything with a bow and arrow. All depends how much you practice."

Dillon's gaze was far off. Hutch could almost see inside his head, where the boy was shooting coins out of the air.

Dillon walked to the table, stuffed his mouth with popcorn, and mumbled, "Can I see it?"

"See wha—?" But Hutch got it before he finished the question.

He felt an attachment to the bow he had used to save their lives in Canada. He supposed it was odd to give an inanimate object such value, but if anyone challenged him on his feelings, he'd tell them, *You clobber Death when he's breathing in your ear and see how you feel about the club.*

"Come on," Hutch said.

They walked out of the living room, through the entryway, and down the hall. Hutch put his hand on the back of Dillon's head and brushed his fingers through his hair. He'd nearly forgotten how much Dillon had come to seem like his own son. Why had he let their phone calls become so infrequent? Why had it taken thirteen months to get Laura and Dillon to Colorado?

As they walked, Dillon put his arm around Hutch's waist. Hutch felt a vague ache in his chest. All the things he'd set aside to pursue Page: the long telephone conversations he'd enjoyed with Dillon and Laura; the times his own children were over and he'd done nothing with them except unveil the latest video game or DVD he'd purchased to keep them busy while he worked.

What a jerk.

He steered Dillon into the master bedroom and went to the closet. He pulled a long nylon bag off the top shelf and brought it to the bed. Unzipping it, he said, "I've done a few things to the bow."

"A *few* things?" Dillon said, excited. "Is that the same one?"

In Canada, Hutch had fashioned a sapling into a longbow, which amounted to a smoothly arching bow with a string running from tip to tip. To make the bow stronger and turn it into a recurve, which he preferred, Hutch had laminated strips of maple to the front and back of the birch sapling. He had then carved a handgrip and arrow rest into the center of the bow, called the riser. Above and below the riser, the limbs arced in toward the shooter. Each tip, to which the string was attached, curved away from the archer.

"I turned it into a recurve, like the one you have," he said. "I'm more comfortable shooting recurves, so it's more accurate for me. See this lighter wood running though the center?" Hutch said. "That's the original sapling, the original bow."

Dillon caressed it. "It's smooth."

"Took a lot of sanding, and some varnish."

"What's this?" The boy was running his fingers over the material on top of the arrow rest, which the arrow slid over as it was drawn back and released.

"Deer fur," Hutch said. "It doesn't interfere with the arrow's flight the way some man-made rests can, and it's practically silent."

"Cool. Can I pick it up?"

"More than that," Hutch said. "Think you can handle a sixty-pound draw?"

Most kids couldn't, but Dillon wasn't most kids; Hutch knew he was tougher than he looked. And bow shooting almost every day? Heck, yeah.

Dillon's eyes flashed wide. "You mean I can *shoot* it?"

"I mean, you can have it."

"Like, for *keeps*?" Dillon's face lit up.

"For keeps."

Hutch picked it up and handed it to Dillon in the manner of a king presenting a sword to his bravest knight.

The boy looked it up and down, turning it in his hands. His expression grew serious, and he held it out to Hutch. "I can't. You made it. It's yours."

"Then it's mine to give away, right? I know you'll take care of it."

Dillon's head bobbed up and down. "I will."

Hutch unzipped an inner pocket of the case and showed Dillon a quiver of arrows. "We'll shoot a few times before you go home, then I'll box it up and mail it to you."

Dillon beamed. "Thank you!"

"For what?" Laura said, coming into the room.

"Hutch gave me his bow." Dillon held it up. "*The* bow!"

"You don't have to do that," she told Hutch.

"He'd get more out of it than I would. Especially up there in the woods. Unless, of course, you don't want him to have it."

She rubbed her son's back and leaned in close to his face. "I think it'd be okay, if you promise to be careful."

Dillon's head went bobbing again. His big grin and sparkling eyes told Hutch he'd done the right thing.

NINE

The doorbell rang.

"Finally," Hutch said.

Dillon put the bow back in its case, then zipped it. Hutch returned it to the closet.

The bell rang again and again, over and over in quick succession.

Laura smiled. "I think one of your kids is having fun."

Hutch made a face. "That's probably my ex." He headed out of the room.

Dillon fell in next to him, and before they reached the front door, the boy gripped his hand.

"Nervous?" Hutch asked.

Dillon shrugged.

"You and Logan are a lot alike. You'll get along fine." He opened the door and stepped back as three people streamed in.

"Why does it always take you five minutes to answer your door?" Janet said.

"Nice to see you too," Hutch said.

Janet's eyes fell on Laura and narrowed.

Hutch introduced them. Laura held out her hand, which Janet predictably ignored.

"So you're Macie?" Laura said. "You know, you're prettier than your dad said. I didn't think that was possible."

Macie beamed.

Laura extended her hand to Logan. "Nice to meet you, Logan."

He lowered his eyes and shook her hand.

"I heard you have a pretty cool set of grillz," Laura said. "May I see?"

The briefest of smiles touched his tight lips. He showed her his teeth.

"There's blue in them," Dillon said. "Cool."

Logan's lips closed over the sparkling metal. He glared at Dillon. His eyes settled on his and Hutch's hands, clasped together. He managed to turn up the intensity of his expression.

Dillon released his grip. "Hello," he said.

"Hi!" Macie chimed. "Daddy talks about you a lot."

Logan said, "You're smaller than I thought."

"Logan," Hutch warned.

"He is!" Logan made a point of sizing Dillon up with his eyes, clearly unimpressed.

"Come here," Hutch said, and walked Logan onto the front porch. He closed the door. "Look, Dillon's anxious enough about being here, meeting you guys and all. What's with the attitude?"

"He's a little kid," Logan said. "You made it sound like he was . . . I don't know, some tough guy or something."

"He's a brave boy," Hutch said. "He saved my skin—"

Logan rolled his eyes. "I know. He showed you how to get out of the mine. You told us all about it a thousand times."

"Just get along. Play with him."

"He's too little."

"He's ten. You're only two years older. You can find something the two of you can do together." Hutch gave his son's shoulder a squeeze. "I told Dillon how cool you are. Don't make a liar out me, all right?"

Logan lowered his head. "I guess. Can we at least do something fun, maybe tomorrow?"

"Like what?" Hutch knew what was coming.

"Casa Bonita?"

"Of course," Hutch said. "I told Dillon I'd take him back."

"Take him back?"

Okay, my bad, Hutch thought. Not only was Casa Bonita Logan's favorite restaurant, but he considered it his special place.

Hutch said, "I just thought . . . I mean, *you* like it so much, and I wanted to kick off their visit right. I took them on the way home from the airport. Doesn't mean *we* can't go tomorrow."

Logan nodded.

The front door opened, and Janet stepped out. She said, "Go inside, Logan. I want to talk to your father." After he left and closed the door, she said, "I am not thrilled about that woman being here."

"Since when am I supposed to care what you're thrilled about?"

"You don't see a problem, your girlfriend staying here in front of the kids?"

"She's not my girlfriend. She's a houseguest."

Janet's eyebrows went up. "Really? Where is she sleeping?"

Hutch let out a heavy sigh. He leaned against the doorjamb and crossed his arms. "In Macie's room."

"With Macie?"

"Macie said it was okay. I put a cot in there. Dillon's sleeping in Logan's room."

"Oh, Logan will love that."

"Stop looking for trouble, Janet. I don't grill you about your various boyfriends."

"Various boyfriends? I've been with George over six months. I don't have *various* boyfriends."

He came off the jamb and gripped the door handle. He was glad the porch light wasn't any brighter. He didn't want her to see how tightly he was gripping it, how easily she had gotten under his skin—again.

He said, "Whatever, Janet. It's my week with the kids. You dropped them off. Adios."

It had taken his heart a long time to move her from soul-mate status to friend to someone he had to tolerate—despite her every attempt to make the transition easy for him.

She scowled at him. He tried to look bored and unaffected. Finally she spun around and took off for her car.

When Hutch stepped back in, Logan was pushing fistfuls of popcorn into his mouth. Dillon watched from across the room. Macie's and Laura's voices drifted to him from Macie's bedroom down the hall.

Hutch felt his office tugging at him, like the gravitational pull of a planet.

Not tonight, he thought. *Well . . . maybe after everyone goes to bed.*

He rubbed his palms together. "Okay, who's up for a game of Monopoly?"

Macie held up a small red car. "Shelby GT500 convertible," she said. "Logan likes the Viper better, but I think convertibles are way cooler."

Laura was sitting on the floor in the little girl's room, her legs tucked under her. A fleet of Matchbox cars and trucks fanned out before her. Mini briefcases holding entire parking lots of the tiny rides, from classics to fantasy vehicles, lay open around them.

Macie would sit for a moment to point out a prized automobile, then hop up to retrieve a new one from a bookshelf, drawer, or dresser top. She returned from the closet to dump twin handfuls of cars in front of Laura.

She said, "My friend McKenna collects horses. Not real ones, little ones." Her eyes grew big. "Some not so little. They're all over her room. She keeps one in her school backpack. She says it's weird for a girl to collect cars. Do you think it's weird? I don't. Look."

She plucked up an ordinary sedan. Hairlines of blue metal showed where brushstrokes of silver had not quite met. Paint had encroached onto the plastic windows.

"I recognize that," Laura said.

"Dad's car," Macie said with a big grin. "I made it silver to match his. What do you drive?"

"A Jeep."

"What kind?" Macie said, plopping down and pulling a case closer. "A lot of people like the Grand Cherokee." She displayed one in her palm.

"I have a CJ7."

Macie nodded appreciatively. "Ragtop. Cool." She pulled a miniature version of Laura's car from the same case and held it up proudly.

"Wow," Laura said. "I keep a hardtop on most of the time. It's pretty cold where I live."

Macie shrugged. "That's okay. Dad has a four-wheel-drive too. For hunting. An XTerra." She scanned the collection, apparently looking for one.

Laura had seen it in the garage. FOR SALE signs were taped to the rear windows.

"Oh," Macie said. She showed Laura a Volvo painted white. "Mom's car. And here's George's car." She drove a black BMW up to Laura's knees.

"George?"

Macie made a face. "Mom's boyfriend." She appraised the Matchbox as though it were the man. "Before him, she dated Steve." She set a yellow Corvette next to the Beemer. She pulled a gray Hummer beside it. "Mark."

"Looks like your mother has good taste in cars," Laura said.

Macie grinned at her. She studied Laura's face. "You're pretty," she said. "Do you wear makeup?"

"Sometimes."

"Mom wears a lot. She says I can use her eye shadow and lipstick in a few years, when I'm older." The girl ran a fingertip over an eyelid.

Laura tried to picture her all dolled up, crashing toy cars into each other. She leaned forward and flipped one of Macie's pigtails. "I like your hair like that."

Macie shook her head, flicking the pigtails back and forth. "Mom did it. Dad can't braid. He tries, but they always come loose."

"Boys," Laura said.

She and Tom had talked about having another child, and she had imagined life with a daughter: sitting on the bed, brushing through long hair; baking cookies; picking out frilly dresses. But who knew? With Tom and Dillon around, her daughter would probably have been more interested in camouflage overalls and setting traps. That would have been fine as well; Laura wasn't exactly debutante material herself.

Macie stood and walked behind her. Little eight-year-old hands brushed against Laura's temples, sweeping her hair back.

"Can I put your hair in a ponytail?" Macie asked.

"Sure."

Macie ran to the dresser and returned with a multicolored scrunchie. She began raking Laura's hair back with her fingers.

Laura closed her eyes, enjoying the moment.

TEN

Julian Page rocked his chair back from the table, trying to get it to balance on its rear legs. Tired of his own quarters, which he shared with no one, he had wandered into Fireteam Bravo's quad. Now he was in their common area, which consisted of a kitchenette, a dining area, and a den. Doors set into each of the two long walls led to four bedrooms.

The barracks here at Outis's Washington state compound were modeled on the U.S. military's "four-plus-one" design, which had replaced the long rooms of bunks most civilians thought of when they heard the word *barracks*. The switch began before Julian was born fourteen years before, but even recent movies about the modern military showed the old style. Either Hollywood was slow on the uptake, or the filmmakers simply refused to give up the feeling of camaraderie and tension, and the romantic notion of a soldier's monastic existence that those halls of bunks and lockers implied.

Oh man, he thought. *Monastic existence. Where'd I hear that? Too much time reading in my room and listening to these guys shoot the crap.*

Which is what he was doing at that moment. The four fireteam members were in the den, ten feet away, arrayed in front of a big-screen monitor. Three of them were wiping out opposing teams who were unlucky enough to encounter them in the online version of a war game developed by one of Julian's dad's companies.

Disgusted by the thrashing they'd gotten, many of their opponents summarily added Ben, Emile, and Anton's player IDs to their "don't play" list, which ordinarily prevented another matchup. The Outis system, however, granted the fireteam special privileges, which included ignoring "don't play" lists and spontaneously changing their IDs.

Which override these guys chose depended on whether they wanted to merely continue owning their frustrated opponents or also wanted to taunt them, stalking them through game after game. Their game play, now as always, was punctuated by whooping and hollering, rude appraisals of their opponents' skills, and equally crass assessments of movies, actors, books, music, weapons, tactics, their own training—whatever struck their decidedly diverse fancy.

Only Michael wasn't participating—in the game or the bantering. He sat cross-legged on a couch, hugging himself, rocking slightly. A wireless controller rested upside down in his lap, as if one of the others had tossed it there. He'd been quiet like that since returning from a training mission a few days before. Normally he was the loudest, the most energetic, the first to plug into a game after a day's grueling drills. Now he was lifeless. If he expressed any emotion, it was a flash of disdain or sadness.

Julian had asked him what was wrong. Michael had frowned, told Julian to leave him alone. The problem must be related to something

Michael had done. These past days, his teammates had either given him the cold shoulder or gone out of their way to razz him.

Julian saw it coming again.

One of their opponents took too long getting his gun around, giving Ben time to blow him away.

"Ha!" Anton said. "That dude pulled a Michael. Gotta be quicker than that!"

The three of them laughed.

"Hey, kid," Ben said, "don't start bawling, you hear? You might slobber on the controls . . . then I'd have to shoot you."

More snickers.

"I don't think he's listening," Anton said. "Better pass this down." He punched Ben lightly on the arm. Ben punched Emile. Emile leaned from his chair, couldn't reach Michael, and stood up. He stepped closer, and gave Michael a serious jab to his shoulder, hard enough for Julian to hear it.

Michael grimaced, tilted sideways, and caught himself from tumbling over. He pushed himself up, rubbed the spot, and stared up at Emile.

Grinning, Emile turned. Even through the darkness of the dining area, he made eye contact with Julian. Emile's smiled faded. He said, "What?"

Julian rocked, keeping his balance by touching the table with his fingertips. He said, "I didn't say anything."

"Better not." Emile plopped back into his chair.

Julian bit his tongue, choosing instead to run his fingers through his hair. Or going through the motion. He no longer had the long hair he was accustomed to flipping out of his eyes, playing with when he was nervous. These days, he sported the close-cropped Marine cut that adorned the heads of all the recruits.

Shortly after Julian's return from Canada, his father had switched his educational program from private tutors to the Outis Military Academy. Not long after that, Outis had started the Quarterback program to instruct squads of soldiers in special skills, à la SWAT teams or Navy SEALs. Julian had been "repositioned" as a loose entity within it. No doubt his old man intended to turn Julian into one of his elite soldiers. All the better to control his wayward son.

Julian's mind kept returning to a story he'd read in the Bible. This was back when his mother had been bringing him to church and Sunday school, before his father had moved on to another wife, separated Julian from his mother, and put an end to the "religious lunacy"—his father's words. The story Julian couldn't get out of his head was about King David. When he'd desired Uriah's wife, Bathsheba, David ordered his commander to put Uriah at the front of a battle. He had known Uriah would be killed, and he was.

Half of Julian's workday was spent training with the others, though his body was ill matched to the program's physical rigors. The rest was spent teaching himself from a homeschool curriculum. Then he'd watch a movie, read a novel, hang with the guys, or go for a walk in the woods. Long ago, he'd lost his taste for video games.

Usually, the guys in Fireteam Bravo were cool. Hard talking and short-tempered when someone didn't agree with them or displayed any sort of weakness, mentally or physically—but otherwise cool. The way they treated Julian may have stemmed from his being the boss's kid, but Michael had once told him they had strict orders to behave as though Julian was just another recruit, no favoritism.

Julian had been relieved to hear the orders weren't for everyone to be especially hard on him. That would have been more like his father—to give Julian that extra opportunity to "become a man."

At twenty-seven, Ben was the oldest and toughest. He had seen actual combat in Iraq, had the scars to prove it. During close-quarter tactical training missions he was the most violent, pumping extra rounds into a downed enemy, choosing to kill with a knife or his hands when he could get away with it. He'd laugh at movie bloodshed, comparing it unfavorably to the real thing. In any situation that could turn either way, peacefully or through physical force, there was no question which Ben would choose. He often egged his teammates into aggressive thinking: "Don't take that from him! Punch him" and "Man, if my girl ever did that to me, I'd smack her down on the spot."

Julian wondered if Ben, as team leader, had been given the directive to talk like that, to toughen the men in his charge.

Still, he was cool to Julian. He'd let Julian in on practical jokes he was pulling on the others, and he always encouraged him on the training field. The other team members were too concerned with their own performance to take the time to show Julian a faster way to exchange ammo clips or climb a rope or whatever it was they were doing.

Anton was a few years younger than Ben. A little high-strung, but he called Julian his "brother from another mother," and sometimes acted like it. He'd bring Julian leftovers when the team went to the steak place in nearby Gold Bar, and insist on letting him have a vote if Julian was there when the team picked out a DVD to watch.

But Emile treated him more like a brother than Anton did. He said he had a younger brother Julian's age. He shared his comic books—G.I. Joe, Avengers, Wolverine—and wrestled with him in the grass. Emile was moody, though, and got into funks for long stretches at a time, during which he'd push Julian away and generally act the way Michael was acting now.

Michael was the youngest on the team, only four years older than Julian. They didn't have a lot in common, since Michael's sole reason for living, it seemed, was to play video games and be a soldier. Sometimes the drills were as hard for Michael to finish as they were for Julian, and that made Julian feel better. But while Julian didn't care that much, Michael was hard on himself about it.

Julian also saw a softer side to Michael than he did in the others. When they'd first been assembled as a team, Michael would debate with Ben about the need for violence in certain situations. Ben always beat him down, so now Michael only listened without getting involved.

Yeah, Julian noticed such things. He'd picked up his philosophical streak from Declan, and he hoped it was the only thing of his older brother's that had rubbed off on him. For as long as he could remember, both his father and Declan had pushed him to think and act older than he was. He'd been taught to field clean a machine gun when he was seven, taken a course on business management at the University of Washington at eleven, and received a subscription to *Playboy* from his father when he turned thirteen. Now *this*, hanging out with mostly guys in their twenties, learning how to fight in war zones. He'd had just about enough, but what could he do?

The volume of the voices in front of the game grew louder.

"Get in the half-track! Get in the half-track!" Ben ordered.

"Hold on!" Emile said. His fingers blurred over the controls.

"Oh!" Anton said. "They got behind us!"

"I'm on 'em," Ben said.

A rap came from the open door. Colonel Bryson stepped in.

"Ten-hut!" Ben said, springing to his feet.

The other men hopped up. Michael took longer, but in the end managed to straighten himself as stiffly as his teammates.

"At ease," Colonel Bryson said. He squinted into the gloom. "That you, Julian?"

"Yes, sir."

Colonel Bryson nodded, obviously displeased.

Not for the first time, Julian thought the longish hair of the faculty and administrative staff somehow conveyed their superior positions over the recruits. If that were true, Colonel Bryson's curly locks, as much as his rank and position as executive vice president of Outis, put him at the top of the heap.

Colonel Bryson stepped into the den. His eyes flicked up to Michael. "You hanging in there, son?"

Michael cleared his throat. "Yes, sir."

Colonel Bryson scanned him up and down, as though doubting Michael's response. "Whadda you got, Ben?" he said.

"This one kid," Ben said. He gestured at Emile, who snatched up his controller and began flipping through menus on the screen. Emile found a video file and started the playback. On the screen, a digitized soldier ran, jumped, cycled through weapons and fired, every move fluid, intentional. The left portion of the screen was dedicated to statistics: number of games played, hours online, frags—or kills—number of wins, both as a solo player and part of a team, overall points accumulated. Under the stats was information about the player: name, address, date of birth, the credit card used to pay for online access to the game. None of this data was available to other players. Only to Outis recruiters.

"Seventeen," Colonel Bryson said, referring to the player's age. "Perfect. You played him?"

"Oh yeah," Ben said. "Kicked his butt."

"Wasn't easy," Anton said. "Kid knows how to move."

Colonel Bryson nodded. "Okay. Watch him a couple more weeks. If he looks right for us, let me know. We'll insert our AI avatars into a few of his games, get a reading on how he handles special situations."

Julian knew "special situations" meant more than tough opponents. The Outis system would have the player face old women planting IEDs—improvised explosive devices—on the sides of roads, little kids who whip machine guns out of their soccer bags, civilians clambering to board a military vehicle. The player would be expected to shoot them.

"Shows a willingness to do what's necessary," Ben had told him.

"All right, guys," Colonel Bryson continued. "You've already been debriefed about the other night's fiasco."

"Sir, with all due respect, sir," Ben said, "I think you mean Michael's screwup."

Colonel Bryson gave Ben an I'll-eat-you-for-breakfast look—with his bushy eyebrows and all-terrain features, he didn't need to change his expression much to accomplish it. "I just said we've already been there. No need beating that horse, got it?"

"Yes, sir," Ben said dutifully.

Colonel Bryson scanned the team. "I'm here to inform you that you're going to have a chance to redeem yourselves."

"Another mission, sir?" Anton said.

"Another mission, yes."

Michael paled visibly. Julian thought he was going to collapse back onto the couch, but he only wavered.

"This one's like eating your grandma's apple pie, nothing to it," Colonel Bryson said. "Recon, that's all."

Ben rolled his head. "Sir, how is that going to make up for—"

"It's Priority One," Colonel Bryson interrupted. "Straight from the top."

Julian thought his eyes flicked his way for a half second.

"MOOTW, gentlemen. Military Operations Other Than War. You've studied it. You know it can be as crucial to U.S. security as combat. Though perhaps not as much fun." He winked at Ben. "We head out at 1200 tomorrow, so no morning drills."

"Yeah," Emile said, tugging the air with his fist.

"Ben, make sure your team is ready. Get a good night's sleep. Gentlemen." He strode out of the room.

Anton held his palm up, and Ben slapped it. "I thought they were going to ground us," Anton said.

"Us?" Ben said. "Not us. We're goooood." He made like he was shooting a machine gun. His aim came around to Michael, and he continued shooting. He pretended to raise the barrel and blow at the smoke. "Don't make me do that for real, man. I mean it."

Michael limped toward his bedroom.

"Hey," Ben said. "Where do you think you're going?"

"You heard him," Michael said at the door. "I'm going to bed."

"Just be ready in the morning, dude," Ben said. "No sudden bouts of stomach flu. You'll come with us anyway."

"Nighty night," Anton said.

Michael disappeared into his room and shut the door.

"Man," Anton said, "that kid's going to ruin it for all of us."

"He'll be all right," Emile said.

"Better be," Anton snapped. "Else we can take Julian. Huh, Julie?"

"Leave me out of it," Julian said, letting the chair settle back to the floor. He stood up and headed for the door. "And stop calling me that."

"Oooh," Ben said. "Watch out, Anton. You'll make him mad."

They all laughed.

Julian flipped them the finger and walked out.

ELEVEN

From the heavy odor of tobacco, Julian knew his father was waiting for him as soon as he stepped into his quarters. The den and kitchen were dark, the only illumination coming from a dim light in the stove's ventilation hood. Light seeped out from under his bedroom's closed door. He considered going back to Fireteam Bravo's room, see if he could convince them to put on a movie. But his dad would wait until Julian showed, stinking up his room with that smoke. Or he'd have him paged. One way or another, Dad would not be denied whatever lesson it was he wanted to bestow on Julian this time.

He opened the door and stepped into a gray cloud. He coughed and waved it away from his face. His father was standing at his dresser, a pistol in his hands. It was the replica Springfield Custom Professional Model 1911A1 semiautomatic his father had given him. Apparently it was a copy of the pistol Page had used when he was a Special Ops officer in Vietnam. *Dropped plenty of gooks*, his father had said of the original.

"Hey, kid," his dad said, putting the pistol back into its stand.

"Hey." Julian spun onto the bed, fluffed his pillow, and lay down. He began fingering the peyote root bracelet his brother had given him. It was supposed to make him brave. He didn't have any problems rappelling, riding the zip line, stuff like that. But the thing was worth spit when it came to helping him stand up to his father.

"What've you been up to?"

"You should know."

His dad sat on the bed beside him. He blew out a plume of smoke. "Like the way this cigar smells?"

"Not really."

His father puffed on the thing, filling the space between them with nauseating fumes.

Julian coughed. He waved a hand in front of his face. As the cloud cleared, his father's cold stare emerged, like a specter from grave-yard fog.

His dad said, "Sergeant Wilson tells me you couldn't finish the all-terrain course."

Julian shrugged.

"You have to try harder. You're only hurting yourself."

"What happened to Michael?" Julian said.

"What do you mean? Nothing, as far as I know."

"He's acting funny, sad. The others are picking on him."

"Picking on him how?" His dad shifted to see him better.

"I don't know. Calling him names, punching him."

His dad laughed. "Sounds like they're in fifth grade. Boys being boys."

"It just seems like . . . something happened to him the other night, on that mission they went on."

His dad made a dismissive face. "He didn't do so well, let his team down. That's why I push you so hard. You don't want to be like him."

"You're right," Julian said. He scooted himself up and pressed his back against the wall. "I don't want to be a soldier at all."

His father scowled. He turned his face away and puffed on the cigar. He pulled it from his mouth to examine it. He said, "Julie," and stopped.

Julian bit his bottom lip. His father knew he hated being called that. Julian used the silence to add, "I want to go home. I want to go to my old school. I don't want to teach myself from homeschool books. I don't want . . ." His hand stirred the air. "I don't want any of this."

His emotions rolled up from his chest, made his lip quiver, threatened to pour out of his eyes. He tried pushing it back. He told himself to be strong. It was the only thing his father respected . . . and expected.

His father used his free hand to smooth back his hair. "This is the best thing for you."

"Why?"

His dad squinted at him. He said, "Because of *this*. You're on the brink of tears. That's no good, Julie, you've got to toughen up."

Julian turned his head away. "You sound like Declan."

When Page remained silent, the boy turned a hard glare on him.

"I know what this is," Julian said. "I know what you're doing."

His dad raised his eyebrows. "Oh?"

"It's punishment," Julian continued. "For . . . for what happened in Canada."

His father raised a shoulder. "That's in the past."

"Then why are you doing this, making me be here? I'm *fourteen*," he said. "Everyone else is, like, eighteen, nineteen, twenty. I don't belong here. All they do is talk about war and fighting. Even my school curriculum focuses on war. I don't know how you pulled that off. For English . . ." He twisted, grabbed a paperback book off a nightstand, and tried to hand it to Page. "*The Red Badge of Courage*. Before that, it was *War and Peace* . . . *The Art of War* . . . *A Farewell to Arms* . . . *Slaughterhouse Five*."

"You do other things," Page said. "Movies. Video games."

Julian pointed at a wall. "Go ask those guys what they watched last. How much you wanna bet it was something like *Enemy at the Gates* or *Saving Private Ryan*? Some documentary. Same with the video games. There's not one racing game in this whole complex. Or a role-playing adventure. They're all personal shooters or war strategies like *Command & Conquer*." He looked away again. "It's not very subtle, you know."

"It's not supposed to be. It works."

"It works, how? Okay, I get it," Julian said. "You make soldiers here. That's what Outis does. And apparently they're really good soldiers, because everybody wants them. There's, what? Thousands of Outis soldiers fighting in wars all over the world?"

His father smiled.

"What I want to know, Dad, is why am *I* here, *me*? I never wanted to be a soldier."

"It's good to know the family business."

"It's *your* business. But if you want me to learn it, that's *not* what they're teaching me! This isn't business. It's . . ." He searched for a word. "It's death."

They stared into each other's eyes. His father's were dark, unreadable. Julian knew his revealed every emotion raging behind them. That's just how he was made. He couldn't help it and didn't want to. He knew his father saw that as a weakness, as giving too much away.

Well, Daddy, he thought, *you're not going to change me by putting me through this boot camp. You're not.*

But deep down, he wasn't so sure. He'd seen the people who'd come through here: normal kids at the beginning, hardened automatons by the time they were sent off to kill other people's enemies for six hundred dollars a day.

His father stood. He leaned over to lay his hand on Julian's head.

Julian flinched.

"You'll do well here," his father whispered. "I know it."

Julian blinked, and tears spilled out. He resisted wiping at them. When his father raised his head, Julian tightened his jaw and glared at him.

"See?" his father said. "It's working already." He went to the door and began pulling it shut behind him. He said, "You'll do the all-terrain course again next weekend. Finish it this time, Julie." The door clicked shut.

Julian grabbed the paperback off the bed and threw it at the door. He fell onto his pillow. Smoke swirled against the ceiling like a brewing storm.

TWELVE

Hutch sat on Logan's bed and brushed the hair off his son's forehead. He said, "I noticed you were trying to be nice."

Logan wiggled his head deeper into the pillow. He tugged a blanket up to his chin. Smiling, he said, "Just *trying*?"

"You got in a few jabs."

"It's just . . ." He shook his head. "I don't know."

Hutch turned to look toward the bedroom door. Dillon had not returned from the bathroom.

Hutch leaned closer to his son. "I think I understand," he said quietly. "Your mother and I . . ." He thought about it, then started again: "Divorce is never good. It's hard on everyone, especially kids. I know I started drifting away. Then when I came back from Canada, I was full of stories about how another boy and I survived this life-and-death adventure. It's like I abandoned you twice. I'm sorry for that, but don't take it out on Dillon, okay? When I was up there, trying to figure out how I was going to handle this mess your mother and I made, he reminded me how important *you* are to me."

Logan smiled again, but there was sadness in his eyes.

A long time ago, Hutch had sensed Logan's resentment toward Dillon, but he'd thought his son would shrug it off in time. He'd denied the depth of Logan's pain. What he now saw in his son's eyes was grief—for the family they had been, for the easygoing dad Hutch had been, for the way things used to be. It broke Hutch's heart.

He said, "So, Casa Bonita tomorrow?"

"Just you and me?"

"Logan, Dillon's only going to be here a week."

Logan frowned. "So?"

"So let's show him a good time," Hutch said. "We'll do something together, just you and me, after he leaves, okay?"

Logan looked away. "Yeah."

"Really." He knew Logan had heard it before, and Hutch had let him down. His words didn't cut it anymore. He held up a finger and wiggled it. "You know, this guy still packs a mean bite."

Logan slapped at it. "Don't."

Hutch jabbed the finger into the blanket over his son's ribs. "He remembers . . . just . . . where . . ." The finger scratched around, digging and prodding.

"Dad, I mean it, don't." Logan tried to push his hand away, but he was smiling, then laughing, raising his knees.

Hutch stopped to let the boy catch his breath, and Logan's joyous expression turned into a scowl. He was looking past Hutch. Hutch didn't have to look to know what—*who*—had sparked his ire. He mirrored Logan's sour face and whispered, "You be nice."

"Hey, Dillon!" Logan called, too cheerfully. "Come on in, old buddy, old pal!"

Hutch shook his head. He turned to see a pajama-clad Dillon staring with confusion.

"Ready for bed?" Hutch said. He went to the other side of the room to a cot. He flipped back a blanket and sheet.

Dillon slipped in.

Hutch touched his head. "You okay?"

"Yeah. I'm glad I'm here. Finally."

"Me too. Good night." He walked to Logan, squeezed his shoulder. "'Night, son."

Logan rolled onto his side. "'Night."

At the door, Hutch switched off the light. The moon and a streetlamp conspired to keep the room well lit. He moved toward the window.

Dillon's small voice reached him: "Could you keep the blinds open . . . please?"

"Oh, come on," Logan said.

Hutch paused, didn't say a word.

After a moment, Logan said, "Oh, all right."

"'Night, guys," Hutch said, and shut the door.

Hutch looked in on Macie. The lights were out, and he heard rhythmic breathing. He was closing the door when she called to him.

"Thought you were sleeping," he said. He went in and sat on her bed.

"I like them, Laura and Dillon," she said.

"They like you back, I can tell." He pulled the blanket up to her neck.

Her eyelids drooped. "Sing me a song."

"Scoot over," he said, nudging down beside her. "'Puff'?" he asked.

She liked "Puff the Magic Dragon," especially when he changed

Little Jackie Paper to Little Macie and the land of Honah Lee to Highlands Ranch, the Denver suburb where they lived.

She shook her head. "'Sunshine.'"

He began to stroke her hair and quietly sing "You Are My Sunshine." Before the third verse, she was out.

In the kitchen, Hutch poured two glasses of merlot. It was cheap stuff, but he liked it. He brought the wine to Laura in the living room. She was on the couch again, watching the fire, which had died to a few spindly fingers.

He handed her a glass. "You seem to have found a favorite spot," he said.

"I like fire." Her eyes sparkled in the glow. "It's always beautiful."

"Unless it's burning something you don't want burned."

"Even then," she said. "Socrates' destructive beauty. Speaking of . . . this is a beautiful house."

"It's a rental," Hutch said, sitting beside her. "Best one I could afford. I wanted the kids to be in a safe neighborhood."

But that wasn't all he liked about it. As a one-story ranch, it looked bigger than it was. The garage doors opened on the side of the house, so they didn't mar the Mediterranean styling of the facade. And the driveway arced from the garage to the street, leaving a big front yard. Columns flanked the front porch. None of this truly mattered to Hutch, except that it rankled Janet to see him in a nice home and gave her boyfriends one less thing over which to stick their noses up at him.

He held up his glass. "To you and Dillon."

"To all of us," she said. Their glasses clinked. She shifted to face him. "I have to say, you look great, really fit."

He looked at the fire. "I got into working out a bit to burn off frustration. There's been a lot of that, investigating Page."

She frowned. "Did that guy call back, the one who called you at the restaurant?"

"Dorian Nichols. No." He shook his head. "And he may be my best angle into Page's crimes."

"How so?"

"He was a lead psychiatrist at Outis. I'd spoken to him a few times, but he didn't want to have anything to do with me. About a month ago, he quit. Three days ago, police found his family slaughtered in a rental house in Eureka, California."

Laura covered her mouth. "How terrible."

"Wife, two boys, a little girl. News reports said police suspected Dr. Nichols of the crime, but he'd disappeared. I figured he really had flipped out or Page had got him."

"Then he calls you." She sipped from her wineglass. "What did he do at Outis?"

"I found a bio from a lecture he gave about a year ago. Said he worked with software designers and military training specialists to maximize the effectiveness of tactical drills. Stuff like that."

"Software designers?"

"That's part of Page's voodoo, how he makes such efficient soldiers in months instead of years. You know how the military uses video games to train pilots and now even ground forces?"

"I've heard something about it."

Hutch nodded. "Apparently, Page has taken video-simulation training to a new level. He's got at least four concrete things going on. I don't know how they fit together, but I suspect they do." He held up his index finger. "He's been recruiting the best video game and virtual reality programmers from other companies. Right now, his video game company puts out only two games a year, but he's staffed to produce four times that number. What are all those programmers doing?"

He held up a second finger. "Outis soldiers are growing increasingly aggressive. Remember hearing about the soldiers who tore through Fallujah, shooting at civilians they claimed opened fire on them? New Outis soldiers. Twenty-one dead. Several women, children. The soldiers kept driving until they were back at their base. One investigator noted that they displayed a marked indifference for their victims. There have been mounting reports of similar violence by Outis soldiers. How does that happen, that one company churns out such ruthless people?"

Finger number three: "The ages of Outis's recruits and the contractors it puts into the field has plummeted. It's not unusual for kids to go there right out of high school and hit the battlegrounds by nineteen or twenty. Used to be, Outis would recruit only seasoned military men in their late twenties, early thirties."

"And four, Dr. Nichols's degree is in *child* psychology. Years ago, he published studies on the effects of war and violence on adolescents. Then his emphasis seemed to skew toward how young soldiers psychologically handled being in battle. The last reference to his work I found addressed how boot camps could adjust their regimens to more effectively prepare young soldiers to handle the warrior life, including killing. That's about the time he began working for Outis. I haven't been able to get numbers or even anecdotal evidence, but I'll bet Outis has a good number of people like Dr. Nichols on the payroll."

He polished off his wine.

Laura thought about it. She said, "So you think Outis is recruiting young people because—what?—they're more open to psychological manipulation?"

"There may be moral considerations as well," Hutch said. "Their ideas of right and wrong are still developing at that age. I think, too, young people are more susceptible to the influence of video games. They know how to play them, and they readily accept them as part of life. Dr. Nichols added something else to the equation, something that I had considered, but thought, *Nah*."

"What's that?"

"*Xĭ năo*," Hutch said. "It's one of the terms he told me to research. It refers to Chinese methods of coercive persuasion. It literally means 'to wash the brain.'"

Laura flinched. "What?"

"I'm not saying Jim Jones or David Koresh. This is something more sophisticated, less . . . I don't know, less obvious. Subtle. But think about it: child psychologists who specialize in training soldiers, video games, more aggression—which some people will tell you equates to a better warrior."

Laura held her palm to her forehead. "My head hurts."

"Tell me about it," Hutch said.

THIRTEEN

The doorbell chimed.

Hutch scowled at Laura. Checked his watch. "After eleven."

It rang again and Hutch went for it, convinced now it was Janet, back for round two. Whatever she said, he wasn't giving up Logan and Macie this week. No way.

He pulled the door open. His boss from the newspaper stood outside, a strange expression on his already unusual face. Larry was fifty years old but had the wrinkle-free, hairless face of a fifteen-year-old. He had a child's large eyes and the hint of buckteeth. The glow of the porch light gave him a jaundiced appearance.

"Larry?"

"I wanted to tell you in person," Larry said, striding past Hutch. "I don't know how I feel about it, so how could you know what to do?"

"Feel about what? Larry?"

Spotting Laura, Larry stopped in midstride. A big grin pushed his cheeks into rosy balls. "Laura Fuller. I forgot you were coming."

Uncertain, Laura smiled and hooked her hair over one ear. She set her glass on the coffee table and stood.

Larry moved in, extending his hand. "It is such a pleasure to meet you."

"Laura," Hutch said behind them, "this is Larry Waters, a good friend."

"And his editor," Larry said. "Sometimes I think he forgets that part."

Hutch said, "Larry, what are you doing here this late?"

Larry pulled off his overcoat and dropped into the La-Z-Boy.

Hutch and Laura sat on the couch facing him.

Larry folded his coat neatly on his lap. He patted it down, then said, "Okay, I got a call. Brendan Page's assistant, secretary, somebody. He's agreed to meet with you."

"When?"

"Right away. Tomorrow. At his headquarters in Washington state. But only tomorrow, she was very clear about that. What did you do? What magic button did you push?"

Hutch gaped at Laura. He said, "Nichols." Had to be. The same call that had sent Hutch to his office for half the afternoon, and had gotten Laura and Hutch talking about his investigation . . . Page had somehow found out about it. Page's sudden interest in him could not be a coincidence.

Maybe the trigger had been Hutch conducting Internet research on the other term Nichols had given him: *Genjuros*. Or one of the people Hutch had called about it, including a few of Nichols's former colleagues. He hoped for the doctor's sake it hadn't been his call to

Hutch that had caught Page's attention—that would mean Page had a bead on Nichols's location.

Larry said, "This is it, buddy. You've been trying to get a sit-down with him for a year."

Hutch stood and paced away from the sofa. He looked at the darkened hallway leading to the bedrooms. "I can't," he said. "I've got the kids this week." He turned back to Laura. "You and Dillon. I can't just *leave*."

"Don't worry about us, Hutch," Laura said. "Do what you have to do. Maybe Janet could take the kids back."

Hutch shook his head. "It took me six months to get joint custody. Something like this . . . taking off for work—not even work—she'll find a way to use it against me, try to get sole custody again."

"So don't tell her," Larry said. He looked from Hutch's gaping expression to Laura's and back. "It's one day, up and back. Laura can watch them for *one day*. Right?"

"Uh . . ." Laura said. "I guess."

"Parents have babysitters," Larry continued. "It's not like you're leaving them alone. Hutch, we're talking Brendan Page here. Face-to-face."

"I can watch them," Laura said. "That's not a problem. But, Hutch, isn't your whole point that the man is dangerous?"

"I thought of that," Larry said. "That's what had me going back and forth. But the more I think about it, if Page wanted to get Hutch, he wouldn't do it this way, calling me, asking Hutch to meet him there."

Hutch nodded. "He'd do something like rig my brakes. Make it look like an accident."

Laura said, "I know it's none of my business, but I don't like it. That guy really, really scares me."

Hutch retrieved his wineglass from the table, saw it was empty, and set it back down. He looked pleadingly at Laura and said, "I can't *not* do this. It's my chance to see his headquarters with my own eyes. To get a read on the man, maybe draw him out some, get him to say something that will help me put the rest of the puzzle together."

She reached out and grabbed his hand. "Then do it. Dillon will understand. And Larry's right, I'll just be the babysitter for a day."

Hutch frowned. "It couldn't come at a worse time."

"But it came," Larry said. "You never thought it would. But listen, don't give him any clues about what you know. Nothing. Guy like that, prone to violence? You never know where his tipping point is. What will be the one person you talk to, the one thing you say that makes him decide that his life would be easier dealing with your disappearance than dealing with *you*?"

FOURTEEN

Lying in the darkness of his bedroom, Michael thought he might be going crazy. He could not stop his mind from reeling out snippet after snippet of memory—all of them seeming random, none of them lasting more than a few seconds. Here he was meeting Ben, his team leader, for the first time. The elation he felt upon breezing through the video game Outis recruiters had asked him to play. Tearing open a Christmas present, then giving his dad a bear hug for scraping together enough to buy a used Xbox 360.

And right when he started to discern a pattern to his churning thoughts, something like learning how to ride a bicycle without training wheels would present itself. Mint chip ice cream on a sugar cone. The dead boy bleeding at his feet. His dad escorting him for the first time to an Outis dorm room—saying, "Are you sure you want to do this?"

Mastering the weapon of a video game still in development—and the following week Colonel Bryson handing him that very weapon in real life. Feeling the pressure of a trigger under his finger, the kick of the recoil—how it felt like Hawthorne, his childhood cocker spaniel, scurrying to get out of his arms. The child he'd shot, how—looking like an adult through the visor—he'd crashed against the television. Little-kid cartoons on the screen.

Each memory felt like a punch: two jabs to his face, one to his gut. Over and over. Even the sweet images—the bicycle, the ice cream—cut him with their innocence. He felt so far removed from them, from their simple joys. And thinking of them now made the harsh memories even harsher.

He could not stop sobbing. He tried to be quiet, but his tears wanted to scream. His inhalations stuttered with effort. Exhaling, he moaned or cried out, depending on the horror of the memory, the severity of its blow. He was on his side in bed, curled up, hugging himself. His face was wet, as was the pillow under his cheek.

A noise reached him. He tried to listen but heard only his own wrenching breaths. The noise again: a soft rap on the door.

He pressed his eyes closed, held his breath. *Go away*, he thought.

He heard the latch and looked. Someone had opened the door. A black silhouette appeared against the grayness of the den behind it. Lights-out was some time ago; the only illumination out there was from a dim bulb in the hood over the stove.

The figure whispered: "Michael?"

"Go away."

"Can I come in?"

Michael didn't say anything. If *go away* wasn't answer enough, this person was coming in no matter what.

The door opened wider, then closed.

"Can I turn on the light?"

"No."

"Turn on your bedside light, then."

Michael didn't move. After what felt like minutes, the voice came again.

"Michael?"

Michael sniffed and wiped at his face. He felt for the small reading lamp on the nightstand. He switched it on. Daggers pierced his eyes. His lids refused to open. He held up his hand; he did not want anyone to approach him like this. He sniffed again and pushed a thumb and index finger into his sockets. Pinching the bridge of his nose, he blinked. Behind his eyes, his brain throbbed.

A figure was standing at the door. Michael blinked away more tears—he remembered his dad called them clouds, after some Elton John song. The figure flickered and became Julian.

Michael said, "Are you . . . real?"

"I think so."

"What do you want?"

Julian walked to the bed. He set something on it. It was a roll of toilet paper. Michael tried to laugh but just snorted.

"I heard you," the younger boy said.

"Yeah, well . . ." Michael unraveled some of the TP and wiped his nose with it. "Probably everybody did, but I guess they're tired of razzing me."

"Funny, huh?" Julian said. "They try to make us think of our teammates as family—even insisting we use our first names on missions, instead of handles. They think the tighter we are, the more we'll fight to protect each other. But do one stupid thing, and the guys come down on you like they hate you."

Michael shrugged. "With friends like that . . ."

"So . . . what'd you do?"

Michael got more tissue and started drying his eyes. "Nothing." He studied Julian's face. "I've heard *you* . . . at night."

Julian nodded. He lowered himself onto the bed. He said, "Probably every night."

"I didn't come rushing in to catch you slobbering all over yourself."

"Why not?" He smiled.

Michael dropped the crumpled tissue to the floor. He pushed himself up and leaned his back against the wall. "So you got problems," Michael said. "It's none of my business how you handle them." When Julian didn't say anything, he continued. "I mean, you're like a little kid—and you're *here*." He said the word the way he would have said *in hell*. "You're Brendan Page's son—and you're *here*. I heard about your brother and what happened."

Julian said, "Then you know why I'm here. And I cry at night because I'm here. What's your story?"

"No story, just . . . *life*." Michael closed his eyes, tried to take in a breath without his chest hitching, but found it impossible. He clamped his teeth together, willing himself to get control. He felt a fresh tear break free and slide over his cheek. He brushed at it as though it burned. Eyes closed, he waited. Maybe the kid would take a hint and leave. When he didn't, Michael said, "Why don't you just go?"

Julian said, "You just got back from a mission. Did something happen?"

As much as Michael thought it wasn't possible, his chest grew even tighter. He opened his eyes. Those clouds again, making Julian's image shift. He reached out and touched Julian's arm. "What . . ." Michael cleared his throat. "What color's your hair?"

Julian's brow furrowed. "Dark brown."

"Your eyes?"

"Green-blue."

Michael relaxed. "I guess you're . . ."

"I'm what?"

"It's only that, I don't know what's real anymore. I saw things the other day, things that weren't there."

"Like what?"

"A guy . . . a guy reaching for a gun. Wasn't even a guy, a man."

"An avatar, then," Julian said. "Outis uses actors and avatars. You know that."

"It wasn't an avatar *or* an actor."

"What then?"

"A child," Michael snapped. "I think a little boy. I shot him."

"Like, during a simulation or war game?"

Michael shook his head. "I thought it was a war game, a tactical training mission. I *think* I thought it was. I don't know anymore. Sometimes they say, 'Okay, here's the operation, and this time it's for real, so heads up.' But they've done that so many times, then showed us we were engaging actors in a simulacrum. We never know what's real, what's not. I knew the VR environment in the helmets *added* things to reality. But it does more than that. It *changes* reality."

Julian's eyes wandered away. "If that's true . . ."

"If that's true, we can't know what's real and what isn't. They can make you see an EC, some guy coming at you with a knife. So you shoot him and it turns out to be your mother."

The boy said, "I don't think they can do that."

"I saw a man. I fought with him. Turned out to be a teenager, about your age."

"How do you know?"

"I took off my helmet. I saw with my own eyes."

"And the little boy?"

Michael stared into Julian's eyes a long time. "He was real. They made me kill a kid, a real kid. Why would they do that?"

Julian lowered his head.

"I've been thinking," Michael continued. "What if they can make you see things they want you to see, even without the helmets, without the visors?"

"Don't get paranoid."

"Paranoid? I *killed* people the other night, based on what they wanted me to see. You hear? What they *wanted* me to see, not reality." That got Michael thinking about who "they" were and who it was sitting on his bed. "How do I know you're not here for your dad or Colonel Bryson? Trying to find out if I've lost it, snapped?"

"I'm not here for that," Julian said simply.

"Then why?"

Julian shrugged. "Like I said, I heard you. Michael, if what you're saying is true, if you *believe* it's true, you gotta get out of here, man. Just go. Run. I mean it."

"They won't let me go," Michael said. "Especially with what I know." Quietly he added, "What I *think* I know. They'll kill me first."

Julian's head came up. The sadness in his eyes went deep, all the way to his soul. He was an eternal spirit who had seen all the world's tragedies. Then Julian blinked, and he was only a kid again.

Michael felt uncomfortable under Julian's gaze. He turned his face away. He sniffed, then wiped a forearm under his nose. He did it again.

Julian picked up the TP and held it out to him.

Michael swung his fist around and knocked the roll out of the boy's hand. He was on Julian in a second, had two fistfuls of his T-shirt. He shook Julian with everything he had. Witnessing his concern and sadness changing to fright was immensely satisfying.

"I don't need your pity," Michael said. "I don't need anything from a little rich brat like you. Just leave me alone!"

He shoved Julian off the bed.

Julian staggered back. Caught himself against the wall. Concern had found his face again.

Michael spread his arms. "What?"

Julian tugged on the bottom of his shirt, flattening the wrinkles Michael had made with his fists. "I'm just saying . . ."

"What?"

"You're not alone, okay? You don't have to go through this by yourself."

Michael narrowed his eyes at him. "Through what?"

Julian shook his head. "Whatever . . . you know? You're scared, freaking out. I would be too. If you want a friend, you know where to find me, okay?"

The kid looked sincere, but so what if he was? What was Michael supposed to do with him? He didn't have time for friends, and he certainly wasn't going to cry on anyone's shoulder. All Julian's caring did was make him feel worse. Another flash of ice cream to make the rest of it that much more awful.

Okay, so Julian was a nice guy. Around here, nice guys—and their friends—didn't just finish last, they finished dead.

Julian said, "I'm mean, I'm here, if . . ."

"What?"

"If you stay. I don't think you should."

Michael lowered his head. "Just go, all right?"

The boy stood quietly for a long time. Finally the door opened and closed, and he was gone.

FIFTEEN

Page Industries was headquartered east of Gold Bar, Washington, ninety minutes from the Sea-Tac Airport by the clock in Hutch's rented Pacifica. At the foot of the Cascade Mountains, the region was heavily forested. From Stevens Pass Highway, Hutch could see sheer cliffs and deep ravines, as if nature had experienced a violent outburst and gouged at the hills with long nails. The topographical map Hutch had picked up in Seattle showed a spattering of lakes, both large and small, as well as a complicated network of rivers and streams. The map also indicated large areas of flatlands hidden among the blanket folds of earth. Toss its isolation into the mix, and it made a perfect place to prepare soldiers for fighting in any terrain.

Hutch knew Outis managed training facilities around the world, but according to reports and its own literature, this was its primary "base of operations," through which all recruits were processed.

Hutch had reconnoitered the area using Google Earth. Most of the Page Industries campus, with its roads and buildings, was visible on the satellite images. A large square to the west, however, appeared to be replaced with a photograph of the land before construction had begun. No doubt this was where the Outis facilities were located. It was similar to some of the places the government intentionally blotted out for security reasons. It was conceivable Outis would be a terrorist target, but Hutch suspected its censoring had more to do with Page's clout.

The main gate onto the campus resembled the ones guarding military bases: set well back from the main road, the area between cleared of all trees, the better to spot approaching attacks; concrete barriers that required vehicles to slow down and weave between them; a metal-brace vehicle barrier that retracted into the roadway. The guard shack resembled a small stone cottage. As he approached, the shack's glass appeared tinted. Closer, he realized it was the panes' thickness that distorted its clarity. Bulletproof.

The guard took Hutch's driver's license and became a shadowy image behind a sliding window. When he reappeared, he said, "Sorry, Mr. Hutchinson, you're not authorized."

"I was invited," Hutch said. "I flew out from Colorado for this meeting."

"I'm sorry. Reach the exit lane by turning left right here."

"Look, I didn't come this far to be turned away. Call Page's office. They're expecting me."

"What time was your appointment, sir?"

"Sometime today. I didn't get a time."

"Then I'd wait by your phone. Please, sir." The guard twirled his finger and held it toward the main road.

Hutch drove around the shack and back to Stevens Pass Highway, which here was nothing but a two-lane blacktop.

If this is Page's idea of a joke . . .

But whatever the man was—brilliant, narcissistic, homicidal—Hutch had not run into any anecdotes that hinted at his being juvenile. He remembered an interview in which Page praised William the Conqueror's strategic skills in battle. "He always delayed confrontation," Page had said, "and in doing so, he let his enemy expend its resources in fruitless attempts to commit him to battle."

But Page had nothing to worry about on that score: Hutch's bank accounts were running on fumes. He'd had to buy his ticket—especially pricey because of the short notice—with the last of his credit.

Yeah, a billionaire's going to worry about my financial resources, even in the best of times.

All Hutch could do was wait. He had wanted to keep the entire day open for Page's meeting. Since all the late-night flights home had been full, he'd scheduled his return for the next day at noon. Any way you cut it, he'd have to stay the night. He'd passed a motel half an hour ago, as good a place as any to wait, he supposed. He turned onto the road.

A few minutes later he spotted a car on the opposite shoulder with its hood up. A man was leaning over the engine. Hutch slowed, then stopped in line with the car, a few-years-old Mustang.

"Need anything?" he said.

"No, thanks," the man said, without looking up. "Almost got it, I think."

As Hutch pulled away, the man looked, pushing up his glasses with a finger. He squinted, then scowled. Hutch watched him in the mirror. The man stepped into the center of the road, hands on his hips, watching the Pacifica accelerate away.

SIXTEEN

The Call, as Hutch had starting thinking of it, the way a death row inmate might refer to a hoped-for clemency call from the governor, came at two fifteen. Short and sweet: "Mr. Page will see you at four o'clock."

When Hutch returned to the gate, the same guard gave him two passes, one for his dashboard, the other to pin to his jacket. The guard handed him a map of the campus, with the route to the Outis facilities marked in red. As he'd suspected, they were located on the west side of the campus, where the satellite photos had been retouched. The map showed five other distinct clusters of buildings. Considering Page Industries' Shiva-like reach into all things war and defense, its compactness spoke to Page's fastidiousness and efficiency—appropriate, Hutch figured, for a paramilitary organization.

"We ask that you not deviate from this route, sir," the guard had said. Something in Hutch's expression may have prompted him to add, "If you do, alarms will sound, and a security car will escort you off the premises."

"Hellhounds and helicopters too?" Hutch said, eliciting as stony a face as Michelangelo ever carved. "Are there chips in these passes?"

"Have a good day, sir."

Crap. Hutch had indeed planned on "deviating" to other parts of the campus. He was, after all, a journalist and investigating Brendan Page. Most likely, he'd have found nothing but locked doors and closed mouths, and eventually a security camera would have picked up his activities. *Then* they'd have released the hellhounds.

That guy had made his breach and ejection sound immediate. It made him careful about not making a wrong turn on the way to his destination.

The Outis facilities boasted their own wall, gate, and guardhouse. This entrance, however, appeared more secure than the first. When he pulled up to the shack, no one greeted him. Its nearly opaque windows were almost certainly tinted; he could see nothing beyond his own reflection staring back at him. The gate here was no retractable barrier, but a massive portcullis set in an ancient-looking stone-block wall running in both directions. The wall was topped, anachronistically, with concertina wire. It was an impressive entrance, if you were a visiting politico or parent of a recruit.

As the gate rose, he could hear chain links rattling through sprockets. He drove through, and the illusion of the grand fortifications of King Arthur and Caesar shattered. A tall chain-link fence formed a box on the other side of the gate. He nosed up to a second gate, which didn't open until the one behind him had closed completely.

Like visiting a prison, he thought, which got him wondering whether the setup kept people out or in.

The Outis building to which the map directed him was a brick three-story in a style architects called modern traditionalism. Lots of angles, copper-tinted glass, and fancy masonry work—herringbone patterns around the windows, incised columns, the use of different shades, shapes, and ages of brick. A portion of the roof appeared to be an embattled parapet, giving the entire structure the quality of a contemporary castle.

Hutch stepped out of the elevator on the third floor into a larger outer office. Three secretaries worked at desks concentrically arranged before a large double-doored portal. Like the concrete barriers at the front gate, they forced visitors to weave between them to reach Page's office. A woman at the front desk told him, "We'll be with you in a few minutes, Mr. Hutchinson."

He nodded. Except for the desk, the remainder of the room could have been the lobby of a fancy hotel in a major city, some place like New York's Waldorf Astoria. The décor leaned toward opulent.

Hutch strolled to the windows. They looked out on the front parking lot. Framed and matted pencil sketches filled the walls. One was a perfectly rendered hand that Hutch recognized as one Michelangelo had eventually painted onto the roof of the Sistine Chapel. He had no doubt the sketch was an original.

He saw pieces by van Gogh, daVinci, Picasso, as well as many artists he didn't recognize. Most could have been described in an auction catalog as "a practice sketch, rendered in lead, of an incomplete body part . . ." Several were more complete depictions of a person, and a few of several whole figures together: mother and child, lovers in repose. He was studying one of these fuller sketches when he noticed what the artist had titled it: *Genjuros in Primo Luogo Assassina.*

Genjuros—the word Nichols had instructed him to research.

The artist's signature was clear, as far as artist signatures go. Hutch was pretty sure it read Giovanni Cavalcasello. Maybe the last name's first *l* was an *i*. He committed the title and name to memory, then looked at the sketch again: three people in billowy clothes and death's-head masks stabbing an elderly man, who appeared to have risen from a writing desk.

Hutch moved away from the drawing before the secretaries noticed his interest. His Internet search for *Genjuros* had hit on nothing but a character in a video game. He should have checked if the game developer had been Spiral, which Page owned. Could Nichols have known Hutch would wind up here and see the sketch? Had he thought the reference would be less obscure than it turned out to be? And what the hell did it mean?

He had pretended to study three other sketches when the lead secretary called to him.

"This way, please." She beckoned him into the slalom of desks. The other two women were schoolgirl petite, but this one appeared capable of putting Hutch down with one arm behind her back.

As he passed her desk, she stopped him. "I'm sorry, I'll have to hold your recording device out here until you conclude your meeting with Mr. Page."

Hutch tried to look injured. "I'm a journalist. I thought this was on the record."

She smiled and opened her hand to him.

Hutch said, "Are you guessing, or do you know?"

"Inside pocket of your jacket," she said.

He retrieved his digital recorder and handed it over. "How's my cholesterol?" he asked.

She opened a door and stepped aside for him. The room was roughly the size of a basketball court. The left wall comprised tall, ornately carved bookshelves, a lighted display case, and a floor-to-ceiling rock fireplace. What appeared to be a tree trunk burned within. A coffee table and leather high-back chairs were positioned in front of it. The right wall was paneled in rich wood squares. Four doors were spaced evenly along it. Between each door were framed photographs, paintings, and magazine covers.

A journalist friend who interviewed and profiled movie stars told him all celebrities had a "wall of fame" like this. "It's not ego," he'd said. "It's more as though they're as surprised as everyone else by their success, if not more so. Mementoes remind them how far they've come."

Bet it's ego in Page's case, Hutch thought.

If the far wall was a single pane of glass, it was the largest undivided window he'd ever seen. It was the width of the room and two stories high, peaking in the center. It must have cost what Hutch had paid for his house. Beyond it, in the distance, the Cascades rose in all of their picture-postcard splendor.

"Mr. Page will be with you shortly," the woman said. "Please make yourself at home. May I get you a drink?"

"No, thank you," Hutch said. "Is this Page's main office?"

"At Outis." She stepped back into the outer office and shut the door behind her.

Between Hutch and the display case on the left was a table. As he approached, he realized it was a diorama of a military battle. Hills, rivers, roads were rendered in three dimensions. Fuzzy green clumps obviously represented trees, though most of it was an open field. The troops were pegs the diameter of toothpicks. Red on one side, blue on the other. At the front of the blue army was a disproportionately large horseback rider, a sword held high. By this commander's ornate uniform, the miniature cannons, and wagons, Hutch guessed the battle was not contemporary: maybe from the American Civil War or the Napoleonic Wars. He was about to move on when the horseman's face caught his eye. It was Page. There was no mistaking the high forehead, narrow cheeks, puckered mouth.

Hutch shook his head.

The display case held weapons. Pistols, rifles, swords, knives, throwing stars. All of them appeared old, some of them were oddities. A three-barreled flintlock pistol, a sword with a firearm built into it, a crossbow attached to a sawed-off shotgun, what may have been a ray gun, a few items Hutch could not even guess at. Scattered among these were badges, bullets, and scopes.

To judge by Page's books, his interests ran the gamut from the expected—*Weapons Through the Ages*, Sun Tzu's *The Art of War*—to the inexplicable—*Botany for Lost Souls, Dance Your Way to Fame and Fortune*. The books shared shelf space with items like a rusty cannonball, a feather fountain pen in a glass case, a severed finger floating in murky liquid.

Nothing you wouldn't find in any successful CEO's office, Hutch thought.

He crossed to the wall of fame. Most of the photographs showed Page in action. In one he was in full combat gear, running alongside other soldiers through a town that had seen its share of bombs and bullets. Its destruction was apparently still underway. One soldier was grimacing, flinching away from a puff of dust springing from a stuccoed wall. Similarly, dirt was springing up all around their feet. Page held a monstrous weapon that was spitting out a blur of fire and smoke. The photo must have been taken fairly recently; Page looked no younger than he was now.

Hutch cursed under his breath. *Too bad he didn't take one for the team.*

Another photo showed him riding atop a tank through some other war-torn street. This was no Bush-like "Mission Accomplished!" stunt. Page was squatting outside the turret with other soldiers, one hand on the big barrel, the other raising a rifle in the air. Of course, he had a fat stogie clenched between his teeth.

The other framed images were more of the same. Hutch had seen none of them in the media. The collected impression was of a man who loved his job—not the parts that involved designing, manufacturing, selling, lobbying, or cashing the checks, but the *doing*, the trench action.

Hutch had once written a freelance piece for a business magazine about passion among visionaries. Passion for a particular art or science was the fuel that kept young entrepreneurs going through multiple setbacks, drove them to work ungodly hours, and gave them the creativity to see innovations others missed. It's what pushed them to succeed.

Trouble was, their success often forced them into managerial positions. For some reason shareholders and lenders wanted the people who'd made the breakthroughs in labs to sit behind desks, trying to convince others to do for money what they'd done for passion. Many of them became miserable. Even Bill Gates had finally shrugged off the mantle of Microsoft's CEO and returned to the software engineering role that had catapulted him to riches.

It appeared that Page had never fallen into that trap. He loved war and soldiering, had built companies that exploited that passion, and had remembered to stay involved on the level that interested him most.

All of it confirmed what Hutch had already figured out: Page was a hands-on leader.

Hutch reached the first door. He glanced back at the main entry and turned the knob. A hallway lay on the other side, running toward the front of the building, past the outer office. Obviously a private entrance. On the wall beside the next door was Page looking supremely content on the cover of *Cigar Aficionado*. He held a smoldering cigar chest-high, as though he'd just taken a puff. Hutch opened the door. An air seal broke, and a fragrance of cedar, coffee, and tobacco wafted out. It was a bedroom-sized humidor. Dim lights revealed walls lined with slanted shelves displaying opened boxes of cigars, hundreds of them. The air was cool and moist, and Hutch saw the reason: a digital display reported the humidity level at 68 percent, the temperature 65. He remembered a quote from Mark Twain: "If there are no cigars in heaven, then I'm not going!"

Hutch didn't believe heaven was an option available to Page, whether the good Lord shared his zeal for cigars or not. The image of Page attempting to light one of Havana's best on the flames dancing around him while Satan's minions jabbed him with spears and branding irons made Hutch smile, but just a little.

He shut the door and moved to the next one. It was open a crack, and he could see a bathroom beyond. The last door was near the back wall of glass. This one was wide open, exposing a vestibule. A stainless-steel elevator door consumed the entire back wall of the little room. Stepping up to the window, Hutched realized it looked out on more than the grand vista visible from deeper in the room.

Directly below was a semicircular field of trimmed grass. Along the outside edge of the field, spanning half its perimeter on the right, were various training stations: a ropes course, a shooting range, a monolithic rock wall. A Quonset-hut-shaped structure of white material likely housed a pool. A course for vehicles started at the field and disappeared over a hill. At the field's apex sat a full-sized commercial airplane, a 747, Hutch thought. It was mounted on what appeared to be shock absorbers the diameter of old redwoods, raising it twenty feet off the ground. Running along the outside of the fuselage were cubicles, platforms, and a ventilation system.

The left half of the perimeter marked the beginning of a town. Hutch could make out only a handful of its structures: a gas station, bookstore, hotel, bank, ice-cream parlor. Farther back, larger buildings rose above the others, blotting out the trees. A "Hogan's Alley," he realized, like the one at the FBI's training facility in Quantico. It was used to teach agents investigative techniques, firearms skills, and defensive tactics in a controlled real-world environment. Except Page's was considerably larger.

About a dozen men and a few women were going through the ropes course, walking a high tightrope, climbing rope ladders, swinging between elevated platforms. In the center of the field, a small group wearing black ninja garb had formed a circle around two people going at each other with martial arts moves. The ground was farther below him than the third-floor office accounted for. The back side of the building must have been open to a lower level or two.

Hutch recognized Page as one of the combatants. The man planted a roundhouse kick into his opponent's head, spun, and kicked the other man's feet out from under him. The other man hopped up and snapped Page in the face with a punch so fast Hutch wasn't sure he'd really seen it. Page reeled back. His foot shot up and nailed his opponent between the legs. The guy dropped, rolling and holding himself. Hutch noticed none of the protective gear he'd seen fighters wearing at other sparring events. No cups either, it seemed.

While Page bounced around, urging his opponent to rise, the secretary who had shown Hutch into the office appeared on the field. She walked from the building toward the gathering. If she and Page started exchanging blows, Hutch would not have been very surprised. She raised her hand and got Page's attention.

He bounced over to her, then looked up at Hutch. He nodded and returned to the sparring circle. He pointed at one of the spectators— no, not a man, a boy. It was Julian, Page's son.

Hutch's chest grew tight seeing Julian here, part of Page's insanity. He had met him in Canada, the only decent person among Declan's followers. Hutch had hoped that Julian would somehow find his way clear of his father's influence. He should have known better. It reminded Hutch of why he was so determined to make Page accountable for atrocities he was committing now—deeds Hutch *knew*, but couldn't prove . . . yet.

Page touched his fist to his palm and bowed to his opponent, who struggled to stand and return the gesture. He strode toward the building. Julian stepped into the circle, and another man broke from the circle to face him. The boy turned and gazed up at Hutch.

The first time they'd spoken, Hutch had been hiding from gunmen in a tree. Julian had been with them. He'd spotted Hutch, whispered, "They won't stop looking," and moved on. Hutch often marveled at the core of goodness the boy must possess to keep his moral flame flickering against the black hurricane of his family's evil.

Julian raised his hand in a tentative wave. Hutch waved back. A foot hit Julian's face, and he went down. He rose onto his hands and knees and stayed like that for a while. Finally he pushed himself up, shook his head doglike, and raised his fists to the other guy.

SEVENTEEN

The elevator opened. Page came out of it like a car salesman spotting his first customer.

"I tell you," he said, touching a cut on his brow, "nothing like a little rough play to get the blood pumping." He stopped, cocked his head. "How ya doing?" Rushing toward Hutch, he extended his hand.

When Hutch didn't take it, Page snapped it back. "Hey, I understand. We're enemies, right? That's what I hear, anyway. Excuse me a second." He went into the bathroom, leaving the door open. He began peeing. He called, "Did Nanya offer you a drink?"

Nanya. She'd been one of the secretaries he'd spoken to how-many-times in the last year, trying to get in to see Page. He hadn't recognized her voice, and she hadn't said anything about it.

The toilet flushed. A faucet turned on, lots of splashing. Page emerged, toweling his hair. He'd taken off the ninja top. Gray hair curled over his abs and pecs. The man was fit. Not twenty-year-old fit, a bit thicker and less defined, but impressive for a man in his late fifties.

Page said, "I didn't hear you. Did you get a drink?"

"No, thanks." He looked out the window. Julian was down again.

Page returned to the bathroom. He came out, pulling a gray T-shirt over his head. He walked past Hutch to a desk equidistant between the two side walls. It was close enough to the window for Page to turn in his chair and watch the training grounds anytime he wished. The wood was worn and scarred. Probably had been Eisenhower's or Ulysses S. Grant's. Page undoubtedly thought *his* ownership added to its value.

Julian was dancing around his opponent, who outweighed him by a good fifty pounds. The boy was hunched over, pressing a hand to his ribs.

"What do you think?" Page said. He nodded toward the field.

"What's Julian doing here?" Hutch said.

Page gave him a puzzled expression. "He's my son."

"You've got people twice his age beating on him."

Page took in the match. "Imagine what he's going to be like in a few years. Unstoppable."

"If he lives that long."

Page pushed a button under the desk's ledge. For a moment, everything outside the window appeared to fade. Then the glass turned milky white, as though a great mist were pushing against it. The effect was disorienting. Hutch felt a flush of vertigo. He took a step back to avoid falling over.

Page said, "You didn't come here to discuss my parenting, did you?"

Hutch scanned the window. The entire pane had become opaque, radiating only the light of day.

"Come," Page said. "Let's sit and discuss our grievances like men."

He strolled toward the chairs in front of the fireplace. He stopped at an end table and picked up a crystal decanter of amber liquid. "Can I pour you a Scotch? It's 1926 Macallan. Exquisite."

"Does that mean expensive?" Hutch crossed to a chair and sat.

"Very."

"Tempting, but I'll pass."

Page poured himself two fingers and dropped into the chair opposite Hutch. His lips were bent into a tight smile.

Still, Hutch recognized those smug, pursed lips he had grown to despise.

Page's eyes were dark and calculating. Hutch had seen them before too—in the cold stare of Page's homicidal son, Declan.

Page opened his hand. "Hutch, right?"

"That's what they call me."

On the coffee table between them, magazines were neatly arranged in a semicircle. Hutch noticed Page's smiling countenance on the cover of each: *Time, Newsweek, Fortune* . . . others whose mastheads he couldn't see. Beside them was a wooden container about the size of a shoe box. Its lacquer was so thick and highly polished, it could have been a large ice cube, the wood grain only reflections.

Page set his glass down. He pushed the box closer to Hutch and opened the hinged top. "Cigar?"

"No, thank you."

"Are you sure? They're quite good. Cuban."

The way he said it made Hutch take a closer look. He plucked one up. The band sported a portrait of Simón Bolívar, the South American liberator. The cigar was a Bolívar Royal Corona—the very brand he, Phil, Terry, and David had smoked in Canada the evening before their fatal encounter with Page's son.

Hutch looked up sharply. "Why these?" he said.

"I don't understand." The smile grew—only a little, but it did.

It could not be a coincidence. What was he trying to say? That he'd conducted his own investigation up there? Found details even the authorities didn't know? Was he saying that if he knew such seemingly innocuous things about what had happened, then he knew *everything* there was to know about Hutch himself?

"This cigar," Hutch said, choosing his words carefully, "has special meaning to me."

"How wonderful." Page tilted his head innocently. "Take a few. I'll have a box sent to your house."

Hutch dropped the cigar into the box.

"So," Page said, "let's not play games with each other. You were instrumental in my boy's death."

Hutch's heart picked up pace. "He was trying to kill me and the nine-year-old boy I was with. He did murder two of my friends."

Page raised the glass of Scotch. He swirled the liquid under his nose. He did not so much sip it as he did eat it, taking it in his mouth and appearing to chew. He said, "Of course, I read the police report. I didn't intend to sound accusatory, only factual. You were instrumental, am I right?"

So this was the way it was going to go. Hutch wanted to leap out of the chair and strangle the man. "On second thought, maybe I will have a drink."

Page took pleasure in hoisting himself up, sauntering to the decanter, and pouring the liquor.

Hutch said, "You don't want to play games. So don't. You know the facts, I know the facts. You want to know why I'm snooping around your companies, right?"

Page handed him the drink. He leaned over, selected a cigar from the lacquered box, and took his place on the couch. He ran the unlit cigar under his nose like a harmonica. "From what I hear—and I do hear everything—you imagine Declan was carrying out my orders when he started killing people in Canada. You believe this because my dear friend, Andrew Norton, went up there to investigate, and Declan killed him."

Hutch remembered Larry's words regarding staying mum around Page. If Page believed that Hutch's interest in him began and ended with the events in Canada, a dead horse as far as authorities were concerned, Hutch wasn't going to convince him otherwise. Let him think Hutch had stumbled over a few exposed roots of Page's tree of corruption and didn't care, because they didn't pertain to Canada.

Yeah, Page, he thought, *you keep believing that, fine with me.*

He said, "He saw what Declan was doing and didn't try to stop him."

Page's eyebrows went up. "It's my understanding that he told Declan to shut it down, to get back home. Andrew tried to bring Julian home with him on the spot, but Declan stopped him. In fact, in one of your own depositions, you stated that Andrew yelled at Declan. He told Declan he was supposed to field-test the weapon by blowing up trees and rabbits, but not people and buildings. That is what you told investigators, isn't it?"

Hutch took a swig. He immediately felt his belly warming, but no calming of his anger. "He saw me tied to a tree and did nothing."

"What was he supposed to do? If Declan had obeyed, he would have wrapped everything up, which included cutting you loose."

"Norton told Declan, 'No witnesses.'"

Page gave him a bored expression. "We can go round and round like this forever. Neither of us can ever know what Declan and Andrew had on their minds."

"Okay," Hutch said. He took another sip. "Declan was working for two of your companies. The weapon was one of your designs."

Page shrugged. "If an electrician comes to work on your house and steals some jewelry, do you assume he's acting on company orders? Or is he simply a bad employee, a bad person?"

"Declan was a bad person?"

"He snapped."

Hutch couldn't disagree. What interested him was *when* Declan snapped: in Canada—or years before, under the pressure of a domineering, warmongering father?

Page clipped the cigar into an ashtray. "The point I wanted to make earlier," he said, "is despite your involvement in my son's death, I'm not holding it against you. I have not come after you for it. As far as I'm concerned, you have not wronged me in a way that compels me to set things straight." He put the cigar in his mouth and turned it. He removed it and said, "Yet."

"Let me get this straight," Hutch said. He cracked the glass down on the coffee table and leaned back. "You're more upset that I'm meddling in your business than that I was 'instrumental' in your son's death."

"What Declan did was wrong. We have no argument there. You may believe that because I am wealthy, I think my family and I are above the law. That's not me, never has been. I'm an advocate of personal responsibility. If Declan had been driving drunk and killed someone, I'd want him to stand trial. Of course, I would make sure he had all the advantages our legal system affords, but in the end, if he were convicted and sentenced to jail, I'd tell him, 'Go pay for what you did.'"

Hutch shifted in the chair. "So, Declan got what he deserved."

Holding it away from his face, Page rotated the tip of his cigar over a lighter's flame. He blew on it, then took a puff. He said, "That's a harsh way of wording it. Declan got in over his head. Look, my companies are doing no harm. In fact, they are helping by providing defense systems that ultimately save lives. What gets me is that you are bent on stopping me from saving lives. That, I will fight you over."

For the first time, Hutch saw anger touch Page's eyes. "You're saying it's not that your personal freedom is in jeopardy, or that you'll take a big financial hit because I'm trying to make you accountable for your actions?"

Page leaped up. He held out his hands. "What actions? I raised a child who went wrong. You'll have to put half the parents in the country in jail if you pursue that one. I'm providing our government with weapons that work, with soldiers who are the most efficient in the world. You want me accountable *for what*?"

"If my suspicions are accurate," Hutch said, "that's a rather long list. Here's one: *xǐ nǎo*."

Oh crap, Hutch thought. *Did I really go there?*

Page would not have looked more startled if Hutch had slapped him. "Brainwashing? Come on!"

"That's what I'm hearing. That's how your soldiers become so efficient."

Page puffed on the cigar, like an engine trying to get up to speed. The smoke around him grew thick, and an expression occurred to Hutch: *He has his head in the clouds.* Too caught up in lofty dreams to see reality.

Page said, "Every military in every society since the beginning of time has faced that accusation. Civilians cannot understand how rational people, noncriminals, essentially *good* people can kill their brethren. But all we have to do is point out that their brethren are trying to kill them. All we have to do is show them that the powers for whom the enemy is fighting want to impose their own beliefs on our mothers and sisters and children. They want to kill you, and they want you to live under their rule. It takes no more than that to convince people to kill.

"If you want to call that brainwashing, where does it stop? We educate our children to understand the things we believe to be right. Is that brainwashing? Religions tell their followers what morality is. Is that brainwashing? You write articles that influence what people believe about an event or a person or the world around them. Is that brainwashing?"

"You know it's more than that," Hutch said.

"It is," Page agreed. "For my soldiers to be efficient, they must have special skills." He pointed the cigar at Hutch. "The way you, as a writer, have your own set of skills. My men have to learn to go against their impulses. When the average person hears gunfire, he ducks or runs away. Soldiers run *to* it. Teaching them to do that is not brainwashing. It's called habituation. It's getting them so used to the sound of gunfire, of fighting while bullets and shrapnel fly all around them, that they can do their job without flinching."

Hutch said, "There's a reason we flinch from danger."

"Self-preservation," Page said. "But every society needs a group of people who choose fight over flight when the going gets tough. If I can send a hundred efficient soldiers into battle instead of a thousand who aren't operating at a hundred percent, as a father and a man who loves the youth of his country, wouldn't you want me to do that?"

"Of course," Hutch said, "but I wouldn't want you to force those hundred into being our sacrificial lambs."

"Holy hell, man, nobody comes here unless they want to. I train soldiers faster and cheaper than any government on earth. They come out of my program with skills that help keep them alive, and help them do their jobs better, so the conflict ends sooner."

Page returned to his seat. He set his cigar in an ashtray and picked up his Scotch. He said, "Besides, we can tell quickly who has what it takes to be a soldier."

"Yeah, throw a bunch of kids in a war zone. Whoever comes out alive are the ones you want."

The conversation wasn't going the way Hutch had hoped. He was trying to get Page to pay out more of the rope with which Hutch would eventually hang the man. Instead, it had become the sort of argument Fox News debates every day.

Page leaned forward. "You're right, but not in the way you think," he said. "Nowadays we don't need real battles. Video games, virtual reality, tactical simulations—we can filter out the nonfighters from the heroes without spilling a single drop of blood."

"Heroes?"

"That's what it boils down to. People who are willing to do what it takes to protect what they believe is right." Page laughed. "Like yourself. Seems I can't hear the name John Hutchinson without the word *hero* in the same sentence."

Hutch shook his head. "I'm not a hero."

Page squinted at him. "I wish you weren't. There's a special kind of pain a person feels when someone is called a hero for killing your child."

The tension between them felt as thick as the smoke over Page's head.

Page said, "You're here to gather intelligence, to find out what you can about me. You assume I invited you here to learn what you know."

Or to scare me off, Hutch thought, but he said, "That's not why you invited me?"

"I don't care what you know. I wanted to know who you are, what kind of person I'm dealing with."

"And?"

"You're obsessed," Page said. "I know what it looks like." He relaxed into the sofa. "I know what it *feels* like. There's a simplicity to obsession that frees you from other responsibilities. Most people don't understand that. They don't realize that laser focus means everything else is out of focus, unimportant. There's something refreshing about that.

"You've had a rough time. Lost a few friends. Divorce. You see your kids only every other week. You're struggling to make ends meet. Oh, don't look so violated. You know I have access to that information. And you should have learned enough about me to know I don't go into any situation unprepared."

He set the cigar in an ashtray. He picked up his glass, swirled the liquid, and drank. He said, "With everything else in your life in shambles, you needed an obsession. I'm all you can think about. Isn't that right?"

Hutch said nothing.

Page continued. "You need to take a deep breath and reprioritize your life. I should not be at the top of your list. I should not be on your list at all. Go do something else for a while. You'll see."

"You're saying I need a hobby?"

"Not a bad idea," Page said. "Have you hunted lately?"

"Not animals." Hutch let his words hang between them.

Page finally bent his lips into a full smile. He said, "I don't like being the object of obsession. Let me put it to you plainly: Get off my back. Stop sniffing around my companies, my employees, my former employees. This will end badly for you."

Hutch rose. He said, "You can't suppress the truth forever."

Page thought about it. Finally, he sighed and stood. He stepped around the coffee table. He touched Hutch's shoulder, gently nudging him toward the door. On the way he gestured toward the diorama. "Did you have a chance to examine my war model?"

"I noticed you sitting on the horse."

Page laughed. "Wonderful, isn't it? Napoleon's greatest battle,

Austerlitz. Some say tactically it was the most stunning military victory of all time."

"I'm partial to David and Goliath, myself," Hutch said.

Page ignored the comment. He said, "Smart commanders know when they're outnumbered, when they've been outmaneuvered. They realize when it's time to give up. Are you familiar with Demosthenes, the Athenian orator and statesman?"

When Hutch didn't respond, Page continued. "I'm surprised, given your fondness for famous quotations."

Is there anything about me this guy doesn't know?

"In August of 388 BC, Demosthenes was an infantryman at the Battle of Chaeronea, where the Macedonians slaughtered the Athenians. But Demosthenes ran away. When people asked him why he hadn't stayed on the front line and died with his countrymen, he answered, 'To live and fight another day.'" Page stopped, allowing Hutch to continue alone toward the door. "Find a different bad guy, Hutch. I'm not your man."

Hutch turned. "I call them as I see them."

He could tell Page was considering a catalog of responses. In the end, the man said only, "Don't forget to pick up your tape recorder on the way out."

At the door, Hutch turned around. Page was leaning over Napoleon's grand moment. He pushed his equestrian effigy closer to the opposing forces, acting as though Hutch had already left, as though he had never been there.

"May I . . ." Hutch said, hating to ask this man for anything. "May I speak to Julian, just to say hi?"

Page didn't look up, but he paused, thinking. "Nanya will escort you down."

Nanya opened a door onto a flat rock patio. Hutch brushed past her and stepped onto the field.

Julian was sitting on the brown grass, his head down. He noticed the glares the others threw at Hutch and looked over his shoulder. He smiled, rose—painfully, it seemed to Hutch. He started for Hutch at a fast walk.

Hutch barely knew the boy, but somehow they shared a connection. He suspected Julian admired him for standing up to his brother, for staying to fight instead of running, as he could have. Well, as *someone*, not Hutch, could have. He just didn't have it in him to turn his back on human suffering. And that was part of it as well: Hutch thought Julian saw in him qualities that were lacking in the male role models in his life. They were qualities Julian felt in himself, but they were dying from not being affirmed.

Julian, if you only knew, Hutch thought. *I'm not the hero you think I am.*

Julian reached him and, to Hutch's surprise, kept coming. He pressed himself against Hutch, embraced him, one tight squeeze. The boy broke away and glanced up at his father's office window. Hutch did too. The milky opacity was gone, but Page was nowhere in sight. Julian's eyes flicked to Nanya, hovering a few feet away. He frowned, but when his eyes returned to Hutch, he smiled.

Julian said, "What are you doing here?"

"I was going to ask you the same question. Your dad and I . . ." He was going to say "had some business to discuss," but the idea of doing business with Page turned his stomach. He thought Julian would respond the same way. "I came to talk to him. How are you doing? You look good."

"Except for the black eye and bloody nose."

Julian's short-cropped hair gave Hutch a clear view of a horizontal scar spanning the boy's forehead.

Hutch nodded toward it. He said, "Why do all my friends have scars?"

Julian ran his fingers over the thin, raised tissue. "Unlucky, I guess."

"Lucky, more like it," Hutch said. "Means you lived through something that tried to kill you. I saw you sparring. Looked pretty rough."

"Nothing new." He nervously rubbed a twine bracelet between his forefinger and thumb. He sidestepped to put Hutch between himself and Nanya. He lowered his voice to say, "Are you still after Dad?"

"You know about that?"

"Who doesn't?"

"What do you think?"

"Keep doing it." His eyes became shiny with tears. "Don't stop."

Hutch heard Nanya crunching over the grass, stepping closer. He said, "How can I reach you?"

Julian shook his head. "I wanted to talk to you, but I don't have access to e-mail or a phone."

An idea struck Hutch, one of those *Wanna-bet-I-can-jump-to-that-balcony?* impulses that smart people ignore. He gripped the boy's shoulder. His other hand slipped into his jacket's inside pocket and pulled out his mobile phone.

Julian took his cue from Hutch's intense stare and kept his eyes locked on Hutch's.

"Are they hurting you? I can get family services out here." He realized how lame it sounded as soon as he said it.

"Are you kidding?" Julian said, a twisted smile on his lips.

Hutch tucked the phone into the folds of Julian's *keikogi*. He knew it would slide down his stomach and stop where the belt was tied. He whispered, "Turn it to vibrate."

Nanya stepped so close, her shoulder touched Hutch's.

Hutch ignored her. He said, "What's going on here? I've heard things."

Nanya said, "Mr. Hutchinson, it's time to let Julian get back to his studies. Julian?"

"I'm sure your ears are fine," Julian told Hutch. "It's good to see you."

"To be honest, Julian," Hutch said, "I wish I hadn't seen you. Not here."

The boy shrugged.

Hutch said, "You take care of yourself."

Julian slowly returned to the sparring circle. He sat and looked back. They exchanged a nod, and Hutch turned and strode away.

EIGHTEEN

Hutch climbed into the Pacifica and slammed the door. He sat looking through the windshield at Page's headquarters building. The odor of the man's cigars clung to him. He felt as though a patina of smoke covered him from head to toe. Still, he got the sense that it was having been in Page's presence, and not simply the smoke, that made him want to take a shower.

Page was slick, no doubt about it. There could be no shadows without light. The man knew how to blind people with candor while keeping secrets in the shadows his truthfulness did not reach. It was a tactic practiced by all great manipulators: tell the truth 90 percent of the time, and people tended to forget about the other 10 percent. But lethal things can be hidden in slivers of darkness.

In dealing with Page, Hutch vowed to remember that.

Their conversation had not provided much new information. It merely confirmed what he'd already known or suspected: the charisma, the directness born of confidence and power. Still, the visit had proved worthwhile in ways he could not have imagined. He'd found a reference to *Genjuros*, probably the very drawing that had put the word in Nichols's vocabulary. Hutch had work ahead of him to uncover its meaning, but he believed he'd made an important inroad.

And Julian. The boy's head had to be filled with details that, with the research Hutch already had on hand, were bound to paint a gruesome picture of the debonair Brendan Page. Hutch already felt regret seeping into his consciousness. The phone put Julian at risk, he was sure of it. Hutch ached at the thought of Julian being caught with it, especially if Hutch's motivation was nothing more than furthering his own investigation.

No, he told himself, *somehow, someway, I can help him. If he wants out, I'll try to find a door. If he wants a friend, I'll be there.*

The phone's battery wouldn't last long. They'd have to connect soon and figure out how to reach one another beyond the life of the phone.

He started the car and drove to the main guard shack, where he surrendered his passes. He pulled forward and stopped at the cross street. Up the road a ways, the Mustang he'd seen broken down earlier was parked at the curb. The driver was looking at him through a pair of binoculars.

Surely Page's money could buy better surveillance than that. Even the car wasn't what he would have expected. It was old and worse for wear. Maybe that was part of the gimmick, to use a vehicle that no one looking for a tail would suspect. But then why be so obvious with the binocs? Perhaps that had not been so intentional; the driver brought them down.

Hutch pulled onto the street, heading away from the car. In the mirror, he saw it pull away from the curb, and then a hill blocked it from view.

NINETEEN

Hutch sat on the edge of his motel bed. He moved the motel phone from the nightstand to his lap and dialed Logan's mobile phone number. He had arranged for Laura to use it during her visit, since she had left her satellite phone in Fiddler Falls.

When she answered, he said, "I'm done."

"How'd it go?"

He groaned and went on to describe the meeting.

"He flat-out told you to get off his back?" Laura said.

Her voice sounded thin. From concern or a bad connection, Hutch couldn't tell.

"Did he threaten you?"

"In his way. He said if I continued my investigation, it would end badly for me."

"Sounds like a threat to me," she said. "What are you going to do?"

"What I'm *not* going to do is get off his back." He pushed himself farther onto the bed and leaned against the wall. "I spoke to Julian."

"There, at Outis?"

"That was my reaction. He's working out with the recruits. He wasn't happy. He said he can't even make phone calls."

Her silence conveyed more than words.

Hutch said, "I gave him my cell phone, so don't call it. Tell the kids not to call either. I think he'll be up the creek if they discover him with it."

"I hate to think what 'up the creek' means in a place like that."

Hutch closed his eyes, trying not to think about it. He said, "Is Logan angry I wasn't there when he got up?"

"More like disappointed. I told him something really important came up."

"What'd he say?"

"He said, 'What else is new?'"

Hutch swore. "Sorry. Put Logan on. I'll try to explain."

"They're outside playing. How about calling back before bedtime?"

"I will, but tell him I'll make it up to him."

"I did."

"I'll make it up to all of you."

"I know," Laura said. "I took them to the zoo, got them thinking about real monkeys, not the ape their dad can be."

"Ha, ha."

"We had a nice day," she assured him. "I made breakfast, and we had lunch out. We're going to make cookies tonight."

"I appreciate it, Laura. I know this isn't what you had in mind for your visit."

She said, "Well, the bright side is that I'm getting to know your kids better." She paused. "Are you glad you went?"

"I found out enough to keep me busy for a while," he said. "I'll tell you about it when I get home."

"I wish you could have booked a flight tonight. I don't like you being in Page territory."

"He has a long reach," Hutch said. "I'm not sure any place is safe from him. I think he had me followed."

"What?" Frightened now. "Hutch, you gotta get out of there. Go straight to the airport, get on standby."

"I'm not going to run scared. Page is just making a point. Killing me would draw more attention to him than he wants. That's what this meeting was about. He'd rather scare me off than resort to more drastic action."

"Like what happened to that doctor's family?"

Hutch's stomach rolled over on itself. "I'm not saying the man's incapable of . . . of doing something like that. But he's smart enough not to, not in this case."

Silence.

"Laura?"

Laura's voice was quiet but firm. "Just get back here."

"Tomorrow afternoon," he said, as cheerfully as possible. "I promise."

Two hours later he was still on the bed, typing notes into his laptop. He had the room's phone cradled under his cheek. It had taken Randall Cunningham, an acquaintance at the Denver Museum of Art, only an hour to track down information about the sketch Hutch had seen in Page's outer office. Giovanni Cavalcaselle—Hutch had thought the last letter was an *O*—was an obscure Renaissance artist who'd lived in Florence. He was known as a chronicler of the city's dark side. His paintings depicted murder, double dealings, child abuse. According to art historian Raffaello Sanzio, *Genjuros in Primo Luogo Assassina* was commissioned as a painting but never completed. The preliminary sketch of it was last sold at auction for a modest sum.

"Okay, but what does it mean?" Hutch said impatiently.

"The title?" Randall said. "Genjuros' First Murder."

Hutch waited for more. He glanced around the dark room, realizing night had descended without his noticing. He switched on the bedside lamp. "What's Genjuros?" he asked.

"Apparently the word is derived from the same Latin root from which we get *justice* and *juror*. It was a secret division of the city-state's security force established by Pietro de' Medici in 1435."

"Security force?" Hutch said. "That sounds right. What did it do?"

"Only one function," Randall said. "Supposedly, its members answered solely to Medici, and its missions were limited to the confines of Florence itself."

"What, like a police force?"

"More of an execution squad. It was used against Florentines who were perceived enemies of the Medicis, and they had plenty. Normally citizens of a jurisdiction, then as now, are accorded a trial when accused of a crime. But criminal courts don't address noncriminal offenses. Say, political or romantic rivals, or getting your feelings hurt, for that matter. That's when a Genjuros-type group would come in handy."

"Assassins," Hutch said.

"Ready whenever you wanted them," Randall agreed. "Private, secret, and not at all finicky about whom they kill."

Someone knocked at his motel door.

"Randall, I have to go," Hutch said. "I owe you one."

"Anything for you, Hutch."

Hutch hung up. He called, "Who is it?"

No answer. He cracked the door and looked through. The motel was a single-story U shape. The light next to each door appeared to be controlled as one, and they were all on now. Each room opened onto a concrete walkway and faced the parking lot. When he'd come to the motel in the late afternoon, having picked up dinner at McDonald's, only three vehicles were in the lot. His had made four. Since then, more cars had arrived, but there was no one standing at his door.

However, someone had placed a festive gift bag directly outside. It was the kind of bag you used when you didn't have time to wrap a present. He'd heard of bombs with mercury-controlled switches. As soon as someone moved them, they exploded. He heard Laura telling him that's how Page makes a point and shut the door. Who would leave a bag for him? No one knew he was there. Laura. Larry. The kids. Page—certainly he would be keeping tabs on him.

That brought to mind the beat-up Mustang. Hutch opened the door again and poked his head out. Slowly, he scanned the parking lot and saw it. It was parked on the right, at the end of the hotel's short wing. Only its bumper, hood, and part of its windshield were visible. Then the trees behind it flashed red, and Hutch knew someone inside had touched the brake pedal.

Again, Hutch thought Page could afford more professional surveillance, but what did he know? His knowledge of such things came almost exclusively from television shows. Maybe real PIs were so crass and confident, they didn't concern themselves with nice cars or stealth.

Hutch pulled his head in and shut the door. Was the package from the person who was watching him? Most likely. But what if it was from someone else, someone who wanted to help? As a reporter, he often fielded calls from tattletales who wanted to remain anonymous. If the package was evidence against Page, he *had* to retrieve it . . . before someone else did. If it had not been left by Mr. Mustang, then that guy must have seen someone drop it off. Wouldn't he come for it, score some extra points from the boss?

Hutch cracked the door again and squinted at the colorful bag. He imagined grabbing its hardened-twine handles, spotting the spark of a detonator, then . . . nothing.

He was being stupid. If they wanted to kill him, all they had to do was kick the door in and machine-gun the place. Or shoot at it with a grenade launcher. Or—he thought, disgusted with himself—put a mercury-switched bomb in a bag outside his motel door.

He considered his options, and realized they were pretty slim: retrieve the bag or not. He would like to learn more—and thought of a way to do it.

He opened the door and flipped the bolt so it wouldn't close. He slipped on his leather jacket, crossed the room, and entered the bathroom. Over the toilet was a small window, glazed with pebbled glass. He unlocked it and slid it up. If there had ever been a screen on it, it wasn't there now. Beyond a twenty-foot firebreak, the bathroom light caught the first vestiges of a dense forest.

As he climbed through, the window kept coming down on him: first on his head, then shoulders, lower back, legs. He dropped down onto dirt and gravel and shot quickly to the edge of the forest. If Page's people were watching him with any level of thoroughness, they would be keeping their eye on this open area behind the motel. Light shone through only three of the back windows. Still, he counted the windows from the edge of the building far to his left to make sure he knew which was his. He might have to reenter the way he left.

Moving along the edge of the forest, he kept a lookout for anything that could help him—or anyone who would want to hurt him. He found one thing right away—a twig the diameter of a garden hose. After breaking protrusions off of it, the twig was in the shape of a pistol.

The firebreak extended another twenty feet past the end of the building, where a shorter wing of the motel branched away. It was at the end of this extension that the Mustang had been parked.

Hutch continued along the edge of the forest and turned right when it did. Halfway to the end of the building he stopped. The trees glowed red, then fell back into darkness. The man had touched his brake again, but something else made Hutch's heart leap. In the brief glow in the brake lights, he thought he'd seen movement among the trees. A figure seemed to have darted behind foliage to escape the light.

Did Mr. Mustang have a partner? Did they know that Hutch had sneaked out of his room? If they did, wouldn't the partner have moved deeper into the woods sooner? Why not hide and wait for him?

He decided to treat the movement he'd seen as a man, not an animal or a trick of his eye. He also chose to assume he had not been discovered. He considered moving deeper into the woods and finding the man lurking there. But the man would be difficult to spot in these dense woods, and even harder to sneak up on. That left returning the way he had come or getting to Mr. Mustang too quickly for his partner to react.

The latter idea appealed to him more, since he still wanted to know who Mr. Mustang was and what he knew about the package. He continued edging toward the front of the building and the car, more carefully now. He listened for movement within the forest, watched for another clue to the man's whereabouts. By the time he came even with the Mustang, he had not spotted the second man again.

He crouched low and held his breath. The sound of a television program drifted from one of the rooms. Across the parking lot, the cursive neon words that told travelers the motel had vacancies flickered and hummed. Wind made the treetops sound like surf. If another man was nearby in the woods, he wasn't moving.

Stick to the plan, Hutch thought. *Move fast. Grab him and go.*

A terrible scenario occurred to him: his standing at the driver's door, yanking up and down on the handle, as both the man inside and his partner in the woods took a bead on him. He crawled farther along the tree line until the driver's side was visible. He had hoped to see a window rolled down, maybe the driver's elbow sticking out, but it was late November and the air had teeth. No one in his right mind would sit in weather like this with the windows down.

The brake lights flashed on, illuminating the ground between the Mustang and Hutch—illuminating Hutch. The glow was so bright it allowed him to see Mr. Mustang's face in the side mirror. The man's eyes flicked to the mirror and away, then back again. They had become the size of silver dollars.

Hutch ran for him. If the car door was locked, he would break the window: no hesitation. He pushed even harder, knowing his only chance was to get there before the man could pull a weapon or his partner could get off a shot. The toe of his shoe struck the edge of the blacktop, and he almost went down. Instead, he pinwheeled his arms and used the momentum to crash into the side of the Mustang. Before he could fully gain his feet, he had the door open—not locked! —and was grabbing at the man within. His fingers found a collar. He tugged at it, pulling the man sideways out of the car.

"Whoa, whoa, whoa!" the man was saying.

Hutch jabbed the business end of the pistol-shaped branch into his ribs. He said, "Get up. On your feet."

They stood together. *Now what?* Hutch thought. He looked into the woods, expecting a muzzle flash or someone barreling directly at him. He moved his hand to the back of the man's collar, the branch to his spine. He shoved him forward.

"Okay," Hutch said. "Let's go."

TWENTY

The man didn't move. He said, "Wait! But—"

"Shut up," Hutch said. "Just move. Fast."

They approached the door and the bag sitting in front of it.

Hutch said, "What's in the bag?"

"I don't know."

Hutch cracked him in the head with the branch. He repeated the question.

"I don't . . . I saw someone set it down, knock on the door. That's all I know!"

"Who?" Hutch jerked back on the man's collar, then pushed him forward again.

"I . . . Don't . . . *Know*."

"Don't touch it," Hutch said. "Open the door. Just push it."

Mr. Mustang's foot snagged on the gift bag's handle. He fell into the room, pulling the package with him.

Hutch grimaced—but only for the millisecond he figured it would take for the bomb to detonate. When nothing happened, he once more scanned the area behind him. The porch lights did not reach far into the parking lot, but he saw nothing alarming and didn't hear anything like the scampering of feet, the slamming of car doors, or the chambering of shells in weapons. He stepped inside and slammed the door.

Mr. Mustang was rising to his knees. He was showing Hutch his hands, that they were empty. "I can explain."

Hutch pressed his back against the motel room door. His eyes fell to the thing that had fallen out of the bag. It lay on the floor between him and Mr. Mustang. It was black, about the size of a hardback book—or the box of cigars Page had promised. Could it be? It must have been upside down; he could not make out any lettering or other distinguishing features.

He said, "What is that thing?"

The other man shook his head. "I'm not the one who left it for you. I don't know who did."

"But you saw him. What can you tell me?"

"I didn't see a car or anything. He just walked out of the darkness, set it down, and left. Black pants, black jacket. White guy. Brown or blond hair."

Hutch turned and put his eye to the door's peephole. He sidestepped to the window. He looked through the blinds at the parking lot. His rental and a couple others shone in the light. Nothing else. He closed the curtains over the window. When he turned back to Mr. Mustang, the man had the fingers of both hands interlaced on top of his head. His skin was ashen. His bottom lip—his entire body—quivered. This was no private investigator, let alone one of Page's professional soldiers.

Hutch said, "What do you do?"

"Do?"

"For a living."

"I'm an . . . I'm an . . . accountant."

Hutch had interviewed a few of them over the years. Enough for him to figure out if the guy was telling the truth. He said, "CPA?"

The man nodded. "Small practice in Portland. Just me."

"What's the professional organization most of you guys belong to?"

"You guys who?"

"CPAs."

"The . . . uh . . . AICPA. The American Institute of—"

"Okay. Put your hands down," Hutch said. "Why are you following me?"

"I recognized you. From the newspaper articles. I've been researching Page Industries. Hard not to run into your name and picture lately."

"Why are you researching Page's companies?"

"My son. He joined Outis. He—"

"Wait a sec," Hutch said. He knelt beside the black box. He lifted it: heavy. He turned it over and returned it to the carpet. The other side appeared to be a flat-screen monitor. The only other features were two ventlike grooves running the length of the device above the screen—a speaker or microphone, he guessed.

Mr. Mustang walked on his knees toward Hutch. "What is it?"

"Looks like a TV."

"No switches," the man observed. "Any place to plug a computer into? Anything like that?"

Hutched picked it up and rotated it, inspecting each side carefully. "No," he said. "I can't even find a seam or any way this thing was put together." He kept looking.

Mr. Mustang cleared his throat. "Name's Jim."

"Hutch. What about your son?"

Jim frowned. "They won't let me see him."

"It's a closed academy," Hutch said. "There are designated days for parents."

Jim was shaking his head before Hutch finished. "Something's wrong."

"What makes you say that?"

Jim rose from the floor, sat on the bed. He draped his arms across his legs. "I never liked it, right from the beginning. Too secretive. Too strict. Michael—that's my boy—he wanted to do something with his life, but he didn't do so well in high school, almost didn't graduate. Outis came by his school. He came home with a brochure, an application. He was pretty excited. But ever since he's been there, he's been getting worse."

"Worse how?"

"Temperamental, moody. When he calls, it's not unusual for him to snap at me or his mother about something: we ask too many questions, we didn't put enough beef jerky in our care package, we're not speaking loud enough . . . silly stuff. When he came home for Christmas last year, he spent most of the time in bed. Didn't want to hang out or talk. He hasn't been home since. He told us a few months ago he wouldn't be coming for Thanksgiving or Christmas. His mother is heartbroken." His voice cracked on this last word. He wiped at his eyes. "Hell, *I'm* heartbroken."

"And you're here to—what? Get him? Take him home?" *Fat chance*, Hutch thought.

"I don't know. I just need to see him, know he's all right. He called this morning. He . . ." Jim dropped his face into his palms.

Hutch touched his leg. "What'd he say?"

Jim spoke without looking up. "He just cried." He lowered his hands, found Hutch's eyes. "He didn't say hi, good-bye, Dad, nothing. I answered the phone, and it was him, crying. I tried to talk to him, find out what's wrong, but he continued to *weep* for two, three minutes. Then he hung up."

Hutch's heart ached for the man. He said, "Michael's his name?"

Jim nodded.

"Do you think he'd come home now . . . if they let him?"

Jim smiled sadly. "You're the first person I've talked to who seems to know there's an 'if they let him' factor to Outis. They call it a military academy, a training facility for private soldiers. But it's more like a cult, or like they've kidnapped these kids, knowing they'll come around to wanting to be there. It's like . . ." He shook his head. "What's that thing where hostages grow attached to their captors?"

"Stockholm syndrome." Hutch had heard the term applied to Outis's methods before. He'd discovered a blog on which a mother had complained of this very thing. He tried to contact her, but the blog came down, her phone number was disconnected, and he couldn't uncover an address.

"I'm scared for him," Jim said. "I've talked to other parents whose kids . . ." He stood, rubbed his face, walked to the door, turned back. "It's like Outis simply swallows them. They get moved from facility to facility. I talked to one guy who was trying to get his kid out of there. He finally got his boy back."

"There, see?"

Jim's eyes bore into him. "In a body bag. An 'accident' during a training mission."

Hutch barely discerned a high-pitched whine, similar to the charging of photographic flashes.

"I'm so afraid—" Jim started.

Hutch held his hand up, cutting the man off. He brought his finger to his lips, straining to locate the source of the sound. As his eyes came to rest on the device, its screen flickered to life. He picked it up and sat on the bed. On the screen, a light zipped past and was gone, as though the camera were in a dark room and had panned past a single point of illumination. Different shades of blackness moved on the screen. He could make out nothing.

Jim stepped over. He put a knee on the bed and watched. "What is it?"

"Somebody moving through darkness, I think."

The angle changed, and Hutch gasped. It was his house in Colorado. The camera was outside. It was approaching the three windows that bent around one corner of the dining nook, next to the kitchen. The windows glowed brightly. Each time the camera swept away to capture darkness—Hutch knew it was an angle into the backyard—and returned, the windows flared with blurry whiteness for half a second. Then the camera would adjust, and the image would become as clear as a Spielberg movie.

The camera approached a window, revealing the interior of Hutch's house. The dining table was clear except for a water glass and a dried-flower centerpiece his mother had given him as a housewarming gift. Movement in the background, over the countertop that separated the eating area from the kitchen.

His heart quaked in his chest. Laura was moving around, transferring dishes from counter to sink, wiping a cloth over the surfaces. Hutch touched the screen. Little rings of discoloration radiated out from each fingertip. He moved his hand away, using it to cover his mouth.

"Do you know her?" Jim said. "What is this?"

All Hutch could do was stare.

The camera turned away and caught a figure darting across the yard. The person could have been of either gender, but something—the broadness of the shoulders, the muscular impression of its body and limbs—seemed masculine to Hutch. The man was dressed in black. A utility belt bounced against his waist. He had a low-profile pack strapped to his back. He wore a helmet—similar to a motorcyclist's, the kind with a dark shield that completely masked the face. It was smooth and sleek, more like a mask than a helmet. Close to his chest, the man held a rifle or machine gun.

As alien as his physical appearance was, his movements were more so. Crouching low, he darted to the edge of the back porch in short bursts of speed. His head snapped this way and that, seeming almost robotic, too quick. The man bolted around the corner column, which supported the porch roof, and disappeared. If he continued in that direction, he would pass the living room and reach the patio door into the master bedroom.

The image came back around to the window. Laura walked to the table, picked up the glass, and returned to the kitchen.

"You know what this is?" Jim said.

"My house," Hutch whispered.

TWENTY-ONE

"When was this recorded?"

"I don't know. I—"

The image on the screen angled away from the kitchen to one of the other dining area walls. It zoomed in to a clock: 8:11.

Hutch wanted to scream, but he could barely breathe. He checked his watch, knowing what he would find: one hour behind the time on the screen. When his plane had touched down in Seattle that morning, he had adjusted his watch to Pacific time.

"It's live," he said.

"How can that be?" Jim said. Then: "They can hear us."

The device in Hutch's hand crackled with static. A voice came through. "Indeed, I can."

Hutch almost dropped it. He said, "Page? What the hell are you doing?"

"Just demonstrating my reach. Mr. O'Dey, I see you've joined us. A lesson for you as well."

The image on the screen had returned to the eating area and kitchen, as viewed through the window. Laura opened a cupboard, then another, looking for something. Somebody ran into view from the living room— Logan. The boy scanned the area, then quickly moved past the kitchen and the table. He disappeared off the right edge of the monitor. The camera panned in that direction. It moved over the stuccoed side of the house and stopped on another lighted window. It moved in, showing Hutch's utility room. Logan was squatting on the far side of the dryer, peering over the top toward the room's entrance.

"Does he see something?" Jim said. "What's he doing?"

"See his smile?" Hutch said. "They're playing . . . hide-and-seek by the looks of it."

I knew you'd warm up to Dillon.

He could not believe what he was thinking. Armed men had surrounded his house, the people he loved, and here he was giving his son a thumbs-up for getting along. But he realized at once what was going on; he'd written about it. He was so shocked by the events, his mind had hiccupped. Psychologists disagreed about whether it was a form of denial, one a healthy person quickly overcame, or simply a stunned pause before the brain caught up with reality—like the seconds between conking your head and realizing you just conked your head.

He shook the screen. "Page! Get away from my family. Call your men off now, you hear?"

Jim tapped Hutch's hip. Hutch looked down to see him holding an open cell phone.

Call them. Of course.

He reached for the phone.

Jim pulled it away and shook his head. He mouthed a word: *video.*

Hutch glanced again and saw the bedspread showing on the phone's screen. It was already recording. Jim turned the phone-as-camera in his hand and slowly brought it up, trying to capture the monitor.

Evidence, Hutch thought. But not as important as alerting Laura to the danger. He had to call, tell her to get everyone out of the house, just get away. He reached for his mobile phone in the pocket of his jacket, then remembered he had given it to Julian.

The monitor went black. Hutch gave it a shake.

"What did you do?" Jim said.

"Nothing," Hutch said.

The monitor flicked on again—still peering through the utility room window at Logan.

Page's voice said, "In a few minutes, I'm going to ask you to put the monitor back in the bag and set it outside. I'll need that cell phone as well, Jim. You'll note the monitor you're holding is receiving a live feed. It contains no hard drive, no evidence."

The person watching Logan shifted. The image jarred slightly. Hutch thought he'd hit the window with the camera. Logan's response confirmed it. The boy snapped his gaze toward the window. He squinted, as if seeing something, but not sure what. He rose and stepped toward the window.

The cameraman slowly moved down, making the window appear to rise off the screen. The monitor was dark, then the man turned the camera toward the dining room windows. Back to darkness, the man obviously stood once more, filling the screen with the utility room. Logan was gone.

The camera returned to the other window. Laura was still in the kitchen. Dillon came in from the living room, looking around. He said something to his mother. She shook her head no.

Hutch snatched Jim's phone out of his hand. He watched Dillon open the pantry door and step in. A moment later, he came out. Hutch flipped the phone shut, killing the video. He opened it and dialed his son's number.

"That's unnecessary," Page said. "They are in no danger—for now. I merely wanted to show you how quickly your life could change. I told you earlier I recognized obsession in you. Irrational determination does not go away simply because somebody suggests that it should. It has to be satisfied or completely defeated. Tell me, Hutch, is this enough to defeat yours?"

Hutch held the phone to his ear. It started to ring. On the monitor, Laura perked up, hearing the phone. She walked around the counter to her purse, hanging on a dining room chair.

"Mr. E, respond, please," Page said.

It took Hutch a moment to realize Page was addressing one of the soldiers. If that person responded, Hutch was not privy to that side of the conversation.

Page said, "Can we get some sound from your end?"

An icon of a speaker appeared in a corner of the monitor. "We're on," a different voice said. The sound of breathing also came through.

Through the window, Laura pulled back the chair. The muffled screech of its legs on the hardwood floor emanated from the monitor's speakers. She set her purse on the table and sat to rummage through it.

In Hutch's ear, the far-off phone rang. A second later he heard the jangling melody that Logan had set for his father's incoming calls. The glass quieted, but did not silence, the sound. Laura extracted the phone, opened it, and lifted it to her face.

"Hello?" Her voice echoed out of the monitor's speaker as well.

"Laura," Hutch said. "Listen to me. You have to—"

He heard a short tone. Simultaneously, an icon appeared on the screen: a blue radio tower with a red circle and diagonal line super-imposed over it.

"Hello?" he said. "Laura!"

On the monitor, Laura said, "Hello? Hutch? Hello?" She gazed at the phone, her eyebrows crinkled. She held it up again: "Hello?"

"Page, what have you done?" Hutch said. "Stop this. Stop it now."

"I will, if you will." Page's voice was loud over the cameraman's breathing and Laura's continued inquiries into the phone.

Hutch ground his molars together. He had expected more threats from Page. And he had imagined himself telling the billionaire to go to hell. He had thought, maybe, just maybe, Page would imply violence toward Hutch's family. But he had believed the threats would escalate to that, not *start* there. And he never imagined more than a verbal threat. He never imagined *this*.

"How do I know if I—" Hutch began, then stopped.

Logan's clear voice came through the speaker: "Hey! What are you doing?"

The camera swung around, and Logan's face filled the screen. He scowled into it. His eyes were wide with fear, but his brazen Logan-ness kept his mouth in gear. "This is private property. You're a Peeping Tom. I'm going to call the cops."

Hutch stood up. "Logan! Page, that's my son. Don't you—"

The camera moved in on him. A gloved hand came into view, grab-bing at Logan's head, seizing a handful of hair. Logan tried to duck and pull away, but he only thrashed futilely.

Page said, "Stand down." Rustling, bumping noises. Page again: "Ian, go off-line!"

Logan screamed.

"Page!" Hutch said.

A burst of snow filled the screen, then it went black.

The phone fell out of Laura's hand.

"Hey! What was *that*?" she yelled. "Guys?"

Parents quickly learn the difference between screams that mean *You found me* or *You're driving me crazy* and screams of pain or fear. What she had heard was not the playful kind.

"Guys! Dillon! Logan! Macie! Come here, now!"

Footsteps pounded toward her. She didn't wait to see who they belonged to. She moved toward the utility room and garage—the direction from which the scream had come . . . she thought. Something banged against the window on the other side of the table. She ran to it and looked out. A shadowy figure—a man—was hurrying away. She saw blue jeans, kicking legs, tennis shoes. The man was carrying away a child. She pounded on the glass with her palm.

"Hey! Hey! Stop!"

Behind her, footsteps approached and stopped.

"What is it? What's wrong?" Dillon said.

Outside, the figure rounded a corner. The sneakered feet went up and down, up and down, then were gone.

Ian was leaning over the control console, scanning the monitors. His hand hovered above the communication button.

Page leaned closer and pushed Ian back into his chair. He shook his head and reached for the comm button.

Ian grabbed his wrist. "What are you going to do?" Ian said, his eyes wide.

"I'm going to finish it," Page said, his voice as brittle as bones.

"That's not the plan. We don't have to—"

"You don't know Hutch," Page said. "We just crossed a line. This is never going to end unless we end it here, now."

The men stared into each other's eyes. Page wondered if Ian could read more than the message he wanted to convey—that he was right, that this was the only way to handle a man like Hutch—and saw a deeper motivation—simply, that Page *wanted* this: the most definitive solution. He wanted the blood. Ian's facial muscles relaxed. He sighed and released his grip.

Page whispered, "Our necks are too stiff to spend the day looking over our shoulder." He punched the button that opened a channel to his soldiers. The order came out loud and sharp, a verbal gunshot. "Take 'em out," he said. "Kill them all."

TWENTY-TWO

"Page!" Hutch yelled at the monitor. "Page!"

"What happened?" Jim said.

"My son. They took my son!" Hutch shook the monitor. He wanted to hurl it into a wall, but what if it came back online? He stood it up, on top of the room's television.

"What happened to the monitor?" Jim said.

"Shut up," Hutch said, trying to think. "Please." On the mobile phone, he pushed the redial button. He waited for a ring . . . and waited. He let out a frustrated yell. He disconnected and dialed his own telephone number at home. Same thing: dead air. He disconnected again and punched in 9-1-1.

It's okay. It's okay. Page said they weren't in danger. He just wants to scare me. That's all.

What had happened, however, did not appear planned. Logan had startled one of Page's men, and the man had reacted. Page's last few words had sounded surprised, as unsure of the situation as Hutch was. So what was happening now? What were his men doing at his house? Running? Killing? No, no, no, not that!

He took a deep breath, then another. He opened his eyes. The monitor stared at him with its dead black screen. He jerked the phone away from his face. He'd forgotten to hit the send button. He punched it now.

"9-1-1 operator. What's your—". Then that low tone he'd heard earlier.

"Hello?" Hutch said. He looked at the phone, it read: CALL LOST. The no-service indicator appeared.

"No!" He threw the phone at the door. It snapped in two and shot in different directions.

"Hey!" Jim said.

Hutch pushed past him and picked up the phone on the nightstand. No dial tone. He punched the 0. Nothing. The disconnect button, then 9. Nothing. He dropped the handset. It banged against the table and toppled off.

Jim said, "I saw a pay phone outside the office." He rushed to the door and opened it.

If they were jamming Jim's phone the way they had Laura's, they must be close. He remembered the man he had seen in the woods.

"Wait!" he yelled.

Jim paused on his way out, giving Hutch enough time to reach him. He grabbed the man's collar and yanked him back in. As they fell, three holes appeared in the opening door. *Thunk-thunk-thunk.*

Hutch scrambled to his knees and reached for the door. Two men were coming through the parking lot. They were dressed in black with the same black helmets he had seen on the monitor. One of them stopped. He snapped his weapon up to his shoulder, taking aim.

Hutch slammed the door. Three more holes appeared in it, spraying splinters and sawdust into the room.

TWENTY-THREE

"Where's Logan? Where's Macie?" Laura yelled at Dillon.

"We were playing," Dillon said.

She knew her panicked behavior was scaring him. *Good.*

"Logan!" she called again. "Macie!"

Without a sound, Macie appeared in the living room entranceway.

"What?" the little girl said.

"Where's your brother? Where's Logan?"

Macie's mouth dropped open, but nothing came out.

"Come here, come here." Laura beckoned them to her. She turned to peer out the window at the place where she had last seen the kicking child. It had been Logan, she knew now. Someone had taken Logan.

Something crashed in the garage. Macie screamed. They were no more than ten feet from the utility room door, and it was through that room that you accessed the garage from the house.

"Lock the door," Dillon said.

"What if it's Logan?" Macie said.

Laura had an image of the boy stumbling through the garage, bleeding, scared out of his mind.

Dillon raced past them. Laura grabbed him, but he pulled away.

"Dillon!" Laura was afraid he was going to open the garage door to see who was there—and equally afraid that he *wouldn't*, and would lock Logan out of the house. "Stay here," she told Macie and ran for her son.

She reached him as he was bolting the interior garage door. He'd had no time to look into the garage. She pulled back on his shoulders, turned him, and shoved him out of the utility room. She looked at the locked door, bit her lip, trying to decide what to—

Bullets ripped through the door. She fell back onto the floor. The deadbolt rattled, but did not fall away. Someone kicked at the door. It held.

She scampered on all fours into the eating area, grabbed the corner of the table, and stood. She held her finger to her lips and told the kids, "Shhh."

Behind her, the door splintered and bullets slammed into the wall on the opposite side of the utility room. Metal clanged against the tile floor—the dead bolt. She pointed into the living room. "Go," she whispered. "Go."

Dillon didn't hesitate. He turned, grabbed Macie by the arm, and ran—through the living room and into the entry hall, where he stopped. Right, into the office; left, down a hall to the bedrooms; or straight, through the front door? Laura watched him hesitate.

"Straight!" she said. "We gotta get out of here."

Dillon started for the door. Macie screamed. A man stood on the other side of one of the glass windows that flanked the door. He put his booted foot through the glass, then elbowed it. Next, his helmeted head came through.

"This way! This way!" Laura said, pointing toward the bedrooms.

Dillon ran, tugging on Macie's arm. The little girl's feet slipped out from under her. Dillon stopped to help.

Lifting Macie, Laura said, "Keep going, Dillon! Go!"

The man at the front door had come through the window. Glass fell from his helmet and shoulders to the floor tiles. He was steps away from them.

Macie got her feet under her, and Laura pushed on the girl's back, urging her to hurry. A hand clasped Laura's shoulder. She ducked down, slipped away. The hand grabbed her hair. Another hand, her arm.

"Run, Macie!" she said.

The hallway was long. Dillon had already disappeared into one of the bedrooms.

Laura kicked back at her attacker. Her heel struck something hard and inflexible. She realized the man was wearing shin guards. He probably had some kind of body armor protecting all the vulnerable points at which Tom had taught her to strike. She swung her elbow up and back, going for his head. She knew he wore a helmet, but thought a blow in just the right place would be jarring just the same. All she needed was for him to release his grasp for a few seconds. If she could face him, she would know where to land her kicks and punches.

Just slow him down, she thought. Give Dillon a chance to get out with Macie. If her attacker made a mistake, gave her the slightest chance to put him down, then maybe she, too, could get out of the house alive.

Her hope faded when the man released her hair and encircled her neck with his arm. She felt her windpipe crushing under his muscles.

He released her arm, allowing her to grip his forearm at the front of her neck. As she had expected, it was sheathed in a hard case. She couldn't get a grip on it, let alone pry it away. His left arm came up and then back to his right hand. He used his left arm to leverage his right against her neck.

In his left fist he held a large knife. She could see her own eyes, wide and wet, reflected in the blade.

Her lungs screamed for air. They pulled and pulled in vain, like a bellows whose nozzle had been crimped shut. She reached over her shoulder, hoping to find her attacker's hair or ear. Her sweaty fingers slipped over the plastic helmet. She could find nothing to grip, and she realized it didn't matter anyway. Her strength was coming out of her muscles. Her vision dimmed. She no longer cared about drawing a breath. She wanted only to *let go*, to take the plunge and feel the relief from pain and fear.

She heard a voice calling. It was a beautiful sound.

Panic found her again as she realized it was Dillon.

"Mom!" he yelled.

"No, Dillon, run," she tried to say, but nothing came out.

Don't be here for this, she thought. *Not for this or what they'll do afterward, what they'll do to you.*

More than the pain in her lungs, more than her own fading away, the most horrifying thing was knowing he was still there, still screaming.

"Mom!"

TWENTY-FOUR

"Who's that?" Jim said. "Outside?"

"You have to ask?" Hutch said, tugging on the man's arm. "Let's go. Come on. There's a window in the bathroom."

Jim got up, stumbled forward as Hutch pushed him. "Wait, wait," he said. "Somebody's bound to call the cops. If we can just hold out . . ."

"Are you kidding?" Hutch pushed him a step closer to the bathroom. "Those guys will be in here in seconds. Besides, our room phone is out, which means they probably cut all the lines to the motel. They're using some sort of jamming device on the cell phones. Help's not coming."

"But why?" Jim said. "Page said no one was going to get hurt. He wanted to scare us. What was that, just a ruse?"

"I don't think so. Something went wrong. My son walked up to one of Page's men, and the guy . . . I don't know, freaked out or something.

I think everything Page had in mind went out the window. Now he's trying to clean it all up."

Hutch remembered Andrew Norton's words to Declan: *No witnesses.* He had been Page's best friend, as close as a brother, according to Julian.

Hutch had always suspected that the evil he had witnessed in Canada was encouraged and funded by Brendan Page. Maybe Page had truly intended to scare Hutch away. But as soon as there was a glitch, Page's knee-jerk reaction was to kill. It was the way he lived and the way he thought.

The window beside the door shattered, and kept shattering as bullets tore into the remaining glass and the falling shards. Hutch looked back to see the curtains billowing out, ripping to shreds.

Jim dropped to his hands and knees and crawled the rest of the way to the bathroom. Hutch stepped over him and was reaching for the bathroom window when a shadow fell across it. He clamped his hand over Jim's mouth just as the pebbled privacy glass shattered inward. Jim's startled scream was no louder than a hiccup and lost among the cacophony of falling glass.

Hutch put his lips on Jim's ear and hushed him. He whispered, "Lie down in the tub. Quietly."

The man outside continued striking at the window, giving Hutch the chance to crunch over broken pieces on the floor and position himself almost under the window, next to the toilet.

A pistol entered first. The hand holding it bent at the wrist until the gun pointed toward the shower. It fired. Tile exploded. The pistol shot the floor at Hutch's feet. Flying tile stung his face. Another round downward, puncturing and cracking the toilet seat. Two more shots: one straight into the wall opposite the window, the other into the countertop beside the sink. The arm and pistol disappeared. Five rounds. The weapon was clearly a semiautomatic, which meant it held between seven and fourteen—something like that, if Hutch remembered correctly; he'd never been much of a gun person. Regardless, the man had more than enough bullets left to finish the job.

A silhouette appeared in the window opening. The pistol slid through, followed by the sleek crown of a helmet.

Hutch lifted the lid off the toilet tank and swung it into the helmet. Something cracked. The pistol clattered to the counter, then to the floor. When he brought the lid back for another strike, the opening was empty. He popped his head over the sill, lowered it. A shadow darker than its surroundings and approximating the shape of a man extended out from the building on the ground. Hutch pushed the lid through the window and heaved it toward the shadow. It landed on what was most likely the man's crotch and stomach. The shadow didn't move.

"Okay," Hutch whispered to Jim. "Let's go before those guys out front storm in." He found the pistol and pushed it into his waistband. In the main room, light and shadow played over the window and under the front door. He closed the bathroom door and locked it. *That'll hold them for an extra nanosecond*, he thought.

Jim hoisted himself onto the sill. He got his foot on the tank and tumbled out.

Hutch followed. He crawled to the downed man. A jagged fissure almost split the helmet in half, vertically. Even the face mask was busted. Hutch gripped his neck. He found the carotid artery, but felt no pulse. He must have hit him harder than he thought. Okay, he had put all of his strength into clobbering the guy, but he'd had no intention of *killing* him.

Sure, keep telling yourself that, he thought.

He patted the body down. The soldier was wearing body armor, probably the Kevlar Interceptor. Last year, Hutch had written a column about a teenager who'd held a fund-raiser to buy Interceptors for her brother's unit in Iraq. A utility belt was mostly empty, but he did find two extra magazines for the pistol. By their heft, he guessed they were fully loaded. Hutch had worn one several years ago while doing research for a story about the Denver SWAT team.

From the bedroom came the *thunk-thunk-thunk* of three-round bursts striking one wall or another. Glass shattered and a *pop!*—the TV tube. That reminded him of the monitor. He should have taken it. A loud crash, then another one, less jarring: had to be the front door being kicked open, slamming against the wall.

He pulled Jim close. "Go straight out into the woods. Make some noise, but don't get shot. If you can, keep going. Get to a store or something. Don't trust vehicles on the road, unless it's a marked cruiser."

"Uh . . ." Jim squinted at the trees. "Shouldn't we stay close to the building, walk to the end?"

"No, I need you to draw their fire. Go into the woods."

"Draw their fire? Are you crazy?"

"You have to go, now!"

"You're not coming?"

"No! Go, man!" Hutch grabbed Jim's arm. "No matter what happens, you get your son out of that place! Go!" He pushed him away.

Jim stumbled. He rose, tottered forward, looked back.

"Go!" Hutch said.

Thunk-thunk-thunk. Glass shattered in the bathroom. Hutch thought they had shot through the door and struck the mirror.

Jim glared at the window. His jaw dropped opened. He lurched toward the woods, then plowed into the underbrush.

Hutch edged back to the wall and positioned himself directly under the bathroom window. He crouched down. He pulled the pistol out of his waistband and pointed it straight up at the window.

Inside, the bathroom door slammed open.

TWENTY-FIVE

Laura willed herself not to pass out, and she was surprised to feel a slight energy surge. It was similar to waking yourself up before drifting off. Power of the will. She understood that her renewed consciousness would be short-lived. The man behind her was crushing her windpipe. Her lungs and, consequently, brain had already trudged on far too long without oxygen.

She jerked around to see Dillon. She had to tell him to leave—she didn't want him to see her die, but more, she needed to know that he was running, getting away from these men.

There he was, at the end of the hallway. His eyes were wide, his cheeks wet with tears.

"Mooooom!" he wailed. "Move!"

She saw it: Hutch's bow in his hand, arrowed nocked and ready to fly. She could not tell if he had pulled back yet, but she doubted it. Hutch had taught him about recurve bows. Their draw weight—the power needed to pull back on the bow—was way too heavy to hold at full draw for more than a few seconds.

She did her best to nod at the boy: *Shoot. Don't worry about me. Shoot.* He returned the gesture. His eyes narrowed.

Laura raised her foot, planted it against the hallway wall, and shoved. She turned, and her face hit a picture frame on the opposite wall. Glass under her cheek broke.

But the man—trying to remain perfectly behind her, where he had the best leverage on her neck and the most protection from her flailing—had turned with her. His side was directly exposed to Dillon's arrow.

Laura saw her son's facial muscles tighten. He rocked back, his arms moved, and the arrow sailed.

The man holding her howled in pain. He released her, and she slumped to the floor. She pulled for a breath, but it didn't come. The man had pinched her throat too tightly for too long. She was going to strangle now without the pressure of his arm.

Please, Lord, not in front of my son. Please.

She pressed her forehead into the wall and closed her eyes. She touched her fingers to her neck, feeling a shooting pain, then an aching throb. Closing her eyes against the agony, she squeezed her neck. She hoped to move *something* in there, which would let air pass. She didn't know anything about anatomy at that level, but she thought if it was pinched she had a chance; if it was swollen . . . well, she would miss those blood-red Canadian dawns, and, oh, she would miss everything about Dillon.

"Mom!"

Yeah, that: his sweet voice, the way he didn't just talk *at* her, but *to* her. She felt his hand on her cheek. She'd miss that too, his touch.

"Mom!"

She felt his hands on both sides of her head. He forced her to turn away from the wall. Hot wires shot from her neck into her skull, shoulders, down her spine. She cried out. It was hoarse and gravelly, and she realized she could breathe. She gulped in air. Her lungs ached, as if protesting their having to get back to work. She could almost feel oxygen moving through her body again.

Her eyes opened to Dillon's face. Inches from her own. She had to smile, despite it all.

"Dillon," she rasped. The word came out with broken glass—that's how it felt to her throat.

He tugged on her. "We have to go! Come on!"

She pushed herself onto her knees. *Just let me get a breath here*, she thought, *just a breath*. But Dillon was pulling, demanding she get moving. He tucked himself under her arm to help her walk.

Reaching across his back, she found the bow and a quiver of arrows.

"Way to go, Dillon," she said. Her voice was quiet and not her own. She wasn't sure he'd heard. She gave him a squeeze, trying to put everything she thought about him into it.

She heard a moan and gurgling. She looked back to see the soldier on the floor. An arrow protruded from his neck, just below the lip of his helmet. Blood was everywhere: soaking his uniform, splattered on the walls, forming a growing pool under him. His helmet turned one way and then the other, slowly. He raised his hand a few inches, then it flopped down on his chest.

She moved her hand to block Dillon's view. "No," she said.

"I was— I didn't—" He sounded on the brink of sobs.

"That's okay, honey. You did what you had to do." She disengaged herself from him, and said, "Get Macie. Go into Hutch's room."

"But—"

"I'll be right there."

Footsteps came from the kitchen. "Go," she whispered.

She knelt beside the arrowed soldier. His knife lay next to his head, half in the pool of blood. She didn't want that. His rifle or machine gun or whatever it was had shifted on its strap and was now pinned under an arm. The arrow, pointing almost directly at the ceiling, wavered slightly, like a fading metronome. Moved by his breathing or his pulse, either way it didn't look good for him.

She reached across his body and unclipped the strap from an eyelet in the butt of the gun. Leaning farther, her knee came down on his chest. Air and blood bubbled out of the hole in his neck. She unclipped the strap below the barrel and yanked the gun from under his arm.

She looked up. A soldier was standing in the arch between the living room and entry hall, aiming his weapon at her.

Maybe it was gonna happen tonight one way or another, she thought. Her time.

She fumbled with the rifle. There was no way she could get it into position before he fired. But she did. She pushed the stock into her shoulder and raised the barrel. The soldier continued to aim at her. Why didn't he shoot? She realized her knee was still planted on the chest of the fallen soldier. She wondered if the image had shocked the man into not firing. No, it had to be something else. What she knew about soldiers told her that the sight of his fallen comrade should have driven him into a killing frenzy, not passivity.

She thought about yelling something—*Back off!* or *Drop it!*—but was afraid to speak, to move. She was afraid any movement would nudge the man back into soldier mode, and he would fire. She couldn't just stay like that, however; other soldiers could show up. Even now they could be breaking into the room where Dillon and Macie waited for her. The thought fueled her action.

She stood and took a step back. The blood under her Timberlands had already grown tacky. They made a sickening noise as they pulled away. She backed away, keeping her aim on the soldier.

One of his hands came off his rifle. He held his palm up to her. *Stop.* When she didn't, a staticky *pop* emanated from his helmet, then: "Wait."

She moved faster, glancing back. She was at the master bedroom door when the soldier rushed forward. She sidestepped into the room.

The soldier's tinny electronic voice reached her ahead of the slamming door: "Wait!"

"Bring me that chair," she told Dillon, pointing. He helped her wedge it under the door handle.

"Where's Logan?" Macie cried.

Laura said, "We'll find him, honey. Don't worry."

The little girl didn't buy that for a second, and Laura's stomach flopped over on itself. She didn't buy it either.

The door handle clattered. A solid bang rattled the door.

Dillon reached over his shoulder for an arrow.

Laura grabbed his arm. She said, "No. Dillon, you need to get Macie out of here. Go through the patio door and straight across the backyard. Get help, now."

The door cracked under the force of the soldier on the other side.

Dillon grabbed the arrow. Laura seized his chin.

"Dillon, I said no. I've got this." She lifted the gun.

Dillon nodded. He snatched the soft bow bag off the bed and ran to Macie. He grabbed her wrist and pulled her toward the French door.

The girl resisted. "I want Logan," she said. "I'm not leaving without Logan."

"Come on!" Dillon said.

Laura positioned herself between the bed and the barricaded door.

She brought the rifle up and braced herself. The door quaked. The chair rattled and inched down away from the handle.

"Macie, go!" Laura screamed. "Dillon will drag you out if he has to."

Macie started screaming, and Laura didn't have to look to know her son had taken her suggestion.

The door opened a few inches—as far as the chair would allow it, before catching again under the handle. The soldier's helmet pushed through.

Laura pulled the trigger and nothing happened. Safety, she thought. The man Dillon had arrowed had seemed intent on killing her with his hands. He had broken through the window beside the door and run for her. As far as she knew, he'd never fired the weapon, never taken the safety off.

Panicked, she looked around the trigger for the safety release. Didn't see it. She checked the other side. Not there.

The man rammed his shoulder into the door. The chair cracked. The door opened another few inches. On either side of the helmet, gloved hands slipped around the door edge and jamb. The black curve of the face mask was pointed directly at her. She ran to the door, slammed her back into it. While she pushed, she scanned the length of the weapon for any kind of push button or switch that would let her fire.

The soldier backed off, then rammed the door again. The back of the chair cracked and folded forward. Laura stumbled away from the opening door. She gripped the barrel of the rifle and spun around. The soldier was stepping through. The rifle stock hit the faceplate, and it shattered. The man stumbled, fell to his hands and knees. She lifted the rifle away, then brought it down on the back of the helmet.

The soldier crumpled to the floor. He rolled over. Most of the helmet had broken away. The scared eyes of a young man, no older than seventeen or eighteen, stared up at her. Blood flowed from a cut on the bridge of his nose.

"Shoot me," he said. "Please."

Just a baby. It would not be very many years before Dillon would be this age. She shook her head.

His mouth moved without forming words. He squeezed his eyes closed. Tears ran from them, washing the blood from his face in stark streaks.

A loud noise outside of the bedroom, down the hall, made her jump. It had been a thunderous bang, most likely the front door being kicked in. She had snapped her eyes up with the sound, when she brought them back, he was reaching for her gun.

"If you won't kill me," he said in a harsh whisper, "then take me with you. I can help."

Another crash from the entry hall. Footsteps.

Laura bit her lip. She said, "Yeah, right." She raised the rifle and brought the stock down on his forehead.

TWENTY-SIX

Hutch waited. Someone moved around inside the bathroom. Fingers came into view as the person leaned toward the window, but Hutch could not yet see a face mask or helmet.

As if on cue, Jim broke away from wherever he had hunkered down. Branches cracked under his feet; leaves rustled in his wake.

The man in the bathroom pushed a rifle through the window. A helmet appeared.

Hutch leaped for the rifle barrel. His feet slipped on the loose ground cover. Instead of grabbing hold of the barrel, he merely slapped it aside. At least the burst of bullets fired well away from Jim. Hutch tumbled to the ground. The barrel swung down. He kicked away from the wall and landed on his back, beside the man he had killed with the toilet lid. He aimed the pistol at the bathroom window and fired over and over. Bullets slammed into the exterior wall and window frame, but not even one found the sweet spot—the window opening. His finger kept pumping at the trigger, even after the slide locked open, indicating the pistol was empty.

Hutch reached for the extra magazines he'd put in his back pocket. Before his hand was anywhere near the ammo, the man inside returned to the window. As the rifle came out, Hutch twisted up onto the corpse's arm. He reached across, grabbed the far shoulder, and fell back, pulling the man onto him.

The machine gun clattered mechanically, its reports muffled by a sound suppressor. Hutch felt the bullets strike the body over him. It was a series of hammer blows, jolting him but causing no harm. He remembered that the Interceptor body armor was not the strongest of ballistic vests; it was rated to stop only 9 mm rounds. However, since it covered the front and back of the wearer, he figured he was doubly protected. And that wasn't counting the stopping power of the man's body itself.

He gripped the body armor at the armholes and tugged the corpse up, protecting his head. The man's chest pressed heavily on Hutch's cheek. A thought splashed into his consciousness: his shield was a human being. He probably had parents, maybe a family, who loved him.

No, Hutch thought, *the guy was a murderer. Nothing more.* That was easier to accept.

The hammer blows continued, pounding up and down the body. A few struck the dirt near Hutch's head. The shooter's best bet for wounding him would be to blast away at his feet. Hutch didn't think the man wanted to come out of the window as far as that maneuver required. After all, the soldier knew Hutch was not alone. He would not want to expose himself.

That reminded Hutch that the shooter was also not alone. Squinting along the firebreak toward the end of the building, he didn't see the man's partner running toward him or taking aim. He turned his head and found that direction clear as well. The soldier in the window continued to fire: a three-round burst followed by a pause, then another burst. Did the guy think a round would somehow find him, that it would miraculously come through the corpse or around it? Or was he trying to keep Hutch pinned down while his partner came around? The second man, however, would come slowly, not knowing Jim's location. Then again, the shooter could simply be trying to prevent Hutch from reloading.

So why wasn't Hutch reloading? Because he'd need both hands, and right now one of them had a firm grip on the collar of the body armor, keeping it from shifting. If the corpse rolled off of him, he would be just as dead. Still, he could not lie there waiting for—

Something other than bullets struck the body on top of him. It rolled off and landed in the dirt in front of Hutch's face.

You gotta be kidding, he thought. He grabbed it and tossed it into the woods with one swift motion.

The grenade exploded.

The shock of it should have kept him in place for at least a few seconds, but he knew the soldier would have taken cover, if only for those same few seconds. While dirt, trees, and shrapnel were still striking the building and raining down, Hutch shoved the corpse away and got his feet under him. He leaped toward the motel and pressed himself against the bricks. Crouching low, he began edging away from the bathroom window. He was torn between keeping an eye on the window and watching for things underfoot that could give him away—an empty potato chip bag, a twig.

His ears were ringing. He hoped the grenade had somehow hindered the soldier's hearing as well. Probably not, considering the helmet.

Regardless, he had to do what he had to do. He paused to eject the empty magazine, retrieve a full one from his pocket, and push it into the handle of the pistol. He flipped a thumb switch and moved the slide back into place, automatically chambering a round.

The machine gun clattered against the windowsill, sliding out. It pointed at the body, then moved up and down, left and right, but never close enough to the building to threaten Hutch. The soldier's next logical move would be to lean out and inspect the area closest to the building.

Keeping the pistol pointed at the window, Hutch slid silently along the wall away from it.

He reached his destination: one of the downspouts. It looked heavier duty than the ones on his house. He pushed the fingers of his free hand under it and flexed. The pipe didn't budge.

Decision time. Wait for the helmet to appear, put a couple holes into it—he was feeling optimistic at the moment—or start climbing.

A sound drew his attention toward the far corner of the building, the way he had gone when he'd sneaked up on Jim. Darkness that way. Shadows. Trees. A shadow shifted, moved. Man-shaped. It was the other soldier.

He had stepped out from around the bend in the building and was walking toward the edge of the woods. Smart: the greatest threat of attack was from the woods. The face of the helmet rotated toward Hutch. The man barely gave the area a glance. He must have been confident his partner had it covered.

Knowing something about Page's passion for technology, Hutch suspected the helmets these soldiers wore were decked out in the latest battle gear: communications, night vision, infrared, maybe targeting matrices. If the man had focused his attention on the firebreak—which was essentially a straight alley along the back of the motel—he would have spotted Hutch in a heartbeat.

Something in the woods had the soldier down there excited. He ran to the edge, fired a few rounds. Hutch hoped it was an animal that had drawn his attention and not Jim.

Fifteen feet away, a helmet protruded from the bathroom window—way out, as though the guy was about to climb through. Hutch's heart ricocheted off his sternum and lodged in his throat. The man pulled his machine gun through. He held his position, leaning out, and aimed into the woods toward his partner. He was covering his teammate, who had obviously communicated his sighting of something among the trees.

The soldier in the window pulled his trigger. Hutch could hear, but not see, the rounds cut through leaves and branches. The soldier shifted his aim to the woods on the other side of his partner. He sent a few rounds into that area as well.

Hutch guessed the soldier was completely engrossed in protecting his teammate, especially given that they'd already lost a man. His ears would be attuned to communication coming from the fighter on the front lines, or too desensitized by the constant firing to detect subtle noises.

Hutch pushed the pistol into his waistband, slipped in front of the downspout, and started climbing.

TWENTY-SEVEN

The soldier's eyelids fluttered. He tried to lift his head, but it fell back to the floor, and he was still.

Laura watched him, tapped him with her toe. When she was sure he was unconscious, she started for the children. They'd stopped at the door to watch. "Let's go," she said.

Dillon released Macie's arm. He took several tentative steps toward his mother, meeting her in the center of the bedroom. The whole time, he held his eyes on the soldier.

Laura brushed past him, sweeping her fingers through his hair. "Come on, honey. There're other people in the house."

He gripped her arm, spinning her toward him. His expression was ancient: fear and concern. "We can't leave him," he said.

"The soldier? Yes, we can." She reached for him.

He backed away from her. "No!"

"Dillon, listen," she said. She was not sure if she should keep her patience with him or be crazy-impatient to get all of them out the door ahead of the other soldiers. "We don't have time for this. That boy—"

She immediately regretted the word, which seemed to support Dillon's argument. But he *was* so young. "That man tried to kill us. His friends are still trying to kill us. One of them took Logan."

Behind her Macie said, "Logan? They *took* him?" She started to cry.

Laura held up her hand to the girl. "It'll be okay, sweetie. Everything will work out." It seemed less of a lie than *Logan will be fine* or *We'll get him back*. She wanted both to be true.

"Mom," Dillon said, "we can't leave him. He asked us to take him."

"He also asked me to shoot him. Should I do that?" She turned toward Macie and the patio door. Conversation over.

"Mom, wait!"

"Dillon!" They had been keeping their voices low, but she was ready to lose it. "There are men out there looking for us. They want to kill us or take us. Either way, I don't like it."

Her heart caught the full impact of Dillon's puppy-dog sadness. She hated when he did that. More softly she said, "Even if we wanted to, we can't bring him. He's out cold. He's a grown man." *Sort of.* Her eyes pleaded with Dillon to understand.

"You can do it," he said. "You've hauled whole caribou miles out of the woods."

She gave her son a crooked smile. "They were gutted and quartered."

Dillon began backing up toward the soldier. "He wanted you to kill him or take him. He wasn't hurting us."

Laura pressed her lips tight and closed her eyes. She could thrash Dillon about now, but she also knew he was right. She remembered

Julian. He had been a young teen forced to go with Declan on a murderous rampage. She and Hutch had lamented his fate many times.

Now she had an opportunity to help someone like Julian. Could she walk away? Just reduce the boy's obvious anguish to sad conversations for the rest of her life?

Who was she kidding, thinking about "opportunity" and "rest of her life"? Her own survival was questionable. But between Dillon and her memories of Julian, she knew she could not leave the young soldier.

She strode past Dillon. "Get the door. And not another word."

She listened at the door to the hallway. Noises deeper in the house. She knelt beside the soldier. She unclipped his helmet's chinstrap and pushed away the pieces of helmet. Wires connected the chunks like sinew. She unbuckled his utility belt, checked its contents. Couple meal bars. A wad of twenty-dollar bills. A coil of large zip ties—lightweight, disposable handcuffs. She slipped everything into her pants pockets.

She examined his bulletproof vest. It looked heavy. She considered wearing it herself, but wasn't sure she could handle the weight on top of carrying the soldier. It would be too cumbersome for Macie. She unstrapped it and tugged it off the boy.

"Dillon," she said, "come put this on." She tossed it toward him.

She stood and looked down at the boy. At least he wasn't fat. She planted her knee by his hip and grabbed one of his wrists. She swung it around her shoulder. She slipped her arm behind one of his knees and lifted. Tom had taught her the technique. It distributed the body's weight across both shoulders and her upper back. Since the hand of the arm entwining his leg also held his wrist across her chest, it left her with a free hand. She rose, groaning quietly. She took a step. Not too bad.

Okay, she thought. *My throat feels like raw meat every time I breathe, my neck's on fire, and I have a hundred and fifty pounds of dead weight on my shoulders. No problem.*

Never mind killers were after them. Icing on the cake. She stumbled toward the door. "Macie, you okay?"

"I want Logan."

"Me too. Let's get out of here first. Then we'll figure out how to get him back. Okay?"

Macie nodded.

Laura smiled at Dillon. "Let's do it."

Dwarfed by the bulletproof vest, with arrows protruding behind his head, a bow over one shoulder, a rifle over the other, and a bow bag in his lap, Dillon more closely resembled a pack mule than a boy. Scratch that. He looked like the personification of *resolve.*

He opened the patio door.

TWENTY-EIGHT

Hutch paused under the motel's eaves. He would have to reach out to the metal gutter along the roof's edge, drop away from the wall, and pull himself up. The soldier from the bathroom was still looking the other direction, covering his partner who had stepped into the woods.

Nothing good would come from waiting, so he just did it. Hanging from the gutter, he felt exposed. With the optical aids he was sure the soldiers possessed, he would be impossible to miss if either one glanced his way. He wanted to swing his leg up, hook his heel on the gutter. He imagined the sound that would make and opted instead to pull himself straight up using only arm strength. He rose over the gutters and folded his torso onto the roof.

The roof was pitched to a center peak. The asphalt tiles were gritty with pebbles; he wouldn't slide off. He could not see the soldier protruding from the bathroom window, but he had a direct line of sight to the one coming out of the woods. That meant Hutch was equally visible to him—more so, considering the helmet's technology. But the soldier did not act alarmed. He simply continued his pursuit of whatever he had seen in the woods. He appeared to be casually strolling along the tree line, heading in Hutch's direction.

Maybe a ruse, Hutch thought. *Waiting to get closer before he shoots.*

Perhaps the soldier had already informed his teammate of Hutch's location. Since Hutch could no longer see the man in the window, he couldn't know if he was still there or sneaking around the front to box him in.

He tugged the pistol out of his waistband. Something on it caught on his pants. The gun came out of his hand. It hit the roof, clanged into the gutter, and flipped over the edge.

By the woods, the soldier's helmeted face snapped up to Hutch. The man started to swing his rifle around, but the soldier in the bathroom window must have still been there, and responded more quickly: right where the pistol had disappeared, bullets ripped through the gutter. They tore it into shreds, then began punching through the asphalt tiles. They marched up the roof toward Hutch.

He thought he was farther away from the edge than the width of the eaves, but he wasn't going to hang around to find out. He was scampering up toward the peak when bullets tore into the roof all around him. He glanced to see muzzle flashes from the soldier by the woods. As he rolled over the peak, he saw a second soldier—the man from the bathroom—backpedaling across the firebreak, trying to get a better aim.

Good, Hutch thought, *if he's there, then he's not out front. . . .* And he wasn't in the room to shoot at him through the ceiling. The two soldiers would have to either climb back through a bathroom window or race around the building. Either way bought Hutch some time.

Give me a minute . . . thirty seconds . . . twenty.

He'd take *any* amount of time right now—and he'd make the most of it. Dying here was not an option. Something was happening back home. His son was in danger. Macie. Dillon. Laura. It didn't matter that he might be in a worse situation than they were. He had to reach them. Help them. He had to *know*.

He stood and began a stuttering, controlled descent to the front edge of the roof. The shooting behind him stopped. He thought of the grenade, wondered if that was coming next.

He listened for its thump against the roof. What he heard was a car engine turning over and over, trying to start. A flash of red caught his eye—the same glowing trees that had alerted him to Mr. Mustang's presence. And there he was now, behind the wheel, his eyes big in the glow of the dome lamp because he hadn't bothered to shut the door.

Hutch knew one soldier, probably both, would be coming around that way any second. He waved both arms at Jim. The engine caught, and the car lurched forward. Its rear tires spun on gravel, then found the traction it needed to shoot across the parking lot. The driver's door slammed shut.

"Hey!" Hutch yelled, waving.

Jim didn't see him up on the roof.

He should have jumped down, but it was too late now. "Hey! Jim!"

The Mustang was angling toward the county road that ran in front of the motel. It braked hard and stopped. Jim's face appeared in the passenger window. He was leaning over to look up at Hutch.

Hutch beckoned to him, but he would not have blamed Jim for speeding off. The backup lights came on. The Mustang moved as fast in reverse as it had when it was leaving the parking lot. Hutch grabbed hold of the gutter, swung down, and dropped. He had to jump to keep from being nailed by the car's rear bumper. Jim opened the passenger door, and he jumped in.

"Go! Go!" Hutch said. "They're coming!"

Jim punched it and crossed the parking lot diagonally, building speed.

The van seemed to come out of nowhere. It pulled into the Mustang's path and stopped. A black-helmeted soldier looked out the driver's side window at them.

Jim slammed on the brakes. Hutch was able to yell only "Don't—!" before flying into the dash. He pushed himself back and said, "Don't stop! Go around! Go around!"

Jim looked dazed, wide-eyed and slack jawed.

They were thirty feet from the side of the van. The driver jumped out. He had his machine gun aimed at the windshield before Hutch's mind registered the weapon.

"Go!" he yelled again.

The windshield spiderwebbed as holes opened up in it.

The Mustang shot forward. Hutch caught a glimpse of Jim's crazy-scared face. He braced his arms against the dash. The broken windshield made the gunman appear fragmented, as though he were not one but hundreds, shooting at them.

The car slammed into the shooter and van. The impact shattered the windshield completely. Pellets of safety glass, like drops of water, cascaded over Hutch. His arms buckled, and his forehead struck the dash. He squinted one eye through the windshield opening. The soldier slumped over the crumpled hood. Steam hissed out, making the body appear to be smoldering. Hutch's other eye was gone. He wiped at it and realized it was only blood from a cut in his brow.

A raspy hiss came from Jim. He was slumped against the door, blood on his face, more on his chest. Hutch grabbed his shoulder. "Jim, we gotta go." He looked beyond the injured man to the side of the motel. The soldiers had not yet appeared. He knew they would be there any second.

ROBERT LIPARULO | 193

"Jim?"

The only response was a wheezing breath in, a gurgling breath out.

Hutch saw blood growing on the man's shirt. It wasn't pouring from his head as Hutch had first thought. He yanked Jim's shirt aside, popping buttons. A bullet had struck him midchest.

"Jim."

Hutch had to shoulder his door open. He ran around and opened Jim's, and caught the man as he fell out. The small window behind the door shattered. Apparently the soldiers had made it around to the front of the motel, but Hutch didn't have time to look.

He pulled Jim out of the car and dragged him to the front. Either the van had slid away or the Mustang had bounced back, but three feet separated the front of the Mustang from the side of the van. The collision had damaged the larger vehicle's sheet metal behind the driver's door. Hutch lifted Jim in, letting him fall between the front captain's chairs.

A bullethole appeared in the windshield, then another. One soldier was running toward them from the side of the motel. Another from Hutch's room.

Hutch slammed the transmission into drive, cranked the wheel right, and stepped on it. The van spun away from the gunmen. Its tires bumped up onto the county road. He almost careened off the other side, but got control in time to steer it back into a lane. As he accelerated past the motel sign, a rear window shattered. Bullets plunked into the back and side. They kept striking the van for a lot longer than Hutch would have imagined. Finally the barrage stopped, and the light of the sign was a firefly in his rearview mirror.

TWENTY-NINE

With the soldier draped over her shoulders like a shawl, Laura stepped off the patio and onto the backyard grass. Macie stopped in front of her.

"What about the car?" the girl said.

The weight of the soldier was already cramping Laura's shoulders and numbing her right arm. She considered turning him around to put the bulk of his weight to the other shoulder, but juggling him back and forth every couple minutes wasn't practical. She decided to tough it out a little longer.

"It's in the garage on the other side of the house," she whispered. "The other soldiers are looking for us. We can't risk getting to it."

"But where are we going?" Macie said.

"Just . . . away. And, honey, I know we have to get Logan. That's step two, and we're only on step one."

She wasn't happy about it, but Macie said, "Okay."

They were halfway to the back fence when Dillon grabbed her arm. He said, "Mom, listen!"

All she could hear was her own heavy breathing. "What is it?"

"A siren."

Then she heard it. It was getting louder. She could see the street in the space between houses. A streetlight shined on the blacktop, sidewalk, and some of the yard.

Here, she thought, willing the emergency vehicle to them. *We need you here!*

She didn't understand how they would know to come, though. The gunfire had been quieted by some kind of silencer. Maybe a neighbor had seen Logan being carried away or heard the breaking of the entryway window. For whatever reason, the sirens did seem to be approaching. She felt hope, a surge of energy. Whoever had taken Logan was probably waiting in a vehicle for the other man inside. They would all be apprehended. Logan would be freed. She started toward the side yard, toward the street.

"See, Macie? It's going to be okay."

The siren grew louder. She could hear the car's engine now. Red and blue lights flashed across the house across the street. Then the cruiser flew past her narrow vision of the street. Tires squealed.

"Come on," she said. "Dillon, Macie, come on."

The cruiser's engine revved, and the car backed into view. A police officer in the passenger seat watched them. He was speaking into a microphone. The driver leaned forward to look.

She waved, lost her balance, and staggered sideways. She laughed in relief. A shot rang out. Then another and another, fast. Machine-gun fire. The windshield started to smoke. Laura realized it was glass dust, kicked up by the bullets striking it. The windshield shattered, followed by the driver's-side glass. The policeman spasmed. Blood flew.

She backed away in horror. Hutch's daughter darted ahead, either not seeing the destruction or not understanding its significance.

"Macie!" Laura said. "Get back here. Dillon, get her."

Dillon rushed to her. He grabbed the back of her collar and tugged. Macie screamed.

Dillon cupped his hand over her mouth. He stepped around so she could see his face. He said, "Shhh."

The cop on the driver's side opened his door and disappeared from Laura's view. He rose, extended a gun, and fired at the front of the house. Bullets tore into the cruiser. The right front tire popped. The door-glass next to him shattered. A headlamp exploded. There were too many bullets without cease to be coming from only one gun or one place.

Macie nodded at Dillon, and he removed his hand from her mouth.

"Hurry," Laura said. She jerked her head toward the backyard.

Dillon led Macie past his mother. Laura followed. The boy on her shoulders seemed to have gained fifty pounds. Her knees wanted to collapse under the weight. She knew the feeling came not only from the fatigue of carrying him, but mostly from her dashed hopes and the shock of witnessing the cop's murder.

When they'd reached the backyard again, she said, "Wait, wait. Let's go get the car."

Macie looked puzzled. "But you said . . ."

Laura hefted the body on her shoulders. There was no getting comfortable with it. "The bad guys are busy out front. Let's go."

They trudged through the yard, past the rear of the house. At the living room windows, Laura paused. She leaned close to a pane. She could see through the living room to the front door, which was open.

They had moved the dead soldier from the hall to the entryway, just inside the front door. She wondered how badly the absence of the soldier she carried screwed up their SOP. She guessed that they'd have hightailed it out of there after the first cops arrived, but they couldn't leave without all their members.

The gunfire out front stopped. A few seconds later, a single shot rang out.

Dillon jumped. He found his mother's face, looking for reassurance.

"You're doing great, Dillon," she said.

They passed the kitchen and finally the eating area. It was from these windows that Laura had seen the man carry Logan away. She stopped. "Just a sec."

Dillon said, "Are you tired?"

"Yeah, I need a moment to breathe." But that wasn't it. She remembered Logan's kicking feet disappearing around the next corner. What if they had not kidnapped him, but murdered him? His body might be right there in front of the garage. She could not lead Macie and Dillon into that nightmare.

She dropped to one knee, leaned, and let the soldier slide off her shoulder. Her physical relief was immediate, but her mind ached at the possibility of Logan's death.

The soldier moaned.

The three of them watched him, but he didn't wake or even move.

Dillon squatted and pushed at the man with his fingers. He whispered to his mother, "You knocked him a good one."

"He'll live." She rubbed her shoulders. Standing, she said, "I'm going around the corner. Wait here."

Panic twisted his face. "Can we all go?"

"I want to check it out first. Make sure there are no bad guys. I can do that better alone."

He frowned.

She touched his cheek. "I'll be right back."

She hurried to the corner and pressed her back against the wall. She smiled back at Dillon and Macie. Catching the light from the eating area and utility room windows, their faces looked pale, their eyes glistened with concern. She glanced around the corner. The garage opened to the side of the house. The driveway made a ninety-degree curve toward the screen. From where she stood, a tall potted evergreen blocked most of her view of the drive.

I can do this, she thought. *I have to.*

She took in a deep breath and let it out. Did it again.

Then she slipped around the corner.

THIRTY

Anton kicked the shoulder of the cop on the ground. The guy didn't move, but Anton put two more rounds into his back anyway. He looked through the interior to the open driver's door. Another cop was sprawled on the street on that side. The police-band radio squawked in a half-dozen excited voices. He didn't need to listen to know they were coming. The sirens were howling like wolves, making their way to the kill.

Anton backed away from the car, throwing glances up and down the street. A few heads in lighted windows, someone on the porch of a house half a block away. He considered taking a quick shot at the guy, see if he could do it. The helmets helped with targeting but could do nothing about shaking hands or bad shooting technique.

He let the thought go and scoped out the house. Front door

open—Emile had fired on the cops from there—window beside it shattered, dark windows where front bedrooms probably were. No sign of Emile now.

Anton jogged to the van. The windshield was all but gone, holes pocked the body panels, but the tires appeared fine and the radiator wasn't steaming. He opened the driver's door and stopped. Something had moved in the shadows beside the garage. He lifted the barrel of his machine gun. He stepped closer. He could make out the huge rectangle of the garage door, a plant on either side. Everything else was shadow.

He squinted at the far plant. It swayed gently, as though in a breeze. But the other one was still.

He pulled the trigger.

The bullets ripped off the top of the evergreen. Twigs and needles rained down on Laura. The stucco over her head erupted, adding dust and sand to the debris on her head and shoulders. She pulled in a harsh breath but forced herself to clamp down on the scream pushing out of her lungs. She bit her lip and squeezed her eyes closed.

Here it comes, she thought. *He's going to correct his aim and blast me away.*

She hoped Dillon wouldn't hear, wouldn't come running. When he found her, she prayed the bad guys would be gone.

She pressed her back to the wall, trying to disappear right into the stucco.

Run? Stay? The words cycled in her mind like a flashing beacon.

Running meant giving the man a definite—but moving—target. Staying made her a sure hit, but only if he really knew she was there. She hoped he had been only trying to scare someone out of hiding.

When the next burst of gunfire didn't come, she leaned forward. The gunman, dressed like the others in black clothes and helmet, had turned to a van parked on the street at the bottom of the drive. He opened the door and climbed in.

Logan was not lying on the drive, as she had feared. But he could very well be *inside* the van.

She sawed her teeth over her bottom lip. If he *was* in there, she could not rescue him, not right then. All right, so between them, she and Dillon had killed one soldier and captured another. But an assault on a guarded vehicle? That was entirely different. She had to believe Logan was still alive, and that meant they wanted him for something. Laura would have another opportunity to get him back safely.

Believe that, she told herself. *Hold on to it. Because if you don't, you're going to do something stupid. Then you'll get yourself killed and probably Dillon and Macie too.*

She stared at the van, picturing the boy lying on the van's floor, crying and scared.

Stop!

Okay, okay. Logan, I'm not abandoning you, I'm not. I'll find you, I promise.

She slipped around the plant and back to the garage wall. She slid through the shadows until she came to the side door. She opened it and stepped into the dark garage.

Hutch's XTerra sat in the center of the wide space. When they had returned from the zoo earlier that day, she had backed in, because that's the way Hutch parked. It had been awkward in the curving drive and unfamiliar garage, but now she was glad she had done it. She went to the driver's door and opened it. The keys were still in the center console's cup holder, where she had left them. She checked the rear seat to make sure the soldiers had not put anything there. *Like Logan's body.*

The thought forced its way to the front of her head. She pushed it away. The interior was empty.

She went to the back of the SUV and opened the hatch. She walked to the front of the garage, found the dangling red handle, and disengaged the door from the automatic opener. She manually opened the door—slowly and quietly. By the meager light of a neighbor's porch fixture and a far-off streetlamp, she made sure no one had slashed the tires or stashed a body in the garage.

Another siren filled the night air like a wailing banshee. Close. Tires squealed. Laura peered out of the garage. The soldier hopped out of the van. He darted behind a tree. He crouched, arced around the trunk, and rattled off a stream of bullets. Another machine gun fired, this one coming from the front of the house.

Laura slipped out of the garage and ran to the backyard.

"Mom!" Dillon said. "I thought they were shooting at you!"

"More cops showed up," she said. "Let's get out of here while the soldiers are distracted." She hoisted the soldier onto her shoulders. "Follow me. We have to be fast and quiet and stick really close to the wall." She looked directly at Dillon. "Got that?"

He nodded.

She pointed to the rifle, arrows, and bow. "Make sure none of those hits anything." She turned to Macie. "Can you do this?"

"Yes, ma'am."

She peered around the corner. The soldier had taken cover behind the van. He had a knee on the bumper and was leaning out to fire. She ran into the garage. Macie came in next, then Dillon. She nodded at the XTerra. "Get in. Shut the doors quietly."

She dropped the soldier into the rear cargo area. She flipped him over and pulled his hands behind his back. She retrieved one of the zip ties she'd taken from his utility belt and pulled it tightly around his wrists. Then she slowly lowered the hatch until she heard it click. Sliding in behind the wheel, she said, "Seat belts."

Dillon, in the front passenger seat, had moved the weapons from his back to the footwell. The machine gun was on the floor, and the bow extended up over the center console. The seat cushion had pushed the bulletproof vest up past his ears. He looked like a shy turtle.

"You can take that off," she told him.

"I'm okay." He tried to find the seat belt, but the vest restricted his movements too much.

Laura leaned past him, snagged the belt, and fastened it. She caught Macie's face in the rearview mirror. Laura thought again of Logan. He was probably in the van.

She could think of nothing else to do.

The firefight out front was going full blast.

She couldn't storm the van—not and live. She couldn't ram the van with Hutch's XTerra—not without risking harm to Logan.

She inserted the key.

All she could do was what she was doing: getting everyone else out of there, saving who could be saved.

She started the engine and put the car in gear. She rolled out of the garage, turning away from the street. When the truck came off the driveway, onto the backyard grass, she punched it. The wheels spun, grabbing for traction. The vehicle propelled forward. She clipped a trash can. It clattered against the front quarter panel and spun off.

In the mirror, she saw a soldier running toward them. He took aim.

"Everyone down!" she said.

The kids ducked their heads. Macie whimpered.

Laura flipped on the headlights in time to see three saplings disappear under the front end. The lights splashed against the wood planks of the back fence, growing more focused and brighter as they sped closer.

Dillon yelled. He covered his head with his arms.

They crashed through. Boards splintered and flipped over the hood and windshield. The SUV bounded over something. It crossed the yard in ten seconds and took out another fence. Laura was glad to see an open stretch of grass to the next street. She had not considered the possibility of running into a car or motor home parked beside the house behind Hutch's. Too many things to think about.

They bounced over the sidewalk, then the curb. In the street, Laura braked. She turned the wheel left, accelerated, and didn't stop until the XTerra needed gas in a Colorado mountain town called Idaho Springs.

THIRTY-ONE

Logan shook the glass out of his hair. He tugged at his wrists. They weren't budging, bound behind his back to a brace in the van's side wall.

Okay . . . they're going to kill me. I don't know why, but they are. No, no, I'm a kid. They don't kill kids. They don't. Oh yeah? What about that Bruce Willis movie? The one with the autistic little boy—younger than me. He knew too much, and the whole movie they were trying to kill him. Really splatter him, shoot him, run him over, throw him off a building. But what do I know that's worth killing for? Nothing! Probably easier to kill a kid than a man: not as strong, can't fight back as well, smaller body to get rid of.

Stop it! Stop it!

He forced himself to think about his injuries. His scalp felt torn where the man had grabbed his hair. He wanted to rub it, but couldn't.

His right cheekbone ached. It had struck the floor when he'd been tossed into the van. His shoulders throbbed from the wrenching they'd taken getting tied up. He gritted his teeth against the pain. He poked his tongue at the tape over his mouth. He tasted adhesive, but the grip on his lips would not loosen. He tried to scream—his throat was raw from doing it so many times: a high-pitched whine reached his ears, nothing anyone else could hear. Especially not with all the gunshots.

It felt like forever since he had heard the first sirens and felt a surge of relief. The man in the driver's seat had scrambled out, and the shooting had started. Bullets had hit the van like baseballs. The windshield had shattered. It had seemed to continue shattering, spraying glass into the van, for a long time. Certain a bullet would rip through the metal and strike him, Logan had curled himself into a ball and pressed his face against the cold steel floor. He had screamed and screamed, not to draw attention, but to focus on something other than what was happening around him.

When he heard the door open again, he realized the gunfire had stopped. He had craned his head, hoping hoping hoping to see a rescuer. His stomach had cramped at the sight of the helmeted driver sweeping his hand over the seat to clear the glass and clambering inside. More sirens had swooped in. The man had jumped out, and it had all started again.

Now the driver climbed in once more. He snapped his head around to look at Logan. The helmet swiveled away, then returned, as if the man expected him to have vanished.

Logan's eyes felt so wide he thought his eyeballs would fall out. He wanted to yell, *Why are you doing this? Why are you hurting me? Where are you taking me?*

The man checked his machine gun, swapped ammo clips from a bag between the seats. He spoke—not too muffled for Logan to make out the words: "Command! Command! Come in. What's happening? Ben! Emile! Michael!"

He shook his weapon as if demanding answers from it. He spotted something through the side window. He said, "Okay, okay, Emile, I see you! Who's that? Emile!"

The rear door swung open. A man, helmeted like the driver, stood looking in. He carried someone over his shoulder, just butt and legs showing.

"Emile!" the driver said. "Who is it? Where's—? Who you got there?"

The man at the door—Emile—heaved the body in. It landed beside Logan. Wetness splattered Logan's face. The body rolled toward him. Wide eyes stared at him. The mouth was frozen in a scream. The teeth were coated in blood, which had spilled out, smearing most of the man's face. A stick jutted out of his neck. More blood.

Logan reeled away, kicking. He tried pulling in a breath through his mouth, found nothing. He shifted the effort to his nose. Along with the air came liquid. He smelled blood. He jerked his head back and cracked it against the van wall. He felt a hand clutch his ankle, holding it tight.

Emile was scrambling in. He tossed something forward.

Logan's eyes followed it. When it landed on the ammo bag, it rolled back and clunked to the floor: another helmet.

Emile unslung his machine gun, tossed it onto the bag. The driver grabbed it and put it on the passenger's seat. Emile leaned back to slam the rear door shut.

"Oh crap, man, crap!" the driver said. "Is that Ben? What happened? Is he—?"

"He's dead," Emile said. He rolled the dead man onto his back. He slapped at his own chinstrap and yanked off his helmet.

His youth surprised Logan. His friend Josh's brother was in college. This guy looked about the same age.

Emile leaned close to the dead man's face. His fingers slid over the bloody neck, stopped. After a moment, he said, "Yeah, he's gone."

The driver's head swiveled back and forth. "Where's Michael? We have to go. We have to go before more cops come. What happened? What was that strike order, dude? I thought this was a recon job."

"Go," Emile said. Crouching beside the body, he stretched his neck to see beyond the front seats and out the shattered windshield.

"But Michael . . . is he down too? He went off-line before the cops came. We need to get his body."

"I couldn't find him. I don't know, he might be in pursuit."

Already beating like a race car's engine, Logan's heart went into overdrive. He imagined Macie running for her life—Laura and Dillon too. *Run, Macie!* he thought. *Hide!*

"What was the truck that came burning out of the garage?" the driver said. "I almost got a shot off at it, but those cops were all over me." He paused. "Was Michael in the truck, you think?"

"I don't know," Emile said. "Why would he be in the truck?"

"If he wasn't . . . we can't just leave him." The driver opened his door. "We can't—"

"Yes, we can! He'll know what to do. He'll go native, wait for exfiltration."

"Wait, wait." The driver touched his helmet. "Affirmative, Command. We have—" He slammed the door, rammed the shifter into gear, and reversed. "Command said to get the hell out of here." He changed gears, and the van lurched forward, bounding over a bump.

Emile raised up onto his knees. "Where are we going?"

"Straight through the backyard, the way the truck went, man. To the next street. Shut up. I'm transpo."

The van bounced and rattled. Cold air streamed through the windshield opening.

Logan kneed at the body, trying to move it away.

"Hey, hey," Emile said. He grabbed Logan's T-shirt. "Settle down."

Logan tried to pull away. He kicked out, landing a solid blow to Emile's thigh.

"I mean it," Emile said and punched him in the face, a quick jab.

Logan's head hit the van again. The tears came. He couldn't stop them.

The driver ripped off his helmet. He glared over his shoulder. "A kid! What the hell, man?"

What? Logan thought through a haze of confusion. *The guy didn't know that before?*

"I got it covered, Anton," Emile said. "Just drive."

"You got what covered?" The van bounced over something. It took a hard right, and the body tumbled into Logan.

He squealed and didn't stop: an alarm triggered by his terror. Somehow the sound came through. Emile shook him.

Changing emotions played out on the man's face, visible in flashes as light came and went through the windows: rage, concern, sadness. He released his grip and flattened the material against Logan's chest. He said, "Just . . . *don't*. It'll be . . ." He didn't finish. He watched Logan cry.

"Man, I have no clue what's going on," the driver—Anton—continued. "How did a recon gig turn into a full-scale assault . . . and now we got a hostage, a kid?"

"I don't know," Emile said, seemingly to Logan. "He saw me, confronted me. I was UF, saw he was just a kid."

"Unfiltered? Why?"

"Orders. Part of the recon," Emile said. "I couldn't . . ." He pressed his lips together, shook his head. He turned to the driver. "I took him, okay? I didn't know what else to do. Next thing, the strike order came down."

"So . . . what? We get points for taking him, or lose some?"

"I don't think it matters now."

"I fragged some cops. You did too. We gotta score something for them."

Emile looked at the body. "Not this time."

Anton swore and slapped the steering wheel.

The van turned left. The body rolled off Logan, bumping up against Emile's legs. Without looking, Emile reached down and held the dead man's arm.

"Must have been a setup," Anton said. "They were waiting for us."

"Who?"

"Whoever we were reconning. The people in the house."

Emile frowned. His eyes found Logan's.

He knows that's not true, Logan thought. *Whatever happened, it wasn't that.*

"So what now?" Anton said. "What do we do? What about Michael?"

Emile didn't answer.

Anton said, "We gotta steal new wheels. We won't make it another mile or two in this thing before it starts drawing cops like a Krispy Kreme opening." He laughed, but even Logan could tell he didn't feel it.

"Then do it," Emile said.

"Right, right. Okay." Anton gestured with his head. "What about him, the kid? What are we going to do with him?"

"Contact Command. See what they say." He glanced at Logan, and turned away. "Whatever they want."

THIRTY-TWO

Brendan Page pushed back from the monitors and slumped in his chair. "What just happened?" he said.

Ian scanned the eight screens arrayed before them. Four showed nothing but horizontal bars of color, their feeds terminated. He rolled his chair back and banged his two booted feet up onto the countertop. "We just got our butts handed to us."

Page stared at him. He wanted to say something, but everything that came to mind simply seemed lame under the circumstances. He held his lips tight, shook his head. His eyes went back to the screens. "Four down," he said and waved his hand at the array. "Four down!"

"Three dead, one missing," Ian agreed.

"Two teams of four," Page said. "Eight soldiers. *Half* of them gone."

Ian nodded. "Two from each team."

"So . . . *what just happened?*"

Ian lifted his eyebrows and sighed. He was looking at the monitors, but Page knew he wasn't seeing them; he was replaying the events of the last fifteen minutes, figuring them out.

Page pulled a tube out of his breast pocket and extracted a cigar from it. He felt the moment did not warrant his usual ritual of savoring the stick before lighting it: smelling it, feeling its texture, tasting the wrapper. Instead, he clipped it and lit up. He didn't even care that he had burnt the tip by putting it too close to the flame and puffing too vigorously. He didn't care that it would make the entire cigar taste like crap. He didn't care, because what that cigar tasted like was what he had just witnessed from his fireteams. He puffed and puffed, filling the control room with a blue-gray haze. He took a long draw and blew a stream of smoke directly at Ian.

Ian absently fanned away the plume, deep in concentration.

"Maybe what you need to think about," said Page, "is just who it was that kicked our butts. Let's see. A newspaper columnist and an accountant. And in Colorado, *hmm* . . . a schoolteacher and a bunch of kids." He took a puff, then another one. "I don't mean to sound like a broken record, here, but I can't get it out of my head: what just happened?"

Ian laced the fingers of both hands together over his chest. He sighed again, and his eyes shifted to Page. "I've been telling you, you're moving too fast on this program. It's a sound strategy. Get them while they're young and pliable. Make them fight in real combat as well as they do on video games—and do it by confusing the two in their minds. Make them believe they're not *really* killing. If and when they realize they are, make sure they care more about winning the 'game' than they do about the people they're shooting. I mean, *smart!* It works. Look at the success we've had, with the troops we've supplied to the U.S. and NATO, so far."

Page scowled, but he liked Ian's confirmation of his ideas. He shook his cigar at the man. "It's like what Eisenhower said: humans just get in the way of winning wars."

Ian coughed and fanned more smoke away. "Actually, I think he said, 'God help us if we take the humanity out of war.' But he was talking politics. Commanders need to never forget that it's fathers and brothers and sons—and daughters—they're sending into battle." He shook his head. "That's not our job. Our job is closer to what you just said. We make weapons of war."

Page smiled. "Soldiers are just one of those weapons. Tools to get the job done. Tools, not people."

"I'm on board with you, Brendan, I am," Ian said. "Send soldiers into battle with one purpose, to kill the enemy. It's what war is all about. We just have to get rid of the psychological garbage that hinders that."

Page pulled on the cigar. When he spoke, smoke came out, as though his words were on fire. "Get rid of their *humanity*!" He said it as confidently as he would have told a child the world is round.

Ian poked a finger at him. "That's what I'm saying. We haven't reached that level with these boys. We haven't cut deep enough."

"They've gone through the same programming as the rest of them, the thousands who are fighting successfully as we speak." He spat out a fleck of tobacco.

Ian's head rolled back and forth. "These fireteams are different. We underestimated the psychological impact of using them in our own country, against our own people. Our program is designed to make soldiers, not hit men."

Page closed his eyes and frowned dismissively. "Shouldn't matter. An enemy is an enemy."

"It does matter. That's what I'm saying we underestimated."

"The virtual overlays are supposed to take care of that."

Ian pulled his feet off of the counter and put them on the floor. He leaned forward and rubbed his palms over his face.

Page could hear the rough skin chafing over Ian's whiskers like sandpaper.

His friend said, "It helps, making men look like women, blood appear as meaningless as spilled paint, stuff like that. But our boys know when they're still in the States. They know how far they travel, they know they're dealing with American cars and locks and power supplies. Listen, man, the hit on this Hutch guy was practically up the street. And what *was* that? It wasn't supposed to be a hit."

Page scowled at his cigar. It really was nasty. "It went off the tracks, that kid showing up and all."

Ian stood. He walked to the observation window and looked into the VR chamber.

Page could see his friend's face reflected in the glass—in the best of times it was craggy and just-plain-mean looking; add a dose of displeasure to it, as now, and the man appeared ready to tear the throat out of a lion.

Ian said, "So knock the kid out and carry on. Don't turn what was essentially a reconnaissance mission into a slaughter."

"Emile panicked, grabbed the kid. Hutch saw it and started freaking out." Page dropped the stogie on the floor and ground it out. "It is what it is."

Ian turned around. "The objective was to scare the guy."

Page shrugged. "I guess we did that."

"They weren't ready for your order: 'Take 'em out! Kill them all!'"

"They should have been ready for anything."

"Brendan, *we're* still figuring all of this out: the psychological conditioning, how far we can push them." He started to say something else, but closed his mouth. The lines in his face became bottomless crevices. He returned to his chair and collapsed into it.

"So what you're saying," Page said, "is that this mess is all our fault."

Ian's eyebrows went up. "Essentially, *yeah.*" The man studied Page's face. He said, "Well, they should have responded better. I think they had let their guard down. They were supposed to observe adult civilians. They weren't expecting a fight. Especially not *that* kind of fight."

On two of the monitors, Page watched the soldiers pace back and forth between trees. One of them swung his perspective—in night-vision green—to two bodies on the ground. The view swung away again, quickly, as though in anger. They had decided that retrieving the bodies at the motel and jacking another vehicle would give Hutch and Jim O'Dey more of a lead than the soldiers could safely close. They had carried their fallen comrades into the forest and were now awaiting extraction—which, in this case, entailed an Outis Hummer driving up the road fifteen miles.

Almost to himself, Page said, "Should have known."

"How's that?"

"We've seen the Feds' videos from Canada, read the transcripts, the depositions, Hutch and . . ." He snapped his fingers, trying to remember.

Ian said, "Laura Fuller."

"They were fighters up there. No reason to think they wouldn't be here."

"So we got the kid," Ian said.

"It's not Dillon." The boy's face had been clear enough when the soldier grabbed him, and again in the van when he tied him up. Hutch had even confirmed it. "It's Hutch's boy."

"Changes everything." Ian rubbed his hands together. "Hutch gets him back in exchange for giving up this . . . *vendetta* he's got for you."

"I don't think so." Page was thinking it through, looking at all the pieces, seeing how they fit together. He looked at his friend. "Haven't you ever been obsessed, Ian?"

Ian considered it. "There was this girl once, in Shanghai. . . ."

"Not the same thing. Grabbing his kid? That's just fuel on the fire. He's not gonna stop, even if he gets his kid back. Oh, he'll play the game, tell us he'll do anything to get his son back. He might even believe it. But in a week or a month or a year, he'll be right back at it, pounding at me harder than ever. He'll be smarter, though. He'll stash his family somewhere first. He'll keep moving, so we can't get him. All the while—pound, pound, pound. First there'll be cracks in all the things we've done to protect ourselves. Then he'll find one that looks especially fragile, and he'll work on it until everything I've built comes crashing down."

He was staring at the wall, seeing the future.

"You can't know all that," Ian said.

Page moved his eyes to him. "I know obsession."

Neither man spoke for a long time. They watched the monitors as the local team stowed the bodies into the Hummer. The men removed their helmets, and the screens flicked to black, then to the multicolored test pattern.

"So?" Ian said. "How do you want to handle it?"

"From every angle," Page said. He stood up, touched his finger to the boy's face on the screen. "We got the kid. He's Plan B."

"What's Plan A?"

"There's only one way to handle someone who just won't stop coming at you."

Ian waited, while Page checked his cigar tube and found it empty.

Page tucked it back into a pocket and said, "You *stop* him. Hard. Right in his tracks."

THIRTY-THREE

Jim was bleeding out fast.

Twenty minutes after fleeing the motel, Hutch pulled onto a dark dirt road. Jim had been unconscious. His pulse was weak, his breathing fast and shallow. Hutch ripped off his own shirt and secured it to the wound with his belt.

Now, in a blood-smeared white T-shirt, he was back on the road. He punched prompts on the portable GPS unit suction-cupped to the windshield. The closest hospital was the Kirkland Medical Center, about twenty minutes out.

"Hang in there, buddy," he said. "We're almost there."

Every time he passed a convenience store or gas station, he fought the urge to pull over. He had to reach Laura. *Had to.* His need to find out what had happened, to get the cops to his house, to make sure everyone was okay, made him dizzy. He kept thinking he could *do* something for them—if he only knew the situation. For the hundredth time, Hutch mentally kicked himself for the outburst that had destroyed Jim's phone.

He had to get home as soon as possible. It was necessary to his heart. Hearing Logan's scream, followed by Page's thrusting Hutch into blind oblivion, then sending killers after him . . . His insides felt wrenched completely out of place. His chest hurt, his throat, his stomach. Forget the firefight he'd just gone through. Forget that he was a terrible aim and it had almost got him killed. Even forget—*God help me*—Jim's galloping ride toward Death's eternal parade. What made Hutch ache on every level was the terror that something had happened to his kids and to Dillon and Laura. Every second without knowing they were okay was like being in the dark with creatures that swooped down to gouge his flesh with their claws and teeth.

His eyes kept flipping to the rearview mirror. He kept the van moving at just over the speed limit, which kept cops off him but reduced his ability to detect trouble. At faster speeds, headlights closing in on him would spell trouble. Now it simply meant other drivers knew the road better and were impatient.

The last thing he wanted to see was an Outis team of soldiers bearing down on him. The second-to-last thing was a cop. It wouldn't take Colombo to figure out he'd been part of the chaos at the motel. Even if he could prove his innocence, they would detain him for questioning. And even the thought of delaying his access to Logan, Macie, Laura, and Dillon made him nauseated.

It was obvious the soldiers had stolen the van. A child seat was strapped to the rear bench. The floor was littered with potato chip bags, candy wrappers, and the packaging of other fat-inducing fare he couldn't imagine those soldiers putting into their systems. Of course, the definitive evidence was the lack of an ignition key. Instead, a strip of metal the size of a Popsicle stick protruded out of the ignition.

He had not inspected the complete interior, but he thought the soldiers had left nothing behind. No spare ammo, no maps or notes about their operation. Not even a medical kit. They likely carried everything they needed. That way, they'd have it wherever they were, and if they had to leave the van without returning to it, no evidence would lead to Outis.

The one exception was the GPS. It made sense they would use one. Their success depended on quick ingress and egress, probably into unfamiliar places. Only the motel's address resided in its memory. Undoubtedly, wiping it clean was on some checklist of their post-mission duties, along with cleaning their weapons, stitching their cuts, and cleaning blood spatter off their clothes.

He jumped at the sound of a female voice. "In one mile, take exit 211, on the right." He found the GPS's volume dial and muted it.

He hoped the hospital was a small, quaint place, where Jim's trauma would demand the attention of the entire staff, leaving him to use their phone all he wanted. But Kirkland was an upscale suburb of Seattle, which meant it was probably modern, large, and busy. After wheeling Jim away, there would be plenty of people to ask questions and call the police.

He drove on, following the GPS's directions. When the hospital came into view, he realized no one would have had to call the police; they were already there. Two cruisers crouched near the ER entrance. A uniformed cop stood outside the doors smoking a cigarette. From Hutch's vantage point across a parking lot, he could see another cop inside. The man was leaning over a counter, talking to a nurse.

If anyone from the motel had given the police a description of the van, these two may already have half an eye peeled for it. He found it curious they seemed so nonchalant, since the hotel was only thirty miles away. It was out of Kirkland's jurisdiction, but how often did businesses within earshot get hit with grenades and machine-gun fire? Such pyrotechnics should have drawn cops from around the entire state. At minimum, wouldn't these guys be chattering about it, listening to their radio for more information? Either whatever constituted law enforcement in Gold Bar had not yet responded, which didn't make sense, or Page had something to do with keeping it quiet.

That whole area out there was Outis territory, so the idea of local public servants being on Page's payroll wasn't too far-fetched. According to press releases, Outis's twelve-hundred-acre facility trained thousands of young men and women annually in all aspects of military disciplines. News agencies continually reported on recruits being seriously injured and killed. The way Page operated, Hutch had no doubt the circumstances around those casualties were not always aboveboard. If he had learned anything during the months he'd spent investigating Page Industries, it was that power purchased silence.

He hoped that producing a gunshot victim—who was not only a civilian but also a vocal father of one of Outis's recruits—would stir something up.

Dream on, he thought.

He swung the van around to a side parking lot and pulled into an extra-wide handicapped space. He left the engine running and climbed out. He slipped into his jacket and zipped it up. Most of this side of the building was brick. The few windows he could see were dark. He opened the side door. Jim was still breathing, but only barely. Blood had saturated the shirt Hutch had belted over the wound. He maneuvered Jim from between the seats and lifted him. He carried him to a grassy lawn between the building and the front of the van. He settled Jim into it, then reached under the man for his wallet. He verified the presence of a driver's license—the emergency room staff or police would contact his family. He replaced the wallet.

Jim wheezed. His eyelids fluttered. He called out, "Michael!"

"Shhh," Hutch said. He gently laid him down.

"Michael," Jim repeated.

"It's Hutch, Jim. It's going to be okay."

Jim's eyes opened. "Hutch?"

"Yeah, buddy?"

"It hurts." But he attempted a smile. The expression was infinitely sadder than had he grimaced in pain.

Hutch squeezed the man's shoulder. "We're at a hospital. I have to leave you here, right outside, but I'll tell them where to find you."

"Those men," Jim said. "That's what my boy is dealing with." He closed his eyes and began to weep.

"Jim? Just hang in there. When you're well enough, I'll help you any way I can, you and your son."

When Jim didn't respond, Hutch brushed his fingers over the man's forehead.

He climbed in the van and backed out, trying not to look at the man he had left lying in the grass. A few blocks away, he pulled into a convenience store and called the emergency operator from an outside pay phone. He described Jim's location and his condition, then hung up and drove away.

Several miles farther, he found another pay phone at a gas station. He used his credit card to dial Logan's mobile phone number. A woman answered.

"Laura! What happened? Are you—"

"Who is this?"

"What . . . I . . . Laura?"

"Laura who? Who are you trying to reach?"

"Who is this?"

"Detective Mia Tierno."

Hutch squeezed the phone. For a few moments, all he could hear was his heartbeat pounding in his ears. He said, "This . . . is my son's phone number. Is he there? Where are you?"

"Your son's name is Laura?"

"She had his phone. Is he there? Is she?"

"Sir, what is your name?"

"John Hutchinson. They were supposed to be at my house." Feeling as though he was in one of Dante's circles of hell, and this woman was his tormenter, he said, "*Where is my son!*"

"Sir, where are *you?*"

Hutch was certain she could hear his teeth grinding together. He said nothing, and she let him. Finally, his voice small, almost gone, he said, "What's happened?"

She said, "I believe I'm at your residence. No one is here, except for four dead cops outside and a lot of blood in here." Beat. "Not the officers' blood."

"No one else?" Hope sparked within him like a lighter searching for a flame. But *blood* . . . she'd said blood.

"None that we found. What do you know about this? John, I need you to come—"

He placed the handset into its cradle. He did not dare release his grip on the phone, however; it was the only thing keeping him upright.

Dead cops. Blood. No one there.

That spark, but no flame.

Before Page had cut off the monitor, he had seen the soldier grab Logan. Had Page's men taken all of them? Was the blood the result of a struggle? Whose was it? Given Laura's history, he gave the odds of the blood being a soldier's or hers fifty-fifty.

A siren wailed in the distance. He didn't know if pay phones transmitted their numbers. It probably didn't matter, considering that he had just spoken to a police detective at the scene of a multiple homicide, where cops had been killed. If anyone was motivated to track him down, she was. Until he knew where the people he loved were, he did not want to be tracked down. Sixty seconds later, he was in the van, trawling for another phone.

THIRTY-FOUR

Operators answered calls to Page Industries headquarters twenty-four hours a day. Its employees—engineers, programmers, and janitors alike—were renowned for working at all hours. Business gurus relished debating the benefits and dangers of encouraging workers to spend so much time on the job. The *Wall Street Journal* had once praised the conglomerate for innovatively providing free gourmet coffee bars, NoDoz, and sleep chambers. A year later the publication decried the practice as being antifamily and ultimately unproductive because of the burnout factor. Through it all, Brendan Page stayed true to form, neither basking in the praise nor defending his company's practices. He was more interested in end results than in how his people achieved them.

In turn, Page kept a staff of personal assistants around the clock.

Hutch had read a *Time* magazine profile that claimed the man slept only four hours a day. His business was global. "Daylight's burning somewhere," he had told the reporter.

Hutch waited for the operator to connect him to one of these assistants now. He was at a pay phone in the customer service area of a grocery store. He thought the clerk was eavesdropping, the way he leaned on the counter without moving. Then the man's head slumped down, and he jerked it up with a wide-eyed expression.

A female voice came through the phone. "Mr. Hutchinson?"

Hutch turned his back to the tired grocery worker. "Is this Candace?" He'd spoken to her many times, trying to get an interview.

"This is Mrs. Avery. Ms. Davis is off for the evening. How may I help you?"

"I need to speak to him."

"I'm afraid Mr. Page isn't available."

"Tell him it's me."

"Mr. Page is unavailable to anyone."

"He wants to talk to me."

"One moment, please."

You'd think that with a billion bucks you could find somebody who could mask her disgust over the phone.

He looked over his shoulder and saw that the clerk had fully succumbed to the pull of slumber.

Hutch thought about getting home. When he had made the reservations the night before, all the late-night flights had been full, or their routes to Denver had been so circuitous that it wasn't worth trying to get back the same night. Now he would pay any price and allow a layover in London if it got him home quickly.

"Mr. Hutchinson?" Total boredom.

"Yes?"

"Mr. Page is indeed unavailable."

"You told him it was me?"

"I spoke to him directly, sir, and I did tell him that Mr. John Hutchinson was on the phone."

Hutch shifted the handset to the other ear. What he really wanted to do was smash it into the phone box, as though it were Page's head. "What did he say? *Exactly?*"

"That he would contact you tomorrow."

"I need to talk to him *now*! Do you understand?"

"Sir, I—"

Hutch slammed the phone down. It was as though nothing had changed, as though he were still just a journalist vying for a scoop with the great Mr. Page. The man had attacked him and his family and refused to take his call. He leaned his shoulder against the phone. What was Page doing? Was it his way of pounding his chest? Was he telling Hutch that he could do whatever he wanted? Through the monitor, Page had said he wanted only to frighten him. Then his men had attacked.

Hutch did not know how to reconcile Page's words and his actions. It made him feel like he was wandering in an alien world, where the laws of physics as he understood them did not apply.

Page obviously intended to kill him. Perhaps his not taking Hutch's call was part of that. Distancing himself. Page was good at that. Hutch had to get home as fast as possible, and he had to do it without running into Page's men or being detained by the police.

He pulled his credit card from his back pocket and lifted the handset again. He stood like that for a few moments, thinking. If this was the way it was going to be, he had to do everything right. Even a little slip could cost him his life—and the lives of Logan, Macie, Laura, and Dillon.

He hung up. Remaining here, after calling Page, could be one of those slips. He had to think of everything, how every move would play out over the following ten steps. He had never been much of a chess player, but winning that game required the same sort of forward thinking he needed to apply now.

He had to find another phone.

Pawn to E-4.

THIRTY-FIVE

Hutch sprang out from below the window, blasting away with the handgun.

"Nice move," Ian said.

"The guy can't aim worth squat," Page said.

They were watching a playback of the motel firefight. All four video feeds—one from each soldier—unspooled simultaneously on the monitors. Except, as of several minutes ago, the soldier in the third position—his video had terminated with a bone-crunching crash.

"Still," Ian said, "the guy's got some sharp tactical moves, like sending the other guy into the woods while he waited below the window. And later, when he gets up onto the roof. Oh, oh—" Ian hopped up, excited. He pointed at the screen where Hutch had pulled the soldier's body over himself. He stayed under it perfectly, while the team leader unloaded his clip at him. Ian smiled. "Look at that."

"What are you, a ten-year-old?" Page said. "Julian used to talk like that during Jet Li movies."

They both watched the team leader lob a hand grenade, then drop down beside the toilet to reload.

"Hutch isn't so hot," Page said. "I want to fight him."

Ian scowled. "He's going to be dead by morning."

"Maybe. Whether he is or isn't, I want to play him in the Void. He doesn't fight like a soldier. That's the only thing he's got on us. It's an oversight in our training. Let's figure this guy out." Page stood. Starting to walk away, he flapped a hand at the screens. "Get Andy working on it, and make sure he uses the behavior recognition program."

"What are you going to do?" Ian said.

Page stopped at the door. "Isn't it obvious? I'm going to do what our men seem incapable of doing."

THIRTY-SIX

Hutch cruised the streets of Kirkland, Washington. His head panned back and forth, hoping to spot a pay phone. He'd written a column a few years back documenting the plight of a couple who had sunk their life savings into the pay phone business only to see it collapse under the weight of the popularity of mobile phones. He'd learned that half of all pay phones had been taken out of service. Not finding one now, he thought that figure was way too low.

He let loose with a mental scream. *Just look!* He chided himself. *Stop thinking about it!*

But that's the way it was: A strong wind was blowing through his mind. All the things he had to do, all the things he had to remember, whipped and swirled. He'd grab at one when another would flash by, drawing his attention. What had happened? But he knew. Wasn't the blood the police had found in his home evidence enough? There, see, another thought to grab at: the blood. Whose was it? The faces of Logan and Macie, Laura and Dillon flashed by. The image of any one of them wounded and bleeding made his entire being go dark, as though a blanket had been thrown over his soul.

Desperate not to go there, he snatched at another thought.

But the people he loved refused to leave his mind. There they were, asking him how he'd gotten them in such a mess. Hadn't he vowed to spend more time with his kids? Instead, he'd sicced the lawyers on Janet, demanding joint custody. Then he'd gone after Page, a pursuit that had become, as the man himself had said, an obsession.

Page. Hutch gave the guy credit in one area: he knew people. Hutch had read the stories. When Page was eight his father got sick, and he began running errands for neighbors and local businesses. He would convince potential clients of his usefulness by anticipating their needs: a bottle of milk and a loaf of bread for the banker rushing to get home; sparkling windows for the store owner worried about new competition; and—consistent with Page's future passion—a box of cigars to the mob boss whose right-hand man just became a father. In addressing Congress to justify the huge military contracts his companies received, Page often predicted global hot zones: a South American coup, a dictator threatening U.S. interests in Africa.

Much of Page's prescience was aided by a topflight staff of analysts and advisors, but in one interview he had said something that Hutch thought was the key to it all: "As a species, we tend to think people will do the logical thing. That doesn't mean the *best* thing. Greed is logical, but not necessarily *right*. For example, we think a man will always protect his family and strive for a better life. How, then, do we explain his wild fling that tears the family apart, or his descent into endless bottles of booze? We're more primal than *good*. We seek adventure, but often confuse chaos with adventure. Essentially, we're crazy. Once you accept that, you've got the world figured out."

The interviewer had seized on Page's calling greed "*not necessarily right*"; he'd wanted to know when it was right. Hutch didn't think that was the most telling aspect of the quote. It was that Page considered our unpredictable nature part of our predictability.

Is that what had happened? Had Page said he'd only wanted to scare Hutch, when all along he'd intended to attack him? Had he been intentionally unpredictable to throw Hutch off guard?

Okay, you're thinking too much.

No, not too much, just dwelling on things he couldn't know. He was wasting time and brainpower on things that didn't matter now. What did matter was getting home, back to Colorado. He had to find Laura and the kids. He had a ticket for the next day, leaving Seattle just after noon. That wasn't soon enough. He had to get to the airport, exchange the ticket, leave tonight.

He looked at his watch—a little after nine. Still time, right? He wasn't a seasoned traveler, but weren't there, like, red-eyes that ferried people throughout the night? Maybe between major cities, like Los Angeles and New York. But Seattle to Denver? He didn't know.

Gotta call the airline—and there he was again, lamenting the state of the pay phone industry.

He pulled into a convenience store. No phone on the outside. He yanked open the front door.

"Pay phone?" he said to a pimply-faced teen behind the register.

"It's broken."

"Do you have one I can use? It's local."

"No can do, man. I'll get fired."

Hutch produced a twenty. "I'm desperate."

The bill disappeared into the clerk's back pocket. He brought a corded phone from under the counter and pushed it toward Hutch. "Make it fast."

But it wasn't. Under the clerk's ever-increasing agitation, Hutch learned that his ticketed airline had no seats on its last few flights to Denver. He called three others before finding a seat on a plane with an 11:15 PM departure. It required a layover in Chicago, which meant he wouldn't get to Denver until after seven in the morning. Better than the three o'clock arrival of his current ticket. The woman on the phone informed him that he'd have to check in at the airport an hour early.

He said, "I can make that." *Barely.*

His credit card was declined. He'd used the last of his credit—the amount he'd been planning to use to show Laura and Dillon a good time in Denver—for the flight here. He closed his eyes. He had two other cards, all nearly maxed out. It was expensive keeping up with an ex-wife whose boyfriend had loads of money to spend on your kids.

He ran through his options. Who could help? Who did he know who—Larry. Why hadn't he thought of him before? Laura knew Larry. If she were out there—running from people, unable to reach Hutch—she'd reach out to him, especially since he was the only other person who knew of Hutch's sudden trip to see Page. Of course. He started dialing Larry's number.

"I need to make one long-distance call," he told the clerk.

"Can't, man."

"Just one. It's a matter of life and death. Really."

An irritating tone sounded through the handset.

"I mean, you *can't*," the clerk said. "That phone doesn't allow long distance."

"Oh, come on!" Hutch hung up. "Where . . . uh . . . ." He ran for the door.

"Got another twenty?" the clerk said.

"What?" Hutched whipped it out.

The clerk rolled his eyes. He pulled a cell phone from the same pocket into which the first twenty had gone. They made the swap. Hutch began dialing, then stopped. He told the clerk, "Don't say anything, and I'll mail it back to you with a hundred bucks. I promise."

The guy's face expressed utter bafflement. It changed to alarm. "Hey—"

"I'm sorry," Hutch said, pushing through the door. "Hundred bucks! Promise!"

"No way, dude! Come back!"

As Hutch squealed away, the clerk ran after him through the parking lot. In the rearview, he watched the guy give up.

He dialed Larry's home number. It rang, then rolled him into voice mail. He disconnected and punched in Larry's cell number. Voice mail again. "Larry, I . . ." He groaned. "This is Hutch. I'll call you back. Be by your phone. It's important."

He dialed his own voice mail numbers. No messages at home or work.

As much as he didn't want to call the only other person who could help if she would—a big *if*—he couldn't wait for Larry. He needed that ticket. He dialed Janet's number. She picked up on the second ring.

"Janet, I wouldn't normally—"

"Where are my kids!" Janet demanded.

"They're my kids too." Knee-jerk response. Habit. Something about her voice did that to him.

"Where are they? I'm on my way to your house because I got a call from the police. The cops are there, but you're not, and neither are Macie and Logan."

"Did you talk to Detective Tierno? What happened?"

"That's her. Tierno. She said there'd been an 'incident' at your house. What is that, an 'incident'? I called Logan's phone. Hutch, Detective Tierno answered."

"I know," Hutch said.

Janet's voice had cracked. Tears were a couple syllables away.

"You're supposed to *have* them, Hutch. What's going on?"

As Hutch filtered through possible responses, weighing each against the consequences of telling her too much, Janet continued.

"Hutch." Her voice had softened. "Just tell me they're all right. Please."

"They're with Laura, hon—Janet." He guessed that was habit too; especially when he sensed a bit of softness in her, something he'd forgotten she was capable of. "They're fine."

"*Laura?*" The harshness had returned. "What are they doing with *her?*"

"I'll explain when I see you. But, listen, I need you to do me a really big favor."

Long pause. "What?"

"I'm stuck in Seattle and—"

"Seattle? Are you there with her? Are Macie, Logan, and . . . and . . ."

"Dillon," Hutch said. She knew his name. "No, they're not with me. I got called away on business, but now I can't get home."

"Why not? You drive to the airport, get on a plane, and voilà, you're here. It's that simple, Hutch."

Hutch closed his eyes, as disgusted with himself as she knew he would be. He said, "I'm out of money."

"Didn't you buy a round-trip?"

"I can't use it, because of what's happening. I have to buy a new ticket."

"That's what credit cards are for."

"I've tapped 'em out."

Silence. Hutch waited.

"So you want money?"

"I got the ticket on hold. Just call in with your credit card number."

No response.

"Janet?"

"A commercial flight, right? You're not thinking about chartering a plane, are you?"

A chartered flight! Why hadn't he thought of that? "Janet, you're a genius. I'm sure Seattle has dozens of private—"

"No, Hutch," she said. "That's why you're broke. You think like that."

"Janet, no, really . . . I have to get back fast. It's life and death."

"Whose life and death?" Shrill again. "Logan and Macie's?"

"I just . . ." He slammed on the brakes to avoid running a red light. "Look, let me just look into it, see how much—"

"Do you want me to buy the commercial ticket or not?"

"I'd rather you—"

"So you don't," she said.

He remembered conversations like this when they were married. He recognized the tone, like an iron spike driven into granite. She wasn't going to budge. He sighed. "I do . . . please."

"Let me pull over."

"Thank you. I appreciate it."

"I don't want to hear it, Hutch."

He wanted to remind her that it was she who had left him, but he guessed now wouldn't be the time. He realized he didn't know how to get to the airport. He tucked the phone into his shoulder and punched at the GPS.

"Give me what you got," Janet said.

After he did, he added, "And, Janet, I need you to keep this between us. Don't tell the cops. Don't tell anyone."

"Hutch, I don't like this."

"Believe me, I don't either. But if they pick me up at the airport, I won't be able to get to Laura. It'll delay getting the kids."

She breathed heavily into the phone.

Hutch said, "I realize it's weird and scary. But, please, Janet, you have to trust me."

"Trust you? You left our kids with a stranger, and now they're gone. You're a grown man and you're broke. You're telling me I can't tell the police where you are."

She liked lists, particularly when they enumerated his faults. He knew she could go on and on.

"Let's not do this now, okay? I'm on my way to the airport. Will you get me the ticket? You have to do it now."

More silence then: "Yes." She hung up.

Hutch navigated the van onto I-405. He dialed Larry's number again. When his friend answered, Hutch said, "Larry, thank God."

"Hutch," Larry said. "Just got out of the movies. You know that new one with Matt Damon? It's—"

"Larry, stop. I have to talk to you."

"You still in Washington? What's going on?"

"You don't know?" It didn't seem possible that the whole world wasn't aware of what had been happening to him in the last few hours. It also meant Laura hadn't reached him. "They haven't called you yet. They will."

"Who?"

"Cops," Hutch said. He went on to give Larry the movie-trailer version of events. He ended with: "I thought Laura would have called you."

"I've been out. You can't call her?"

"She was using Logan's phone," Hutch said. "Some detective has it now." He pushed away the image that put in his head: not of a found phone, but of a battered and bloody one at the scene of an accident.

Larry said, "She may have tried to call me at work. I haven't checked my messages there. What about *your* voice mail?"

"Nothing, even the work number. I always have messages there."

"Cops probably picked them up already."

"Don't they need a court order?"

"Technically," Larry said. "But, Hutch, four dead cops? Procedures fly out the window when it's their own. What do you want me to do?"

"Check to see if Laura called. Try to reach her, somehow. Make sure she and the kids are all right." He thought it through. "I need to meet her someplace when I come in."

"Where?"

"Let's see, how about . . . wait a minute. Larry, is there any chance someone's listening?"

"What, like a bug?"

"Or some kind of remote listening device. What do they call those things, parabolic shotguns? Something like that. Page knows we talk. He contacted you to get me out here."

"Now you're being paranoid."

Hutch laughed. "Don't you think I have reason to be?"

"All right," Larry said. "I'll call you back from a pay phone."

"Not in the *Post* building . . . or near your house."

It was Larry's turn to laugh. It sounded as pathetic as Hutch's had. "What's your number?"

"Uh . . . " He looked at the phone. Nothing.

"You don't know your number?"

"It's new. Didn't it come through on caller ID?"

"It said *blocked*."

"It's always something. Always."

"You don't have a place the kids would know to go?"

"Janet's," Hutch said, "but I don't want them going someplace Page knows about."

"Someplace you've prearranged for emergencies? Hutch, I'd think you of all people . . ."

He knew what Larry meant. In Canada, Dillon had known exactly where his mother would look for him. It's what had saved them. So when Hutch had returned home, why hadn't he made contingency plans with *his* family?

He said, "I know, Larry. I screwed up. I—" The phone clicked. The screen said, "Incoming call," followed by a number. He told Larry to hold on and clicked the answer button.

"Dude, that is so uncool." The clerk.

"What's your cell phone number?"

"What? Are you kidding me? Bring it back now, okay? No harm, no foul, no cops."

"I can scroll through the menus and find the number," Hutch told him. "Save me the trouble, and I'll throw another hundred bucks in when I send it back."

"You stole my phone!"

"I told you I'll send it back. With a hundred, two if you tell me the number."

"You don't have it, man. I heard you on the phone. You couldn't pay for a plane ticket. I saw the crappy van you got."

"I have the cash. Come on."

The kid thought about it. Finally he rattled off a number. "But I'm telling you—"

Hutch clicked back over to Larry. He gave him the number. "Call me back. Fast."

He dialed his own mobile number. Maybe Julian knew something or could convince his father to talk to Hutch. It rang until Hutch's voice mail kicked in. He disconnected and tossed the phone onto the passenger seat.

THIRTY-SEVEN

Bound at his wrists and ankles, the man in the SUV's cargo area was going crazy.

Not a man, Laura corrected herself, *a boy.* But it didn't make watching him any easier.

He kicked at the rear seat backs, cracked his head into the glass, and thrashed around like a movie vampire dragged into the sun. Most unsettling were the noises he made. He would utter animal grunts as he rolled and jerked himself into one position or another. Next came the screams; shrieks, really: inhuman and insane. After thirty or forty seconds he'd collapse, hyperventilating. Slowly, he'd start to moan, low and sad.

Macie had first noticed him beginning to stir. Before Laura could pull over, the stranger lunged at the girl. She screamed and pulled away, scrambling into the front seats. Laura had taken the next exit and stopped at the end of a dark off-ramp. Now the three of them were crowded into the front seats. Laura was turned in her seat, holding the machine gun like a bat, stock pointed at the boy. Macie and Dillon had turned around in the passenger seat and were leaning back against the dash. Macie was crying. Dillon held his arm around her, but judging by his facial expression, his emotional state wasn't much better.

"What's wrong with him, Mom?" he asked.

She didn't answer. She was too intent on a change she had detected in the soldier's behavior. His tantrum was subsiding.

The moaning grew quieter, then faded altogether. His breathing slowed. He raised his head—just to where his eyes could appraise them over the seat back. He said, "Are you real?"

Laura and Dillon exchanged a glance.

Laura said, "What's wrong with you?"

His head disappeared. He began to sob. "Are . . . you . . . *real*?"

"We're real," Macie said. "So are you."

He sat up and propped his back against the rear hatch. He sniffed, ran the back of one hand across his nose. Only then did he seem to notice the zip ties binding his wrists. He noticed the one around his ankles as well. To Laura, he said, "Did I hurt you?"

"I think you were going to. The other soldiers did." She rubbed her throat, still sore.

He stared at her.

Dillon said, "What's your name?"

"Michael . . . I think . . . I think . . ." He began rocking forward, moaning. With a screeching yell, he shoved himself off the floor.

Macie screamed as he lurched toward the front of the car, obviously intending to get over the seat backs. His head hit the ceiling, and he dropped onto a headrest and rolled back into the cargo area. Screaming, he kicked the seat back. It canted forward with a crack. He turned and kicked the plastic panel below the window. His foot nailed the FOR SALE sign taped to the side glass. The window shattered, bowing out.

"Mom?" Dillon said.

She leaned into the passenger footwell and grabbed the machine gun. She opened her door and climbed out.

"Mom, no!" Dillon said. He reached for her, but she slammed the door. The door opened, and he hopped out. "Mom, don't!" He was crying.

"Get back in, Dillon," she said firmly. She glanced through the rear window, saw Michael on his back, kicking the headrest. She opened the hatch.

Michael stopped screaming to scowl at her. Yelling again, he kicked off the seat back, propelling himself out of the vehicle. He tumbled over the bumper and fell onto the gravelly asphalt. He spun to swing his tied feet at Laura's legs.

"Don't hurt him!" Dillon yelled behind her.

For the second time that night, she brought the weapon down on his head. This time, however, he only screamed louder and thrashed more wildly. She smacked the gun into his forehead. He stopped moving.

"Did you . . ." Dillon said, stepping up beside her. "Did you *kill* him?"

She squatted and pressed her fingers into Michael's neck. "He's alive," she said. She stood and put her arm around her son. "I just knocked him out again. He could have hurt us, and himself. Help me get him back into the cargo area."

They hoisted him up, pushed him in, and closed the hatch.

Dillon sniffed. "I thought you were going to . . ."

"I know," Laura said. "I'm sorry." She led him back to the driver's door.

"I don't want to sit in the backseat," Macie said.

"I will," volunteered Dillon.

"No," Laura told him. "The both of you sit up here awhile, okay?"

"It's too crowded," Dillon said. "We got all this other stuff." He indicated the weapons and other items they'd taken from the boy.

"Put it in the back," Laura said. "Not the bow and arrow."

"Not the *gun*," Dillon added.

In the front, the XTerra had two bucket seats and a center console. With the stuff Laura didn't want within reach of Michael, there wasn't enough room for everyone.

She said, "Okay, hold on a second." She returned to the rear and opened the hatch. She pulled the coil of zip ties from her pocket and made a chain of about three feet. She fastened one end to Michael's wrist restraints and the other to a metal loop mounted to the floor. She shut the hatch and returned to the driver's seat.

"You can sit in the backseat now, Macie," she said. "It's safe."

Macie considered it, then shook her head.

"You can lie down, go to sleep."

"No, thank you."

"I'll do it," Dillon said. He moved the bow and arrow to the floor behind the front seats. He climbed over Macie and slipped over the console. He sprawled out on the leather bench. He said, "Wake me when we get there."

Back in Silverthorne, Laura had tried to get her act together. She had filled the tank, using the cash she had found on the soldier . . . Michael. She had called Larry's number at the *Denver Post* and left a message. Then she had shut herself in the bathroom and wept. After washing up, she had mulled over their situation. Almost broke, unable to reach Hutch, unwilling to seek help until she knew what was happening.

Logan gone. Logan gone. Logan gone.

She needed Hutch, and he needed to know about his son. Their best chance to find him, she decided, was at the airport. So she had pulled the XTerra onto eastbound I-70, heading back toward Denver. That was thirty minutes ago.

"You got it," Laura told Dillon.

"I don't want to miss anything," he said.

"You won't, sweetheart."

But she hoped he did. She hoped he missed a lot of what she feared was heading toward them.

<hr />

Hutch was pulling in to the airport when Larry called back. Hutch told him, "Hold on." He leaned out his window and pushed the button for a parking stub, raising the barrier in front of him. "Did she call?"

"She left a message on my work line," Larry said. "She sounded crazy out of her mind. Hutch—"

"Did she say where she was? I'm hoping she got somewhere safe, where she can stay."

"She didn't say. If you're right about Page bugging the lines, good thing she didn't."

"She's a smart lady," Hutch said. "She wouldn't want to leave it on voice mail. So nothing about a phone? If she was able to—"

"Hutch," Larry interrupted. "They have Logan."

Hutch's heart fell out of his chest. "No . . ."

"She said she had Macie and Dillon," Larry said, "but they took Logan. She didn't know what to do. She said she'd call back, but I didn't get any more messages."

Hutch brought the van to a stop. He stared out the windshield, dazed. "Just 'they took Logan'?"

"That's the way she said it. Hutch, I'm so sorry."

Behind him, a car honked. Slowly, he took his foot off the brake and let the van roll forward. The car honked again. He waved for the driver to go around.

Larry said, "When you talked to the cops, they didn't say anything? They don't know?"

"If they do, they didn't tell me."

"You have to tell them."

"No," Hutch said. "I can't get pulled into that right now. I've got to make sure the others are safe. Then I'll figure out what to do."

"What to do is go to the cops." Larry's voice was shrill, shaky. "This is a kidnapping. They know how to handle it. The FBI."

"Larry, I can't."

"I can. Let me call them, get them on this."

"Listen," Hutch said, "I know Page. If he thinks the feds are moving in on him for anything, he'll get rid of all the evidence. You hear what I'm saying? He'll kill Logan." He realized he was squeezing the phone tight enough to break it. He eased up. Instead, he crushed his teeth together. He closed his eyes. No tears. No time for that now.

"You're sure it's Page?"

"I'm sure. He has the resources to make this whole thing go away, you know he does."

"Make it go away as far as the law is concerned, you mean."

"I'm not the law," Hutch said. "I can do things they can't. But not if they're all over me, not if they detain me. I need to be free to move."

"Since you didn't know about Logan, that means Page hasn't contacted you. You need to call him."

"I did. He wouldn't talk to me."

"That doesn't make any sense. What is he doing?"

Another vehicle pulled up behind him and honked. Hutch applied some gas. He turned into a stall. He said, "He might still be trying to scare me, but I think he knows it's gone beyond that."

"What do you mean, gone beyond that? That you won't let it go? But you will, Hutch. For your son, you will."

"Yeah, I would. But I don't believe he thinks that. Maybe I'm wrong. Maybe he's just waiting until he gets an exchange arranged."

"You're thinking he's going to set you up?"

"Or get to me without having to risk my getting close to Logan. Or him."

"Kill you now? But he's got your son!"

"You have to know the way the guy thinks."

Larry didn't say anything. Finally, he said, "If you're right, you have to bring the feds in on this. Don't go it alone."

"Larry, if he gets me, then you can call the FBI, okay? It won't matter then."

"Hutch, this is . . . this is . . ."

"A little scarier than Matt Damon's latest?"

"You're joking? How can you joke? But as a matter of fact, it is. So what are you going to do, stroll into the airport and catch a flight home? You can't do that."

"I have no choice. I'll be on the lookout, but I have to trust that he won't do anything here. Maybe he hasn't had time."

"He's a billionaire. Time doesn't work the same way for people like that."

"He's human. Sort of. So are the people he hires. You can't buy god-like powers."

"Tell that to a billionaire."

Hutch sighed. "When I get there, I'll play it smart. Right now, I'm on a blitz."

Larry paused. "What can I do?"

"Go back to your office. Wait by the phone. When she calls, tell her you have to call her back from a pay phone. When you get her again, give her my number. In case she can't reach me, tell her I'll meet her where we had lunch yesterday."

"Hutch, I want to help," Larry said. "There must be something else I can do?"

"Yeah. Pray."

THIRTY-EIGHT

"Do you like my dad?"

Laura glanced over at Macie, sitting in the passenger seat. They had skirted the north side of Denver on I-70 and were quickly approaching the airport. Laura had no way of knowing when Hutch would be coming in. She assumed he'd find a way back from Seattle before his scheduled flight tomorrow. She'd called his mobile phone three times so far, with no luck. Had to be he'd lost it. It was about midnight. No way he could have arrived yet, but she'd rather play it safe. If she missed him at the airport, she had no idea what to do next.

She said, "'Course I do, sweetie."

"I mean do you *like* him?" She showed Laura a sly grin.

It was nice to see her smiling. Most of the ride down from the mountains, she'd moped and asked about Logan: *Why did they take him? Do you think he's okay? Are they feeding him? Can he go to the bathroom?*

To this last question, Laura had made a scary face and said, "I hope so, don't you? Either that or get him a diaper."

Macie had almost laughed then. Almost.

"Well . . ." Laura thought about it. Certainly Hutch occupied a special place in her heart, more than what her dad used to call a "drinking buddy"—meaning a friend you can laugh with, but not count on. She suspected some of her feelings stemmed from Hutch's having taken care of Dillon when she wasn't able to; from Dillon's strong love for him; for the traumatic experience all of them had shared. But then there were the *hours* on the phone during the first few months after he'd returned home. She shook her head—she couldn't think that way! Her life with Tom was still too fresh in her memory for her to allow anybody else in.

She continued: "I do care for him, and it feels like I know him really well. But you know, we haven't spent that much time together. It's hard to like somebody *that* way, just chatting on the phone."

"I think he likes you that way," Macie said.

"Really?"

They drove on for a while. A sign instructed airport-bound vehicles to use the left lanes and exit on Pena Boulevard. She signaled and drifted over.

"You know where you're going?" Macie asked.

"Just following the signs."

"In the airport. Do you know how to find him? My mom and Logan and me used to come get him sometimes when he came back from trips. You can't go to the gate anymore, you know. I don't remember ever going to the gate, but Mom said you used to be able to. Now you have to wait where the trains drop off all the passengers from all the flights, at the top of the escalators. I don't like it."

"Why not?"

The child should have been exhausted, but she seemed to be perking up. Laura thought her talking was a good sign, the way being hungry was after a bout of the flu.

"Too many people waiting and too many people coming from the trains. We missed him a couple times. But that was when he wasn't expecting us, and we wanted to surprise him. He's going to be mad about the windshield."

"I think he'll understand." A warmth went from Laura's stomach up into her chest, and she recognized it as happiness—or at least anticipation—at the prospect of reuniting with Hutch. They passed signs listing airlines and on which side of the airport each was located, east or west.

Macie said, "Do you know what, uh, plane company . . . ?"

"Airline? No," Laura said. "He's not going to be easy to find."

"You can call him on the, you know, speaker." Macie pointed at the ceiling.

"Page him?" Laura said, impressed. "That's a good idea. But since we don't know *when* he's going to come in, that might mean making a lot of calls to the people who do the paging. And who knows, maybe after a while they'll say we can't page anymore."

Macie frowned and nodded. "Then how?"

"I've been thinking. What if we find his car? We know what it looks like, and we have some time. We can go up and down all the aisles until—"

"Turn here!" Macie yelled, pointing.

Her excited voice was a poke at Laura's adrenal gland. Her heart kicked into overdrive and she slammed on the brakes. The SUV skidded, tires smoking. She heard and felt Dillon fly off the rear bench into hers and Macie's seat backs. A second later, she released the brake and eased to the side of the road.

"Dillon, are you all right?" She snapped off her seat belt and spun around.

Dillon moaned. He appeared in the space between the seats, holding his forehead. "What happened?"

"I'm sorry," Laura said. "I got a little startled." She turned to Macie. "What is it?"

The girl smiled guiltily. "You said we needed to find his car." She pointed at a sign indicating an off-airport parking and shuttle service. The lot itself was beyond a hill, out of sight. "He always parks over there."

"But, honey," Laura said, "the airport is still miles away."

"He says it's easier to get in and out, and it's cheaper. When we went to Disney World and to Connecticut to see Grandma, that's where we parked."

Laura smiled. She patted Macie on the knee. "Good job, Macie. You just saved us hours."

"Yeah, good job, Macie," Dillon said, giving her an exaggerated scowl. He was still rubbing his head.

Macie stifled a laugh. "Sorry."

"Really, Dillon," Laura said. "How's your head? Anything else hurt?"

"I'm all right." He climbed back onto the bench, sitting this time. He started to massage his knee. "I was dreaming."

"Something nice?"

He frowned, shook his head.

"Then good thing you woke up!" Macie said.

Leave it to an eight-year-old girl.

Dillon thought of something. He turned in his seat and rose onto his knees. Looking back into the cargo area, he said, "Michael's still sleeping. Maybe you hit him too hard."

"Is he breathing?" Laura said.

"Yeah."

"Put your seat belt on." She steered the XTerra into the parking lot's entrance. She took a stub, rolled forward, looked around. She said, "It's huge. Is there any place your dad liked to park, someplace special?"

Macie shrugged.

Rows of cars marched away from them in both directions. They were idling in a road that ran perpendicular to the rows of cars. A bus emerged from an aisle onto this road and headed for them. Laura pulled ahead farther, into the aisle that was straight ahead of them. The bus roared past their rear bumper. She watched it go to a far corner and turn out toward the busy street that serviced the airport.

"The exit must be over there," she said, more to herself than the kids. She clapped her hands. "Okay, Macie, Dillon, I need your help. We're looking for a Honda Civic."

"Accord," Macie said. "2001 LX. Silver."

Laura said, "Guys, I know it's dark and they don't have enough lights . . . some though, right? Enough to kind of see all the cars."

"The *shapes* of them," Dillon said.

"Just keep your eyes out for a silver Honda. A four-door. We can do this."

"I can't tell what's silver," Dillon said. "Is that one silver?"

She looked at the car he meant. "Yeah . . . or gold, maybe brown."

"Looks yellow to me," Macie said.

Laura let out a tired breath. "If I see the kind of car he drives, I'll point it out, then you can look for ones like it. Think that'll work?"

"You can look for a flip-flop in the window," Macie said.

"A what?" Dillon said.

"A flip-flop, like you wear to the beach. It's pink and white, but I don't think we'd see that."

"Why is there a flip-flop in the window, sweetie?" Laura asked.

"There's a lot of cars that look like Dad's at my school. Dad put the flip-flop right here, so we can find him easier in the carpool lane." She stretched out against the seat belt and touched the top part of the dash by the corner of the windshield. "Before, we had to look in all the cars that looked like his. Logan said it was stupid."

"The flip-flop?" Dillon asked.

"No, looking in all the cars. He likes the flip-flop. He told Mom about it, and she put a little teddy bear in *her* window."

"Smart," Laura said. "So look for the flip-flop."

"Except when it's not there," Macie said. "Sometimes he takes it down when he's not coming to school."

Dillon flopped back in his seat, lifting his hands, like *So much for that!*

"All right," Laura said. She reminded them what they were looking for: a silver car that may look gold or brown or yellow. A four-door Honda Accord, which may or may not have a flip-flop on the dash.

"Got it," Dillon said. "Start driving, already."

Laura said, "Let's start on the far end over there and work our way toward the exit." She backed into the perpendicular lane and headed for the farthest aisle.

THIRTY-NINE

At O'Hare, Hutch let his guard down a bit. He was still keyed up over Logan's kidnapping—probably more so, now that he'd had three hours on a plane to stew. But he couldn't imagine Page's men figuring out the exact flight he'd taken, not this soon.

He hadn't considered it before, but Janet purchasing the ticket for him might have been a wise strategy. Even before the divorce was final, she had legally readopted her maiden name, Brooks. The chances were high that Page had access to credit card databases, but not to airport systems, because of tightened homeland security rules. Hutch didn't think financial transaction records listed specifics like flight times; but if they did, Page wouldn't find Hutch, except on a flight leaving Seattle the next day.

He found his connecting gate and paced among the chairs. He sat, then immediately stood again. He imagined how different things would be if he had picked up Page's lacquered cigar box in his office and brained him with it. The clarity of hindsight could drive you crazy.

He pulled out the phone, dialed Larry. He was there, at his office desk. Laura hadn't called again. Larry wanted to talk. Hutch didn't. He slipped the phone back in his pocket.

He forced himself to sit, slumping low. He thought about Logan, what he was going through at that moment. He wished with bone-aching sincerity that Larry had misunderstood Laura's words. He knew Larry had got it right, but for a few seconds, it was a balm on his nerves to think of his son asleep in bed.

Since his children were babies, Hutch would go into their rooms at night, when they were in deep slumber. He would brush their hair with his fingers and gently sing a lullaby. Every night they had been in his house, without fail, he had performed this ritual.

By lying about his parenting behavior—and thanks to his own unfortunate outburst in court—Janet had secured sole custody of Logan and Macie for more than ten months. During that time, Hutch had sung to his children alone before sleep. More than anything else Janet had done—more than the affair, the lying, the snippiness, the sapping of his bank account—more than any of it, he hated her for taking his kids away.

And yet, since winning joint custody nine months ago, he'd spent more time "with" Page than he had with his kids. He had mapped Page's suspected misdeeds, interviewed people with bad things to say about the man, and dug through public records, looking for Page Industries improprieties. All of these had extended long after what some people called "normal working hours." He'd chosen to spend his time this way, rather than taking Macie and Logan bowling; rather than battling the evil Xbox villain, Dytar, with his boy; rather than playing with his little girl in her room and finding out why she preferred Matchbox cars to Barbie dolls.

Crashed now in the plastic airport chair, he lolled his head back as far as it would go. He did not hate himself for misallocating time. What he felt was worse: a deep disappointment. Not only had his preoccupation deprived Macie and Logan of his time, surely making them wonder why he'd fought for custody at all, but it had directly resulted in Logan's kidnapping. And in the possibility that the harm to them would not be limited to a traumatic experience for his son.

Harm. Traumatic experience. He was a writer, quick with a soft-pedaling euphemism and an editor's pen, even with his own thoughts. What he meant was that his insane obsession could result in the deaths of his children. As well as Laura and Dillon.

Even his lullaby ritual had become a sham. Tired from hunting Page, his mind not on his children, he had mumbled the songs and often ended early. His caress had gone from stroking their hair to touching their foreheads. What once might have taken ten minutes he had reduced to a thirty-second how-do-you-do.

His head came up. He blinked. Still no tears. He was more disgusted with himself than sad for his children.

Isn't that the problem? he thought. *More you than them.*

He thought of some names he had called people over the years, and applied them all to himself.

I'm working on it. I am.

Really? What are you doing?

He lowered his face to his palms. He had caused this. He had gone on a safari and wounded a lion. The beast had circled around to his camp and attacked his children. He had to make it right. Whatever it took. He would give Page what he wanted: every scrap of paper he had accumulated about the man, every note, digital file, phone number.

If it would get his son back, he'd lie prostrate on the floor of Page's office and beg, weep, promise anything. If he never heard Page's name again, he'd not miss a thing. Page had won. He'd struck at Hutch's heel and hit his heart.

He pulled out the mobile phone and dialed Page's number. The operator put him on hold. Page's assistant came on.

"This is Mrs.—"

"Tell him he won," Hutch said. "Tell him John Hutchinson says he won. I give up. I'm done. Whatever he wants . . . just . . . whatever he wants. You got that?"

"Sir, I—"

"Did you hear me or not?"

"Yes, but—"

"And you tell him I want what's mine. That's the deal." He recited the clerk's mobile phone number and listened to the woman repeat it. He hung up. He breathed in deeply, pushed it out.

Hutch looked at his watch. His plane left in two hours. He stood and stretched. He felt good. He'd taken a scalpel to his insides. He'd gouged and prodded. And it hurt like hell. But he considered it necessary, cathartic. He had attacked not the healthy tissue of his soul, but the cancer, the stuff that shouldn't be there.

A phrase kept repeating in his mind. It could have been a condemnation of his present state, but he saw it as a challenge. It made him believe he could be a better father. There was hope for him yet.

Work harder, he thought. *Work harder.*

FORTY

"There," Dillon said.

"Looks like it," Laura said, but she was hardly enthusiastic. They had given closer inspection to dozens of cars—felt like hundreds: stop, clamber out, look, climb in, go. If *go* was what you would call the slow, not-even-registering-on-the-speedometer pace Laura moved at, to make sure they took in every car on either side of each aisle.

Always, there had been something that disqualified the car as Hutch's: a broken window, an out-of-state plate, a BAD AS I WANNA BE bumper sticker. Macie had remembered that Logan had clipped his bicycle handlebars against the door, leaving a distinctive straw-sized scratch above the door handle. That had ruled out several candidates.

They had traversed a little more than half the aisles. Several people had given them long, suspicious looks. Laura was beginning to think they wouldn't find Hutch's car in that lot. But the prospect of continuing the search in the airport's many other garages and lots made her want to give up. If she monitored the passengers arriving in Terminal East, and Dillon did the same in Terminal West, the odds were in their favor that they'd spot him. But considering the stakes, she didn't want any odds; she wanted a sure thing. And that meant finding his car.

"Go look," she told Dillon.

He hopped out, ran to the Honda that to Laura looked older than the one she'd remembered Hutch driving away in the day before.

A sedan with a flashing amber light on top stopped at the end of the aisle. The driver stepped out. He was dressed like a cop, but Laura didn't see a holster. Security guard. His skin was so dark, it blended in with the night. He pushed his hat back on his head, hiked up his pants, and started walking toward them.

"Uh-oh," Macie said.

"No worries," Laura assured her.

"No," Dillon said. He was halfway back to the SUV when he spotted the guard. He froze.

"Come on, baby," Laura said. "Get back in."

The guard stepped up to her window. A hundred wrinkles furled his face. His eyebrows were bushy and mostly white.

"Evening," she said.

"Morning," he replied. "Can't help but notice you been cruising the aisles, checking out cars."

"We're looking for my husband's car," Laura said. "He left his briefcase in the backseat. He needs it for a morning meeting."

"How you going to get it to him?"

"Fax. You know, the important stuff."

The guard looked past her at Macie and Dillon. "You know it's past one in the morning?"

"Gotta do what you gotta do," she said.

"You have a key? To your husband's car?"

"Yes, sir."

"May I see it, please?"

"Oh, you mean on me? No, it's, uh, you know, in a little thing under the bumper."

"What's the license plate number?"

"S . . . A . . ." She laughed. "I don't know. It's *his* car. Do you know yours?"

The driver thought for a moment. A big smile pushed up his cheeks. "It's got a number one and an *L* in it." He slapped his hand on the sill. "All right, ma'am. Just let the lady in the checkout booth know when you find it. We'll record the license plate. Just in case there's a problem. And I'm going to get yours right now—and your driver's license." He held out his hand.

She looked around her, into the footwells. She said, "This isn't looking good for me. I ran out of the house without my purse." And that was true.

The security guard made a face. He peered around, thinking. Laura knew he was about to boot them out of the lot.

"My daddy's getting a new job," Macie said.

"Zat so?" the guard said. The loose skin on his face seemed to move and flow on its own. It dipped into a frown before congregating in his cheeks to form a smile.

Macie bobbed her head up and down, showing all her teeth. The two on either side of her eyeteeth were missing, giving her a bit of rabbit DNA. "Then we can move out of Nana's house and get our *own* apartment."

"Oh, sweetie," Laura said. "That's family stuff." To the guard she said, "I'm sorry."

He was smiling at Macie. "It's okay, I understand. Like you said, you do what you gotta do." He reached out his hand to Laura, startling her. "Name's Charlie."

They shook.

"You need anything while you're looking, flag me down."

"Thank you. I will."

He walked to the front of the XTerra, pulled out a notepad, and jotted down the plate number. He waved, strolled to his car, and drove away.

Laura glared at Macie in disbelief. "Where did *that* come from?"

The girl shrugged. "Jenna Robinson, in my class. She got out of all kinds of homework when her dad lost his job." She lowered her head. "I shouldn't have lied."

Laura patted her leg. "I did it too, sweetheart. It's all right, this time."

Macie grinned.

Fifteen minutes later, they rolled to the next aisle.

Dillon said, "There's one." He hopped out without waiting for the SUV to stop.

Laura glanced at it. Easy to tell it was a Honda. It had been backed in, so the grille with its center logo faced the aisle. But no flip-flop resided on the dash, and it appeared copper-colored to her. Dillon's yelling startled her from a state of bored drowsiness. He was jumping up and down, pointing.

"There's a flip-flop in the front seat!" he said.

She put the XTerra in gear and climbed out. Up close, the brownish hue faded, and it was clearly silver. The scratch from Logan's bicycle was right where Macie said it would be. She held up her palm to Dillon, and he high-fived her.

Hutch's car hunkered about ten vehicles from the end of the row, farthest from the entrances and exit. On one side of the Honda, closer to the center, was a Corvette; a minivan occupied the space on the other side.

She pointed over the 'Vette's roof. "Let's find a spot over that way, so we can see it better."

As they returned to the SUV, she scanned the area. A sign attached to a light pole showed a silhouette of a bighorn sheep and defined the section as S14. A shelter for customers waiting for a shuttle fronted the aisle a few spaces beyond the 'Vette. She could see another shelter way down near the other end. Most of the spaces were filled.

If we have to, she thought, tired of the hurdles, *we'll* push *a car out of the space we need.*

FORTY-ONE

"Don't park yet," Dillon said. "Now that we know where Hutch's car is, can we get some food? I'm starving." He held his stomach dramatically.

"Me too," Macie said.

"It's been awhile since we ate," Laura said. "And I could use a bathroom."

Macie nodded.

"I'm all right," Dillon said. He'd relieved himself earlier between the cars. "It's like being in a metal forest," he'd said.

"There's a McD's way over there," Macie said. "The sign's lit up, so I think it's open."

Laura could see it. Not far, but the way things were going, Hutch would show up while they were gone. It was too far to send Dillon, and the traffic around here made her head spin. Between their stomachs and their bladders, they had to do something. She threw an arm over the seat back to see Dillon.

"What do you think about staying here while Macie and I make a food run?" she said.

"I can do that," her son said, naturally.

The kid would babysit lions in their den if she asked him to. It wasn't that he was blindly obedient. His willingness to do whatever the world required of them was rooted in his trying to be the man of the house, now that his father was gone. He'd never spoken about it, but Laura knew.

"You'd have to hide among the cars, okay? Don't go near the Honda unless you see Hutch. And don't talk to anyone. Not even that security guard, got it?"

He gave her a thumbs-up and hopped out.

She rolled down her window. "It's nippy. Want your gloves?"

He skewed his mouth sideways. "Mom, we live in northern Canada."

She nodded. "What do you want to eat?"

"What do they have?"

The closest Fiddler Falls came to a fast-food restaurant was the Elder Elk Diner. Lars and Barb Jergins flipped a mean caribou burger, with steak fries and a side of homemade soapberry ice cream—all in under ten minutes. The few times Tom or Laura had taken the boy to Wollaston or Saskatoon, they had dined at a friend's establishment, one of those mom-and-pop, old-fashioned places, not so different from the Elder Elk.

Macie said, "You've never eaten at McDonald's?"

Dillon shrugged.

"Whoa," Macie said.

Laura didn't know if it was nobler to keep him pure or to treat him to something different. Finally she said, "Burgers."

"Okay."

She said, "Go hide, now."

He moved away. Before she realized it, he had disappeared from view. She squinted, tilted her head, and even pulled forward slowly, but saw not a flick of hair or flash of eyes. He did that on their walks in the woods. She marveled that he could duplicate the trick here.

"Where'd he go?" Macie said.

"Only the Shadow knows," Laura said in her spookiest voice. She took one last look, then pulled away.

When they returned, Laura found a trash can blocking a parking space. It was across the aisle from Hutch's, about a dozen spaces over. She slowed in front of it. Dillon materialized from nowhere, waved at her, and dragged the can to the shelter. Laura backed into the spot. The only way to get a clearer view of the Honda would be to sit in it. Knowing what Hutch was returning to—his son gone, killers after them—Laura thought the car appeared forlorn. The man who was coming to drive it would be sad and desperate. She wished their reunion could be happier.

As Dillon climbed into the backseat, he said, "A lady came and got her car. It looked like a good place."

"Perfect," Laura agreed.

"What's that smell?"

"Grease." She handed him a box that had been printed to look like a haunted house.

He reached in, pulled out a fry, and examined it.

"Just eat it," Macie said, watching him. She pushed five of her own fries into her mouth.

He did and nodded appreciatively.

The dashboard clock read 2:01. Grains of sand seemed to have slipped under Laura's eyelids. Each time she blinked, she found it harder to open her eyes. She took a bite of a double cheeseburger, felt as though she could barely chew it.

"I'm fading," she said. She nudged Macie. "You should be too."

Macie widened her eyes. "I'm okay." She yawned.

"I had a nap," Dillon said. "You guys sleep. I'll keep watch."

"You sure?" Laura said. He did look spunky.

He said to Macie, "Change places with me. You can lie down back here."

Her eyebrows came together.

Laura said, "Honey, that guy's tied up. He can't get anywhere near you."

Dillon leaned over his seat back, then returned. "Besides, he's still out."

Macie slipped between the seats. Dillon went the other way into the front passenger seat. He leaned over the seat and snagged his Happy Meal. Macie was already sprawled on the bench, eyes closed.

Laura brushed Dillon's hair away from his face. "You doing okay?"

He nodded.

She reclined her seat back and slouched down into it. Her eyes closed. "Wake me if you see anything."

"Don't worry," he said. He looked at the blood on his finger, then smeared it with his thumb. He pressed his lips together, not upset at all that he'd put an arrow in that guy. Not even a smidgen.

FORTY-TWO

Laura woke to Dillon shaking her shoulder. His face was close. Beyond him it was still dark. The gleam of a parking lot light caught his eyes: the blue sparkled in a sea of white. He looked frightened.

She rubbed her face. "What—?"

"Shhh," he said.

"What is it?" She began to sit up, but he pushed her down.

"Some men," he said. "They're checking out Hutch's car."

The skin on her arms and back of her neck tingled and tightened. She licked her lips. "Let me see."

"Stay low." He pulled back into the passenger seat. Slouched, Dillon's head breached the level of the dash only enough to let him see.

She put her hand on the console and pushed herself up. A man dressed in black stood in the aisle near the Honda. His hands were in his pockets and his back was to the car, casual, uninterested. His posture was canted enough away from the XTerra for Laura to believe he was not intentionally facing them. His head swiveled slowly around.

"I only see one," she whispered.

"The shelter."

A man-shaped shadow occupied an edge of the bench. His immobility more than his dark clothing had caused her to overlook him.

"They came from separate directions," Dillon said. "The one standing walked between the rows. He went right to Hutch's car and looked in all the windows. Then he stepped out to where he is now. The other one was more sneaky. He stayed low and weaved through the cars until he reached the shelter."

"You didn't see them looking for it?" she asked.

"A couple cars went by. They could have been in one."

"I think they're soldiers from the house," Laura said. "Same clothes."

"They aren't wearing helmets."

"They want to appear as normal as possible," she said. "Can't do that with futuristic helmets."

The men confirmed her suspicion that they wanted Hutch as well. Whatever had happened in Washington, Hutch had gotten away. He had tried to warn her, but the people after them had cut off their communication.

"What time is it?" she whispered.

He looked at his watch. "It's 3:41."

She'd slept two hours.

The man standing in the aisle rose onto his toes. He craned his neck to catch every direction, then he nodded.

Shadow Man glided off the bench, barely growing in height. Laura realized he was bending his knees, hunching his back. He carried a small duffel bag, which pulled down in the center under the weight of some heavy object within. He floated out of the shelter and drifted toward the back of the lot. He stopped in front of the Honda. Without pausing, he dropped to the blacktop and slid under the front of the car. The duffel bag went with him.

The man in the aisle backed closer to his partner. He turned his head and raised his hand to his mouth.

"I think he's talking," Dillon said.

The man's head snapped around. He crouched, touching his fingers to the pavement.

Laura followed his gaze. At the far end of the aisle, closest to the entrances, the white car with flashing amber lights cruised slowly past.

The man unfolded from his crouch.

The legs and boots protruding from under the Honda wiggled and squirmed, as though he were hard at work on the car's suspension.

"What's he doing?" Dillon asked.

"Nothing good."

Shadow Man slid out from under the car. He got his feet under him and semi-stood. The duffel bag was empty. He flattened and folded it and pushed it into his waistband behind him. He pulled something from a shirt pocket.

Laura thought it was a pack of cigarettes until a light on it illuminated, glowing red. He returned the device to his pocket. Nodding at the other man, he walked to the rear of the car and dropped out of sight. Where his upper torso and head had been, now only the red roof of the Corvette glimmered in the yellow glow of sodium vapor lamps.

The other man twisted his hips and kicked at pebbles. It was a completely relaxed gesture, designed to appear harmless. A minute after his partner had disappeared, he broke into a striding gait. It carried him across the aisle and into the row of cars in which the XTerra was parked.

Dillon tugged off his sneakers. "We have to know where they're hiding," he said, as if in one long word. He spun and opened his door.

"Wait!" Laura said, low and harsh. She slapped her hand over the dome light. "Dillon, no!"

He closed the door softly. It clicked, and the interior light blinked out.

"Dillon!" She scrambled over the console and opened his door. The light came on again, and she didn't care. "Dillon!" she whispered.

He had faded into the shadows of the cars.

FORTY-THREE

Dillon immediately moved toward the rear of the XTerra. He peered around the bumper, between the rows of cars. He crossed to the next car and quickly moved along its length. He stopped at the next aisle. He, Mom, and Macie had not gone down it, because they'd found Hutch's car first. He saw no one. The man must have been walking faster than Dillon thought. He paused to study the car windows. No lights, no head-shaped silhouettes.

He was about to bolt across the aisle when the sound of a shoe scuffing against the pavement made his heart leap into his throat. He ducked and edged his vision past the bumper. A dark figure three cars away peeled itself away from the shadows and stepped into the aisle.

The man had stopped. Waited. Had he heard Dillon leave the car or shuffle over the blacktop? Dillon thought he'd been more than quiet;

he'd been truly silent. He was accustomed to moving over a forest's groundcover, with its twigs and leaves and needles—essentially, a blanket of noisemakers—without alerting keen-eared animals. Surely he could handle flat pavement.

But the most dangerous aspect of this new terrain was precisely that it was new to him. His father had taught him that every terrain, every environment presented its own challenges. *Unless you've spent hours living with it*, he'd said, *don't think you understand how it will respond to your presence.*

So Dillon knew better than to think that simply because he knew how to move with stealth through a forest, he could do it here. He had no clue which seemingly harmless things could trip him up. Did gravel have a way of sticking to socks, only to click against the asphalt as he ran? Would it come off his socks and clink into the side of a car? How much pressure could he put on the metal all around him without it creaking under his weight? Could he peer through automotive glass without a thousand reflections transmitting his image to the person he was hiding from?

He had figured out a few things while waiting for his mother and Macie to return with the food: the blacktop was cracked in places, usually at the margins of the aisles, between driveway and parking space; some of these cracks were inch-high toe catchers; headlights could sweep across your hiding spot at any time; and it was never safe to touch a mirror because too many of them were loose and rattled. Even so, there were too many things he *didn't* know.

The man slipped between two cars.

Dillon crossed the aisle. He was moving parallel to the man, about forty feet behind him. He looked under the cars. He saw the shifting shadows that were the man's feet moving away, between the rows. Touching his fingertips to the metal to keep his balance, he sidled to the bumper of the car. He poked his head into the row. The man was walking away from him, twisting sideways when two cars had parked too close together. Near the back end of the row, the man turned in between two cars. Dillon heard a door open. A front bumper rocked. The door closed.

He heard a soft sound, like clothes rubbing together, and turned his head. A dozen cars away, the other man was duckwalking directly at Dillon.

The man had circled around, for whatever reason: Maybe the two men avoided being seen together—more suspicious in a place like this. Or he had hung back to catch anyone tracking or spying on his partner.

Dillon fought the urge to jump up and run. Instead he pulled his head back. Surely if the guy had seen him, he wouldn't have continued duckwalking. He'd have made an all-out sprint for Dillon.

The man drew closer.

Dillon put his palms on the asphalt and walked his legs out from under him. When he was lying flat, he rolled to the car closest to the approaching man. He went a little farther, so he was lying between the car's right-hand tires. He watched the man come.

The guy's moves were apelike—his knees bent, his hands touching the ground now and then to maintain balance and help his speed. He passed in front of the car under which Dillon lay. He paused at the space between cars, where Dillon had been. Three seconds, then he started moving again.

Dillon waited. When he heard a door open and close, he rolled out from the car. He squatted at the opening to the row and eyed the vehicle the first man had entered. An interior light went on, and Dillon could see both men. Neither was much older than Michael, Dillon thought. They were examining something between them. One of them kept looking toward the back of the van. Dillon wondered why. His breath jammed in his throat.

Logan!

If these were the men from the house, they were the ones who'd taken Logan. Could he still be with them? Macie had cried over her brother for most of the day. She'd made him consider what his new friend, Hutch's son, was going through. It made him sad and scared and, more than anything, angry.

Dillon crossed the row and stopped at the next aisle. The vehicle was pulled in with its rear to the aisle, its windshield facing Hutch's Honda across three rows of cars. That meant the safest approach was from the aisle behind it. He began moving toward it. He crouched, but kept his eyes high enough to see the lighted passenger-side window. The rear windows came into view. They were small, set high in each of two doors. No other windows, except at the front. If Dillon wanted to sneak a peek, it'd have to be through the back.

When he was three cars away, the interior light flicked out. He braced himself to dive under the car should the doors open. He was behind a Volkswagen bug. He wasn't sure he could fit under it. Staying low, he took a step back, then another. He was at the corner of the bug now. He figured he could jump down between cars if he had to. Looking through the VW's windows, he watched the van. It rocked a bit, as though someone were moving around inside.

When, after five minutes, no one came out or showed himself in a window that Dillon could see, he crept forward. He made himself crouch lower as he drew nearer. He stopped behind the car parked beside it, a small, sporty thing. Good thing the van didn't have side windows in the rear. Anyone inside would have been able to stare down on him.

He went to all fours and peered into the space between the van and the sports car. The bad guy's side mirror stared at him like a lizard's eye. No face reflected there. One may have been hidden by the darkness inside, or no one was in the passenger seat. Big difference.

Slowly he moved forward, hands and knees. When he was the most exposed, positioned perfectly in the space between vehicles, he shuffled quicker. He stopped behind the van and sat, touching his back to the bumper, but only lightly.

Okay. Hop up, take a look.

The driver's door opened.

Dillon's heart stopped. At least it felt that way. His whole body turned to marble: lungs, thoughts. His skin felt stiff and crackly.

At the driver's door, a foot came down onto the blacktop. The other joined it. The van rocked down and came back up. Whoever stood there snorted up snot and hawked it out. Dillon heard a zipper, then a splattering flow, hitting the car next to the van on that side. It made a hollow, metallic sound, then stuttered to silence. The zipper again. The man sighed loudly. The van rocked. The door shut.

Dillon pulled in a breath. His vision blurred. He was dizzy, lightheaded. He closed his eyes and sucked in little bites of air. After a time he felt better. He realized he had to pee as well. Bad. Maybe it had been the scare or the suggestion, but if he didn't relieve himself, he would go in his pants.

It'll pass, he told himself. Like in school. It gave him a sour stomach to even think about drawing attention to his need for relief, so he always held it. Half the time, when a break came, he'd forgotten he had to go so bad.

He turned and rose up onto his knees. He put his hands on the bumper and looked up at the windows. They were too high for him to simply stand and peek through. But if he stepped on the bumper . . . Did he weigh enough to cause the van to shift? Ninety pounds. That sounded like a *lot* of weight at that moment. Would the men inside feel the movement? Would they think it was Logan—if Logan was in there and able to move?

An alarm went off: a loud *beep-beep-beep*. His watch! Every morning it went off at four. He slapped his hand over it, pushed the button that silenced the alarm. He listened: no noises from inside. No movements he could feel. It had not been so loud. It had only sounded like it to him.

He thought, *What if it had gone off when the man was outside the van?* and felt dizzy again.

He shifted his gaze back up to the rear windows. He couldn't do it. He did not have enough courage to step on the bumper and look in.

Baby!

I can't. I just can't.

He imagined stepping up, panicking, and grabbing hold of the van as though it were his mother. The guys inside would come out and pull him off. They would toss him in the back with Logan, and that would be that. His mom would go crazy, probably come looking for him, and they would get *her*.

Besides, the interior was probably too dark to see anything. They likely had Logan tied up or drugged, or he was sleeping. Dillon would have risked everything for nothing.

He squeezed his eyes shut and lowered his head. Was he talking himself out of looking through the window because he was scared? Or was he being smart, cautious? His father used to look at it from the other angle: *when is bravery just plain stupidity?*

It was true that his weight on the bumper might alert the men to his presence and that he might not be able to see Logan inside anyway. And what did he stand to gain? If he saw Logan inside, he'd know for sure. If he didn't, then Logan might or might not be in there. If he could tell Hutch without a doubt that Logan was there, he knew Hutch would tear through those guys inside like a hurricane with teeth. He might do it anyway, just for the *chance* of rescuing his son. Dillon believed Hutch would do it for *him*.

Bravery or stupidity?

Gotta know the difference.

Dillon pressed his hand against one of the rear doors.

Logan, are you in there? Hang in there, friend. We'll get you. Your dad will.

He turned and crawled away. He expected to hear the doors opening, voices yelling for him to stop. But nothing happened. He crawled past six cars, then turned in toward the XTerra.

FORTY-FOUR

"Don't you ever do that again! Do you hear me?" Laura yelled into Dillon's wide-eyed face. She yelled in *attitude*, not in volume: Dillon had told her the men they had seen were close.

In the backseat Macie groaned. She sat up, still mostly asleep.

"I'm sorry," Dillon said. "I just thought—"

"No! You don't think! You're a child. This isn't a game. Those men mean to kill us, all of us!" Laura closed her eyes, and tears spilled out. Her breath came in sputtering hitches.

"I'm sorry . . . Mom?"

She felt Dillon's hand on her arm.

She looked at him. The entire time he'd been gone, she had imagined him getting shot, stabbed, strangled. The only thing that had kept her in the car was the fear that her going after him would be the very thing that would draw attention to him and get him killed. He looked at her now with those puppy-dog eyes, that sweet, expressive mouth. She wrapped her arms around him, pulled him close.

"What's going on?" Macie said.

Laura disentangled herself from Dillon. She held her hand to his face, taking it in, relishing his being alive. She turned in the seat. "Macie, did you get some sleep?"

The girl rubbed her eyes. "Yeah."

Laura frowned at her. "You know those guys from the house, the soldiers? They're here."

"Why?"

"They did something to your dad's car. I think they're waiting for him too."

"What'd they do to it?"

Laura looked at Dillon. "I'm afraid to guess."

Macie came fully awake. "What?"

"That guy had something in the duffel bag," Dillon said. "He went under the car with it, and came out without it. There's only one thing it could be."

Laura peered through the window at the Honda. She turned her head, as if following a line, toward the van. "They can see Hutch's car from where they are?"

"It's a clear shot over the roofs of other cars."

She knew Dillon was right: it had to be a bomb. It was the cigarette pack–sized device, the one with the red light, that bothered her more. There was something about their *looking* right at Hutch when they activated it . . .

"Okay," she said. She found Macie's eyes with her own. "This is tough stuff, but I don't know how to make it better without your hearing. Think you can handle it?"

Macie was silent for a long moment. Then she nodded. "If it'll help save Dad and get Logan back, I can handle it."

"Dillon," Laura said, "do you think Logan is in the van?"

"I don't know," he said. "I couldn't look inside."

While she talked, she looked at Dillon, throwing glances at Macie, but her words were really meant for herself. She was getting it out and reeling it back in, organizing it.

"Here's what we know: Some people—probably Brendan Page's people—attacked us and took Logan. They tried to kill us. Hutch called to warn us, but something cut him off. We don't know what happened after that on his end. We have to assume he's coming home, because he knows we need help. We don't have any way to reach him, so we're here at the airport parking lot, waiting for him. Other men—probably the same people who attacked us—are here too. They may or may not have Logan with them. They put something—probably a bomb—under Hutch's car. Have I got it all?"

"We have one of the soldiers who attacked us tied up in the back of our car," Dillon said.

Laura nodded. "We think he wants to get away from his . . . employers." Her eyes grew big. "He's really got some issues."

"So," Dillon said, "take away all the *probably*s, and I think that's it."

To make the girl feel part of it all, Laura looked at her. "Macie?"

"I want Logan back," she said. "I want my dad, and he has to stay away from his car."

Has to stay away from his car . . . Didn't everything boil down to that? At least right now. Logan was next, but they needed Hutch back alive.

"So we watch for Hutch," Laura said. "We make sure he stays away from his car."

"How are we supposed to do that?" Dillon said.

"When we see him, we yell and scream and get him into the XTerra.

Then we drive away before the bad guys get us." She held her palms out, as if to say, *See? Simple as that.*

Dillon squinted at her.

She knew that look: he was assessing whether or not she was serious.

Slowly, as if talking to a child, he said, "He could come from behind the car and we wouldn't see him until he was in it, or so close to it that it wouldn't matter. But if we get closer to the car, so he sees us sooner, those guys watching will spot us."

Laura thought about it. "We have to get to him before he reaches the car. How do we do that?"

"The airport," Marcie said. "Stop him there."

Laura's nod turned into a shake. "We don't know what airline he's using. We don't know when he's coming. Do we wait in the East Terminal or the West? There are too many ways to miss him at the airport. That's why we came here in the first place."

She turned from Macie to Dillon, hoping one of them would some-how pull a magical solution out of the air. They gave her blank stares.

Macie said, "You have to stop him. Please."

"Mom," Dillon said, "why don't two of us go to the airport, one for each terminal. The other can stay here."

"No," she said immediately. "No way. Doing that would put one of you out in the open, alone. I can't risk that."

"But we don't have any choice," Macie said.

"I have a choice about putting you guys in more danger or not." She looked between them. "I choose not."

They were silent for a while. Laura wondered if the kids felt the sense of claustrophobia that she did—like all the bad in the world was swirling around them, pressing in. The XTerra was a bubble, tempo-rarily keeping them safe, but she felt the air pressure changing outside. It was building, threatening to crush them.

Dillon said, "We can't let Hutch get to his car."

She squeezed her eyes closed. Despite the bad guys and what was probably a bomb in Hutch's car, she felt the airport was even more dangerous. At least here, they could hunker down, stay out of sight. She hated Page for putting her in this position. "I'll go," she said. "*I'll* watch for him at the airport. You guys stay here. If you see him, stop him. Yell and scream, but don't go near the Honda, you hear? Get him in the XTerra and get out of here fast."

Their faces were twin expressions of hopelessness.

Laura said, "It's not perfect, but it is what it is." She took a deep breath.

It hurt, leaving them, but waiting wouldn't help and could be a terrible mistake, if she missed Hutch.

"I better get going. If Hutch rushed to the airport as soon as he called to warn us, he could be here anytime now. I'll get to one of the shelters on the other side of the lot and wait for the shuttle there."

"Stay low," Dillon said. "Don't let the bad guys see you. They know what we look like." His eyes followed the path she would take. "You should probably crawl. Or do what that guy did, duckwalk. Fast."

"You're the expert," Laura said.

"What about *him*?" Macie said, looking over the back of her seat. From her expression, she could have been watching an autopsy.

"Michael," Dillon said.

"When he wakes up, give him some food, but stay away from him."

"No problem there," Macie said.

Laura touched Dillon's neck. She kissed him. "You guys stay down too. Those men might decide to take a look around. And, Dillon, no matter what happens, don't be a hero, you understand?"

He smiled. "You too."

When Laura put her hand on the door handle, Dillon covered the dome light. She opened the door and slipped to the ground. Then she crawled back inside and tugged the door closed.

"I can't," she said. "I can't leave you here. Not with . . . them." She squinted through the side window toward the van. Macie's face rose into her field of vision.

"Please," the little girl said. "You said those men are watching my dad's car. They don't know we're here. We'll be quiet. Please." She seemed on the edge of tears.

"Mom," Dillon said, "if Hutch gets to his car . . ." He shot a glance at Macie.

Laura shook her head. "I hate this."

Dillon squeezed her hand. "We'll be okay."

Laura opened the door and forced herself to climb out. Everything told her to stay; everything except the part of her that wanted to stop Hutch before he showed up at his car. She gave them a final look, drawing courage from their sweet, frightened expressions, and pushed the door shut.

FORTY-FIVE

Laura followed Dillon's advice, crawling and duckwalking all the way to the end of the aisle. She stopped twice and almost returned to the XTerra. Then she remembered Macie's face, so much pain carved into her porcelain features. The lines would cut deep into the child's soul if they didn't reach Hutch in time. She thought of Dillon, how his resolve would slip away at night—as though it retired before the rest of him did—and he'd cry quietly in bed. She would often lie down with him, holding him and gently rocking him until he fell asleep. Who would do that for Macie? The question got her moving again.

Two cars and a bus passed on the cross street ahead of her, but no vehicles turned in. She saw no pedestrians until she herself became one, walking upright and purposeful. The cold night air raked itself over her arms and legs, cut through her thin blouse. Her breath plumed out in front of her. Soon enough she'd be on the shuttle, then in the airport.

For a few minutes she was alone in the shelter. She thought of Dillon and Macie hunkered down in the XTerra seats, peering over the dash at Hutch's Honda. As courageous as Dillon was, she knew he had to be scared. She hoped that Macie's presence helped him be brave. She was another person to help bear his burden, but also she was someone he could protect.

He was like Hutch that way; maybe he got it from Hutch: he was at his best when doing for others, especially when that doing entailed protecting. But the longer those children sat in the car, watching for Hutch, jumping at the slightest sound, the more frayed their nerves would become. She hoped that didn't translate into doing something foolish.

In her own frazzled state she imagined all those foolish things: returning for another shot at seeing Logan in the van; sneaking to Hutch's car to find out just what the heck it was those men had put under it; untying Michael for whatever reason. In her mind, none of those scenarios ended well.

What was she doing, leaving the kids alone? There were killers fewer than a hundred yards from them, a bomb closer than that.

Just stand up and walk back, she thought. *Well, walk, crouch, and crawl back.*

They could figure out another way to warn Hutch. But how? Nothing was sure. Even leaving the kids in the car and going to the airport wasn't sure, but it seemed the *most* sure of everything she could think of doing.

She could get both Dillon and Macie to watch the other side of the terminal. Then both of them would be in peril. And what if Hutch slipped them anyway? No one would be at the car for a final chance at keeping him away from the explosion.

They could leave a note or write something on the Honda. That would be an invitation for the bad guys to come get them. Besides, they could just remove the message, and it was a bomb, for crying out loud: they'd just set it off while Hutch was standing next to it, reading the message.

They could call the cops, but doing that with Logan in the bad guys' possession felt wrong. There could be a shoot-out, and Logan would be caught in the middle, maybe used as a shield. Or they could hurt him in retaliation.

She sat erect, clamped her hands in her lap, and closed her eyes. What they had decided to do was the best plan.

She put the phrase on a continuous loop in her head: *this is best, this is best. . . .*

A lady's heels clacked on the pavement, coming toward her. The low rumble of a wheeled suitcase joined the sound. It was a soundtrack to accompany the early-rising, hardworking traveler. The woman clacked her way through a pool of light. She was trim, well dressed, professional. Laura and she were from different planets.

Laura had never regretted the life she had, being a schoolteacher in a tiny, rugged town. She enjoyed being so intimate with nature and being part of a community small enough that everyone felt like family. But at that moment she would have given anything not to be herself, not to be the woman who had to decide between putting children in the path of killers and letting a good friend die.

The woman strode up to the shelter. Her smiled greeting changed to a puzzled frown as she took in Laura's bird's-nest hair and crawling-through-the-parking-lot knees.

Don't ever play poker, lady, Laura thought, forcing a tight smile. *You give away too many of your thoughts.*

Trying for nonchalance, Laura brought her hand to her hair. Yep, a bird's nest. She tugged out a few snarls before giving up. She'd buy a brush in the airport and clean up a bit. Not that she cared about appearances all that much, but looking the way she did would draw attention. She brushed her hands over her scraped and dirty knees.

"Hey!"

She looked up to see the security guard from earlier—Charlie, she remembered. He was scowling at her from his cruiser.

"Where are your kids?" he said.

"They, uh . . ." She pushed her bangs off her forehead, felt the tangles. "We couldn't find my husband's car, so I took them home and came back."

His eyebrows worked like agitated caterpillars as he thought it through. "You still haven't found it?"

She shook her head.

"Where's your car?"

She started to wave toward it, then gestured in the opposite direction. "Over there, somewhere. I figured I'd have a better chance to find it if I walked."

"Looks like you been crawling."

She smiled down at her knees. She shrugged. "A little."

"Where's your *coat*?"

She smiled at him. "With my purse."

"So what're you doing now? Taking the shuttle?"

"I thought I'd go get a coffee or something. Take a break."

He gestured with his head. "Why don't you hop in? I'll give you a ride."

She frowned.

He laughed. "You don't have to," he said. "I don't have the authority to *make* you. I'm just your average, everyday rent-a-cop. Don't even pack a gun."

She stood and absently brushed herself off. The woman with the clackity heels sat on the bench, eyeing Laura with what may have been disgust. Laura straightened her spine and walked around to the other side of the car. Charlie leaned over to open the door for her. She sat and immediately appreciated the car's warmth.

Charlie pushed a button to raise his window. He dropped the car into drive, and they pulled away from the shelter.

"So, the airport?" Charlie said.

"Yeah, anywhere's fine. Thanks."

He drove into the exit lane. The barrier arm went up as he approached. He waved at the woman in the booth. At that hour the traffic was light, allowing him to pull right out onto Pena Boulevard.

He glanced at Laura. He said, "You want to tell me what's really going on?"

She held her hands in her lap and watched her thumbs take turns rubbing each other. She shook her head.

He said, "If I go back there and cruise around a bit, am I going to find your car . . . and your kids?"

She snapped her face toward him. His eyes were sad.

She said, "It's a long story. If you could just . . . give us till morning, we'll get out of your hair."

"Honey, you got a husband what's beating on you, the kids? You trying to get away?"

She made her expression flat. All those wrinkles on his face. She thought each one could tell a story.

"I'm no dummy," he said. "I may not have the best job in the world, made a few wrong turns, but I been around enough to know what's what."

She didn't trust herself to say anything.

He continued: "'Member what we said before? You do what you

gotta do. You figure out what that is and get yourself outta my little corner of the universe. Not that I don't like having you, but it's no place to spend time, no place for kids. Or pretty ladies." He smiled.

His teeth were perfect.

"You get yourself away, go back to your family. Whoever said 'you can never go home again' didn't know nothing. He was probably a jerk, and nobody liked him. You're not a jerk, are you?"

"I don't think so."

"I don't either." He pulled to the curb in front of the Frontier Airlines counters. He tugged a wallet out of his back pocket. "You need a little gettin'-away money? I don't have much, but—"

She bit her lip, watching him finger through the bills. After getting gas and food, she had about a hundred left from the money she'd taken off Michael. She hoped Hutch would have some. She touched his arm. "No, thank you."

"You got a place to go?"

"We're working on it," she said.

"The kids, they eat lately? Going to be able to eat today?"

"Got that covered." She pulled her lower lip into her mouth. "About the kids . . ."

"Don't worry, they don't need some old stranger scaring them. And they gotta know their mom's handling things. That's important."

She wanted to tell him, *No, no, please check on them, sit with them, protect them.* But she realized his presence at the XTerra would most likely catch their pursuers' eye, and another brick from the kiln of good intentions would settle into the road to hell.

She said, "You're a good man, Charlie. I'm Laura, by the way."

"Nice to know you, Laura." His eyes turned to gaze through the windshield. "You know," he said, "been through my own hard times.

One thing I can say. They make life interesting, make fantastic stories to tell your grandkids." He smiled at her.

She nodded.

"Now," he said, "go make things right."

"I intend to." She gave him a firm nod and climbed out. He drove away slowly, those rotating amber lights looking to her like waving hands.

FORTY-SIX

It seemed that every airline had flights coming from Seattle. She went to the Frontier counter, hoping for information that would narrow the possibilities. Instead, the clerk told her that in addition to the direct flights, it was also a popular layover route: "The departure city could be listed as Cleveland, Houston, Dallas/Fort Worth, Ontario, Chicago, or LA," the clerk said. "It would help if you knew the airline."

As she had feared, the gates for the various Seattle-serving airlines were split between East Terminal and West Terminal, so passengers from the Emerald City would pour into two separate areas of the airport. Each terminal boasted its own baggage claim, elevators, exits, parking garages. There was no single place for Laura to observe all the travelers moving through the airport. Catching Hutch was pure hit-or-miss.

She picked up a white paging telephone. "I'd like to page John . . . no, make it for David Ryder." He was the friend whose quote Hutch kept on his office wall.

"To meet you, ma'am?" the male voice said.

"Yes. Which door is the farthest north?"

"What level?"

"Where do people catch shuttles to the off-airport parking lots?"

"Level five, same as baggage claim."

"That one then."

"In Terminal West, the northernmost door on that level is 502."

It was six thirty in the morning—still dark outside, but not for long. More people were in the airport than when she'd arrived forty minutes earlier. The attack on the house had occurred shortly after eight the night before. Laura could hardly believe they'd been on the run only ten hours. It felt like days.

She reached door number 502—stenciled within a red circle on the glass—without hearing the page she'd left for Hutch.

Come on, people. How difficult can it be?

She stepped close to the sliding door, and it opened. Another door lay beyond a sort of airlock. She walked to the outside door and stepped onto a wide sidewalk next to a drive where shuttles, limos, and taxicabs waited. The sidewalk ran the length of the building, about three hundred yards. She marched toward the far end. At the last door, she entered the terminal and went to the matching door on the east side of the terminal. Everything on that side of the building was a mirror image of the other side. Getting lost there would be a nightmare. Before she'd completed the first lap around the airport, she heard the page. Among a string of other names came, "Mr. Ryder, Mr. David Ryder, please pick up a white paging telephone."

Yes, Mr. Ryder, she thought. *Pick up the phone! Please!*

She crossed through the building and again exited through door 502. She turned left and headed for the other end. As she went, she gave a second's worth of scrutiny to each person she passed.

FORTY-SEVEN

"Look *that* way," Dillon said, pointing to their right, down the aisle.

"I was!" Macie snapped.

She was crouched in the passenger seat. Dillon was behind the steering wheel. He had his sneakers back on and pressed into the top edge of the seat. His knees were bent and pressing against the wheel.

She rotated her head back and forth, causing her ponytails to fly out from her head. She said, "I can turn my head sometimes, you know."

"I've got this side covered," Dillon said.

"Why do you get to watch the Honda, and I have to stare down toward nothing?" she whined. "It's *my* car."

"It's Hutch's."

"That makes it mine."

"Anyway," Dillon said, "he's going to come from that way, so you can see him first."

"Not unless he comes around." She waved her finger, illustrating her point. "He could go straight up the aisle from one of the entrances, like we did, then take the back road to this aisle and his car. Then you'd see him first."

"See? You said *his* car."

They'd been on the lookout for Hutch for over an hour. It wasn't easy work. When people appeared—either getting off a shuttle or walking from somewhere else in the lot—their hearts would jump, and they'd almost strain their eyes trying to identify Hutch in the darkness. The pools of light from streetlights, too few and far between, actually made it worse. Their eyes couldn't adjust to the night. Then there were the shadows, which seemed to always shift and move because of headlights from the main road to the airport. The vigil in general and the false alarms in specific were getting to both of them.

"*His* car because he drives it. It's my car too."

"He's not going to come from behind," Dillon said. He sighed. "If my mom doesn't find him at the airport, he'll take a shuttle. They've all been coming up the aisle from the front." He pointed. "*That* way."

"You think you're so smart," she said.

He shrugged.

"Logan says there's nothing special about you," she said. "You think there is, but there isn't."

"I don't think that," Dillon said.

"What about my dad?"

"Hutch *is* special." He gave her a mean look. He shouldn't have to defend Hutch to his own daughter.

"No, my dad thinks *you're* special. He said so. But Logan says you're not."

Dillon stared at the Honda. "Logan doesn't know me." He thought for a moment. "I don't know why he doesn't like me. I like him all right."

"See, you don't know everything," she said. "Logan doesn't like you because Dad *does*. I heard the two of them talking about it."

Dillon frowned. "That's just stupid."

Silence fell over them. Dillon scanned the area around the Honda. Macie kept her head turned the other way.

She said, "Do you love my dad?"

"Yes."

"That's weird."

"Why?"

"He's not *your* dad."

It took him a moment to reply. "He saved my life. He was nice to me."

The sky was starting to lighten. It was like someone was blotting away the inky night, making it white again. It was a long cleanup job. In Fiddler Falls, night's blackness didn't so much fade away as got pushed away, first by a deep purple, then a bright red.

Right now, Dillon didn't care *how* the sun made its appearance, just that it did. He felt fingers graze his arm.

Macie was staring at him. A tear had streaked down her cheek. "I'm sorry I said that, about what Logan thinks."

"That's okay."

"I think you're special."

"Thanks."

"I'm glad you love my dad."

Dillon turned back to the area of the parking lot he was responsible for watching. He vowed not to coach her in the art of watching for her dad. Even if she looked away, her peripheral vision would catch someone walking into it. He'd spotted a lot of animals in the forest when he was looking away.

When Macie spoke again, Dillon jumped.

"Why are those men after us?"

"'Cause Hutch wants to put that rich guy in jail. He's . . . I don't know . . . after him."

"So why doesn't he stop?"

"Maybe he will now."

"Then maybe those men will stop coming after us, stop trying to kill my dad, if that's what they're doing."

"What, just stop? As in go away, and we never see them again?"

"Yeah, why not?"

The voice came from the rear of the SUV: "Because that's not what they do."

They spun in their seats. Dillon's knee tapped the horn, giving audible expression to their surprise. Michael was sitting up in the cargo area. His eyes, catching the brightening light of day, appeared keen and alert.

FORTY-EIGHT

Hutch hurried through the jetway. He pushed past other disembarking passengers, tossing out apologies as he went. "Excuse me . . . sorry . . ."

Home, finally.

He pulled the mobile phone out of his pocket and pushed a button to turn it on. As he jogged for the trams to the terminal, he watched the phone slowly come online.

Come on, come on!

When it chimed and a bar graph appeared, showing signal strength, he dialed Larry's number.

"Did she call?" he said when Larry answered.

"What time is it?"

"Don't tell me you fell asleep!"

"Only a little. *Your* call woke me up. No, no, she didn't call. Where are you?"

"I'm in town, I'm home."

"Hutch, this came in last night," Larry said. "Nichols is dead. They found his body in a motel room in a place called Pinedale, California. They're thinking suicide, but it's still under investigation."

"Last night?"

"They found him yesterday. Released his name last night. They believe the time of death was the night before."

"When Page's people invited me to see him," Hutch said. "It *was* his call to me that triggered this. They kicked into cleanup mode."

Larry said, "I'm ready to call the cops."

"Larry, hold on, hold on." Hutch stopped at the top of an escalator leading to the tram platform. People from his own flight bumped into him, grumbled as they went around. He stepped sideways to clear the way. He cocked his head to one side. But the voice over the intercom had moved on: ". . . Mr. Jack Johnson, Ms. René, Ms. Lynda René, please pick up . . ."

"Larry," Hutch said into the phone. "I think someone is paging me. I'll call you back. And don't call anyone. Not until I get Logan back." He hit the disconnect button, scanning the area for a phone. He saw one on a pillar by the food court. Ran to it and picked it up.

"Paging operator," said a pleasant-sounding woman.

"You paged me. David Ryder." It had to be from Laura.

"It was just cleared."

"Cleared? Expired? I just heard it."

"It was picked up."

"No, I'm David Ryder. I didn't pick it up."

"We show it cleared, sir."

"Okay, what was it?"

"It's cleared, sir. We no longer have it in our system."

"You have to have a record of it." He took a deep breath. "Please."

"One moment, please."

Be Laura, he thought. *No, no. Be Page.*

Could it be him, calling to accept Hutch's deal? Why wouldn't he have called the mobile? Hutch looked at the mobile phone's screen. There was no indication that he'd missed a call or that a message was waiting to be picked up.

Be Page, he thought again. *Be Page ready to give me my son.*

"Mr. Ryder?"

"Yes."

"The message was: Please wait for your party at door number 502 in Terminal West."

"Who's the 'party'?"

"It doesn't say."

He hung up and headed for the tram platform. It was either Laura or . . . His steps quickened. What if Page's men were here with Logan? Page had made his point. Hutch had agreed to get off his back. Could it be this easy? Were they here to release his son?

Another possibility presented itself. That it was a setup. They were here, but not with Logan.

He pushed the thought away. It went kicking and scratching, because Hutch knew that this last scenario was the most likely, the most like Page.

He'd know soon enough. There was no way he could avoid the rendezvous, not with the chance that Logan or Laura was waiting for him there.

FORTY-NINE

Laura had watched the sun bleaching the sky and the photostatic lights outside turning off one at a time. She had traversed the airport a dozen or more times. All she could think about was how every step brought her closer to the time the men after Hutch—and Laura and the kids, she reminded herself—showed up to look for them at the airport.

Come on, Hutch. Where are you?

It was still early—not even seven. She expected him earlier than his scheduled flight, which had been midafternoon, but dawn shouldn't be her patience's breaking point.

She reached the door that marked another complete circumnavigation, but didn't go through it. She slowed her pace, turned in a circle, and leaned into a wall. She stretched her back against it and raised her right knee up high, then the left, as though she'd just completed a long run. She bent over, gripping her thighs above the knees.

Her clumpy hair fell over her face. She never did get to a store for a brush. She hadn't wanted to waste a minute doing anything other than looking for Hutch. He would simply have to tolerate her lack of hygiene. She raised herself up to her full height, snapping her head to flip her hair back off her face.

One of the men from the parking lot was heading for her. Black boots, pants, jacket. He was young and fit—there was no mistaking him. He had come out of the elevator and was taking great strides, trying to rush without drawing attention.

She turned and slammed through a metal fire door. She had discovered the possible getaway earlier, which was one reason she'd chosen that spot to rest. It opened onto a long, doorless hallway, which led to a labyrinth of connecting corridors. She had gone only a few intersections in, enough to get the idea that she could lose a pursuer in there.

Behind her, the door *ka-chunked* open and banged against the wall. As she darted around the first corner, something struck the wall. Sharp debris struck her face. He had shot at her.

In an airport!

No sound from the gun, but that didn't matter to the bullet. Of all the places she could have scouted for Hutch, this one lay way outside the security checkpoints. He'd have been able to carry a firearm without anyone challenging him.

The man's footsteps, surprisingly quiet, picked up pace. She turned right, then left. She hoped she was too quick for him to catch every turn. Eventually, the combination of directional changes she could have taken would force him to give up. While she ran, she thought about how he'd found her. Could be, he'd simply stumbled onto her. More likely, the men had made the connection between David Ryder and Hutch, and picked up the page.

She believed the man had missed her last few turns. It was time to get out of town. She opened a door: storage room. Another door: janitor's closet. Finally she found a short hallway leading to a door labeled DENVER COFFEE BAR. She stepped around a stack of boxes to the door—and heard the man's footsteps, approaching fast. A flap of the top box was tipped up, revealing four coffee decanters. She pulled one out, gripped the handle, and edged to the corner of the hallway.

The footsteps grew louder.

She swung around the corner, swinging the coffeepot. It cracked into the man's forehead. He flew back, staggering, his arm flying up over his head. She had already set the coffeepot on top of the box and was at the door when she heard him hit the floor with a loud *oomph!* Metal clattered against the floor. She hadn't knocked him cold, but he might have lost his gun, at least for a few seconds.

She pulled open the door and stepped through. She was behind the counter of a coffee bar she had passed a dozen times. A young woman was handing a customer a tall paper cup. Her mouth dropped when she saw Laura.

"Security," Laura said, knowing full well her appearance didn't fit the part. "This door is supposed to be locked. You have the key?"

The woman pointed to a key hanging from a nail by the jamb.

Laura grabbed it and locked the door.

"My partner's right behind me," she told the barista with a wink. "Don't let him in."

She went around the counter and hurried to the escalator to the fourth level. She still needed to find Hutch, but she had to take care of a few things first.

FIFTY

Hutch exited the terminal on the third level, which connected directly to the parking garage complex. He climbed the garage stairs to the fifth level. He watched door 502 for a minute from an island where a few limousines idled. No one waited for him. He walked to the other end of the building and entered. He worked his way back toward the meeting place. When it came into view, he went to a row of chairs, picked up a stray newspaper, and sat. He peered over the sports section toward the rendezvous spot.

A man burst through an interior door. Holding one hand to his forehead, he swung his head around, looking, looking. . . . His hand fiddled with something behind his back. No doubt, a gun stashed in his waistband.

Hutch's insides felt blowtorched. Stomach, heart, muscles ached with disappointment. Page's man wasn't here to return Logan. He was here to kill Hutch. Page had communicated his answer: no deal.

On the plane, Hutch had clicked through Page's options. Several scenarios involved stashing Logan in Colorado until Hutch gave himself up to Page's men. Most entailed Logan being taken back to Page's campus and compound, where he had a thousand places to hide him and many times that number of people to help. A couple scenarios required Logan's quick death, but Hutch had tried not to dwell on those.

Page had told Hutch, "This isn't going to end well." Hutch's hope lay in short-circuiting Page's plans before they reached their conclusion.

You're right again, Page, he thought. *This isn't going to end well. But for you, not me.*

The man walked through the glass exit doors. A few seconds later, he reappeared. He crossed toward the center of the level and walked out of Hutch's view.

Hutch beelined it for the exit.

Names rattled out of the airport speaker: "Mr. Neil Savona . . . Mr. Zhou Tong . . ."

The RapidParking shuttle wasn't in sight. He hopped in a cab. The driver grumbled about giving up his place in the queue for a five-mile, ten-dollar fare.

"I'll make it a twenty," Hutch said. "Just get moving, will you?"

He watched the doors as they passed, but he didn't see the man with the gun or anyone else he would identify as a likely Outis soldier.

The cab turned left, and the building fell away. When he could see all of the airport's roof of thirty-four white spires, which represented the Rocky Mountains, he relaxed a bit.

He rubbed his hands over his face. He should have caught some z's on the two-and-a-half-hour flight from Chicago. His body had been more than willing, but his mind had refused to slow down. It had reeled out everything from practical action items—*get a gun*—to memories of Logan—*the first time he'd taken him fishing: the kid had fallen in, twice.* From considering Page's motivations—*protecting his freedom, his image, his pride . . . some kind of macho, competitive crap . . . the guy was just plain nuts*—to guessing the man's next moves—*keep after Hutch . . . negotiate for Logan . . . nothing, let Hutch stew.*

He did not put it past Page to play dumb, pretend he hadn't taken Logan. At some point Hutch would have to call in the cops, which would not rattle Page in the slightest. The man had the kind of real estate holdings that made looking for Logan akin to finding a specific grain of sand in the Mojave. But *stew* didn't describe what Hutch would do if Page ignored him. If Page thought a crate of old dynamite, sweating nitroglycerin, was volatile, he didn't know volatile.

Those had been Hutch's thoughts on the plane. The man in the airport told Hutch which option Page had chosen. The man was coming after him. Didn't matter that he had Hutch's son. Page liked edgier games than that. He—

Zhou Tong.

Hutch had heard the name announced on the airport intercom while he was peering over the newspaper at Page's man. He'd heard it . . . but hadn't. He'd been concentrating on the killer, then on getting away from the airport without being seen.

Zhou Tong had been a famous archery teacher and military arts tutor in the Song Dynasty. He and Dillon had had long telephone conversations about him, because of Tong's blending of archery skills and self-discipline. He was an inspirational figure to Hutch. Dillon had sensed that and wanted to know everything about him. This time the page could only have been left by Laura.

The driver said something.

"Sorry?" Hutch said, pulling the phone from his pocket.

"Where's your car?" They were stopped just past the entrance barrier.

"Oh," Hutch tried to remember. "The aisle with the bighorn sheep, S. Way down toward the far end."

The driver cranked the wheel left and pulled onto the road that traversed the parking aisles.

Hutch called the information operator and asked for the airport's paging service.

A robotic female voice said, "You are being connected to that number."

He touched the driver's shoulder and pointed. "Right here." After the cab turned into the aisle, he said, "Almost to the end, on the right. Just go until I tell you to stop."

A man came on: "DIA Paging. May I help you?"

"You have a message for Zhou Tong."

"Hold, please."

Hutch pinched the phone between his shoulder and ear. He fished his wallet out of his back pocket and selected a twenty. "Little farther," he told the cabbie. "Here." The guy grabbed the bill from him.

The paging operator returned. "Mr. Tong?"

"Yes. Hold on a sec." He extended his arm past the seat back to point. "Right there, the silver Accord." Into the phone, he said, "Okay, sorry."

The operator said, "Umm, this message is marked urgent."

The cab stopped in front of the Honda. Hutch opened the door and stood. "Yes?"

The operator said, "It says, 'Do not go to the Honda.'"

"What?"

"'Do not go to the Honda.'"

Hutch stopped breathing. He looked at his car, snapped his eyes up to the vehicles behind it, then swung around to the ones parked on the other side of the aisle. Movement caught his attention—several rows away, a man rose up from the open driver's door of a tall vehicle, a truck or SUV. He was staring directly at Hutch, something in his hands.

Hutch dropped the phone. He ducked back into the cab and slammed the door.

"Go! Go!" he yelled.

The driver crooked his elbow over the seat back. "What are you—?"

"Drive!"

The Honda exploded.

FIFTY-ONE

The explosion shattered the cab's windows. Fragments of glass flew into the interior. Hutch saw a blinding flash of fire, a glimpse of the Honda's front end starting to rise, as though it were a dragster popping a wheelie. Sheet metal blew apart. The sound was a thousand shotgun blasts in his ears.

The taxi's right side buckled in. Hutch was thrown into the opposite door. A hand of fire and smoke pushed against the taxi, tossing it over. Sky filled a gaping rent the length of the passenger side. Hutch's legs, then hips, then torso tumbled over his head. His face smashed against the glass in the left-hand door. It cracked and shattered, breaking inward as the asphalt road pushed in on it. Hutch continued to tumble. He hit his head on the ceiling, which was now the floor.

Through a side window, narrowed by a pushed-in roof, he saw the

pieces of burning metal that had been his Honda—something uniden-
tifiable jutted from the side of an adjacent minivan, which in turn had
tipped into the car beside *it*. The engine had landed on the hood of a
Corvette. Windows all around had shattered. Fenders and hoods and
trunk lids and roofs were blackened, bent, torn away. Heavy smoke
billowed up from burning oil. The pungent odor of gasoline and fry-
ing seat-foam stung his nostrils.

Liquid poured from his face. Blood, he realized. He spat. His forearms and knees against the ceiling of the upside-down cab, he turned
his head, felt pain streak over his shoulder, down his left arm. He
moved again. More pain. He ignored it.

The cabbie lay slumped on the other side of the partition. His face
was pushed against the Plexiglas. If he had let a child finger-paint his
face in reds and browns, it could not have been messier, less defiling.
His sightless eyes stared at Hutch in horror and disbelief. The
Plexiglas itself was scratched and pocked. The windshield was shattered. Hutch realized that it had imploded into the cab like a million
shotgun pellets. The divider had saved his life.

Hutch coughed, spat more blood. He reached out to the cabbie's
wrist. He felt no pulse.

A loud, steady moan filled his ears. Slowly it diminished, and he
could hear car alarms, screams, crackling fire.

He backed through a window opening. When both knees and hands
were on the road—on the glass and detritus that littered the road—he
attempted to stand. He pressed his fingers against the mangled door
and heard them sizzle on the scalding metal. He pulled them away,
staggered back, fell.

Voices, sounding underwater, came at him: "Hutch!" "Daddy!"

Hands grabbed him, at first tentative, then greedily. Macie squeezed
his neck. An icicle of agony penetrated his head. He closed his eyes

against it. He held his daughter close, basking in her embrace despite the pain it caused. On his other side, Dillon smiled worriedly. The boy's hand gripped Hutch's shoulder. Hutch pulled him close and squeezed.

He remembered the guy standing in the open door and looked. The man was still there, scowling. He slid back into the vehicle. He reappeared and leveled a weapon at Hutch—at them.

"Move," Hutch said. The word came out as a grasping croak. He pushed Dillon away, swung Macie around and pushed her as well. "Move!" He hit the ground. Bullets thunked into the taxi beside him. Divots of asphalt exploded into the air. He crawled, grabbing and pushing the kids ahead of him.

The shooter was a good forty yards away. Three rows of cars lay between them. It should not take that much to get out of his line of fire.

"Closer to the cars!" he told Dillon and Macie. "Go that way!" He pointed and recognized his XTerra. It was parked nose out on the other side of the aisle from where the Honda had been. It was right where he had directed them to go. "Go to the car," he said.

The taxi's tire exploded. Big holes appeared in the fender. *Thunk! Thunk! Thunk!*

"Dillon! Macie! Hutch!"

Laura ran at them from the front access road. Behind her, a taxi had stopped. The driver stared out the windshield, trying to assess the situation. His eyes widened, and his mouth moved in a silent string of obscenities—Hutch knew it from the expression on his face. The taxi's tires kicked up smoke as the driver reversed.

Laura was still thirty yards away when Hutch gestured wildly with his arms. "Get down! Get down!"

She looked beyond him at the gunman. Her jaw unhinged, and she dropped to the road. A windshield behind her shattered as three bullets struck it. Laura had covered her head with her arms. She raised her face to him. "There's a gun!" she yelled. "In the car, the XTerra!"

Hutch and the kids were close enough to touch the SUV's front bumper. Hutch pushed them. "Go around the next car. Crouch down. Hide there."

"But—" Dillon started.

"Do it!" Hutch said. He gave them both a hard look that said, *Don't even think of questioning me!*

Macie tripped over Dillon getting past him. Dillon gave Hutch an anguished expression, turned fast enough to catch Macie, and, hunched, they ran together to the other side of the next car.

Hutch darted to the XTerra's passenger door. Knowing it would be locked, of course, he tried the handle. It opened. He blinked, trying to see the objects inside, but a liquid blindfold had slid over his eyes. He rubbed at them, squinted at his fingers. Blood. He must have received a new head wound that hadn't started hurting yet, or he'd reopened the one from when the Mustang had hit the van. He pulled up the collar of his shirt and wiped his eyes.

He saw the weapon. It was the same model the soldiers had used in the attack at the motel.

How did Laura—?

No time for questions. Just move.

He pulled the machine gun out of the footwell. He toggled the safety switch in front of the trigger guard with his thumb, revealing a triangle of red paint. Hunkering down, breathing hard, he returned to the front of the XTerra.

He didn't hear gunfire—then *pop-pop-pop!* It seemed as though someone slapped an open hand against the XTerra's hood in time with the sounds.

Hutch turned and pressed his back against the bumper. He squatted down onto his heels. Laura hadn't moved. She lay in the center of the road, her arms over her head, her eyes peering out at him.

"Can you see him, the shooter?" Hutch called in a stage whisper.

She shook her head quickly.

"Then stay there!"

She probably would have been safe crawling to him, but he didn't want to risk her moving into his line of fire. Besides, the gunman seemed more interested in shooting Hutch. She was better off away from him.

He breathed out slowly, concentrating on what he had to do. He wished he were a better aim with a firearm. It'd never been his thing, rifle hunting, target shooting with a pistol. Give him a bow and arrow, point him toward the woods, and he was good to go. Give him a firearm, and whatever he was shooting at better be within arm's reach.

This guy wasn't. Hutch thought about what lay between him and the gunman: the XTerra's row of cars, the row behind it, the next aisle over, and another row of cars. *Then* the guy, standing on some tall vehicle, taking potshots at him. One thing was sure. Outis recruits could outshoot Hutch in their sleep.

But he doesn't know that, Hutch thought. *At least right now he doesn't. If I don't blow it completely—shoot off my own hand or something—maybe I can keep him from moving in until help comes.*

But the gunman wasn't going to be frightened away by Hutch brandishing a weapon he didn't have the skill to aim. Hutch knew from somewhere—maybe a History Channel documentary—that most battles were won through attrition: the combatants simply kept fighting until the other side had too few able-bodied men to continue. If that was the strategy taught at Outis, then that guy wasn't going away until more men and firepower became aligned against him or they zipped him up in a body bag.

So bring in the cops—he'd worry about the repercussions later. Just don't let Macie, Laura, and Dillon get hurt.

God, don't let them get hurt.

FIFTY-TWO

Hutch waited until the man shot at the hood again—his bullets striking the metal and the asphalt beyond. As soon as Hutch detected a pause, he rose and spun. The man was ready. He fired. The bullets broke the driver's-side glass, punched holes in the windshield. Glass sprayed Hutch's face. He started to drop down, changed his mind, and held his ground. He aimed and fired. Fist-sized holes appeared in the windshield in front of the gunman, who ducked. Hutch did the same.

Yeah, he thought. *Weren't expecting that, were you?*

He couldn't believe he'd placed the rounds so close to his target.

Nice.

Maybe he could do this after all.

At the far other end of the aisle, a taxicab rolled slowly toward them. The driver's door opened and a man tumbled out. He rolled

away, scrambled to his feet, and began yelling. A shaking fist punctuated his words.

Shadows shifted behind the taxi's windshield, then another man leaned out to grab hold of the door. It was the Outis soldier from the airport. The man yanked the door closed, and the yellow vehicle accelerated. It was heading directly for Laura, who was lying on her stomach in the middle of the aisle. She had lowered her face to the street, wrapping her head with her arms as though they would protect her from machine-gun fire.

"Laura!" Hutch yelled. "Laura!"

She couldn't hear him over the car alarms, screaming people, revved engine, and gunfire—the man Hutch had shot at had recovered and was punishing him with a barrage of bullets. He would never be able to reach her in time—not crawling, and as soon as he moved away from the XTerra's bumper, he'd feel the hot burn of lead.

"Laura!"

He raised the machine gun and pulled the trigger, releasing a three-round burst. Pulled it again, and again. Two of his bullets hit the windshield of the approaching car—in the upper corner on the passenger side. The glass wall of a faraway shelter shattered. Spectators at the end of the aisle began a new volley of screams and yells.

Hutch fired again. The next time he pulled the trigger, nothing happened. The weapon was either jammed or empty.

The taxi kept coming. The driver aligned the wheels with Laura's prone body.

Hutch tried firing again. Nothing.

"Laura!" he yelled.

"Hutch!" Dillon was crouched next to the XTerra. He raised something to him: the bow. Hutch let the machine gun clatter to the ground.

He grabbed the bow, then the arrow Dillon held out in his other hand. He had the arrow nocked on the string and ready to shoot in three seconds. It was like slipping into his favorite jeans. One fingertip touched the string above the arrow, two below it. It took him another half second to realize the cab's windows would easily deflect the arrow, especially considering the shot's acute angle.

Laura glanced up. She registered the direction of his aim and craned her head around. The car was a hundred feet from her . . . ninety: less than ten seconds.

He lowered his aim. Instantly, he calculated the speed and trajectory of his arrow in relation to the speed and trajectory of the car—a skill honed on deer, which ran faster than the thirty miles an hour he guessed the car was moving. In one fluid movement, he pulled back to full draw, where the thumb of his string hand grazed his earlobe, and released. The arrow sailed away from him at 240 feet per second. He grimaced when he realized he had miscalculated. It struck the lip of the wheel well in front of the tire he had aimed for. It glanced off the metal and penetrated the tire, which exploded as surely as it would have had Hutch hit it with a bullet. The car pulled sharply to the left.

It ran over Laura.

The taxi's front-end mercifully blocked Hutch's view.

His stomach cramped. His mouth dropped open.

The taxi continued its sharp leftward incline and crashed into a parked car before reaching Hutch's position.

Hutch leaned and pushed Dillon back between the cars. He yanked the quiver of arrows the boy gripped in both hands.

Laura stood up. She had not been run over; Hutch's perspective had only made it appear so. Her knees wobbled, and she swayed. She looked dazed, but she slapped the hair back from her face and smiled.

Way to go, he thought, then immediately remembered why she'd been lying there in the first place and yelled, "Get down!"

A bullet struck her right shoulder. Laura's face twisted in pain and shock. Her feet seemed to take flight, sailing out in front of her. She landed hard on her back. She grabbed her shoulder and rolled toward the cars on the opposite side of the aisle.

But she was *moving*. She was all right.

Relief washed over Hutch like ice water on a parched throat.

She kept rolling until she was mostly under a bumper. Then she turned like a watch hand, getting her legs under the car farther. She began wiggling backward into the shadow of the undercarriage.

Hutch's mind could hardly keep up with the situation. As Laura had, he had momentarily forgotten about the shooter two aisles over.

"Daddy!" Macie was leaning out from the spot where he had sent her. A car lay between them.

"No, baby, go back," he said.

She ducked back between the cars, giving him a clear view of the wrecked taxicab. The man inside battered down the airbag and shoved his shoulder into the driver's door. It was crumpled and smashed up against the car it had struck. He saw Hutch looking and bared his teeth. The man's head mimicked a chicken's as he searched the interior for something—Hutch didn't have to be Stephen Hawking to figure out what.

Hutch pulled an arrow from the quiver and nocked it. He said, "Dillon, crawl under the car." He nodded his head toward the sedan beside the XTerra. "Get Macie under there with you. Don't come out till I tell you. Got it?"

The boy dropped to the blacktop. He scrambled away, getting his entire body underneath the car. Hutch heard him calling to Macie.

The man inside the taxicab raised a pistol. Hutch saw the flash, a billow of smoke, and the windshield became opaque with cracks. Another shot and the glass fell away, cascading over the hood.

Hutch plucked at the bow's string. The arrow sailed into the glassless windshield opening. The man jerked his head sideways. The arrow pierced a headrest. A starburst of cracks appeared in the Plexiglas partition behind it.

The man glared at the eighteen inches of shaft and feathers vibrating a hand's-breath from his head. He disappeared beneath the dash. The passenger door swung open.

Hutch pulled out another arrow.

The man's feet appeared below the door.

Hutch positioned his fingers, raised the bow, and waited for a clean shot.

The soldier rose up behind the door, swinging his pistol over the window frame.

Hutch plucked the string back and—

The string snapped. The arrow pinwheeled into the air, sailing back over his shoulder. It happened in the field enough that most bow hunters carried extra strings.

But now? Now?

Behind a big pistol, the man at the car smiled and closed one eye.

Then man and car door exploded forward. Both flipped up and landed on the hood of a car that had plowed into them from behind. The door spun away as though it weighed nothing. The man hit the windshield, made a head-sized concavity in it, and kept tumbling— over the roof and out of sight.

The car screeched to a stop beside Hutch. Its tires coughed out smoke, which washed over the vehicle and drifted off. A single amber strobe flashed on the roof. Behind the glass of the driver's door an old black man looked as though he'd just been shot out of a cannon.

A security company's patch had been sewn to the man's sleeve over his bicep.

The window slid down, and the man looked out at Hutch. He said, "You better be one of the good guys."

FIFTY-THREE

"Get down!" Hutch said to the man in the security car.

"Wha—?"

Bullets pinged into the roof and took out the remaining amber strobe.

The security guard opened the door and spilled to the ground. He crawled to Hutch and said, "What the Sam Hill is happ'nin,' man?"

The machine gun kept firing—*pop-pop-pop* . . . *pop-pop-pop*—but Hutch couldn't see or hear what the bullets were hitting. Then they slammed into the cruiser's trunk, and Laura came crawling around the rear of the car. When she was close enough to be out of the gunman's line of sight, the gunfire stopped. She rolled onto her side and grabbed her shoulder. Her hand couldn't cover the swath of blood.

"Laura," Hutch said. "Your shoulder."

She bit her lip, but said, "Flesh wound." Her eyes took on all the world's sorrows. "Hutch, Logan—"

"Larry told me."

Their words came fast, rushing as they huddled closer together in front of the XTerra.

Laura frowned at the guard. "Charlie . . ."

"That your old man, the one with the machine gun?" the old man said, peering over the grille toward the gunman. "Hell's bells, woman, you should have told me!"

"Not my husband. These guys are professional soldiers," Laura said.

Charlie shook his head. "Killers, not soldiers. Soldiers got more honor than what I seen here."

She said, "You could have been killed."

"No fooling. What's that guy *doing*?"

Hutch popped his head up. "Shooting from that van over there. I got a few shots at him. I think he was in contact with his buddy, the one you took care of. I don't know what he's going to do now that his backup is out of the picture."

Charlie squatted low. "How many of them are there?"

"I saw two," Laura said. "I think they're it."

Charlie took in the bow. He said, "Haven't you ever heard you shouldn't bring a knife to a gunfight? I think that applies to a bow and arrow, too, my friend."

Hutch nodded. "I'm better with this than I am with that." He indicated the TMP at his feet.

"Whoa," Charlie said. "Now you're talking." He picked up the machine gun, pushed a button that released its magazine, looked into it, and tossed the magazine away. He pulled back on a small tab, which showed him the chamber. "Empty gun's worse than a knife or a bow," he said.

"You know your way around those things?" Hutch asked.

"Two tours in 'Nam. Third Brigade, First Air Cavalry Division. Didn't have that weapon back then, but a gun's a gun, pretty much."

"So you can shoot?" Laura said.

"With bullets I can."

"How about that?" Laura said, pointing. The pistol the soldier had aimed at Hutch rested against the tire of the car under which Dillon and Macie hid; their wide faces peered out from the shadows.

"You kids stay right where you are," Charlie instructed. He crawled a few feet, grabbed the gun. He checked it for ammo. He hefted it. "This I can use."

"Hey!" The yell was muffled. It had come from *inside* the car.

Charlie and Hutch shared a startled expression. Crouched in front of the grille, Charlie wiggled like a cat about to pounce. He held the pistol in both hands.

Before he could spring up, Laura grabbed his shoulder. "It's one of the soldiers," she said. "I got him tied up in the cargo area."

"What?" Hutch said.

"I'll explain later."

"Get me out of here," the voice yelled. "Untie me. They're shooting at me!"

"Michael," Laura yelled. "Stay down."

Hutch looked at the van. He dropped down and scanned under the cars. "I don't see the gunman," he said. "He might be out of the van, trying to get around to us."

Charlie's head snapped around in all directions. He said, "Cops'll be here soon. I didn't have time to call it in myself, but I saw a lot of excited mouthin' into cell phones."

"Shouldn't they already be here?" Hutch said. "I mean—" He realized only about three minutes had passed since the explosion. It seemed like ten times that.

"Airport's a few miles away," Charlie said. "It's a bear getting here. You have to pass the lot, then circle back on the front road."

Hutch snapped his head around. He swore. "He's on foot, I know it!"

"Wait, wait," Laura said. "There."

The man had reappeared above the door of the van. He lifted a black object and fitted it over his head. One of the helmets Hutch had seen at the motel.

Laura said, "Hutch, those helmets, I think they have all kinds of stuff that'll help him—"

"I know," Hutch said.

"I don't like the looks of it, no matter what it does," Charlie said. He rose straight up. Holding the pistol in his right hand, with his left bracing the butt of the gun, he raised it a foot in front of his face. Without pause he squeezed off a round.

The bullet struck the face mask—a white circle, dead center. The gunman's head snapped back. He grabbed the window frame to keep from toppling backward. He pulled himself up, shook off the shock, gave a final look at them, and slipped into the vehicle. The door shut.

Hutch slapped Charlie on the back. "Nice, man!"

Laura grabbed Hutch's arm. "Hutch, Logan might be in that van!"

Hutch felt a dumbfounded expression touch his features. His face tightened with determination. He brushed past Charlie and shot between the cars toward the gunman's vehicle.

"Hutch—" Laura called.

"Stay with the kids," he said. Charlie fell in behind him. He reached the next aisle—still one away from the van. He cut across it diagonally, directly toward the van, which was pulling away. It headed for the back road, was already there.

Hutch slammed into a fender and ran between two cars. He reached the spot where the van had been. It turned right onto the back road, heading the opposite direction from the way Hutch had expected. Instead of going toward the exit, it accelerated the way it had been facing when it was parked—toward the destroyed Honda. Hutch reversed and ran between the parked cars, parallel to the back road.

He caught a glimpse of Charlie leveling the pistol off the roof, aiming at the speeding van. He waved at him.

"No!" he said. "Don't shoot! My boy's in there." Of course he was. Where else would he be?

The van turned into the Honda's aisle, which was also where the XTerra was parked—the aisle with Laura and the kids.

Putting everything he had into his legs, Hutch pushed harder.

"Laura!" he yelled. "Run! Hide! Get away!" He didn't know what she should do, didn't know where she was.

The van picked up speed. It crashed into the upside-down taxicab, knocking it aside. But it didn't move enough for the van to get past. Its rear tires spun on the asphalt, generating plumes of smoke. Metal squealed. Stuck between the Corvette that boasted the Honda's engine as a hood ornament and the taxi, the van wasn't going anywhere.

As Hutch bolted around a car, into the aisle, the gunman kicked his door open and jumped out. He swung the machine gun and fired.

Hutch dived between two cars.

Hurrying, hunched over, Charlie came up behind him. He said, "Whaddaya want me to do?"

"If you can take the guy out without hitting the van, do it."

They peered out. The driver was leaning into the van.

Logan. What were the killers' orders? In the event of imminent capture, were they supposed to kill their hostage? Would Page consider that a victory? Tit for tat? Hutch's son for Page's?

"Wait! Wait!" he yelled at the gunman. "Just go! Don't hurt—"

The gunman stood. He threw the strap of a duffel bag over his head and pushed the bag behind him. He fired, hitting the bumper beside Hutch. He slammed his door, jumped and slid over the front end of the Corvette, and began running up the aisle.

The bag was big, loaded down—but large enough to hold a twelve-year-old boy? Could the man be strong enough to move that fast carrying so much weight?

Charlie pushed past Hutch. He reached the taxi—pushed into a parked car—and squeezed through. He tore after the soldier.

Hutch bolted for the van's rear doors. Locked. He looked in a window, cupping his hands around his face. For a moment he considered that another gunman waited inside, at that moment ready to fire through the glass. He could see nothing through the dark tinting. He beat his fist against the window. He turned to run around to the passenger side.

A single shot rang out. Then another. Charlie was shooting.

The machine gun returned fire.

Hutch skittered up to the van door. He could see the gunman now. He was squatting down beside the body of his partner, his machine gun wavering back toward where Hutch knew Charlie must be. He draped the corpse over his shoulder and rose. Gun protruding straight out like a lineman's arm, he spun in a circle. Laying eyes on Hutch, he paused. He turned away, took a staggering step, got his balance, and darted away between two cars.

Hutch yanked the front door open. "Logan!"

Let him be alive.

He scrambled onto the seat. He pulled his feet up and pumped them forward, hopping into the space between the seats. He jumped into the back, squinting against the darkness, feeling, feeling. "Logan?"

The van was empty.

FIFTY-FOUR

Laura crouched beside the XTerra. The kids were still under the car beside it. The gunman had run past. Charlie was back the other way, exchanging fire. She stood to scope out the situation.

Now the gunman was running away, darting between cars. He carried a body over one shoulder. A duffel bag bounced against his back. He continually swung his face and machine gun around toward them.

Charlie came toward her at a fast clip. His eyes were on the gunman's. He held his pistol up, ready to squeeze off a shot.

As he passed, she grabbed his arm. "Don't," she said.

He turned intense eyes on her. He looked at the man getting away. The gunman's head was just visible over the roofs of cars several aisles over.

Charlie lifted the pistol. "I can—"

"Don't," she repeated. "He's leaving. Let him go."

He stared at the retreating figure, almost longingly, she thought. He nodded and said, "Tail between his legs."

She patted his shoulder. She slipped past him and went to the van. She leaned in, saw Hutch squatting in the rear. His head hung low.

"Hutch? Is—"

"He's not here." His voice was flat, far away.

"I'm sorry."

His breathing changed, and she thought he was crying, or trying not to.

Sirens reached her. They were in the distance, but growing louder. From the time she'd heard the explosion, seen the smoke from the backseat of the taxicab as it pulled into parking aisle S, no more than ten minutes had passed. So much had happened, so *fast*. She said, "We have to go."

She left him and returned to Charlie. He was sitting cross-legged on the road, the pistol in his lap. She picked it up and tossed it under a nearby car. "Let them know what happened," she said. "But you don't want to be holding it when they come. Not—"

She scanned the parking lot: the burning ruin of the Honda, the shattered and flipped taxicab—its driver she hadn't seen emerge—the other cab, crashed into more damaged cars, bulletholes everywhere.

"Not with all this," she finished.

He looked up at her. "You turned out to be one interesting story."

"We're in your debt."

He blew air out. "If I'da given it half a thought, I'd still be in my car, watching like the others."

"I don't think so."

Hutch walked up. His face, arms, and T-shirt were a bloody mess. His eyes were nearly as red, glistening. He nodded at Charlie. "Thanks."

Charlie's wrinkles deepened. He glanced back at the van. "Your boy?"

"Not there."

The old man shook his head. "Ain't right."

The sirens were almost on them. Laura could see the flashing red and blue lights coming from both directions on the main road. She said, "We can't be here when they come. We have to keep working to get his son back."

Charlie said, "'Course."

Laura helped him stand, and he groaned and pressed a hand into the small of his back.

"Look here," he said. "Take the back road to aisle—"

The sound of crunching metal reached them. In a far-off aisle, a panel van backed away from the parked car it had struck. It roared off, breaking though an entrance barrier without slowing.

"There he goes," Charlie observed. "Just had to leave his mark one more time on the way out." He looked sideways at Laura. "Not your hubby, you say? So who were they?"

"Wayward youth," she said. She was serious about that, but it seemed too kind, too dismissive for the damage they'd wreaked. She shook the thought away. "You said we should go to what aisle?"

"B, the bear. There's a hidden gate in the perimeter fence. Just tap it with your bumper. Take the service road—just a rutty dirt thing—west. It'll sweep you 'round to a freight company's parking lot. Should be able to bypass the craziness that's 'bout to converge on this place." He cast his eyes out on the approaching cherry tops. "Go." He pointed at Hutch. "Get your boy. Don't stop till you do."

Hutch inclined his head and brushed past him. Macie and Dillon ran out from between the cars. They leaped at Hutch. He knelt and embraced them.

Laura gave Charlie a sad smile. She reached Hutch and touched his head. "We have to go," she said.

Macie and Dillon had their faces buried in Hutch's neck. He turned and looked up at her. "Who's the guy in the back of the XTerra?"

She covered her mouth. "One of the soldiers who attacked us. Kind of a long story."

"He's tied up?"

She nodded.

Hutch gently extricated himself from the children. He stood. "Get in the car. Go on, now." To Laura he said, "We've got a lot to sort out. Let's get someplace where we can think. A motel."

She hugged him, and they hurried to the XTerra.

FIFTY-FIVE

Emile maneuvered the van through Denver's rush hour traffic. He kept checking the rearview mirror to see if one of the cops heading to the parking lot had spotted him. If so, the traffic would kill him; as it was, however, it kept him from transferring his adrenaline-fueled tension to the gas pedal. He reminded himself to drive with caution and awareness. It would be too easy right now to run a red light or change lanes into some other car.

He held a hand up, still and horizontal. Shaky. No wonder his shots missed so many times. Twice in one day, seemingly simple missions had spiraled out of control.

His teammates were all gone, either dead or vanished. Ben, the team leader, had bitten it at the house. An arrow through the neck. An *arrow*! It was also there that Michael had disappeared. Command Center had reported his going after the woman and kids when his helmet went off-line. Now Anton—run down by a car! Taken out by some security cop! 'Course, that guard was something. He'd taken one shot, under fire, and decommissioned Emile's helmet, just like that.

This whole op had been screwed up from the get-go. Spy on a family through their windows—what was that? Then the kid had shown up, calling Emile a Peeping Tom, surely ready to scream for his mom and get the cops all over them. What was he supposed to do? He'd grabbed the kid, thinking he'd restrain him in the van, let him go later. That's when it had hit the fan: "Keep the boy, kill everyone else."

It was the sort of order that got Ben revved up. He just loved that kind of stuff. Didn't matter who it was they were after. He liked the chase, the victory. Once, after a VR simulation in which they'd wiped out a village of mostly women and old folks, Ben had acted like he had just reached the top of Mount Everest—freestyle, no oxygen for that boy. He had been whoopin' and grinnin' and ready for more. The others had been happy to have achieved high score among all the fireteams, but it wasn't exactly the mission they had signed up for.

"Dude," Anton had said, pushing Ben and his enthusiasm away, "ain't winning better when your opponents are firing back?"

Ben had flashed his crazy ear-to-ear grin. He'd said, "As long as I get the points, I don't care if I'm taking out dogs. All of the points and none of the risk—that's my kind of mission."

So Command Center's unexpected order had pushed Ben's let's-get-it-on button. He must have been flying high. Until that arrow got him.

All of the risk had been there. They just hadn't known it.

Emile still didn't know what to do with the kid. "Take him back with us," Anton had suggested. And it made sense. Colonel Bryson had told them the mission involved pressuring people into doing something.

"Blackmail," Ben had interpreted.

"Or extortion," Anton had said.

Emile had asked, "What's the difference?"

"Blackmail's for money," Anton had said. "Extortion's for making people do things." He'd frowned. "I think."

Later, after they had the kid in the back of the van—along with Ben's body—Emile had thought about the mission, its objectives and such. Kidnapping seemed to accomplish the goal: it could be for money or to force a person into compliance. That had to be why the order had been to take the boy and not kill him.

So they had been thinking "bring the kid back" when the order to intercept a different target at the airport had come through. To preserve the integrity of the previous mission, they had stashed the boy at a motel. That way, he'd be available for blackmail or extortion or whatever it was.

Also, he and Anton would not be tripping over him at the airport.

They hadn't known for sure whether the second mission was related to the first. They thought probably it was, but it didn't matter. They'd figured it out, however, after Anton had spotted the same woman from the house, waiting for their current target. It had been Colonel Bryson's directive to monitor the airport announcements to help them locate the target. He had been running all the names through Command Center's databases, looking for known associates, et cetera, when a name had hit.

It was these kinds of twists and turns that made the game so fun.

Fun—not the word he would use now, not with Ben's body back at the motel and Anton's in the backseat. He knew many of the fireteams' members—on other teams, not just his—reconciled the danger with the entertainment by applying the philosophy *If you can't lose, why play the game?*

This was what losing looked like. Dead and missing teammates. Fireteam Bravo's score on this one was going to suck.

The second mission's requirement to mingle with civilians—in the parking lot, at the airport, driving—meant not wearing their helmets for much of the time. Command Center would not have many of the details it required to properly score a team and its members. He'd have to fill them in as best he could. That was a debriefing he wasn't looking forward to.

Emile knew Colonel Bryson was expecting a call and would be ready to give Fireteam Bravo their next order. It would probably be to return to base, since the team amounted now to only him. With or without the kid, he didn't know. Didn't care.

As he drove back to the motel, he decided Colonel Bryson would just have to wait for his call. Emile was dog tired, starving, and completely fragmented. Remedying the first two would certainly mitigate the last, making him sharper when he checked in.

Besides, how many more points could they deduct from a mission that had scored a big goose egg?

FIFTY-SIX

Julian peered through his quad's door into the hallway. By this time on most mornings, the fireteams were whipping up breakfast in their kitchenettes. Julian didn't smell burning bacon grease or pungent eggs. None of the usual guffaws and wisecracks drifted to him. They hadn't returned yet. Good.

He shut the door and crossed the den to his bedroom. He closed the door and knelt beside his bed, as if to pray. He snaked an arm between his mattresses and found Hutch's phone. Not the most original hiding place, but if his superiors searched the room—which they did periodically—they'd find it no matter how well he stashed it.

He detected a soft click and snapped his head toward the door, pressing the phone against his chest. After a quarter minute, he suspected the sound had come from the refrigerator in the other room.

He stood and went into the bathroom. He locked the door, lowered the toilet lid, and sat on it. Leaning over, he rested his forearms on his thighs. Between his knees, his hands turned the phone over and over. He thumbed it opened and turned it on. To conserve the battery, he kept it off when he wasn't around to hear it ring. He watched it power up.

His stomach sent a message of distress. He ignored it. Next, his throat tightened, and he ignored that too.

Something occurred to him. He stood, turned on the shower, and returned to the seat. The screen's backlight had gone out.

He took a deep breath, held it a few seconds, then let his lungs deflate. His finger punched a button. The screen lit up, displaying the first digit. He tapped out the rest of the number. The phone felt cold against his face.

Half a continent away, a phone rang. He pictured the setting: a bedroom in a middle-class home. Nothing extravagant, because his father never gave anything away if he could help it, and he could almost always help it. Two hours later there, so the sun would have had a chance to heat up and fill the room with bright yellow light.

Three rings.

Julian's guts felt loose, like he'd almost reached the top of a tall roller-coaster hill when the car plunged in reverse.

"Hello?" Her voice was soft, careful.

He remembered the last time he'd seen her. He'd thought then that she was going through life walking on eggshells, afraid of cracking one. She had not always been that way. Nearly the opposite: bold, happy, gung-ho for life.

"Mom?" Julian said. "It's me."

"Jul . . . Julian?"

"I just, just . . . I miss you."

Silence . . . too long, the silence. Maybe her heart couldn't take it after over a year. "Mom," he said, "please don't hang up."

Her sobs came over the line. They were the final blows, or they were *permission*. His own tears came. They welled up from his chest and poured out, loud and scalding on his cheeks.

Logan Hutchinson twisted against the duct tape that secured his neck to the bathtub faucet. He had long ago given up trying to free himself. He wanted only to *move*. Every muscle in his body ached from all sorts of abuses: getting tossed into van interiors, motel walls, the bathtub; having his arms wrenched backward, his wrists tied to his ankles, tape wrapped completely around him, even his knees bound together with a plastic ziplock thing; then not being able to move out of an awkward, uncomfortable position for hours.

The washcloth stuffed in his mouth was soaked with spit. He kept gagging on it, choking because the snot that came when he cried clogged his nose. To breathe he'd had to first blow the gunk out of his nostrils—over the bulging tape that covered his mouth, down his chin. His chest and stomach were covered with it, snot and tears.

The man who'd tied him up had been the van's driver—Anton, Emile had called him. He'd said, "Don't barf, kid, or you're dead."

He almost had barfed. But he knew there was no place for it to go but in his throat, maybe his lungs. He realized only then that the man had been serious. When he'd felt the urge, when his stomach had churned and wanted to get rid of the KFC Laura had picked up for dinner, Logan closed his eyes and thought of tough guys in the movies enduring worse without puking. Did Will Smith lose his lunch when he was hanging by his leg in *I Am Legend*? No way. Never.

Logan had, however, peed himself. More than once. He wasn't embarrassed; it was just a thing people had to do. What he didn't like was the slow-drying wetness and the odor he had to endure since the first time, how many hours ago. It didn't help that he could also smell blood, like a jar of pennies. It was all over him, but mostly on his jeans over his right thigh—slowly darkening, becoming stiff. The blood had come from a body the two guys had tossed into the back of the van with Logan. He tried not to think about it.

Anton had bound him so thoroughly, he could barely wiggle his shoulders or move his knees a few inches in either direction. He had heard the two men talking and knew they were worried about more than his getting loose; they didn't want him making any noise. They didn't want him screaming or pounding or kicking. Nothing. That told him they were going to leave him alone.

They never said so, but after leaving the bathroom light on—Anton had flipped the switch up and down, saying, "On or off, on or off?"— knowing Logan couldn't even shake his head or nod—and shutting the door, Logan was pretty sure both of them had left. Someone had turned on the television out there, but he hadn't heard voices that were louder than the TV. He hadn't heard laughter or bumps against the wall. No one had come in to check on him or use the bathroom—that alone told him something.

He wondered how long they were going to keep him tied up like this. Were they gone for good? Would they tell someone where to find him? Was his dad or Laura or the police negotiating with them? What if the cops killed all of them? Or it might be Dad who killed them; he'd done it before. If the people who'd taken him died without telling anyone where he was, he could die here. He'd starve to death. He was already hungry.

And that was something he thought was strange, being hungry in a situation like this. Weren't fear and worry supposed to override everything else? Well, it didn't stop his bladder, so maybe bodily needs like eating just marched on regardless. Yeah, fear might make you forget your stomach for a while, but not forever. He wondered if the pain of it went away or if you got used to it. Maybe he would last longer, not *have* to eat, since he wasn't moving around, burning energy. After football practice, he was famished. Watching TV, not so much.

He liked it when his mind wandered. Even to contemplation—vocab word; he thought he was using it right—even to contemplation of his own death. It made him forget the pain in his muscles, how his joints felt twisted. It made him forget that he'd almost died in ways even Stephen King couldn't dream up: Death by Vomit; Death by Suffocation Because Your Nose Is Full of Snot. He didn't think you could die from smelling your own pee, but it got pretty bad.

What about a maid coming in? Didn't even crappy motels like this have maid service? Wouldn't someone come in to change the sheets, vacuum, and untie the kid in the bathtub? But those guys seemed to know what they were doing. They probably paid for the room a week in advance and told the front desk clerk they didn't want to be disturbed.

No maid service. No inquiries. No calls. He hadn't heard the phone ring, come to think of it. But who'd call? Maybe Dad, wondering where to drop the ransom money.

Dad. Logan *hoped* he was trying to get him back. If it were Dillon who'd been taken, Dad would be calling molten lava down from the sky on anyone he even thought wasn't helping find him.

That wasn't fair. He knew his father loved him. When he had the time, Dad liked to roughhouse and talk about things Logan wanted to talk about. Logan could tell when someone was only tolerating him because he had to, even if he did say "I love you" a thousand times and bought him the latest, coolest doodads. He sensed it sometimes, a little, with his mom. And *definitely* with George, the heir apparent to Dad's rightful place in the family.

His dad had never been that way. When they were doing something together, even something blah like cleaning the kitchen, the conversation often came around to how much Dad loved him. Sounded corny thinking about it now, but it never was at the time. Even that time when Dad broke into some mushy song called "You Light Up My Life." Logan had loved it, even though at the time he'd said it was stupid.

Problem was, his dad never had time for him anymore. Even when he was there, he wasn't *really* there. He was thinking of the next thing he had to do, some person he had to interview, or what the last person said that sounded wrong.

But he did talk about what happened in Canada. How awful it had been. How some of them had beaten the odds and survived. That always got him talking about Dillon.

And Dillon was someone Logan absolutely didn't want on his mind right now. Wouldn't that be just the kicks if the last thing he thought about on this planet was that little punk?

He tried to pull away from the faucet again. Just . . . the . . . smallest . . . amount. He couldn't tell if there was some new looseness to the tape or if it had stretched a bit or if it was the flesh in his neck giving a little.

He wiggled his jaw. It caused spit to squeeze out of the cloth, trickle down through the tape, and run over his chin. Another feeling he didn't like. It also pulled the hair on the back of his head. Not so much now as before. Probably it had pulled out all the hair it could.

Aaahhhhhh!

He couldn't take this anymore. Couldn't take the wondering if they were coming back, wondering if they were going to kill him. Couldn't take trying to think of things—anything, everything—to stop thinking about *how* they would kill him. To stop thinking about whether he was dead already, because they'd left him and nobody would find him until he was so dead and decayed they'd have to identify him with dental records. Couldn't take not being able to *move, move,* just *move.* He strained against his bonds. Jerked his muscles without moving. Wiggled what he could—his knees, his shoulders, his head. *Not* his fingers! Anton had taped his *fingers!*

Aaahhhhhh!

A door slammed. Louder than the others he'd occasionally heard. This time he'd felt it: a vibration coming up through the tub, air coming through the crack under the door.

The television turned off. The bed creaked. Something fell to the floor. Something else.

Logan's heart took off. It pounded like a fist against his ribs.

Be a maid, he thought, but he knew better.

The door opened, and he hissed air into his nostrils. He got a throat full of snot and swallowed it. His eyes stung. He hadn't blinked since he'd heard the door. *Blink!* He couldn't. He stared at the man in the doorway. It was Emile. He was dressed as he was before, all in black. He had blood and something black smeared on one cheek and his forehead.

Emile glared down at him. His lips were so tightly clamped, they were white. The muscles in his jaws flexed. A vein in his temple throbbed.

"I hope you're worth it," he said. "Whatever it is they're trying to do, I hope you're worth it."

The guy's hand went behind his back, returned with a big knife.

Logan couldn't get enough air. *In, out, in, out—fast.* That beating fist in his chest squeezed. His heart hurt like a pulled muscle. It *hurt.*

Calm down, Logan, he thought. *It's like the movies . . . like the movies . . .*

The man stepped in. He leaned over the tub, putting his free hand on the tile wall.

Like the movies . . . like the movies . . .

Emile brought the knife down and sliced the ziplock between Logan's knees. He lowered his other hand and pushed a finger under the tape at the corner of his mouth.

"Hold still," he said. He brought the knife in, and the tape fell away.

See? Just like in the movies.

But Logan didn't think he'd be as nasty minded as before to the characters who freaked out, thinking they were about to be killed when everyone in the audience knew they were just going to get cut loose.

Emile pulled the washcloth out of his mouth.

Logan let spit pour off his tongue onto his chest. He spat. He gulped in big, deep breaths. He started to cry.

Emile backed away. He leaned against the sink, crossed his arms, and watched.

Logan closed his eyes, pinching off the tears. He looked at the man, who said, "You done?"

"Yeah." It came out a whisper.

Emile knelt at the edge of the tub. He cut the tape between Logan's arms and body, but his wrists were still bound to his ankles at his butt. Emile slipped the knife behind Logan, and his neck sprang free from the faucet.

The man said, "What's your name, kid?"

"Don't you know?"

Emile said nothing. He pushed Logan, rocking him forward. His head fell toward the bottom of the tub. A hand on his shoulder stopped him, then eased him down. Logan's hands sprang free, but he couldn't bring them around; his shoulders flared in pain when he tried. Next, Emile released his feet.

Logan rolled onto his side, sliding down to the bottom of the tub. He groaned. He couldn't move his arms or legs. His neck and shoulders were so stiff, it occurred to him that Emile might have stabbed him; he'd let Logan bleed out in the tub and be done with it. But there was no blood pooling under him, so he guessed he was all right.

"Work it out," Emile said, standing.

Logan said, "My name is Logan. You're Emile, right?"

The guy walked out.

Logan slowly did work out the kinks, at least enough to move. The soreness remained.

Emile came back in. He lifted a short stack of clothes for Logan to see. He set them on the counter. "They'll be too big for you, but I think you'll feel better getting out of what you're wearing."

He didn't wait for a thank-you—good thing, because Logan wouldn't have given one. He left, pulling the door shut behind him. He said, "Don't lock it."

When he pulled himself out of the tub, Logan realized how much he hurt—everywhere. Getting undressed was worse. Even as the blood returned to his limbs, and the muscles loosened, he found new areas of pain. Either the tape around his neck had been tighter than he'd thought, or he'd pulled at it too much. His throat—from skin to . . . whatever was in there . . . felt like it was on fire. With his clothes off, he examined the stack Emile had given him: white boxers; black pants with lots of pockets; a black T-shirt. All of it was big enough to be his dad's.

Emile opened the door. He held open a plastic bag. "Your stuff."

When Logan had scooped up his soiled clothes and dumped them in the bag, the man said, "Take a shower."

Logan looked at the tub, back to the man. The last thing he wanted to do was get in *there* again.

"I'm not your old man," Emile said. "I'm not trying to teach you good hygiene, but I have to be with you for a while, so . . ." He gestured toward the shower.

"What's 'a while'?" Logan said.

Emile stared at him a moment, then pulled the door closed.

FIFTY-SEVEN

"Michael O'Dey?" Hutch said.

Sitting on the bed, the young man nodded. His arms were crossed tightly over his chest, his back pressed against the wall. He rocked slowly forward and back.

The motel room was dingy and small, but it seemed quiet. Hutch liked that it was close to the highway, in case they had to travel quickly.

Earlier, Laura and Macie had gone into the bathroom with the XTerra's small first-aid kit to tend to Laura's shoulder wound. After they'd returned, the kit nearly empty, Laura and Hutch had gone into the adjoining room to talk to Michael. Laura had closed the drapes against the eye-aching sunlight.

Now the only illumination came from a dim bulb behind a grime-covered shade beside the bed. Laura and Hutch were leaning against a low dresser across from the foot of the bed.

"Son," Hutch said, "I met your father last night."

Michael's eyes snapped up.

"Jim, right?" Hutch said.

Michael nodded. His eyes were hungry, waiting for information.

"He'd . . . um, come to help you," Hutch said. "You called him the other day, and he'd driven up from . . ." He tried to remember.

"Portland," Michael said.

Hutch's eyes caught Laura's. He turned back to the boy. "He wanted to get you out of Outis. He approached me because he thought I could help."

"Is he still there?" Michael said slowly. "We have to let him know I left."

Hutch considered sitting near Michael on the bed. If it had been anyone else, he would have. The boy appeared subdued, but so did alligators before they lurched for their next meal. Given the erratic behavior he had exhibited, he needed to show a lot more restraint before Hutch could trust him.

"Michael," Hutch said, "your father got hurt. One of Page's men shot him."

Michael's eyes flashed open. His lips formed words, but no sound emerged.

"He was alive when I dropped him off at the hospital," Hutch said. "As soon as I can, I'll try to find out his condition."

Michael focused on something far away and frowned. He rocked over his crossed legs, then bumped his head into the wall, producing a hollow thump.

After a few minutes Laura said, "Michael, we need to know about Outis. What can you tell us?"

Nothing about him changed. He continued to rock, gazing into a dark corner of the room.

"Outis soldiers kidnapped my son last night," Hutch said. "He's only twelve."

Michael stopped rocking. His eyes shifted to meet Hutch's.

Hutch said, "I think you can help me. Will you do that, will you help?"

Michael nodded, and when Hutch thought that was all he *could* do, Michael said, "How?"

He sounded lucid, together. It was as though a breakdown were hitting him in waves. Hutch didn't know if the waters of mental collapse were at low tide or had merely ebbed out until the next breaker. Slowly at first, then more rapidly, he lobbed questions at the boy. Laura stepped in when she felt an answer needed more elaboration or Hutch's question seemed unclear.

They learned about Michael's recruitment, how an invitation to "try out" at Outis had come through a massively multiplayer online game. He told them about his being selected for an elite division called Quarterback. Most interesting to Hutch was Outis's use of video games and virtual reality to train their soldiers. He realized that Outis was using the technology for more than honing skills.

"They desensitized you to violence," Hutch said. He turned to Laura. "You know how everyone complains that violent video games and television shows and movies eventually numb people to the horrors of death? Page is using that, accelerating the process to make his soldiers killers without emotions."

"Sounds like *A Clockwork Orange*," Laura said.

"In reverse," Hutch agreed. "Instead of using images of violence to try to make people so sick of it they become nonviolent, Page uses it to intentionally create people who thrive on it."

"No," Michael said. He looked from one to the other. "You don't get it."

Hutch narrowed his eyes at him.

"Outis isn't desensitizing us," Michael said. "They're *confusing* us."

"I don't understand," Laura said.

"They make it so we don't know when we're really killing or when it's a game. We don't even know *who* we're killing." He told them about the hit on the rebel leader, and how his team had wiped out a family, children and all.

Laura covered her mouth as he spoke. Hutch, knowing something about Nichols's family, put faces to Michael's words. He found himself taking quick, short breaths and forced himself to slow down.

The last few minutes of Michael's tale was told through his tears. He stuttered through how his team had ostracized him and how he suspected his own inability to distinguish reality from fantasy. He turned and dropped his face into a pillow. His shoulder hitched up and down as the intensity of his wrenching sobs rose and dipped.

Hutch touched Laura's arm. He whispered, "Blind adherence to orders doesn't work in war. When we give a soldier a weapon, we expect some sort of . . . I don't know, moral double-checking. Otherwise, what's the difference between a nuclear bomb and a squad of killers wiping out everything in their path?"

"Deceiving them takes away their ability to chose, to agree or disagree with their orders," she said. "Making people think they're shooting adults who mean them harm when they're actually killing children is simple trickery. Evil, but simple." She watched Michael weep.

"But confusing the soldiers makes a sort of twisted sense," she continued. "It allows the soldier to believe, rightly or wrongly, that he hasn't done anything wrong. All the atrocities he's committed weren't real, even if some or all of them were. It's an escape hatch. Like at least one weapon in a firing squad containing a blank cartridge. It makes all of the executioners better shots, because it eliminates the 'taking life' aspect of the task. Each chooses to believe he was the one with the blank."

Hutch gestured toward the connecting door, and Laura went to it.

"Michael," Hutch said, "Laura, the kids, and I are in the next room. We're going to get some sleep. Knock on the connecting door if you need anything. You're not our prisoner, you know that. You can leave anytime you want. But if you stay, we'll find help for you. Whatever it takes. All right?"

Michael turned his head. His eyes were red and wet. He nodded.

Laura opened the door, and they slipped into the next room. Macie and Dillon were lying on the bed, watching a kids' show. They both smiled, then turned back to the television. They were wiped out. Hutch locked the connecting door. Laura leaned around him to check it.

"I feel sorry for him," she said quietly. "But he still scares me."

Hutch sighed. "Between his knowledge of Outis and Julian on the inside, I'm starting to think we can really do this, that we can get Logan back."

"Of course we can," she said. "You still think we should drive up there, to Washington?" She shook her head. "It seems like such a long shot."

"I need to get to either Page or Logan. I have no clue where Logan is, but I do know Page is at the compound."

Laura blinked slowly and yawned.

"Get some sleep," he said, rubbing her shoulder. "I'm going to find a pay phone and call Larry. I'm hoping he can pick up a few things for us."

"Like what?"

"Cash, mostly," Hutch said. "And we can all use a change of clothes." He unzipped his leather jacket and held it open for her to see the shirt underneath, which looked as though he'd drenched it in a brownish-maroon liquid.

"Hutch!" she said.

The kids turned to look.

"Daddy!" Macie squealed. She began scrambling over Dillon to reach her father.

"Whoa, honey," Hutch said, holding up his hand. "It's not my blood. Not the majority of it, anyway." He made eye contact with Laura and nodded toward the connecting door. "Michael's dad."

Laura pinched the bloody material over his chest and tugged on it. It resisted, then pulled away with a Velcro sound.

"Oww," Hutch said.

Laura grimaced. She said, "There's a gas station and convenience store up the street. I bet they have a cheap T-shirt."

He nodded. "We'll top off the tank too. Let's get some sleep and plan on heading out tonight."

Laura bobbed her head up and down. Her hair fell over her face, and she looked utterly exhausted.

"It's going to be okay," Hutch said. "You'll see."

She smiled at him. "I'm supposed to tell *you* that."

"When I forget to say it," Hutch said, "then it's your turn."

FIFTY-EIGHT

When Logan stepped out of the bathroom, Emile was sitting on one of the room's two beds, flipping though news channels. A machine gun leaned against the wall by the door, within Emile's grasp. A canvas tote bag occupied the bed behind him. He looked Logan up and down.

"I need a belt," Logan said. He was holding a wad of excess waistband in front.

Emile looked at the other bed. Logan followed his gaze and screamed. Two bodies lay on top of the bedspread, shoulder to shoulder. He recognized one of them as the man who had tied him up: Anton. One of his forearms was bent as though he had another elbow there. Something under his shirt didn't look right either; it was bumpy and poking up where it shouldn't be. His face was battered and bruised. Someone—Emile, most likely—had wiped some of the gore away, but a lot remained.

The other guy Logan had seen earlier as well. He was the corpse from the back of the van, the one Logan had kept rolling into and trying not to look at. It was this guy's blood that had soaked Logan's pant leg. The nub of an arrow protruded from the left side of his neck. It was broken off before the fletchings, probably to make the body easier to move. Brownish goop—dried blood, Logan knew—covered half his face, his left arm and chest.

Logan started hyperventilating again.

"Knock it off," Emile said. "They're bodies, kid. You'll leave yours behind one day too."

"What . . . what happened to them?"

"Isn't that obvious?" Emile punched the remote. Another news station came on.

"Why are they here?"

"Where should they be?"

"Not *here*. Your car?"

Emile flipped to another channel.

The bodies hovered at the corner of Logan's vision, like ghosts trying to sneak up on him. He turned his back to them. He said, "Could you cover them up? Please?"

Emile threw an exasperated glance at him. He sighed. He stood and walked between the beds. When no sounds came, Logan looked. Emile was frozen there, just staring at the dead men.

"They were your friends," Logan said.

Emile's face became hard, the way it had been when he'd come into the bathroom to cut Logan loose. He said, "They were soldiers."

He bent over Anton and unbuckled the man's belt. He yanked it free of the loops and held it out to Logan.

"I don't want it," Logan said.

"Don't be a baby."

Logan took it, examined it for blood, didn't find any. He threaded it around his waist, but it was too long to do any good.

Emile grabbed it. His knife came out and sliced off a foot of leather. With the knife's tip, he made an extra hole where Logan needed it. He turned from Logan, sheathing the knife. He moved the canvas tote from the unused bed to the floor, pulled off the bedspread, and billowed it over the bodies.

Logan crinkled his nose. "Are they going to . . ."

"What?"

"You know, start *smelling*?"

Emile went back to the end of the bed, snatched up the remote, and sat. Staring at the screen, he said, "Not as bad as you did in the tub." His boot bumped a white paper bag on the floor. He picked it up, said, "Here," and tossed it at Logan. It was a fast-food breakfast: hash browns, a sausage-and-egg biscuit sandwich, a croissant. Logan's stomach reminded him how much it wanted that food. But the bodies on the bed . . .

It felt like someone had dropped a bowling ball on his gut.

Better eat, he thought. *Who knows when you'll get more food.*

He stepped near the bathroom door, where he couldn't see the bodies. He sat on the carpet and put the bag in his lap. Once he bit into the biscuit sandwich, he forgot about who else . . . *what* else . . . besides Emile shared the room. He shoved it in as fast as he could.

"You're going to choke," Emile said.

Logan licked his lips and nodded. He squinted at Emile. "How old are you?"

Emile hit a button, muting the television's volume. He said, "What's it to you?"

"You don't seem very old." Logan checked the bag: no napkins. He wiped his lips on the bag.

"So?"

Logan shrugged. He grimaced at the pain in his neck and shoulder. "Doing all this," he said. "Kidnapping, guns, almost getting killed."

"That's what soldiers do."

"*Kidnapping*? I mean, *kids*? In the United States? You sound American. Are you American?"

Emile scowled. "Shut up and eat."

Logan chewed. He watched Emile glaring at the TV screen with the volume turned off. He said, "What time is it?"

Emile brought his wristwatch up. "Eight thirty."

"What are we going to do?"

"You're going to shut up, and I'm going to get some sleep." He glanced at Logan. "Don't think that means you're getting away. I'm going to tie you up again."

Logan felt sick.

"Not like you were," Emile said. "If I can trust you to be quiet, I'll just—" His eyes roamed the room. He indicated the heating/air-conditioning unit under the window next to the door. "I'll just zip tie you to that. You can sleep on the floor."

Zip tie, Logan thought. In his mind, he'd been calling it ziplock. The vocabulary lesson helped him not think about sleeping in the same room with dead people. He said, "Then what?"

"Then we'll see." Emile waved the remote like a wand at the television and clicked it off. He stood up. "You done?"

Logan pushed half a croissant in his mouth. He nodded. He got up, crumpled the bag, and tossed it into a wastebasket.

Emile was fishing through the tote bag. He pulled out a handful of zip ties. He said, "Hit the head, dude. I don't want you waking me up, and I don't have any more pants for you." He knelt beside the bulky contraption that would be Logan's prison for the next few hours—

better than the way he'd been hogtied in the bathtub—and began searching for anchor points.

Logan continued chewing. He wiped his fingers on the T-shirt. He wondered how someone as young as Emile could wind up where he was, doing what he did.

Emile spotted him watching. "Hey," he said, pulling out his knife, twisting the point into the air-conditioning unit. "We're, like, getting along and everything, right? Kind of two guys hanging out?" He waggled the knife back and forth between the two of them. "But you need to remember that's not the way it is. If you try to get away, if you try to signal somebody . . . anything like that, I will kill you. Won't even hesitate. You understand?"

Logan caught a whiff of something unpleasant and thought it was coming from one of the bodies.

"Well?" Emile said.

Logan nodded. He went into the bathroom and shut the door. Emile reminded him not to lock it. He frowned at his image in the mirror. Just in time, he turned to the toilet, lifted the lid, and puked up his breakfast.

FIFTY-NINE

Shortly before midnight, Hutch edged the XTerra to the heavy gate at the entrance to the *Denver Post*'s parking garage. He waved his pass card in front of a reader, and the gate rattled open. The next day's issue would have been put to bed about half an hour before. Evening-shift employees were leaving, but the paper's graveyard shift kept a good number of cars in the garage through the night. Hutch steered the SUV onto an ascending spiral ramp.

They had slept through the afternoon and early evening. None of them had truly rested the night before—the kids a little in the car, and Michael, though Hutch wasn't sure you could count getting knocked out as sleeping. The crash that followed adrenaline-fueled activity and emotional chaos, like intense fear, had hit them hard. A few times during the day, Hutch had awakened. When he had checked on Michael in the next room, the boy had seemed to be sleeping soundly, normally. Sometime after Dillon and Macie had turned on the television, and Laura had gone out for food, Michael had rapped gently on the connecting door. He had climbed on the bed with the younger children and sat with his back against the headboard, quietly watching cartoons.

Laura and Hutch had decided to get a late start, which allowed them to rest more and meet Larry when the chance of the building being watched was smallest. They would drive through the night and assess their energy level in the morning, and decide whether one of them was up to continuing or it was time to find a place to rest. Hutch had argued for coffee and NoDoz until they reached Page's compound, until they rescued Logan, but Laura had made the point that he would have to be in better condition when they arrived in Washington than he was in now.

Hutch had agreed, but had said, "Every second Logan's gone feels like a lifetime of failing him."

"Don't go to a movie," Laura had said, giving his arm an encouraging squeeze. "But sleep when you need to, eat when you can. Staying sharp and fit is part of what you have to do right now."

Her advice had reminded him of one of the reasons he had enjoyed being married. It had tempered him; he had shared life's blessings and had someone to ease its disappointments.

Maybe Page had been right: Hutch possessed an obsessive personality. It simply never had a chance to blossom into nuttiness while he'd been married to Miss "Let's Be Reasonable." Since finding another guy and hitting Hutch with divorce papers—in that order, he thought bitterly—Janet had become Queen B of the Universe. Prior to that, however, Hutch had loved her dearly.

It had surprised him when Laura had started stirring similar feelings during their long telephone conversations after he'd returned from

Canada. But his kids were here, and she was there—and newly widowed, he'd reminded himself. So he'd pushed her out of his mind. And that had been about the time his outrage at Page had ratcheted up. *Filling a void*, he thought now.

Hutch pulled past an empty parking space. His name was stenciled to the wall.

"Hey, that's you," Dillon said. "Cool."

It struck Hutch how not just physically, but mentally limber kids were. The world could be ending around them, and they would acknowledge a school chum in the distance or lament missing their favorite TV show. Most adults would label it *lack of focus*—but Hutch thought there was something more important at play, some kind of creative and intuitive energy.

A survivalist he had interviewed told him that getting in a rut, figuratively speaking, was the worst thing that could happen to people lost in the wilderness. The man had said, "It doesn't matter if the rut is thinking you're dead no matter what you do, or being determined to get out alive. Focusing too sharply on one thing means everything else is blurry."

He described an incident in which a lost hiker was so focused on getting over the next mountain, he'd walked right past a canoe that would have floated him to a nearby town. Instead, the guy had died. Hutch had dedicated a column to one fact the man had told him: businesspeople are more likely than tradesmen to die in survival situations. "Not because they're wussies," he'd said. "They're just too tunnel-visioned on an outcome, and not so open to the various ways to reach it. They make a plan and stick to it, regardless."

Hutch thought it boiled down to the age-old wisdom of bending like a young tree, not breaking like an old, dry one. He hoped he could keep that in mind as he faced whatever chaos Page had planned for him.

He put the car in reverse and backed into the space.

"I shouldn't be long, then we'll be off," he said. He looked over the seat back at Macie. "It's not the kind of car trip I wanted to take with you, sweetie. When we get Logan back, we'll do something really fun, Disney or something like that."

"Me too?" Dillon said.

"I think we can work something out." Hutch glanced at Laura, who nodded. He gave Michael a wry smile. "You want to come?"

"I told you I'm ready to help," Michael said. He opened the car door.

"I meant to Disneyland," Hutch said.

Michael frowned, then smiled. "Yeah, sure. What about here? You need a hand?"

"Help Laura watch out for dangers. We'll have a few days on the road to figure out how all of us can pull together to get Logan back." He nodded at the notepad in Michael's lap. They had picked it up for him at Wal-Mart. He said, "The best thing you can do right now is keep writing down everything you know about Outis. The layout, its security, any weaknesses. Think about where you'd stash a twelve-year-old boy."

Michael flinched as though Hutch had accused him. Hutch believed the damage Outis had done crackled just under the surface. Like cleansing a cult's influence from a former member's conscious and subconscious, it would take years to detoxify this boy.

Michael's flinch, though, was something else, something Hutch had not thought about at the motel. It was guilt by association. Michael had not taken Logan, but his team had: close enough.

Thinking it would shift the blame to the proper shoulders, Hutch added, "If you were Page."

Michael nodded. He lowered his eyes to the notepad. He put pen to paper, but his hand didn't move. He seemed to stare at the speck of ink the pen had deposited as if waiting for it to snake out across the page and answer Hutch's questions of its own accord.

Hutch felt little fingers pressing on his shoulder. Macie was leaning forward in her seat. He gave her a reassuring smile.

She said, "I don't care about Disneyland, Daddy. I just want Logan home."

"Me too, sweetheart. He'll be tearing up the house and back to insulting you before you know it."

"That'd be okay," she said. "He can if he wants to."

"That's what big brothers do, right?"

"I wish he was my big brother," Dillon said.

Hutch narrowed his eyes at Dillon. He said, "You just want somebody to help you with the chores."

"And to go hunting and camping with."

Dillon's smile was so broad, Hutch thought he could see every one of the boy's teeth.

"Well . . ." Hutch said. "Logan never really got into the hunting thing. He kind of liked camping when he was little. Not so much anymore."

Macie said, "He likes video games now. And football and skate-boarding."

"Video games of playing football on skateboards," Hutch said.

Macie smiled, and he could tell she was thinking of her brother. He raised his eyebrows at her. "And drawing," he said. "He's been really getting into drawing lately."

She wrinkled her nose. "Gross stuff. People with big swords, fight-ing . . ."

"I don't know," Hutch said. "What about those cartoons?"

Macie laughed. It was a sparkling sound, free of the tension that had tightened her face all day. She glanced around at Laura, Dillon, and Michael, pulling them into her memories of Logan. "He did this one," she said, barely containing herself. "These babies are sitting around a table in their diapers. They're playing poker and drinking beer and smoking cigars. Under it he wrote, 'Why guys should not babysit.'"

Laura and Dillon laughed. Michael was too intent on the ink spot to have even heard.

Hutch said, "He did that one after I asked him to babysit Macie while I went to the store. I made him stop playing *Zelda* so he could pay attention to her."

"Logan showed me some of his cartoons," Dillon said. "They were good." He shrugged. "It's okay that he doesn't like hunting and camping."

Hutch opened his door. It lightened his heart to leave them like this, rather than the gloom-and-doom that had been hanging over them. They could not be in a worse situation: Logan kidnapped; the man who took him bent on making a point or revenge or . . . Hutch didn't know; all of them—kids!—on a trek to the dragon's lair.

Still, the mind could be wound only so tightly for so long. They needed relief, a breather. They needed reminders, however brief, of what made life worth living.

According to Laura, adversity was what gave meaning to Hutch. He understood how it could look that way. He sprang to action when a situation required it. Did he feel more alive going after Brendan Page than he did hugging his son, hearing his daughter laugh? He didn't think so. He didn't think that action necessarily translated into living life to its fullest. Otherwise, what was sitting on a grassy knoll, watching the sunset with a person you love? What was falling asleep on the couch, your children cuddled up next to you?

No, Laura had witnessed Hutch's kicking into gear because that's what was required of him. She did not see his heart, what truly made it beat.

"Start the car, if you need the heater or the radio or something," he told Laura.

"My CD!" Macie said.

"Carrie Underwood," Hutch said. "It's in there. Disc number four, I think."

"Got it," Laura said. She reached for the key in the ignition to give the stereo some juice.

Hutch shut the door and went to the back of the car to fetch the hockey equipment bag they'd picked up at the store. It was full of the Outis items he wanted to show Larry. As he came back around, Laura was leaning over the driver's seat to lower the window.

"What about cops?" she said.

Hutch looked around. He didn't see any guards, just a few stragglers making their way home. He said, "Larry said they'd come by. They think I'm in Washington, but it won't be long for them to figure out I returned. Just keep a lookout." He slung the bow bag strap over his shoulder, patted the windowsill, and said, "Be right back."

SIXTY

Hutch's desk was on the fifth floor. It was a level above the newsroom, where people bustled 24/7. His floor housed the staff concerned with less timely issues—entertainment, food, fashion, home and garden. Hutch's column covered people who epitomized the "spirit of Colorado." To fully embrace his subjects' crises and triumphs—often the impetus for drawing out that spirit—Hutch spent most of his time in the field, interviewing, taking it all in. During the past year, focused as he was on Page, he'd relied heavily on telephone interviews and worked more increasingly from his home office. He didn't get around to his desk here all that much anymore. In fact, he'd learned recently that his cubicle wasn't only his anymore. He now shared his space with the guy who covered little communities around the state and a woman who wrote a column called Women and Wheels. Consequently, he kept nothing here that would help him now.

He traversed the central passageway between cubicles, toward Larry's office. The overhead fluorescents had been turned off. Light from one of the cubicles glowed against the ceiling on the other side of the big room. Fingernails clicked over a keyboard. He thought it was Joanne Macintire, the society columnist, probably back from some black-tie affair. How she cranked out coherent columns after partying, Hutch never knew. When Joanne had heard about his divorce, she had invited him to something like a soirée or debutante ball. Knowing he'd feel as awkward as Hulk Hogan having tea and crumpets at Buckingham Palace, he'd declined.

He was almost at Larry's office. Through the glass wall, he could see his friend behind the desk. His face was buried in his hands.

"Hutch!" Joanne was hurrying toward him in a fancy chiffon dress. "'Bout time you came in."

"How's it going, Joanne? I just stopped in to see Larry for a minute."

"What are you doing with that?" She slapped at the bow bag. Metal rattled within.

He turned it away from her. "Camping," he said.

She looked at him as though he'd said *brain surgery*. A second later, she'd forgotten it. She touched his arm. "Listen, the Governor's Ball is coming up and—just hear me out. You're kind of a local celebrity now, you know, with the saving-a-whole-town-in-Canada stuff and the news stories, *60 Minutes*, oh my goodness. Anyway, I just happened to mention to the mayor that you could maybe be persuaded to come."

Larry was looking at him now, his eyes wide, his hands spread to say, *Come on!*

"Let me think about it," Hutch said.

"Really? Hey, I'll take anything that's not *no*. I've got a press kit about it . . . hold on." She flitted toward her cubicle. Her backless dinner gown was way too backless.

"Catch me next time, Joanne," Hutch said. "I really gotta run."

She waved her hand at him, and he stepped into Larry's office.

"Shut the door," Larry said, coming around the desk. He pulled a cord, closing the blinds over his view of the cubicles. Beyond his desk, a large window looked out on the building across the street, a turn-of-the-century brick structure with lots of interesting architectural features—vastly different from the modern design of the *Post* building.

Hutch always told Larry he had the better end of the deal: "I'd rather be *in* this building, *looking* at that one, than vice versa." It wasn't the grand vista Page looked out on, but at least the *Post*'s "decorative" Plexiglas-faced balcony-like structure didn't run up over his windows, as it did the science editor's office next to Larry's.

Larry swept his arm over his desk, pushing aside a pen holder, a paper tray, books. "What do you have?" he asked.

Hutch clunked the bag onto the desk. "You'd think I robbed Fort Knox, the way you said that."

"Hey, evidence that could put Brendan Page behind bars? You bet I'm excited."

"I don't know about evidence," Hutch said, unzipping the bag. "I'm sure Page has distanced himself from all of this stuff." He held the flaps closed and simply stared at Larry, thinking.

"And you know something?" he said. "I don't even care. I don't care if I've got his fingerprints, his DNA, and a video of him stabbing somebody. I just want my son back."

Larry shook his head. "I know, I know. That's all that matters. You haven't heard anything?"

"He's toying with me, driving me crazy with silence."

"But you still think he had Logan brought to Outis?"

"It's the only move that makes sense. Even if Logan's not there, Page is. I have to get to one of them."

Larry said, "And you're willing to let everything you know about Page go? Cut bait and run?" He looked at Hutch skeptically.

"Larry, this is my family. . . ."

Larry's eyes dropped to the bag. "So, what's *this*?"

Hutch pulled out the machine pistol. "I wasn't thinking of evidence. More like, how can these things help us get Logan back?" Hutch handed Larry the weapon.

Larry held it at arm's length by the tips of his fingers.

"It's not loaded," Hutch said. He pulled a spent shell from his pocket and showed it to Larry. "It fires 9mm. Pretty common. You don't happen to have any or know someone who does?"

"*Me?* Not me."

"I can probably pick some up on my way to Washington," Hutch said.

Larry turned the gun over in his hands, growing more comfortable.

Hutch said, "When I was at Outis, I saw Julian."

"Julian Page, Brendan's son? The one who . . . ?"

Hutch nodded. "I gave him my cell phone. I think he can help me get into the complex."

Larry read the look on Hutch's face. "What is it?"

"I've tried calling a few times," Hutch said. "He hasn't called back."

"Maybe they took it from him." Larry handed the weapon to Hutch.

"I'm hoping I tried at the wrong times. You know, when he couldn't answer or was away from wherever he stashed it." He looked at his watch. "Probably in bed now."

"So call," Larry said. "Does he have roommates?"

Hutch shrugged.

Larry said, "If you can't call him in the middle of the night, when can you?"

Hutch placed the gun on the desk. He turned Larry's phone around to face him. He picked up the handset, thought about Nichols and the phone tap that Page must have used to find him, and replaced it. "Larry, you got your cell phone?"

Larry shook his head. "Battery died. It's charging in the car. What's wrong with that one?"

"Page."

Larry's eyes snapped to it as though it had hopped up and run across the desk.

"You know," Hutch said, picking up the desk phone, "as far as Julian goes, Page probably has my mobile bugged anyway, so it doesn't matter what phone I use. As for me, I'll be out of here in a few minutes." He dialed. Before the first ring he said, "I hate asking, Larry, but did you have a chance to get some cash?"

"I hope a couple grand will do," Larry said. He went to his desk chair and sat. He opened a drawer.

"That's great, man, thank—"

A groggy voice answered. "Hello?"

"Julian, it's me. Did I wake you?" He nodded at Larry.

"Yeah, but . . . I put the phone under my pillow. It's on vibrate, like you said, but I felt it."

"Can you talk?"

"Yeah, I'm alone." Sleep still clung to his words. "Where are you?"

"I'm at a friend's place in Vail." Worth a try. Maybe it would throw off Page's men for a time. "Have you heard what's happened? About Logan and the attacks on me and Laura?"

"Logan?"

"My son. Julian, your father had him kidnapped."

"What? Why?" The voice was fully awake now.

"Soldiers attacked us," Hutch said. "Me up there in Washington; Laura, Dillon, Logan, and my daughter in Colorado. Something went wrong, and they took Logan."

"What did they look like, the people who attacked you?"

"Black everything. Pants, jackets . . ."

"Full-face helmets?"

"High-tech ones, I think."

"That's Outis," Julian said. "My dad has these new teams of soldiers—"

"Genjuros?" Hutch said.

Pause. "What?"

"Is that what he calls them, these teams?"

"I haven't heard that one," Julian said. "The program's called Quarterback—Quick-Response Black-Ops."

Michael had mentioned Quarterback, but not what the name meant. Sounded to Hutch like a military take on the Genjuros model.

Julian continued. "It's less than a year old. There are only three teams right now, sort of prototypes. One returned yesterday morning from an overnight training mission."

Nichols, Hutch thought. Larry had told him Nichols had died the night before Hutch and Laura were attacked.

"The other two left yesterday afternoon," the boy said. "They were still gone when I went to bed."

"Julian, listen," Hutch said. "I think they're taking Logan back to Outis. I'm going to—"

Larry extended his hand across the desk, a thick wad of cash in it. Hutch reached for it.

It all happened at once: With a sound like a branch snapping, the window pane behind Larry cracked. A fissure instantly appeared, running straight up to the top from a half-dollar-sized hole. Larry slammed his head down onto the desk. Blood splattered over Hutch's face. Hutch flinched, dropped the phone, and hit the floor.

"Larry!" he said. "Larry!"

He scampered around the desk on all fours. He grabbed Larry's arm and shook it.

"Larry!"

He tugged him out of the chair, catching him before he hit the floor. He didn't have to check for vital signs. The exit wound said it all.

The office door burst open.

"Here it is, dear," Joanne said. "Hutch?" She saw the body in his arms and screamed. The folder in her hand fluttered to the floor.

"Go!" Hutch said. "Get out of here, now!"

She was frozen, a Madame Tussauds wax figure with a siren mouth—wailing out an alarm.

"Joanne!"

She stumbled back against the blinds. Her hand covered her mouth. She rolled out of the door and fell.

"Run!" Hutch said. He gently laid Larry's head on the floor.

He wiped a hand over his own face and gaped at the blood smeared across his fingers and palm. He crawled over Larry's body, trying not to bump it or put weight on it, as though that mattered now. He crouched below the windowsill. The glass continued to crack, making a noise like a knife tip scratching tile. Wind whistled through the hole, a mournful soundtrack to Larry's death.

Hutch popped his head up, down. He did it three more times before spotting the man standing on the terrace of the building across the street. It was the outdoor dining area of a restaurant Hutch had patronized many times. It was on the sixth floor, which put the man slightly above Hutch's position.

When he looked again, the man's head was obscured by a cloud of smoke, which caught the terrace's dim after-hour lights. It drifted away, revealing Brendan Page's smirky, devil-may-care face. He wore the same black uniform as the soldiers. Under one arm he held a black helmet, in the manner of a motor racer posing for the press. Extending up behind his shoulder was the long barrel of a rifle.

Hutch clamped his fists on the sill. "*Paaaaage!*"

Page plucked a cigar from his lips and waved.

"Hutch!" Julian yelled into the phone. He swung his legs out from under the covers and hooked them over the edge of the bed. He reached for the bedside lamp, flipped it on. The lamp tipped over. Julian caught sight of himself in a mirror over the dresser, pale, terrified. The shadows on his face and the long shadow cast against the opposite wall stretched and rose up, and the light came down. His heart skipped as, for a moment, it appeared as though his soul were seeping from his pores and flying away. The lamp struck the floor, and the light blinked out.

He'd heard Hutch yelling a name—*Larry*—and the clattering of things being tossed around. A woman had spoken, then he heard screaming, a whooping, high-pitched sound even over the phone lines.

The coup de grâce to Julian's heart still echoed in his ears: "*Paaaaage!*"

"Hutch!" he called into the phone. He found the speaker button and pushed it. Indistinct rattles, bumps, and shuffling came from the tiny speaker. He dropped it to the bed and began pulling on his clothes.

SIXTY-ONE

Page was *waving* at him.

Hutch ducked under the windowsill. The rifle on Page's back didn't mean that another soldier wasn't taking aim at him. He peered over the sill, but didn't spot a shooter. Page was now gesturing for Hutch to stand.

Hutch hunkered lower. Page clearly intended on killing him, then Laura, Dillon, Macie, and Logan. Hutch wasn't about to let that happen, certainly not as easily as Page apparently hoped.

Hutch scurried to the desk. He snagged the phone and pulled it down into his lap, then scooted back to the wall under the window. His finger shook as he punched in the number of the mobile phone he had taken from the convenience store clerk in Washington. He had left it in one of the XTerra's cup holders. As soon as he heard the first tone, he realized he had not dialed 9 to access an outside line.

Think! Don't panic now!

He closed his eyes and took a deep breath.

You have to do this, you have to do this. Don't think of Larry. Don't think about the man across the street trying to kill you. Just do this.

Another error tone. Different this time. A recorded voice told him the number he had dialed had been disconnected.

No!

He thought of the phone's owner. Had he reported it stolen? Had service to it been terminated? Had Hutch dialed the right number?

He dialed again, slowly this time. Every push of the button called up their faces: Macie . . . Dillon . . . Laura.

It rang, and Laura answered.

"Page is here," Hutch said. "He killed Larry."

"Hutch, no—"

"Listen. You have to go. Just take off now. I don't know how many people Page brought with him. Someone here saw what happened. I'm sure she called the police. You have to leave before they come. You can't get pinned down."

"Hutch . . . um, where . . . I . . ."

"Shhh, shhh." He had to think. He said, "Page might be monitoring the phones. He has that number, the mobile phone you're on. So get out now, before he blocks you in."

He could hear the kids in the background, panicky, asking for details. The loudest voice was Michael's.

"Laura? Can you hear me?"

"Michael wants to help."

"No! Tell him he can help by staying with you. Go to the restaurant we ate at the other day, when you and Dillon first came."

"Okay, okay," she said.

Hutch heard the seat belt warning chime, indicating she had started the car. She was doing it, staying together, making it happen.

Thumping, scraping came through the earpiece.

"Laura?"

Distant, she said, "Michael, no . . ."

Michael came on the line. "Hutch, let me help. I know these guys. I can get them, I know I can."

"Michael, stay with Laura. Give her the phone."

He heard Macie crying loudly in the background . . . Laura calling, "Get back in! Mic—"

A door slammed, and the voices cut off.

"Michael?" Hutch said. He was pressing the phone against his face so hard, his ear hurt. "Where are you?"

"I'm coming. What floor?"

"You've got to get out of here!" Hutch was screaming now. "Get back in the car. You're endangering their lives, Michael, the kids—"

"They're gone," he said. "I waved them on, said it was okay. They left."

"Are you sure? They left?"

"What floor are you on?"

Something clanged over the phone—a fire door, Hutch thought. He said, "Just stay there. It's the safest place."

Silence.

"Michael?"

He'd hung up. Hutch dropped the handset. What had Michael just done?

Flipped out, Hutch thought. *He went into attack mode or something.*

Thank God Laura had the sense to leave anyway. It was that ol' Mama Bear thing. *Let's see, who do I save: my son and my friend's little girl, or . . . a crazy kid who attacked us?* No contest.

He thought about where she would exit. It fed into Grant Street, a one-way avenue that would force her to cross the street running in front of the building. He poked his head up. Page was patiently waiting, standing there like he'd ordered an espresso. His hands were spread in the same *Come on!* shrug Larry had done not ten minutes earlier.

Hutch rose higher, and without being obvious, he leaned until Grant Street came into view.

Where are you, Laura? Get out of here.

Page tossed the cigar over the terrace balustrade. He reached behind him. His hand came back gripping an object.

Hutch jerked down, responsively. When he stood again, he saw the XTerra. It crossed Broadway, moving too slowly for Hutch's taste, but away . . . away. It disappeared beyond the building across the street.

Dropping down, he stopped. Page held a flashlight, flicking it on and off. When he was sure he had Hutch's attention, he left the light off. He strolled to the left edge of the terrace and peered into the shadows beyond. He held the flashlight up and out, like the Statue of Liberty with a tired arm, and turned it on.

Hutch caught his breath. His heart became a lead ball and plunged into his stomach.

Logan dangled below a window cleaner's platform that extended a few feet past the edge of the roof. His arms were wrenched over his head. The rope that bound his wrists was in turn tied to the bottom of the platform. He had managed to catch a ledge with the toes of his sneakers. Hutch could tell it lessened the weight on his arms, but it forced him to slant out from the building—giving him an unimpeded view of the seven-story plunge under him. He must be terrified.

As if intending to verify Hutch's thought, Page's light glinted off the boy's wet face and wide eyes. Duct tape covered his mouth, but the movements of Logan's jaws and cheeks told Hutch he was working his mouth, screaming.

His boy was screaming in terror.

Page looked across the open space at Hutch. He held an index finger up to pursed lips: *shhh*.

"What do you want!" Hutch screamed into the window.

Page beckoned to him.

Hutch found Logan again, just as Page snapped off the light. Darkness blotted his son from view. Hutch kept his eyes on the spot where he knew Logan was, the way lifeguards were taught to keep their eyes locked on the place a drowning victim was last seen.

Page had not simply tossed the boy to his death in front of Hutch. He wanted to talk. Or get Hutch closer, then kill them both. Either way, it bought them time. As long as Hutch was breathing they stood a chance, however slim, to get out of this alive.

Shhh, Page had instructed. *Shhh*. Why did that tighten Hutch's stomach?

He was pretty sure Page's "be quiet" gesture had meant *Don't call the cops*. The last thing Page would want was to be caught here with a kidnapped boy. Most likely he was still playing games, trying to make Hutch believe he was there for an exchange: Logan for Hutch's silence. They both knew, however, it would never play out like that—not with Page murdering Larry, not with Page's cold, black heart.

Still, if it meant Hutch getting closer to Page, to Logan, then he would act his part. And who knew what Page would do if he thought Hutch was setting him up, trapping him in?

But Joanne had seen Larry. No way she *wouldn't* have grabbed the first phone she'd seen. If she hadn't already made the call, Hutch would consider it a miracle.

He pushed away from the window and ran to the door. "Joanne! Joanne!"

He started into Cubicle City, then ducked back into Larry's office.

He grabbed the bow bag off the desk. Halfway to the elevator, he called for her again. No response. She was gone. He pictured her wringing her hands and telling her story between sobs to a knot of security guards as they waited for the DPD to respond.

What would Page do if he saw flashing lights? Would he take the time to get Logan down? Would he take him back to Washington with him, try again another day? Would he leave Logan dangling there for Hutch to rescue? Hutch didn't have many answers, but he knew this: if Page ever allowed Hutch to embrace his son again, this side of heaven, it would be on his terms.

And that just wouldn't do. Not in Hutch's book.

SIXTY-TWO

Hutch ran past the elevators. He noticed the floor indicators above the doors. The lifts that were not already on the first floor were heading for it. Standard procedure in an emergency: building security called all the elevators to the first floor and locked them down. They'd also lower and disable any parking garage gates in place. Laura had gotten out just in time.

Hutch pushed through the door into the stairwell and started down. Several floors below, a door crashed open. Shoes pounded up the stairs. Hutch gazed between the rails down the center of the staircase, but saw only a shadow gliding along with the staccato beat.

"Michael?" he called.

The person kept coming.

Hutch propped his foot on a low railing, rested the bag on his thigh, and opened it up. He rummaged through it and found what he wanted.

He had the bow, which he'd re-strung at the hotel, partially out when the quiver snagged on something. He shook the bow in vain, then released his grip on the bag to fish his hand inside.

"Freeze!"

A building security guard stood on the landing directly below, waving a revolver at him. He was huffing for breath, but wide-eyed, full of adrenaline.

"Someone shot at us from across the street," Hutch said. "He's holding my boy hostage. I need to get over there. *He has my son!*"

"What's that?" the guard said.

"A bow . . . arrows. I'm a hunter. It's the only weapon I have. Listen—"

"No, *you* listen." The guard's facial muscles tightened. "Let go of that bow, slip your hand out of the bag—slowly!—and let the bag and bow and whatever else is in there just fall off your leg. Is that clear?"

"Officer, you don't understand. The man across the street has kidnapped my son. He killed Larry Waters. My name is John Hutchinson, I'm a columnist here."

"We're not having this conversation until you drop the—"

If a bull had ripped the fourth-floor door out of the jamb with its horns and flung it aside, it couldn't have startled Hutch more—or appeared more indomitably forceful—than Michael bursting through and tackling the guard. The pistol fired, zinging off the concrete underside of higher steps above Hutch's head. The bag slipped off his leg and bounced down the stairs. Michael sat on the guard's chest, beating him in the head with both fists. The guard weakly struck Michael in the arm and side with his gun.

"Michael," Hutch said. "Stop!"

The boy was wild, screaming. Out of his wailing rage, a single word began to take form: "No . . . no . . . no . . . no . . . !"

Hutch descended to the landing. He seized Michael's collar and arm, and tugged.

Michael's knees squeezed the guard's torso, holding him in place.

Hutch pulled again. The boy fell sideways, jerked his arm out of Hutch's grasp, pushed at Hutch.

"Leave me alone!" Michael said. "It's not real, don't you understand?"

"Get off him, Michael," Hutch said. He got two fistfuls of Michael's shirt and yanked him off the man.

The guard kicked his legs away from Michael. He pushed himself into a sitting position and fumbled with the gun, trying to get a better grip on it.

Michael cried out and spun around. One hand clutched the guard's gun; the other arm wrapped around the man's head. Together, the two tumbled down the flight of stairs. Michael's leg slipped between the concrete steps and metal railing. As he continued to descend, tangled with the guard, his leg twisted, wedged, and snapped—Hutch heard it over the scuffling and grunting. It slipped free, and the men rolled the rest of the way down.

The guard sprawled facedown on the next landing. Michael scrambled for the pistol, got it, and held it to the motionless guard's head.

"Michael, don't!" Hutch said.

The guard's back rose and fell. He was alive, for now.

Michael sat, his back pressed against the wall. His legs stretched out before him. The right leg was broken. A jagged tip of his tibia protruded from a rip in his jeans. Blood soaked his pants.

"You're hurt," Hutch said, aware that he meant Michael's injuries extended much deeper than the shattered bone.

Michael squeezed his eyelids tight. He crossed his arms over his head. He groaned.

Hutch thought it wasn't his leg Michael agonized over. He didn't even seem aware of it. Hutch took a step down.

"No!" Michael said. He pointed the gun at Hutch. "Stay away! I don't know . . ." Tears streamed out. His frown was more pronounced than Dionysus's tragic mask. His bottom lip quivered. His proclamation poured out with all the agony and sorrow of a parent who has lost a child: "I don't know what's real anymore!"

"I'm real, Michael," Hutch said. "He's real. You're real." He held out his palms. "We can get you help. Let me have the gun."

Michael pulled the trigger. The bullet hit the wall beside Hutch's face. Bits of concrete stung his cheek.

Hutch said, "Wait . . ."

Michael fired again, one shot after another. Thunder clapped in the confined space with each trigger-pull. The bullets ricocheted in the stairwell. Then the hammer fell on spent cartridges. *Click, click, click.* He gazed up at Hutch. He looked younger than Logan, younger than Dillon. He was a little boy who needed someone to tell him how the world worked, which monsters were real and which had no teeth. Hutch wondered if he would have done any better, with someone turning stone into sand under his feet, bending even the most fundamental laws of the universe. Waking up to find you'd only dreamed of reality.

Hutch whispered, "You're going to be all right. I'll do what I can to help. I promise."

Only I can't do it now, he thought. He'd already lost too much precious time.

The part of the guard's belt he could see held no extra ammo, no speed-reload pouches or bullet loops. But half the belt was out of sight. Hutch couldn't leave Michael with the gun if bullets were within his reach. Not in the kid's state. He stepped down, and Michael resolved the issue for him. He yelled and threw the revolver at Hutch. It clattered on the landing and slid into a wall. Hutch picked it up. He retrieved the bow bag and dropped the gun inside.

Below, another door banged opened. More feet pounded up the stairs—a whole shoe store of them.

SIXTY-THREE

With the way below blocked by guards or cops or both, Hutch went up. He took the stairs three at a time. He pulled open a door and found himself back where he had started, the fifth floor. Sirens grew louder, winding down as a cruiser screeched up to the building. Hutch ran into Larry's office. Page was gone from the terrace. In the street below, off to Hutch's left, two cruisers had parked at the corner of the building, in front of the main entrance. Directly below, a twenty-foot swath of grass ran the length of the facade, separating the building from the sidewalk.

He lifted his gaze. A faint luminance touched Logan's body. It was enough for Hutch to see only that the boy was still dangling from the platform. His toes balanced on the ledge, keeping him angled horribly over the empty space.

Page stepped from a shadowy corner of the terrace. He looked over the balustrade at the cop cars below. His head lifted, and he leveled his eyes at Hutch. He shook his head. He turned Logan's way before striding toward the restaurant's glass doors. He pulled on his helmet and entered.

"No!" Hutch yelled.

Hutch stood no chance at all of beating the man to Logan. If he called 9-1-1 and used magic words that convinced the operator on the first crack that a crime was taking place on the roof, Page would still have time to kill Logan and get away.

There was no time to think, only to act.

He grabbed Larry's chair and swung it into the cracked window. The glass buckled. A hundred cracks fanned out from the bullethole and the chair's point of impact. He pulled back and heaved it at the window. It crashed through, plunging down to the street in a glittering, spiraling ballet troupe of glass shards. Cold wind blew in, whipping papers off the floor. Hutch kicked and elbowed the glass fangs still clinging to the frame. He dropped the bow bag onto the desk and worked the bow out of it. He returned to the window.

No good, he thought. The distance to the opposite roof was a shootable fifty, fifty-five yards. It was ten yards farther than his comfortable shooting distance, but he had practiced at greater ranges. What he didn't like was the angle. Shooting down or up always presented special challenges. It changed the dynamics of the arrow's velocity and drop. Unless an archer regularly practiced incline shooting, which he hadn't, accuracy could not be assured. Worse, in this case, was his lack of a vantage point. He could not see the roof's door, or the path Page would take to Logan. His target would have to be at the junction of the roof's edge and the window cleaning unit. By then, however, Page would be seconds away from shooting Logan or releasing the rope. Hutch would have one shot—if that.

Without giving himself time to analyze, plan, or rethink his options, Hutch slipped the bow and bag over his head and stepped out of the window. He clung to the frame and felt with his feet for the ledge he believed was there. The building had been designed with horizontal lines in mind. The facade gave the subtle impression that the floors were stacked one upon the other. There had to be a ledge—didn't there?

But Hutch's toes slid over only smooth surface of the facade. Then he felt it against his shin. Higher than he'd expected; his feet had arced past it on his way out. He got his feet on it—all three or four inches of it—and stood. He would not have to venture far. In fact, he could almost reach the building's cosmetic scaffold without releasing his grip on the window frame. But not quite: his outstretched fingers came short of the crossbeams, a foot, maybe more.

Don't think! Do!

He leaped. One hand, then the other gripped the balcony. His body swung under the brace. His foot hit a Plexiglas panel, almost jarring his hands loose. As he pendulumed back, he worked his fingers for a better grip. He pulled himself up, feeling the burn in his arms. Could be that exercising to relieve his frustration would prove to be one of the few benefits of his obsession with Brendan Page.

No, he thought. There were no benefits. Nothing. He would have gladly become a fat mushroom, swigging beer and channel surfing, if he could take it all back, if Laura and the kids had never seen an Outis soldier, if Logan at that moment could be playing *Halo* on the Xbox and razzing Dillon and *not* be hanging over a hundred-foot drop.

He continued to climb, sloppily, hastily, until the other building's roof came into view. He was positioned slightly above it—not enough of an incline to worry about. Here he could see the roof's door, faintly outlined by the light behind it. It was ten yards from the edge of the roof, but more in line with the scaffold than the window cleaning platform was to Larry's window: the distance was about the same.

He draped the hockey bag, and the ballistic vest inside it, on a brace. He threw a leg over it and sat. He hooked an elbow around a vertical beam. Wiggling, he assessed his stability. Not bad, not so very different from balancing on a tree limb, waiting for an elk to pass.

He slipped the bow off his back. He selected an arrow from the quiver and nocked it onto the string. All of his arrows were graphite, which provided the most consistency from arrow to arrow.

Consistency was key to instinctive shooting: the hunter needed to practice the same style of shooting—placement of hand on the bow and fingers on the string, the position of his eyes in relation to the bow and arrow, the point in his draw where he released the string. In the field these habits kicked in, allowing him to shoot quickly and accurately without having to think about it.

But that worked only when one could count on the bow and arrows performing the same way every time as well. Hutch had inserted metal tubes into his arrows, giving them more weight and rigidity. Otherwise they would wobble in flight, under the power of his bow's sixty-pound draw weight.

The cold bristled against his skin. His fingers felt it down to the bone. He saw Larry's blood on them. He wanted to spit on them and wipe the traces of his friend's death away. He didn't dare take the time. But he did lean close to blow into his hands. So much of bow shooting depended on the sensitivity and dexterity of the archer's fingers. The slightest tremble or early release would send the arrow off target. Positioning the fingertips even a millimeter away from their usual position on the string would affect the timing of the release and the way the string slid off his skin. A hair's-breadth variance, when compounded by distance, could translate into his missing his mark by several feet. The effect of wind on an arrow's flight would be even worse. It would be especially so between buildings, where the breeze funneled through in sporadic gusts.

If he dwelt too long on all the factors working against him, he'd be tempted to give up. Instead, he plucked the string back and let the arrow fly.

Against the shadows' multihued grays and blacks, he lost sight of it. He saw it break against the bricks just below the lip of the parapet. It had dropped five feet and drifted right by the same amount. He had aimed for the door, but the arrow had not come anywhere close to it. Had the shot been directed at Page, the man likely would have been completely unaware of it.

Kentucky windage was a term used to describe adjusting your aim to compensate for the weather's influence on an arrow. It usually worked for light breezes that stole a few inches of accuracy. Five feet? No way.

A shadow broke the thread of light outlining the roof's door.

SIXTY-FOUR

Hutch nocked another arrow and set his aim high and to the left—*too* high and *too* left, he knew.

When the door didn't open, he wondered if the shadow had been a trick of his eyes, or if Page was waiting on the other side. Would he come out, running straight for Logan? Slip out and around the stairwell shelter, to approach Logan circuitously, denying Hutch a shot? Or was he marshaling more soldiers to storm the roof?

Risking his chance, but feeling that accuracy was more crucial than timing, Hutch disengaged the arrow from the string. He pressed the tip of the bow's lower limb into the top of his foot. He pulled the upper limb down, arcing the bow and loosening the string. He worked the loop of the string out of the notches that held it in place. He twisted the string between his fingertips, tightening it, then slipped the loop back into place. The length of the string from limb to limb was now just a little shorter. It was more taut, which would result in a heavier draw weight. And that, Hutch thought, with some hopeful satisfaction, meant more power.

In the span of seven seconds, he re-nocked the arrow and shot it at the door. It thunked into the door frame, waist-high. He looked at the back of his knuckles. They had been sliced open by the tip of the arrow. It was a broadhead, two triangular razors that fit together to form a lethal, pointed plus sign. Shortening the string made the bow arc more, which lengthened the distance between the draw point and the arrow rest. It required longer arrows, a luxury he didn't have.

As he pulled another arrow from the quiver, the light around the door darkened again. Hutch nocked the arrow and adjusted his aim. He pulled back on the string, just half an inch, enough to feel its tautness on his fingertips. The door opened, and Hutch stopped himself from pulling the string back and letting the arrow fly. It was like reversing a jump in midair. His muscles were ready. They were trained to shoot as habitually, as quickly, as the blink of an eye.

But the doorway was empty. Page's helmet broke into the lighted rectangle and disappeared again.

Hutch anticipated Page taking the most direct route to Logan. He moved his aim to a point along that path. If those archers he had told Dillon about could hit aspirins and dimes flying through the air, certainly Hutch could hit a running man. He hoped.

He didn't have to wait long for the answer.

Page bolted out of the doorway, heading directly for Logan. With the police coming, Hutch had figured Page would take the direct route. The surprise—Page's "unpredictability factor"—came in the form of a machine gun in Page's hands. The man began firing at Hutch as soon as his feet hit the rooftop. Apparently he had spotted Hutch in the few seconds when the helmet had shown itself. Hutch had suspected the helmets were equipped with electronic optics that enhanced the wearer's vision. This proved it.

He gauged Page's trajectory and let the arrow fly.

Page ducked. The arrow glanced off his helmet. The hit, however ineffectual, got Page to stop his dash for Logan.

His son was hanging lower than the parapet wall at the roof's edge, out of Page's line of fire. Page braced his legs and took careful aim at Hutch.

His weapon appeared to be a machine pistol. Designed for close-quarter combat, its long-range accuracy was poor. Bullets shattered the Plexiglas panel beside Hutch, sparked off of the scaffold frame, and blew chunks of concrete from the building's facade. Even before the last arrow had struck Page's helmet, Hutch had begun the movements required to fire again: *arrow from quiver to bowstring . . . fingers in place . . . aim . . . shoot.*

The arrow sailed over Page's shoulder.

. . . arrow from quiver to bowstring . . .

Page yanked the magazine out of the bottom of his weapon.

. . . fingers in place . . .

Page retrieved another magazine from a pouch at his waist.

. . . aim . . .

Page fired. Starbursts flashed from the barrel. Bullets zipped past Hutch. A fist punched into his right calf. A branding iron seared into it. He gritted his teeth, concentrating on keeping all of his muscles and thoughts locked on one objective.

Hutch shot.

Page saw it coming. He twisted his body away. The arrow pierced his bicep and continued into his side. For a few moments, he stood, staring at his arm pinned to his torso. He dropped to his knees, then onto his helmeted face.

Julian pounded on the control room door. He stared into the camera that transmitted his image to the people inside.

The intercom crackled. Colonel Bryson's voice came through. "Go away, Julian. I'm up to my eyeballs right now."

"But—"

"Go away."

He pounded and pushed the buzzer, but the intercom had said everything it was going to.

The door was at the top of a flight of stairs inside a building that housed the Void—the virtual reality room—and the facilities that serviced it: a locker room, briefing rooms, programming workstations, and a climate-controlled environment for servers and computers. The control room was windowless, except for the one that looked into the Void.

Julian's security badge granted him access to the building and some of the rooms, but not the control room. Whenever he wanted to observe, Colonel Bryson would let him in. Except tonight.

Giving the camera one last glance, Julian stepped away from the door and started down the stairs.

SIXTY-FIVE

The bow nearly dropped out of Hutch's hand. He leaned forward into a metal bar and gulped cold air into his lungs. He wasn't sure how long he had been holding his breath. Before his first shot at Page, out of habit he would have released half the air in his lungs and held his breath. The procedure minimized the transference of movement from his body into the bow. He didn't remember pulling in air between shots. The oxygen now quenched his aching lungs.

He slipped the bow over his head and let it rest against his back. He raised his leg. His jeans were ripped, and a dark stain was spreading. He touched the wound. A white-hot wire of pain shot up his leg. Rotating his ankle caused less-intense shooting pains, like the wire wasn't so hot, smaller in gauge. The bone wasn't broken, no major arteries severed. He'd hurt himself worse falling out of trees.

He glanced over at Logan, barely visible.

I'm coming, son.

On the street below him, another cruiser had parked at the corner by an entrance. Hutch had not noticed its arrival. He saw no one moving around in Larry's office, peering out to find the source of the machine-gun fire. They had probably stopped in the stairwell to figure out what Michael was doing sitting next to an unconscious security guard. No doubt the kid was keeping their hands full.

He leaned, getting his foot on the brace under the one he was sitting on. He swung his other leg over and slipped the bow bag's strap over his shoulder. Standing, he tested his injured leg. An invisible knife jabbed at his calf, but the leg functioned. He started to descend the balconies.

Movement caught his eye, and he stopped. He pulled himself up again, and there . . . Page was moving. He had crawled several feet toward the edge of the roof, where the wall concealed the upper half of his body. As Hutch watched, Page's legs pulled in, and he was completely gone. He would be able to crawl like that, safely out of reach from Hutch's arrows, all the way to Logan. Leave it to Page to make killing a child his last act on this earth. He would do it to have the last word in his struggle with Hutch.

Hutch gripped the vertical brace that formed the outside corner of the scaffold structure. He began sliding down it. His feet and arms knocked into and over each brace. Where he encountered tinted panels, he plunged down, slowing himself again under them. He was thinking about the bottom of the scaffold—how it was positioned above the tall first floor of the building and what he was going to do when he reached it—when the scaffold ended and he fell. He landed in grass. The jabs in his injured leg became a sledgehammer blow. He tumbled. The upper limb of the bow cracked into the back of his head.

But before he had fully stopped, he was up, limping over the sidewalk into the street. A kaleidoscope of red and blue lights from cruisers streaked over his face and the building in front of him. Sirens heralded the approach of more cops. He picked up his pace but didn't want to be seen running.

As if the bow and arrows strung over my back aren't enough to make them stop me, he thought. Or chase him. Nothing would stop him from getting to that roof.

He examined his fingers, where the broadheads had sliced them. One fingernail was split in half, from cuticle to tip. Blood oozed from it and from several other cuts. He shook it off.

The glass door of the building had been kept from locking shut with a security guard's hat. No one sat behind the security desk. Hutch didn't look behind it. Ignoring the pain in his leg as much as he could, he ran through the lobby and down a corridor to the stairway door. He did not know how many soldiers Page had brought with him, and he wasn't taking precautions to avoid an ambush. If they were lying in wait, he hoped his speed would throw them off. He realized it was naive thinking, but all he wanted to do was save Logan.

Can't do that if you're dead, he heard Laura say in his head.

Shhh.

He pulled the door open and raced—hobbled—up the stairs, only vaguely aware of the doors he passed. He'd already witnessed one ambush through such a door tonight—Michael's attack on the guard. It would be his own stupid fault if one of Page's men nailed him.

Inexplicably, he recalled a scene from a Charles Bronson movie. The way he remembered it, Bronson had some bad guy boss by the neck, and he was pinned down by a horde of the guy's minions. Bronson, being Bronson, put a bullet in the boss's head. He tossed the body where the minions could see it and said, "Your boss is dead. Go home." And they did. They just walked away.

He doubted it would work with Outis soldiers, but he still felt the compulsion to yell *Go home! Your boss is dead!*

Or will be soon enough, Hutch thought. As he climbed, he pulled the bow off his back, plucked the arrow from the quiver, and nocked it onto the string. Passing a door marked 6, he thought of the ballistic vest in the bag. No time. He pulled the bag around to his front and yanked on the strap so the bag hung over his chest. He reached the roof door and burst through it.

Page was at the window cleaner's rig. He had pulled himself up and was leaning over the parapet, reaching out for the rope with his uninjured arm. He held a knife.

"Page! Stop!" Hutch yelled.

Page's helmet swiveled around. He held the machine pistol in his other hand. His upper arm was skewered to his body, but he managed to bend it at the elbow and fire. Bullets marched along the roof toward Hutch, kicking up gravel. Page corrected his aim. Holes opened up in the roof door, the wall behind Hutch.

Hutch shot the arrow. It struck the roof at Page's feet, skipped, and pinged off the window-cleaning equipment.

Page's gun jammed or ran out of bullets. He dropped it, turned, and lunged for the rope with his knife. His feet kicked and pushed. He was inches from cutting away Logan's life.

Hutch tossed aside the bow and ran. The knife tip touched the rope, and Hutch hit Page full force and shoved. The man went over. He plunged without a sound, clutching the knife all the way down. The helmet hit the sidewalk first. It made the sound of a gunshot and shattered. Hutch was pretty sure all the debris that flew away wasn't only pieces of helmet.

SIXTY-SIX

Hutch reached out for his son, touched the top of his head. He said, "Logan, Logan, it's me, it's Dad. I'm here, son. It's okay."

Logan twisted, his eyes rolling to see Hutch. His feet slipped off the ledge and he swung away. He squealed through the tape over his mouth.

"You're okay," Hutch said. "I'll get you."

The rope was frayed where the knife had cut it. It was made of black nylon and appeared strong, even at the fray. Hutch tracked the rope to where it was attached to the platform. Steps led from the platform to the roof. He pushed back from the parapet and stood. He surveyed the roof, as much of it as he could see in the darkness. He listened for noises. As far as he could tell, no one waited to catch him off guard. He slipped the bag over his head and dropped it on the roof. He mounted the platform, sprawled on his stomach, and grabbed the rope. He pulled it up, hand over hand. He groaned with the strain, and was glad the bullet had hit his leg and not an arm.

"You're getting heavy, kid," he said between breaths. "No more Big Macs for you."

He got hold of Logan's arms and tugged him up onto the platform. He resisted the urge to squeeze and hold and cry over his boy. Instead he took him in his arms and carried him to the roof.

Okay, he thought. *Now I can squeeze and hold and cry over him.*

He set Logan down. Their eyes locked. Tears streamed out of Logan's.

Hutch cupped Logan's face in his hand. "I know, I know. I got you. You're safe." He got a finger under the tape and yanked it off.

"Daddy!" Logan said. "Oh, Daddy . . . Daddy!"

Hutch kissed him on his cheeks, his nose, his chin, his forehead. He squeezed him in his arms. He had to force himself to break away.

"Hey, you know," he said, "it's kind of cool, you tied up like this. I get to kiss you all I want." He smiled and wiped tears out of his own eyes. "But I guess that's kind of unfair, huh? Hold on a sec." He started to stand.

Logan grabbed his arm. "No, Daddy, don't go!"

"Look, my arrow's right there, on the roof. I'm going to cut you free with it. Okay?"

Logan looked. He tried to say something, but could only hitch in short breaths. He moaned and released Hutch's arm.

Hutch ran his hand over Logan's hair, pressed it against the side of his face. "I'm so sorry, Logan. I am. I . . ." He stood, retrieved the arrow, and returned. He sat in front of Logan and sawed at the rope with the broadhead.

"You're . . . you're bleeding," Logan said. He was looking at Hutch's knuckles.

"That's nothing. Look at this." He shifted his leg to show Logan the bloody pant leg. "It's not too bad either, really. You're bleeding too."

The rope had fallen away, revealing torn, bleeding wrists. The skin around them was red and bruised. Hutch held one of Logan's hands and gently fingered the flesh surrounding the wound. "Can you move your wrists?"

Logan did. He tried to lift an arm. His face twisted up. "My arms and shoulders," he cried out.

"No kidding," Hutch said. "Hanging like that, I can just . . ." He rocked up onto his knees, leaned into Logan, and hugged him. He ran his hands over the boy's back and head.

Logan felt so good, so alive. He pressed his palm into his son's shoulder blade until he felt Logan's heart beating under it.

Logan encircled his arm around Hutch and pressed his face into his chest. "I thought I was going to die," he said. "Then I saw you on that thing across the street, getting shot at. I thought *you* were going to die too." He started crying again, deep sobs.

Hutch didn't have anything to say that his embrace couldn't say better. After a while, they released each other. Hutch stood, then sat down again. "I just want to look at you a minute longer, that okay?"

Logan nodded. He used his fingers to wipe his eyes and nose. He rubbed his fingers on his pants. He prodded his lips gingerly. "I can't feel them," he said.

Hutch nodded. "You're a handsome boy, you know that?"

Logan shrugged, grimacing as he did. "I heard Abbie Walters told one of her friends I was."

"She did? Who's this Abbie girl? Do you like her?"

Another shrug, another grimace.

Hutch slapped Logan's knee. "Hey, I was just kidding. About Big Macs, I mean. You can have anything you want. Really, you name it."

"Okay," Logan said. He blinked slowly.

"Tired?"

"Dead . . ." He frowned. "I mean, *really* tired."

Hutch hoisted himself up. He walked behind Logan, put his hands under his son's arms, and helped him up. "Can you walk?"

Logan appeared a bit shaky, but he began walking slowly toward the roof door. "I'm all right," he said.

Hutch picked up the bow bag and caught up with Logan. He put the arrow inside and slipped the strap over his head.

"Hey," Logan said, pointing.

The bag had a perfectly round hole in it, the size of a dime. Hutch reached in and pulled out the ballistic vest. He held it up, turned it around. Near the edge was a larger circle where the covering material had been torn away, exposing wire mesh.

"Wow," Logan said.

"I guess these things work." Hutch felt around the inside the bag and held up a flattened slug.

"Keep it," Logan said. "It's cool."

Hutch nodded. He dropped the slug into his pocket. He replaced the vest, picked up the bow, and pushed it into the bag. At the door, he gripped the arrow that was sticking out of the frame and worked it loose. It went into the bag. He played his eyes over the rooftop, not sure what he thought he'd find.

More to himself, he said, "Leave it to Brendan Page to come alone."

"There were two of them," Logan said.

Hutch's stomach tightened. He willed himself to relax. If the other soldier were around and wanted to hurt them, he'd had plenty of chance to do it by now. He said, "I guess the cops scared him off."

"His name was Emile," Logan said. "He picked up the older guy earlier today. I was in . . ." He started to cry again.

It was all so right there, so fresh, Hutch thought. He rubbed his son's back and said, "It's okay. You don't have to talk about it."

"They tied me up in the back of a van, with *dead bodies*." Logan dropped his head, covered his face.

Hutch held him. He had hoped to bring a little normality back to Logan with the casual chitchat about Big Macs and how handsome the young ladies thought he was. If only things were that easy.

Naive me, he thought. *I have a lot to learn about so many things*. Two of them were his kids. For their father, he didn't know nearly enough about them. Laura's and Dillon's smiling faces appeared on the screen of his mind, fading in like in a Hallmark commercial. Yeah, them too. This time it was Page who left a void in his obsessed personality. Hutch wouldn't mind at all if these four people filled it. That was an obsession he could handle.

"Do we have to talk to the cops?" Logan said.

Hutch thought about it. He heard Ricky Ricardo's voice in his head: *You gotta lotta 'splainin' to do!* But nothing was going to help Larry, and his killer was dead.

He said, "We will, but not right now. Let's go get your sister, and Laura and Dillon. They gotta be going crazy about now."

"Can't we just go home?"

"As soon as we pick up the others, okay?" Hutch said. "They're not too far. And if the cops want to talk, they can come to us, can't they?"

Logan hugged him.

They left the building through a back door.

SIXTY-SEVEN

In the locker room, Julian pulled handfuls of paper towels from the dispenser. He soaked them in one of the sinks, then covered the floor drains with them. The clumps appeared too flimsy to withstand much water. He pulled off his shirt, pants, and socks, and added them to the plugs. He stuffed more paper towels into each of the sink drains. Five faucets: three sinks and two showers. He turned them all on, full blast.

Then he backed into the short hallway that led to the Void.

He leaned his shoulder against the wall, crossed his arms, and waited.

Hutch and Logan walked west on Colfax Avenue, staying close to the buildings and turning away whenever a vehicle passed. Hutch thought they must have looked like the poster family for Denver's homeless and destitute: father and son, limping along, supporting one another; their clothes stained and tattered; carrying a duffel-like bag stuffed, undoubtedly, with all their worldly possessions; shielding themselves from prying eyes.

Cruisers flew by, heading toward the *Denver Post* building. Hutch's brain seemed to throb in time with their sirens. Their strobing lights jabbed at his eyes. But it was all right. He had Logan. If he were walking the Via Dolorosa, carrying a cross and ducking from a thousand thrown stones, he would take it all with a grin because he had his son.

He spotted a cab and nearly leaped in front of it. The driver took one look at him standing at the front of the hood and shook his head. Hutch pulled out the wad of money Larry had gotten for him and fanned the bills for the driver to see. The driver jerked his head, gesturing for them to get in.

"Go ahead," Hutch told Logan. Only after the boy opened the rear door and started inside did Hutch move from the front of the car. With the cops on full alert, another Outis soldier somewhere on the loose, and Macie, Laura, and Dillon not yet within his reach, he didn't want to be stranded in the street.

He pushed in beside Logan, set the bow bag beside him, and handed the driver two twenties. "Casa Bonita," he said.

Logan laughed, what little he could, and said, "I guess you were serious about taking me there."

The driver eyed them suspiciously. He said, "What happened to you two?"

"Rough day," Hutch said. He couldn't help himself from looking through the rear window to the convergence of Denver's finest several blocks away. The *Post* building was just out of sight where the road curved around Civic Center Park. The lights, however, flickered and flashed on the surrounding buildings as though a bonfire had erupted.

"What's going on back there?" the driver said. "You part of that?"

"Just curious," Hutch said. "What do you say we get going, huh? Casa Bonita." He considered peeling off another twenty and pushing it in the guy's hand, but he figured that would be about the same as telling him to drive them back to the cops.

The cab pulled away from the curb, and Hutch felt the tension in Logan's muscles relax a little. His son was leaning into him, one hand draped over his shoulder, the other crossing Hutch's stomach to grip his side. Hutch pulled him closer. He brushed Logan's bangs off his forehead, let them fall back, and did it again, over and over.

When he thought the boy had fallen asleep, Logan whispered, "We had an adventure, didn't we?"

"Did we ever."

"Like you and Dillon?"

Hutch caught the faintest scent of Logan's meaning, like knowing a fire was nearby, but not yet comprehending its implications. "Something like that, I guess."

"So . . ." Logan shifted against Hutch. "So, will you talk about *me*, now? Will you tell everybody how we got through this together?"

Hutch felt that his heart and not his leg had taken Page's bullet. Had he been that callous, that superficial, that Logan felt unloved because he had not experienced all that had happened in Canada? Did Logan really believe that it took being kidnapped and almost killed to stake a claim in his father's life?

Hutch closed his eyes tight, knowing he had asked the wrong question. It was not whether Logan believed that, but whether it was actually true.

"Oh, Logan." He pressed his cheek to Logan's head, turned and kissed his hair. "You have always had my love. We've always shared the greatest adventure there can ever be. We share each other's lives. I'm sorry I haven't made you feel that way."

As his mind searched for the words that would express how he felt, but did not always behave, Logan relieved him of that duty. His son hugged him tightly, as though he wanted to pull himself right into Hutch's chest.

"Thank you for saving me, Dad. I love you."

Hutch's inclination was to recite the words back to Logan, but he stopped himself. He knew that on Logan's tongue those three words were precious and as weighted in meaning as they were intended to be. But Hutch had tossed them around like treats to a dog without supporting them with his time and attention. Over the past year they had become cheap, costing him nothing.

He worked with words every day. He knew they had power, but by using them without tethering them to the objects they described—in this case to his heart—they just floated away, so much air. Even now he wanted to caress his son with words, to wrap a blanket of *I love you*s and *Here are all the things we're going to do together* around him. But he had no right to expect those words to mean anything to Logan. All he could do was *do*. One hug at a time, one day at a time—one day of giving his children everything he had.

He squeezed Logan now and kissed him again. It wasn't enough, but he hoped his son understood.

The driver hitched his elbow over the seat back and looked at his watch. "Casa Bonita at twelve thirty in the morning? It's closed, dude."

"That's all right," Hutch said, peering through the windshield as the cab pulled into the near-empty lot. In truth, he hadn't thought about the restaurant being closed. Traveling all night and sleeping all day had knocked his biorhythms out of sync. It had *felt* twelve hours earlier when he'd told Laura to take off and meet him here. Somewhere in his head he had pictured Laura, Macie, and Dillon munching on sopaipillas until he and Logan arrived.

He tapped the driver's elbow and pointed. "See that SUV? Drop us there."

The XTerra was parked at the far end of the lot behind a large Dumpster-like box designed to receive donations of clothes and other items that could be sold. Leave it to Laura to park out of sight from the street. A pursuer would have to pull into the lot to spot the vehicle. When he had last talked to her, Larry had just been shot and hell was breaking loose. She had left in a panic and would have had no way of knowing who had won: Hutch or hell.

Hutch watched the taxicab pull away. He said, "We better hurry. They must be worried out of their minds."

"What happened?" Logan said, putting his finger in one of the bulletholes. He poked at a shattered window. Safety glass cascaded over the sheet metal, tinkling musically. Hutch had taped cardboard behind the broken glass, but had not bothered to clear the rest away.

"The guys who took you had friends," Hutch said.

He and Logan simultaneously pressed their faces to the rear-door window, the only one not broken on the driver's side. They cupped their hands around their eyes to block the reflection of a nearby sodium vapor lamp.

"They're not in here," Logan said.

Hutch turned to stare at the restaurant's big pink facade. He said, "She probably figured it was safer inside."

"But it's closed."

Hutch shook his head. "That wouldn't stop Laura." He gently slapped Logan on the shoulder. "Let's go see what's what."

The fountain out front had been turned off, but lights in the portico's ceiling cast a dim, yellow glow over the entrance area. Hutch pulled on one of the doors, then another. "Locked," he said. He walked out from under the portico to survey the building. "If I know Laura, she would keep looking until she found a way in."

"Do they have guards?" Logan said.

"I don't know. It's big enough, draws enough attention . . . you'd think they'd have an after-hours guy."

"Can't we knock?" Logan said.

"Let's make that the last resort. Laura could have talked her way in, convinced the guy to let her and the kids stay." He scratched the stubble on his cheek and squinted at a window twenty feet up. Wrought-iron bars covered it, but in the dark they looked rusty and unstable. "Or she could have found another way in. If they're hiding in there, I don't want to blow their cover."

"Does it matter?" Logan said. "Now?"

That struck Hutch as a profound comment, not only true, but one that marked a critical change in their circumstances. They no longer had to worry about being chased or caught or killed. It didn't matter if the police came, threw them all in the pokey for a day or two. They were finished with all of that.

"I guess you're right," Hutch said. He noticed a van in the parking lot, hidden by shadows. He could barely make out the logo on the side: CRAZY CARPET CLEANERS. If not a security guard, then perhaps a janitorial crew was in there. "I was just thinking—"

"Dad?" Logan was holding a front door open.

Hutch said, "It was unlocked?"

Logan nodded.

Hutch hurried toward it. He whispered, "Wouldn't you know it'd be the one I didn't try. Laura must have got in somehow and left it open for us."

"It's dark in there," Logan said.

"They're closed," Hutch said, keeping his voice low.

They stepped in, and the door closed behind them. A hallway broke left. If they were there to eat, they'd head that way, pay at a bank of cash registers, and pick up their meals from a cafeteria-style food bar. Straight ahead, a chain blocked an arched passage to the seating areas. Hutch unhooked the chain and reattached it to the other side.

"If you see anyone, just—" He stopped. He sniffed the air. The subtle, lingering odors of flour, cheese, grease, and . . . the grassy-tea aroma of an expensive cigar. He stumbled back into Logan and turned. He lifted his son in his arms and crashed back through the door, spilling outside onto the tiled patio beyond.

SIXTY-EIGHT

"What is it?" Logan said.

Sprawled on the tiles outside the restaurant doors, Hutch scanned all directions. He expected to hear the crack of a rifle at any moment and feel a brief, hot pain in his head, before . . . nothing. Unless the bullet reached him before the sound. Unless Logan was hit first!

Rolling onto all fours, he pulled Logan into a corner near the front door and a perpendicular wall. He pressed his chest into Logan's head, trying to cover as much of him as he could. He spun around and leaned his back into the boy's upraised knees.

"Dad," Logan said. "What is it? I'm—" Then he gasped, started to whine, then sob.

"What, Logan?" Hutch said. He pushed up into a crouch so that his torso completely protected Logan's head. "What do you see?"

This is it, he thought. *This is how it ends. Please, Lord, not Logan.*

He remembered news footage of a Jewish father and son in Jerusalem. They were heading to the boy's school when a firefight broke out between Israeli guardsmen and Palestinian militants. The father had pushed the boy into a corner and covered him with his body. Bullets kicked up dust and dirt all around them. As it cleared, the father fell away dead. The son fell on top of him, dead. The video had been the talk of the newsroom. It had been painful to watch, and a lot of lunches had gone uneaten that day.

What Hutch remembered now was how fast it had happened—mere seconds—and that the father, regardless of his resolve, regardless of his love, had been unable to protect his child.

He wasn't going to let that happen. If Page wanted him, he could have him, but not his boy. "What is it, Logan?" he said. "What?"

Logan's arm came out from behind him, pointing into the parking lot. "That van."

The carpet-cleaning van Hutch had noticed on the way in. But he saw no one in the windows, no one standing around it.

Logan said, "That's the van Emile put me in, the one he used to pick up that other man and bring me downtown. They . . . there's . . ."

Hutch saw Logan's eyes grow moist. "What is it, son?"

"There are bodies in the back. He *tied* me to them. My face . . ." He wiped a hand over his cheek, back and forth, taking off something that wasn't there anymore. "The *smell*."

Hutch hated Page for many things, but at that moment, he hated him for exposing Logan to human death and decay. Hutch felt his fury rising. Page—or someone working for him—had *tied* his son to corpses.

"It's okay now," Hutch said. "Shhh. It'll be all right." He gripped Logan's shoulders and held them until the boy's breathing slowed and their eyes met. He said, "Listen, I want you to run. Just start running that way. Run far. Then find a place to hide. Watch for me."

"No! I'm not leaving, you can't make me!" Logan grabbed two handfuls of Hutch's jacket. "No!" His head drooped, and he started sobbing.

Maybe it would be best to keep Logan with him, Hutch thought. What if Page's men were outside somewhere, watching? He was sure nothing would please Page more than snatching back what Hutch had taken from him—what had been Hutch's in the first place, but he didn't think Page would care about that. He hoped he was not simply justifying a stupid decision because he could not stand to see Logan cry—and because he himself did not want to be separated from him.

He said, "Okay. You stay with me, but do exactly as I say right when I say it, got it? No trying to be a hero or anything. Deal?"

Logan repeated the instructions, fast, as though they were the magic words that would keep him with his dad.

Hutch pulled the bag around to his front, unzipped it, and withdrew the bow. He set it on the tiles beside him. He tugged out the ballistic vest. "Put this on."

"No," Logan said, pushing it away. "You'll need it."

"Logan! What did we just talk about?"

Logan nodded. He let Hutch slip the vest onto him.

Hutch pulled the Velcro belts as tight as they'd go, but the vest still fit Logan as poorly as his pants did. "That'll have to do," he said.

He picked up the bow. The attached quiver held the two arrows he had retrieved from the roof. He grabbed one of them and nocked it onto his string. He held the arrow in place with the index finger of his bow hand. That kept one hand free, while positioning the bow and arrow for quick use.

He gestured toward the van. He said, "I should go check it out, see if anyone's hiding there, waiting to sneak up behind us when we go in."

"Don't," Logan said. "What if it's a trap, an ambush?"

"More likely there'd be one *inside* the restaurant," Hutch said. But Logan was right. To reach the van he'd have to walk forty feet in the open. And for what? Weapons, maybe, but he wasn't much good with firearms. Besides, he had to reach Macie, Laura, and Dillon before Page did. He prayed it was not already too late.

"Okay," Hutch said. "You saw only two men?"

Logan nodded.

"I got one of them, so it must be only Page inside."

Page, he thought. *How can it be Page?*

Hutch had seen him on the terrace. He'd signaled his displeasure at the arrival of the police, and he'd taken off for Logan. But had it been Page who came through the roof's door, guns blazing? Hutch had seen a helmeted soldier and had assumed it was Page.

He remembered Page's words: *What's real? Everything is an illusion.*

That's the way Page saw the world, the way he lived his life. Michael had been fooled into believing he had been playing combat games. In his mind, he had shot only at actors and computerized renderings of enemy targets, avatars. But Page had sent him to kill real people. He had shown Michael a bad guy, so Michael had shot him—and had killed a child. Illusions.

Page had not been merely making a case for relativism, for the sub-jectivity of his actions. When he'd said *Everything is an illusion*, he'd really meant *everything*. The success of Outis depended on illusion. His ability to control his soldiers, not only to wage war on his client's enemies, but also to eliminate his own perceived foes—it all depended on illusion.

Page had made Hutch believe they had fought each other, and that

Hutch had won. Now it appeared that Hutch had arrowed someone else, had pushed someone else off the roof. Still, Hutch could not shake the sense that Page had come back from the dead. He thought he had *seen* Page die, and even now it was hard to grasp that the man was alive.

For how many centuries had people clung to the idea that seeing is believing? How long would it take to realize the eyes could no longer be trusted? Pictures were Photoshopped. Characters in video games and even some movies looked real, but never were. Page had recognized the potential of technology to manipulate perception and had built an industry around it.

Whatever had happened back on the roof, however the man had found his way here, Hutch was sure it was Page who waited inside. Who else was cocky enough to smoke cigars while trying to assassinate people?

Hutch looked at the door to the restaurant. Above it should have been mounted the inscription Dante attributed to hell's entrance: "All hope abandon, ye who enter here."

No, no, he thought. *I won't do that. I can't.*

"Logan," he whispered. "Grab hold of my belt. Squeeze it tight. Don't let go."

He closed his eyes. He imagined that he was about to enter the woods on a hunting excursion: stealth mode, high sensitivity to sounds, every move intentional, no wasted energy. He called to mind his objectives: Macie, Laura, Dillon, alive and away from Page; Logan and himself too.

He pictured the hurdle to reaching those objectives: Page. He'd be armed, wearing the black SWAT-type clothes he'd worn on the terrace, and he'd have that helmet. Hutch would have to find a way to combat the advantages the helmet gave Page. He thought of a few things that might work. He felt the bow in his left hand, the arrow under his index finger. He took a deep breath, rose, and opened the door.

Crouching low, feeling the tug of Logan's hand on his belt, he stepped inside.

SIXTY-NINE

Hutch eased the door closed, and darkness engulfed them like a fist. He felt a curving wall on his right. He knew it circled around to the exit doors and a small room. He followed it, Logan clinging to him, until the lighted green letters of an exit sign showed him the doorway he wanted: a small security office. Here, a guard could monitor the closed-circuit cameras positioned around the restaurant and control the lighting and other features.

Hutch felt a desk, a Styrofoam coffee cup—still warm, and the glass screens of the monitors. He pushed a button and a screen came on, displaying static. He pushed another button, lighting up another screen. He found a panel of switches next to the monitors and began flipping them. The static on the screens changed to black. A distant exit light in the corner of one told Hutch they were working, staring into the darkened building. He found another bank of switches and toggled one up.

"A light just came on in one of the eating areas," Logan whispered from the doorway.

"I did that," Hutch said. He toggled the switches, one after the other.

The monitors showed the restaurant springing to life. Every few seconds the images changed as the monitors cycled through the cameras, showing the lagoon at the restaurant's epicenter, trees with twinkling lights, whole areas of empty tables, the kitchen . . . where Page was leaning against a stainless-steel countertop, puffing on a cigar. He lifted his gaze to the fluorescents overhead, nodded, and tossed the stogie aside. He raised a helmet off the counter and slipped it over his head.

"What are you doing?" Logan said. "Aren't we safer with them off?"

Hutch pointed at Page on the screen. "Not when our enemy can see in the dark. The lights even things up a bit." He continued flipping switches. Lights in the ceiling and mounted to the walls came on, marching toward them from deeper within the big space. Overhead lights illuminated the security room and exit area.

Logan hissed out a scream. His hand covered his mouth.

Hutch looked past him to a body facedown on the floor. It was an older man, wearing a security guard's uniform. His hat lay a few feet away. A puddle of blood fanned out behind his head like a halo in a Renaissance painting. The liquid had found the cracks between the floor's tiles and fingered out from the main pool along them. The man's holster was unsnapped and empty.

"Don't look," Hutch said. A flash of thought, like a poke on his shoulder, reminded him to be glad the boy's experience with the corpses in the van hadn't jaded him to the horror of death.

He turned back to the controls and flipped a switch labeled WATERFALL. The humming of a pump kicked in somewhere. Next came the sound of splashing water. He said, "I think those helmets enhance sound. The water should mess things up for him."

A monitor flipped back to the kitchen. Page, still helmeted, was stretching his back, rotating his arms. He picked up one of the machine pistols Outis favored, slung its strap over his head, and headed for a steel-covered door with a port window. The image changed to the arcade room: flashing pinball machines, stand-up video games, and skeet ball lanes.

Hutch stepped past Logan, knelt beside the guard, and felt for a pulse. Nothing.

He moved with Logan to the bottom of the wide ramp that would take them to a viewing area in front of the lagoon and waterfall. The pool's surface was one level down, but this higher ground offered better views of the diving platform and kept customers from getting wet when the performers plunged into the water. At the viewing area, diners could go left and back into a faux Mexican village, angle slightly left around the lagoon into the arcade and game rooms, or take a sharp right into what resembled a beachside resort. It was in this resort area that Hutch, Laura, and Dillon had eaten lunch.

Logan tugged at his belt and whispered, "Are you after the soldier guy, or do you want to find Macie and them?"

Good question, Hutch thought. Take on the threat, or go right for the goal? He said, "Macie, Laura, and Dillon. If we can get out of here without a showdown, all the better."

"Did you tell Dillon about the bridge in Black Bart's Hideaway?"

Hutch nodded.

Logan said, "Then that's where they'll be."

He was right. Out of all the places to hide, the one in which Logan had once eluded his parents and the restaurant staff for three hours was clearly the best. Hutch had told Laura and Dillon about that.

He tried to remember the layout. The kitchen was behind the food bar, which placed it way off to the left, on the ground floor. That's where Page would be coming from. He'd have to traverse the Sierra Madre mines and would come out . . . Hutch had no idea where. Why hadn't he ever written a column about this place? Too bad they weren't in the Denver Mint. He'd covered it twice.

Black Bart's Hideaway was behind the lagoon, between the waterfall and the arcade. They could reach it from the viewing area at the top of the ramp.

He leaned back. "Ready?"

Logan gave his belt a quick tug.

Staying as close to the right-hand wall as the sconces, plants, and mounted artifacts would let them, they started up the ramp. At the top, where the wall curved to the right into the resort area, Hutch stopped. He crouched low, and Logan nestled up beside him. Directly in front of them, the waterfall roared. While the sound should help their movements remain undetected by Page's electronics, it also prevented Hutch from hearing Page.

If they veered to the left side of the lagoon opening, they'd wind up right at Black Bart's Hideaway. But they would be more exposed. If they followed the wall around into the resort area, they could move through a cantina, then behind the waterfall, and reach Black Bart's that way: a fifteen-second run versus five minutes of wending around walls, tables, and who-knew-what. He signaled to Logan his intention to dash straight across the open area.

Wide-eyed, Logan nodded.

Hutch held up three fingers. He lowered one, then another. As he made a fist, he sprang up and ran. Logan was slower and tugged him back. By the third stride, they were in sync. On the fourth, Page appeared.

On the right, he rose up from a narrow staircase. To Hutch, he appeared to lift out of the floor like a warrior robot in a James Cameron movie. Among the platform for a mariachi band and the complicated arrangement of fake buildings, the staircase was nearly invisible.

Hutch swerved to cut across the viewing area, which was designed to resemble a bridge. He swung his free arm back to get it around Logan.

"Let go of my belt, Logan," he yelled. "Let go!" He propelled Logan forward, putting himself between the gunman and his son.

Page fired. Apparently not worried about pinpoint targeting, he panned the machine gun across the wide area. Divots tore out of the wall at the far side of the resort.

Hutch caught up to Logan and ran alongside. As his faster legs moved him ahead of his son, he grabbed Logan's wrist. Inexplicably, Logan yanked it out of his grasp. Continuing to move forward, Hutch turned.

Logan tumbled over the bridge's handrail.

"No!" Hutch yelled, braking hard, heading back.

Bullets tore into the handrail. They zinged past Hutch, forcing him back. Over the rattling gunfire and the waterfall's susurration, he heard a heavy splash.

"Logan! Logan!" Hutch stepped forward and swung the bow toward Page, who was heading toward the handrail. Seeming to act faster than Hutch thought possible, certainly faster than Page could have registered Hutch's switch to offensive mode, Page dived away. He rolled into the Mexican village, disappearing behind a family of stuffed burros.

Hutch took a step toward the handrail.

Page popped up, shooting wildly. A light shattered above Hutch. Glass and bits of ceiling rained down.

"Dad!" Logan yelled. He coughed. "Dad!"

"Are you okay?"

Logan sputtered. "Y-yeah."

"Run, Logan," Hutch yelled, backpedaling out of Page's line of fire. "Hide! Logan, hide!"

He heard more splashing—either the boy climbing out into the mines beneath him or swimming to the waterfall and the dark cavern behind it. "Hide! Hide!" he yelled again. His mind told him to keep yelling it until his throat gave out.

Page was out of sight. He had stopped firing. Hutch caught the man's shadow. It stretched along the floor, nearly to the bridge. It joggled and reached the bridge. His shadow's head slipped over the edge, where Logan had tumbled away. Hutch darted forward. Catching the merest glimpse of a solid body, he plucked back on the string and let the arrow fly.

Page hit the ground and rolled. The arrow thunked into the head of the lead burro.

SEVENTY

Hutch had stopped yelling for Logan to hide.

He wanted now to call out to him, make sure he was still okay. But more than needing that reassurance, he needed Logan to be silent. He turned and ran through the resort, and jogged sharply into the cantina. He dropped to all fours and scrambled to the wall beside the entrance, where he sat and pushed his back against the wall. He leaned his head toward the opening, listening for Page's approach. The cantina was its own room, boxcar shaped and open at each end. The bar ran the length of the room on Hutch's right, across an aisle. Booths formed a scalloped pattern along the other wall, which separated the cantina from the resort area. It was this wall that Page had shot up, aiming at Hutch and Logan.

Hutch stretched his injured leg out in front of him. Blood dyed his jeans from the knee down. His sock was soaked. Other than a dull throb, however, he felt no pain.

Logan, he thought. What had happened to make him go into the lagoon like that? Could he have been shot? Odd as it seemed, he hoped that if a bullet had struck him, it would have hit his torso, where the ballistic vest would have absorbed most of the impact. He knew that even through vests, bullets stung like getting punched with an iron fist. A SWAT officer had once shown him a nasty yellowish black-and-blue mark where he'd been hit. That would have been enough to drive Logan over the handrail. He thought his son would still be screaming for him if it was any worse than that.

Hutch hated being separated from him. He could not think of a nightmare more hellish than for Page to get his hands on Logan again.

Which way would Logan have gone? Behind the waterfall or into the mines? The Sierra Madres—here as well as the real ones, Hutch imagined—offered plenty of hidey-holes and crevices in which to hide. On the other hand, the waterfall side of the lagoon was nearer their destination, Black Bart's Hideaway. Logan probably would head that direction. If not because he thought Hutch would continue toward it, then to reach his favorite hiding place and possibly his sister and the others.

Hutch looked along the length of the cantina to the opposite entrance. It was dark through there—a few lights, walls, and ceiling painted black. It was supposed to represent a cavern behind a waterfall. He thought of the movie *The Last of the Mohicans*. Hiding in a cave just like this one, Daniel Day-Lewis tells Madeleine Stowe, "You stay alive! I will find you. No matter how long it takes, no matter how far, I will find you"—then he jumps through the waterfall.

Hutch wished he could tell Logan the same thing. Macie, Laura, and Dillon too. *Stay alive. I will find you.*

He heaved himself onto his feet and crouched to sit on one heel. He looked at his quiver: four arrows left. He selected one and nocked it.

Page called out to him. "Hutch! So you thought you killed me, did you?"

His voice sounded amplified and a little distorted. No doubt coming through a speaker in the helmet.

"The playback in my monitor was rich: 'Page, stop!' Poor Emile. Just doing his job the way I programmed him to do."

He slowly turned in a circle, using the helmet's optics to scan for them, Hutch thought.

"Bet you're wondering how I knew to come here," Page continued. "Rather simple, really. Frankly, I'm shocked you didn't know better. You gave me the number of the cell phone you used to call your lady friend. The restaurant you ate at the other day? Hutch, you used a *credit card*. Don't you think I have access to those databases?"

Hutch squeezed his eyes closed. There were just too many things to think about—all while running, trying to save lives. Hutch hunted animals and knew how to do it. He knew how to read broken branches, antler marks on trees. One glance at their prints and he knew how many animals, how big they were, and how long ago they had passed through. He knew where they had bedded down and where they were heading by the freshness of their spoor.

Page hunted humans, and knew this task as well as Hutch knew his. People left electronic clues to their whereabouts and even their destinations. Human trackers needed only to know where to look, how to read the signs.

"I have to say," Page went on, "this place is wonderful. Exactly what I would expect from you. I feel like I'm outdoors. There's even a kind of woodsy feel here, don't you think? You must feel right at home."

Hutch rose and hurried to the far end of the cantina. Stepping out of it into the cave, the rushing water of the falls all but obscured Page's diatribe.

"You must know by now that you can't win," the man said. "I've got the technology, the superior firepower. Best of all, I don't have people I love to worry about—running all over the place, getting in the line of fire. Like right there!" The machine gun rattled.

Hutch jumped. His heart wedged itself in his throat.

Page's laugh stuttered electronically. He said, "Bet that scared the crap out of you, didn't it?"

Hutch raised his bow. He saw that his hand was trembling. He wondered if that had been Page's intention. Hutch had hunted in the most adverse conditions: freezing cold, hail, tired and hungry. Even, he thought, while being hunted himself. He believed when he found another opportunity to fire at Page—and he would, he would—his instinctual shooting abilities would kick in, trembling hand or not.

He moved to the waterfall showing through a floor-to-ceiling opening in the cavern's wall. Through its flowing veil, he saw Page. The man was standing on the bridge on the opposite side of the lagoon, facing the resort and the cantina entrance Hutch had ducked into. It dawned on him that Page was unfamiliar with the restaurant's layout. He would have no way of knowing about the cantina's back exit into this cavern. The opportunity had arrived sooner than Hutch had expected. He looked at his feet to brace himself for the best shot.

Looking up at him from the floor below was Logan. The boy was in the water, clinging to the lagoon's edge on Hutch's side of the waterfall. Hutch held his palm out to him and mouthed the words *Stay there*.

"I'd say we could still work this out," Page was saying, "but we're beyond that now, aren't we? My only regret is that I won't have a photograph of this for my wall. Can't you see it? Me standing in this great place, next to a pile of bod—"

Hutch let loose—pulling back and releasing in one smooth, two-second motion. The arrow pierced the water without the slightest deflection.

Page bent backward, and the arrow sliced through the air his body had occupied a second earlier.

Hutch already had the next arrow nocked . . . and rocketing at Page.

But Page was dancing away. *Dancing.* As he disappeared down the main ramp, his voice trailed back: "Technology, Hutch! It's a wonderful thing."

Hutch shook his head. What was he up against? Not just a man. No wonder Page's soldiers were known as the best in the world: bloodlust, firepower, unimaginable technology. And Outis had ten thousand soldiers in the field.

Man! The way Page had dodged that arrow!

He found Logan still gazing up at him, wet, shivering, scared. Hutch slung his bow over his shoulder and stepped over the short rope netting that kept kids from spilling into the lagoon. The waterfall grabbed at his bow and tried to pull him down. He lowered himself, hung from the floor's edge, and dropped to the level below. He landed on something soft and almost fell. He kicked away the ballistic vest, which Logan had draped on the edge.

"D-D-D-Dad," Logan whispered through chattering teeth. Hutch pulled his son out of the water, and sidestepped with him behind a wall. The boy's entire body shook. His lips were as blue as his braces.

Hutch knelt in front of him, removed the bow, and set it on the floor. He removed his jacket and draped it around Logan's shoulders. He embraced him, squeezing—he imagined—the cold and fear away.

"I . . . I . . . I . . ." Logan said, "took off . . . the vest. It was . . . dragging me down."

"That's okay," Hutch said.

"It saved me, though," Logan said. "I felt . . . the bullet hit my back."

Hutch's hand rubbed over Logan's back. "Does it hurt?"

He felt Logan shake his head.

"It's the cold," Hutch said. "It might start hurting as you warm up, but you'll be okay." He broke away to hold Logan at arm's length. He brushed the wet hair away from his son's face. "You did well."

Logan nodded. He smiled in that lopsided way he did when he thought of something smart. "You too," he said. "Except you *missed*."

That brought a grin to Hutch's face. "That's my boy." He looked around the cavern, half expecting Page's black figure to step out of the shadows.

Logan pointed. "Black . . . Bart's . . ."

"I know, it's just around the corner. You ready?"

"Let's . . . let's do it."

SEVENTY-ONE

At the control room door once again.

Julian pushed the buzzer button and pounded. He gave the camera a panicked expression.

Come on!

He hoped he wasn't too late. The water had taken longer to reach the Void's door than he'd expected.

Now he stood outside the door again, this time in only his boxers. He rubbed the bravery bracelet on his wrist. *Do your job*, he thought.

Colonel Bryson's voice came over the intercom. "Julian, what are you doing? Where are your clothes?"

"The locker room, Colonel Bryson! Something's wrong. It's overflowing. Quick!"

"What? What were you doing at this hour? I'm tied up right—"

"Colonel Bryson!" Julian pointed in the direction of the Void. "Look!"

He imagined the man leaning up over the control panel to peer into the Void. He'd flip on the lights and see two inches of water shimmering on the floor, drawing closer to the VR equipment and various plugs, monitors, and cables.

"What the—?" came the voice over the intercom.

A bolt released in the door mechanism, and Bryson appeared in the doorway. All that hair and sharp features. He looked like something from *Where the Wild Things Are*.

"What did you do?" he said and bolted past.

Julian let him descend two steps. He whipped the replica 1911 pistol from his boxers' waistband at the small of his back. He put everything he had into cracking the butt of it into the back of Colonel Bryson's head.

Page crossed through the cashier lanes to the other side of the building. He found the entrance to the kitchen and went in. It was time to wrap this up, stop messing around. He believed the video his helmet had sent back to Command was enough to show recruits what could be done. He'd incorporated many of the features built into the helmet: Night vision prior to Hutch turning on the lights, when he'd scared the woman and kids into hiding. The targeting system on the guard and that punk kid. The helmet's trajectory warning had saved his butt when Hutch had shot through the waterfall.

The Behavioral Pattern Analysis software had even predicted Hutch's quick second shot. Page had read about archers of old who could fire twelve, fourteen well-placed arrows in a single minute. He'd had no idea people still practiced that archaic skill, and certainly no clue that

Hutch was one of them. But the system had known. It had analyzed Hutch's pattern of fighting—at the motel, the parking lot, and the downtown rooftop.

Page could not remember Hutch shooting his bow like that. He had not seen all the action on the rooftop. Ian had replayed for him only the "Page, stop!" clip, because Ian had thought it hilarious. Apparently somewhere during those battles, the system picked up on the hunter's skill and inclination to quickly reshoot, and it had warned Page. That's what it was all about. Page himself did not have to know everything, did not have to keep everything in mind. Not when he had systems to do it for him.

Page felt immensely satisfied. He was wrapping up a problem that had confounded two fireteams, the one that had blown it at the motel in Washington and the one here. He had scratched the itch for action he'd felt since returning from Baghdad six months earlier. And he was about to pluck from his side the thorn named John Hutchinson. Overall, it had been a good day.

After taking care of the people in this building, he'd have some cleanup to do. Their bodies. Michael in police custody. Michael's father in the hospital in Kirkland. And leaving Emile's corpse at the scene downtown was no good at all. He believed Ian had already put into motion everything they needed to come out smelling as sweet as a vintage Havana . . . as he had done with that fiasco in Canada.

He left the kitchen through the door that serviced the dining area in the caves, mines, whatever. Who in their right mind would eat in here anyway? Instead of ascending the stairs as he had done before, he crossed through a hallway to a game room. Coming to another arched entryway, he poked his head out and pulled it back in. He'd seen a cobblestoned area with a wishing well and an empty easel and chairs. Signs and sample drawings advertised caricatures.

On the far side of the space were two flights of stairs. One led to the cavern behind the waterfall, the other to a dark, cavelike opening, above which were a Jolly Roger skull and crossbones and the sign marked BLACK BART'S HIDEAWAY. Minutes ago, Hutch had been in the cavern. Since his enemy had seen him head down the ramp on the other side of the building, Page suspected that this was the way Hutch would come next.

Page eased out onto the cobblestoned area. He stayed close to the wall, where a thatch overhang provided a shadowy spot to wait. Movement *under* the cavern steps caught him off guard. But that was fine, just a matter of lowering his aim a few feet. The infrared overlay in his face mask picked up Hutch's body heat before he was visible in the light. The helmet's targeting system placed blue crosshairs on him. Another set of crosshairs appeared, as a second, smaller, and much less radiant body-heat signature came into view, clinging to Hutch's side.

Well, how nice, Page thought. *They found each other, father and son.* The boy must have stayed in the water, the cold shielding him from the helmet's infrared. Warming up now, he was starting to glow. The two stepped cautiously into the light, passing the cavern stairs. Hutch had his bow in hand, the arrow ready to shoot.

Won't help you this time, Page thought. He lifted his machine pistol, and the blue crosshairs over Hutch turned red. He shifted it slightly until the boy's crosshairs turned red. He kept his aim as the two stepped onto the stairs leading into Black Bart's cave.

Footsteps pounded on the cobblestones. Page spun to see a police officer running toward him, gun drawn and pointing. Page fired his machine gun into the man's chest. The cop screamed and flew backward. When he hit the ground, something happened, a trick of the light. He flickered and seemed to fade. A yell off to Page's left gave him no time to think. He pivoted to find a ninja.

"Ian!" Page yelled. He slammed his fist into the side of the helmet. "Ian!"

The ninja spun his weapons before him and ran for Page.

Page shot him and turned back to finish off Hutch and his son. They were gone. His heads-up display flashed an icon, and a beep sounded in his ears. He sidestepped in time to avoid an arrow that came out of the cave's mouth and stuck into a wall beside him. He rolled through the archway into the game room. A soldier thrust a bayoneted rifle at him. He dodged and fired.

"Ian, what are you doing? Ian!"

A small screen appeared in the corner of his display—picture-in-picture was the technical term. Julian glared at him from it.

"Sorry, Dad," Julian said, "Colonel Bryson is, uh . . . I guess you could say he's *out* right now."

"Julian, what the hell are you doing? This is not a game. Now is not the time to be—"

"Just learning the system, like you said I should."

"Where is Ian? Put him on now."

Julian's hand filled the screen. The control room flashed by. The camera moved toward the door, which opened. It tilted and settled on Ian, sprawled facedown on stairs. His feet were closest to the camera, several steps above his body. His head, a mass of dark curly locks, rested on the landing below. The camera panned and jiggled again, then settled in its usual position. Julian reappeared. The boy said, "I told you, he's out."

"Julian, what have you done? Leave the control room now. Get back to your quarters before I—"

Julian squinted at something, reached for it, and another ninja came screaming out of the dining room. Page shot it—he had found long ago that he could not stand ignoring the avatars while they pranced around him, hacking and shooting. They would not go away until killed or turned off by Command.

"Julian . . ." Page did not know what to say.

Julian leaned close to the camera. His cheeks were flushed, his lips white from being pressed together so tightly. A tear streaked down his face. He said, "Leave those people alone. Leave all of us alone. I won't be here when you get back." He lowered his head.

Page heard clicking, a lot of clicking. A soldier appeared between the skeet ball machines. Another from a different era popped into being near a glass display of trinkets. A Pygmy warrior, blow dart in hand—

Page fumbled for his chinstrap, unsnapped it, and tore off his helmet. He sent it flying into a pinball machine. His heart raced—and not in the way it did when he conquered an enemy, not in a way it had for a long time. This was frustration, fury. He stepped to the trinket display case and set down his weapon. His hands roamed over his pockets, found his cigar holder, and pulled it out. One left, a Romeo y Julieta Churchill. He closed the holder and slipped it back into his pocket: better to wait, to make a celebratory smoke after he'd bagged his prey.

Okay, he thought. *Let's do this.*

He snatched up the machine gun and strode toward the mines.

SEVENTY-TWO

"What happened?" Logan said.

Hutch squatted just inside the mouth of Black Bart's Hideaway. "I don't know," he whispered. "He started firing, but not at us."

"Are there other people here?"

Hutch shook his head. He stood, touched Logan's shoulder, and said, "Come on."

They wound deeper into the cave, which was Casa Bonita's version of a haunted house. Hutch rounded a corner. A light flashed onto a skeleton. The thing screamed pathetically. Hutch almost put an arrow in it. A couple more scares, and they reached the plank bridge. He knelt and craned his head to look under it. "Laura," he said. "Macie, Dillon, you there?"

No one—no movement, no sound.

"Logan, how far back does it go?"

"Not very. They're not there. Dad, where do you think—?"

Something touched Hutch's shoulder. He whirled, swinging his bow around.

"It's me, it's me," Laura said. "I'm sorry. I whispered. You didn't hear me."

Hutch reached out and grabbed her arm. "Where—?"

Macie pushed around Laura and jumped at Logan. She wrapped her arms around him. "Logie!"

Logan returned the embrace. "I never thought I'd say this, but I missed you, Macie."

Laura stepped aside, and Dillon leaned in to give Hutch a quick squeeze.

"I thought you'd be under the bridge," Hutch said.

"We were," Dillon said, "for a long time."

Laura said, "We heard the shooting. It sounded like it was getting close. I wanted to see if there was a better place to hide or an exit or something."

"Page is out there," Hutch said. "That guy . . ." He shook his head. "He seems to know my every move. He was tracking me perfectly." He thought a moment. "Then he just started shooting at I don't know what and ran into the game room. It's been quiet for a while. He's pulling something, maybe sneaking back around."

"What are we gonna do?" Dillon said.

Hutch locked on Laura's eyes. "I need you to stay here with the kids. Hide a little longer. Can you do that?"

"Yes, but—"

"I'm going to try to draw him away," Hutch said. "There's kind of a house setup. It's above the main ramp, pretty high. If I can get onto the roof, I'll have a good vantage point. When you hear shooting, run as fast as you can through the game room, then into the mines. I think that will lead you to the kitchen. It'll have an exit."

"I'm not leaving you," Logan said.

Hutch cupped his hand against the boy's cheek. "You have to, son. I'll be right behind you."

"Promise?"

Hutch could only look into Logan's eyes, which started brimming. "None of that," Hutch said. "I'm counting on you to be strong."

The muscles in Logan's face tightened. He nodded firmly.

Hutch smiled at Macie. Words were forming in his mouth, when Dillon said, "Mom has a gun."

Hutch snapped his eyes to her.

She held it out to him. It was a large automatic, .40 or 9mm. "Got it off the dead security guard," she said with a shaky smile. "I heard Page in another part of the building and went looking for anything that would help. I should have taken the kids. We could have gotten out. I just . . . I just . . ."

"You didn't know," Hutch said. He closed her fingers around the pistol. "You keep it," he said. "I'm no good with guns, and I'll feel better knowing you have it." He looked around at all of their faces, said, "Can all of you fit under the bridge until it's time to run? Just in case he comes through this way."

"Not all of us," Logan said.

Laura said, "You kids get under. I'll stand back in the shadows."

Hutch stood. He watched the children slip under the bridge and disappear into the darkness.

Laura whispered, "You can't do this."

"What choice do we have?" he said.

"You said he knows your every move. He'll get you before you get there, you know it. Hutch, you can't— What is it?"

"I'm thinking," he said. "All right, all right. You know something?"

"Tell me."

"He doesn't know me as well as he thinks he does."

SEVENTY-THREE

Page heard Hutch coming.

He knew Hutch preferred high ground—a tree, a roof, a scaffold. Page had noticed how the structures in the restaurant climbed higher as they approached the right front corner of the building. There were two routes to that area, maybe more. He figured Hutch would choose the one he was most recently familiar with. So Page had slipped into the cantina and ducked down behind the bar. Now he heard a floorboard groan near the door to the cavern behind the waterfall: Hutch had entered the cantina. He waited until Hutch had passed and stepped through the opposite exit. He rose and came up behind Hutch as he started up a flight of stairs. "Even without technology," he said.

Hutch froze.

"Drop the bow," Page said. "You're fast with it, but not faster than my trigger finger."

He watched the bow and arrow fall out of Hutch's hand. They clattered on the tile steps and tumbled down. Hutch turned to face him. He said, "Listen, it doesn't have to end this way. I know you want me off your back."

Page said, "Oh, I want much more than that, now." He began backing away from the cantina, through the resort. "Join me, won't you? I just want to get my . . ." He leaned over to a table where he had balanced his cigar on the edge. He puffed on it, getting a heady billow of smoke. He plucked it from between his lips and held it up. "This is how sure I was I had you. My victory smoke."

Page's finger stiffened over his machine gun's trigger as Hutch descended the stairs. If Hutch so much as blinked wrong, he'd end it here and now. His muscles and joints were beginning to feel the day's exertions. He had better things to do than continue chasing this guy.

Hutch walked closer. He said, "You're not going to tell me how smart you are before shooting me, are you? I've seen that movie."

Page nodded. He pulled in more smoke, blew it out. "Me too. I just want to give you one chance, a very *brief* chance, to save your children."

Hutch's eyes narrowed.

"There are many ways to win a game," Page said. "I'll let you choose how I win. I shoot you, then run through the building, lobbing hand grenades into the places I can't see. Just for good measure, I'll chain the doors and set the place on fire before I leave. Or . . ."

Another puff—this thing was *fantastic*, despite having not been toasted correctly.

"Or you call everybody out. I shoot only you and the woman."

Hutch scowled at him skeptically. "Not the kids?"

"Call me gracious. Besides, thanks to you, I'm short a few soldiers.

From what I've seen, these kids would fit right into my program. Just call them, Hutch. I know you will. Same way I knew where you would be heading." He shook his head. "Predictable." He smiled and drew in a big breath of smoke.

The shot rang out behind him. His cigar tilted out of his fingers. Hutch was moving for his bow.

Page pulled the trigger—or tried to. His hand wasn't working. The gun slipped loose and fell to the floor. He turned to see the woman, not ten feet away, holding a pistol in her shaking hands. He dropped to his knees, keeping his body upright; at least he could do that. Tasted something. Cedar, coffee, blood. He felt the air escaping from his lungs. He looked down to see blood oozing from a hole in his shirt. It bubbled, and smoke came out. He watched it form a perfect ring and drift away. He glared at it until all the color was gone from his vision.

He heard the woman say, "Did you predict that?"

Everything . . . smoky . . . gray . . . black . . .

Page fell backward. His feet and lower legs were tucked under him. He appeared to be staring at the smoke drifting from his nose, mouth, and incredibly, from the hole in his chest Laura had made.

"I thought you were going to just push the gun into his back, tell him to drop it," Hutch said.

"Did you hear what he wanted to do with our children?" she said. She dropped the pistol. "Do you think we would have ever been rid of him? He would have found a way . . ." She dropped the gun and lowered her face into her palms.

Hutch pulled off his jacket. He unstrapped the ballistic vest he had retrieved from the floor beside the lagoon. Wearing it had made walking into Page's ambush a little less frightening, but only a little. He let it drop away. He stepped forward and kicked Page's gun over the edge, where it splashed into the lagoon below. He patted down the body, finding a big knife and a pistol in an ankle holster. These went into the water as well. He stepped over Page and went to Laura. He wrapped her in his arms. "Shhh."

Logan's face appeared from around the stonelike structure that was Black Bart's Hideaway. Hutch gave him a thumbs-up. He came running out, Macie and Dillon right on his heels.

"Look," he said, turning Laura to see the children coming around the lagoon. "You did it for them."

She let out a shaky laugh, and knelt to receive their hugs.

SEVENTY-FOUR

Two weeks later

"Can you live with having killed a man?" Hutch asked.

He was standing next to a bench, one foot propped up on it. Laura sat on the bench. They watched Logan, Macie, and Dillon playing in a park. Logan searched a wooden fort, looking for Dillon, who had slipped away and was watching from the branches of a nearby tree. Hutch marveled at how the boy's stillness and positioning made him nearly invisible, even in a defoliated cottonwood. Macie had watched Dillon ascend, and now she stood at the top of the fort's big green slide, waving at him. Whenever she sensed Logan turning her way, she stopped and whistled a light-hearted tune.

The air was nippy, but the sun was bright. The small park adjoined St. Anthony's Hospital, and every so often Hutch would look over at an ambulance waiting in a driveway.

Laura squinted up at him. She said, "I guess most people struggle with having to take a life." She tilted her face toward the sun, mulling over his question. "I'm not most people."

He touched a scab on his left eyebrow. His fingers moved up a bit to another scab on his forehead. One of the lacerations he had sustained in Jim's Mustang. The other in the taxi when the Honda had blown up. He didn't know which was which. He resisted the temptation to scratch the healing bullet wound on his calf. For a few days after the "Casa Bonita Shoot-out," as the media called it, he'd often found himself quietly enumerating his many injuries. Macie had noticed and would start counting with him.

Logan would show the burns from the ropes around his wrists, the spot on his head where the soldier had yanked out a clump of hair, and the bruise on his cheek where he'd been punched.

Laura remained quiet about the bullet-grazed shoulder and her various bangs and cuts. Dillon and Macie had emerged unscathed, though Macie always pointed to the scraped knee she'd suffered crawling under the car at the RapidPark lot.

Hutch eyed Laura now. She was smiling up at him. He said, "No regrets then?"

"About shooting him?" she said. "When I was sneaking up behind him, I thought about how we would all be dead if he'd had his way. I thought of poor Logan, kidnapped, terrified. I even thought of Dr. Nichols's family, though I didn't know them."

Hutch said, "Never mind that he had me in his machine gun's sights and was ready to pull the trigger."

She waved her hand dismissively and tossed her head back. She said, "I know somewhere inside I should hurt for having taken a human life." She shook her head. "But I don't." She pulled in a breath. Fog, like smoke, billowed out of her nose. "I do have nightmares, though."

Hutch's eyes widened. "About shooting him?"

"About *not* shooting him. I play the nice girl and say, 'Put it down or I'll shoot.' He ends up killing both of us and turns the kids into perfect little killing machines."

Hutch glanced over at the children. He said, "You think it's that easy, turning good people bad?"

"I think that's what he was doing," she said. "We make choices, sure, but who can withstand the mind games Page was getting into?"

"Julian." Hutch shook his head at the thought of the boy. "That kid wallowed in blackness, but he stayed pure. He did what was right. More than once."

"Outis had just started on him," Laura said.

"You're a nihilist," Hutch said.

"Me? No, I love life. That's why I don't mind defending it." She looked over at the playground. "Especially when it's theirs."

Hutch was glad she included Macie and Logan in the Don't-Mess-with-Mama-Bear deal. He'd felt protective of Dillon since he'd first met him, and it seemed only right that it had come full circle. He straightened and crossed his arms over his chest. He watched the kids play, especially the little brown-haired kid who'd just leaped ten feet to the ground.

"What about Dillon?" he said. "He shot that soldier."

"He's more together about it than I am," Laura said. She squinted up at him. She blocked the sun with her hand. "Remember, he'd seen people like that murder his dad. He wasn't about to let it happen to his mom. He's a tough kid."

She watched him watching them. She said, "What is it?"

He shook his head.

"No, what?" She put her hand on his knee.

"Maybe I'm a slow learner. . . ." He smiled and took her hand in his.

"But I want to do it right this time. I want to be in their lives while they want me to be, you know?"

He saw that she was right with him. Slowly he said, "I feel that way about you and Dillon too. I can't believe you're going back, now that your depositions are finished."

He felt his face flush under her gaze. He looked away.

"What are you saying, Hutch?"

He looked up at the sky, back to her. "Maybe you could . . . find a reason to stay?"

"Maybe I could."

He smiled. "Hey," he said, gesturing with his head.

An attendant had pushed a wheelchair through a back door and was rolling it toward the ambulance. A uniformed police officer and a man in a suit strolled alongside. Sitting in the chair, his leg in a cast straight in front of him, Michael spotted them. His hand rose a few inches off his lap. He gave a tentative wave.

"Come on," Hutch said. As they walked, Laura clasped her hand around his.

The cop saw them coming and nodded. He'd been stationed outside Michael's room most of the times they'd come to visit. He spoke to the other man, who nodded.

They reached Michael at the rear of the ambulance. The attendant opened the doors.

Hutch squeezed Michael's shoulder. "How's it feel, going home?"

Michael nodded. "They haven't set a venue for the trials yet, so they figured I can be in a cage near my parents as well as here." He hitched a thumb at the man in the suit. "I have my own U.S. marshal."

The guy tilted his head. Sunglasses prevented Hutch from seeing his eyes.

Laura crouched beside the wheelchair. She touched Michael's hair. "I hear your dad's going to be okay."

That brought a smile to Michael's face. "Yeah, they finally got the slug out of his chest. This close to his heart." He held up his thumb and forefinger, as though holding a pellet between them.

"He's going to be proud of you," Hutch said, "breaking away from Outis like you did. Turning state's evidence."

Michael rolled his eyes. "Lot of good it will do, a conglomerate that big."

"They've already had all of their licenses and contracts frozen," Hutch said. "And the investigation's going to make it worse for them, not better."

Michael lowered his head. "Too bad he's dead. Page, I mean. I would have liked to strap a helmet on his head and show him a thing or two."

Laura said, "I think what you have in mind is pretty close to what's happening to him."

"Let's go," the marshal said. He waved his hand at the attendant, who began folding parts of the wheelchair so Michael could stand.

"Michael," Hutch said. "I won't forget that you helped save Logan. I promised to help you any way I could, and I meant it. I'll be in touch, okay?"

Michael wrinkled his nose. "I'm pretty messed up," he said.

"Who isn't?" Hutch said.

They watched him shift into the ambulance. The marshal joined him, and the vehicle pulled away. The cop strolled back toward the hospital.

Hutch and Laura returned to the park. The kids saw them and came running. The sun glinted off Logan's braces—his grillz. It lifted Hutch's heart to see the boy smiling.

They barreled into him, knocking him to the grass. All three of them began tickling him. His hands weren't fast enough to stop them from pushing their little fingers into his sides, neck, underarms.

"Wait, wait, wait," he said. "How about dinner and a movie?"

A chorus of whoops and cheers.

"First one to the car gets to pick the restaurant; second one, the movie. Go!"

Dillon and Macie scrambled to their feet. Laura laughed and followed.

Logan lay on Hutch's chest, his arm propping up his head.

"You're going to let them pick our food and entertainment?" Hutch said.

The boy nodded. "How long is this going to last?" he said.

"What?"

"You being cool. Spending time with us."

"I hope a long, long time," Hutch said. "I have to work, of course. But I'll try to keep it pretty much nine-to-five, okay?"

"No obsessions?"

Hutch mussed his hair. "You've been talking to Laura." He smiled. "My only obsessions will be the people I love."

"No one's going to replace Brendan Page?"

Hutch turned to gaze at Logan from the corner of his eye. He squinted.

"Brendan *who*?"